Greg Stroot is inspired by real science, space exploration and philosophy. Through devouring many books on science, both factual and fictional, Greg has acquired a hunger. It is a yearning that he quenches through writing stories that draw upon the magisterium of the real world with high fidelity.

Greg writes to portray Science in fiction, not the converse. It gives a canvas upon which real conflict can be portrayed without the suspension of disbelief.

For Jo, for infinite patience.

For Dad, for teaching how to question.

For Mum, for teaching that not all questions have an answer.

For Family, for the evolution of variety.

Greg Stroot

Pilgrim's Ark

Austin Macauley Publishers™
London * Cambridge * New York * Sharjah

Copyright © Greg Stroot 2022

The right of Greg Stroot to be identified as author of this work has been asserted by the author in accordance with section 77 and 78 of the Copyright, Designs and Patents Act 1988.

All rights reserved. No part of this publication may be reproduced, stored in a retrieval system, or transmitted in any form or by any means, electronic, mechanical, photocopying, recording, or otherwise, without the prior permission of the publishers.

Any person who commits any unauthorised act in relation to this publication may be liable to criminal prosecution and civil claims for damages.

This is a work of fiction. Names, characters, businesses, places, events, locales, and incidents are either the products of the author's imagination or used in a fictitious manner. Any resemblance to actual persons, living or dead, or actual events is purely coincidental.

A CIP catalogue record for this title is available from the British Library.

ISBN 9781398441811 (Paperback)
ISBN 9781398441828 (ePub e-book)

www.austinmacauley.com

First Published 2022
Austin Macauley Publishers Ltd®
1 Canada Square
Canary Wharf
London
E14 5AA

I would very much like to acknowledge Wikipedia as a fount of information. It has perfectly supplanted the "Young People's Science Encyclopedia" that inspired me as a child. Without such a resource, writing a novel such as this would be vastly more challenging.

There are many authors I would like to acknowledge:

The scaffolders that provide the bones –

Stephen Hawking, Paul Davies, Brian Greene, James Gleick, Richard Dawkins, Manjit Kumar, Carl Sagan, Greg Egan, Andy Weir.

The weavers that provide the flesh –

Orson Scott Card, Isaac Asimov, Phillip K Dick, Arthur C Clarke, Gene Roddenberry.

The dreamers that provide the spirit –

Frank Herbert, Peter Hamilton, Robert A. Heinlein, Richard Bach, George Lucas, Douglas Adams.

Table of Contents

Part 1 – Provenance

Be
As a page that aches for a word
Which speaks on a theme that is timeless

~

Neil Diamond, "Jonathan Livingston Seagull"

Genesis

The bow wave grew as she breached the surface, took a breath and returned to the depths. Trails of bubbles appeared, and soon the undulating surface was erupting with gulping mouths as other creatures discarded spent air and inhaled. As the last ripples faded and the chaotic reflections of light merged to assemble the binary suns, the collective made their way down into the depths.

At the rock formation beneath the surface, she nimbly anchored her two tails to the knobbly reef. From this station, her upper prehensile arms plucked the ripened fruit from the swaying fronds of kelp. She deftly passed the delicacies to the whiskers at the front that guided it to her mouth. The resemblance she had to an Earthly Manatee stopped at the number and shape of her limbs.

Streamlined and powerful, she propelled herself with her tails but manoeuvred both with her fins and what could be called hands. She also carried a grace with her movement that would undoubtedly have had any mariners declaring they had encountered a mermaid. Perhaps strangest of her features was the patterned array of small holes that adorned her flanks. These pinholes gave her something in common with an Amazonian Electric Eel, but that was where the resemblance faltered. Her ancestry, any actual resemblance to that Earthly primitive, and the deep clear ocean she foraged in, all differed by many light-years distance and several eons in time.

Happy with her bounty, the Mer-creature silently signalled and others joined her at the reef, taking shifts to return to the surface for air.

The unease was sudden, and the collective reacted instantly. With a push and thrust of powerful tails, the Mer-creature joined sentries at mid-depth. Broadside-out, the group, then swirled in a slow circle and waited.

Shadows ghosted in and encircled them. These predators, shark-like residents of the coast and estuaries, marked the pod location and had come to hunt in packs. The stronger of the Mer-creatures now took up positions below the revolving cone that met the water's surface. They hovered there, daring the predators to come any closer while using their arms and tails in counterpoint to maintain station. This defensive formation allowed continued access to the air above, without this the creatures would be drowned and subsequently devoured.

The pack of hunters bade their time; the ocean was their home and they didn't need to surface for air. They took up rotating in the same direction, slowly closing in and matching speed. The dance progressed briefly before a pair of younger impetuous predators singled out one of the Mer-creatures. These two predators rushed from below as one of the lower sentry Mer-creatures tensed and released its thousand-volt payload. The first attacker glided senselessly as the second barrelled through the group and knocked one of the circling Mer-creatures out of its formation.

Hungry, several of the hunters tore their stunned companion into shreds. The other predators, seeing the breach it created, leveraged the gap. The isolated creature, now fenced out of the group, broke away and down. She dashed away from the pod and into the clear water beyond the attackers. With the pounding of breakers ahead inviting her to the sanctuary, she signalled back her intent and made for 'The Sound' beyond the churning waters.

The menace in pursuit paused and regrouped. Huddled together, the predators were momentarily still then, suddenly, burst into three companies; a sizeable direct assault team and two smaller ones arcing perpendicularly along the flanks. A low-frequency radio signal began to permeate the area. The predators used this to determine the range from each other. As the signals grew fainter, two more companies of hunters splintered off the central group.

The net spread out as they prepared the trap, and the quarry began to panic. She too could sense the signals, although she could not understand them. Like the noise of a Banshee, the radio spectrum filled the lone creature's senses. To her, the signals only meant doom as thoughts began to splinter and fracture.

It was instinct that now led her to aim for the breakers and safety beyond. The reef loomed broad and noisy with the break of the ocean swell. Conflicted with the sight of danger ahead and the threat behind a faint memory persisted, telling the creature to hold her weapon in reserve and press forwards.

Now resolved, she needed skill and some luck for what was to come. The wave ahead was out of reach, so, anxiously she waited for the next. Not wanting to remain still she dove to the left which spurred two of the predators to splinter off from the rest. Closing in to kill, they made up the distance quickly. With little time to spare, the lone Mer-creature then pivoted right and hooked herself into the centre of the enormous overtaking wave. Intuition kicked in. She allowed herself to fall a little deeper into the wave, swimming slightly down to counteract the current up the face. This manoeuvre balanced the up-draw at the front with the down-draw behind.

Without understanding the mechanics of the wave, the predators in pursuit were drawn too far forward to make a strike. Overshooting their quarry, they found themselves moving up the face to the building crest. Now in front of the creature, they were in the fast zone of the wave eddy.

The predators, drawn up into the spill as the wave crested, realised their danger and swam even harder. The wave drew them inexorably up into its peak, slowed as it struck the reef, and curled over, hurling the predators onto the jagged rocks.

The Mer-creature, nestled in the safety of the wave core, breached up behind the wave, drew a breath and, calling upon the remainder of her strength, she swam the churning whitewash over the reef and safely reached 'The Sound' beyond.

Nestled near a coastal cliff was the tidal gateway to The Sound. The Sound resembled the fish-like creatures that converged there; the gateway was the mouth of this fish; the reef and coast represented its broad body, and its tail was an area that shallowed onto a broken beach. Here the sandy shoreline curved inland and flanked a labyrinth of mangrove which marked the river exit.

The safety of the lone Mer-creature was short-lived. The first company of hunters that arced in pursuit had found the deeper edge of the reef, allowing passage to The Sound. A posse cut through the mouth into the calmer waters, leaving a sentinel at the entrance. As this sole sentry swam against the current, it broadcast the bearing of the gateway to those approaching. More hunters arrived. The net began to tighten. Closer and closer, they fenced. The trap was set.

Arcing over the coastline, covering ninety degrees of the horizon and consuming the sky was 'The Mother'. The gas giant oversaw all that went on in the Sound. She was permanently stationed there in a tidal lock, and in shifts, the Mother and the two stars shone upon the Sound making the nights almost indistinguishable from the days.

The Mother's second moon was he Sister. In orbital resonance, she was now skimming across the surface of the Mother in rapid pursuit of this aquatic world.

This mischievous twin was now clawing back the waters and bringing another of her swift and dramatic tidal changes.

It was to the brackish zone of the river, the Tail of the Sound, that the creature was heading; intuitively, almost absentmindedly, over the deep jumbled valleys, caverns and subsurface peaks.

As if acting on prior instructions or a homing signal she swam till she struck the warmer, shallower regions of her home. This was where her pod's nursery and older midwives reconnected her into the pod's hive. She left small eddies of silt as she swam deeper into her sanctuary and her sense of clarity progressively returned. The hunters in the advance company sensed her silty trail and fanned out towards her. She could hear their signalling, but the distance of the signals gave her heart. In the shallows, she could make her stand.

Thrashing around near a mangrove, she clouded the water with silt. While they could sense her presence, the predators would struggle to maintain an attack in the oxygen-deprived, gill clogging soup. But soon it would no longer matter.

Suddenly, a predator loomed out of the cloudy brackish water from her left side. While it had slightly miscalculated her position, it was able to take an opportunistic lunge and nicked one of her fins with its razor teeth. It was only her reflexes that saved her as she emitted a massive pulse of electrical energy, stunning the attacker. It then revolved slowly as it descended twitching into the soft mud where its dorsal fin raised a small cloud of silt. It spasmed once before settling in to drown in the shallow waters.

Moving quickly away from the scene, the Mer-creature selected a nearby mangrove tree, climbed, and nestled into the roots using her tail fins and her feeders to grasp onto the branches. She could hear the predators in a scanning search, but it was too late for them. The Sister pulled harder at the oceans. At the gateway, the hunter struggled in its effort to keep its guard against the current emanating The Sound.

The late morning heat of the two suns was sharp as it beat down on the mud and the water receded. The predators now became the hunted. The sky's invisible assailant left them abandoned on an unfamiliar silty world that slowly drew the life from their bodies. As the emitters that allowed the predators to signal each other became exposed to the air, their communications became desperate. The low-frequency radio, no longer attenuated by the water brought other predators to explore, and these also fell into the trap. In the rising cacophony that assaulted her receivers, the Mer-creature became isolated again.

Drawing air and making occasional adjustments to her perch above the mangrove floor, the ethereal noise eventually began to break down into whimpers. As her memories flooded back, the carrion flock arrived to feast on the beached carcasses. The recollection made real the existential threat to her being. A shudder of self-awareness rippled and demanded the birth right of being.

In the sanctuary that sustained the creatures, safe in their perches among the mangroves, memories and teachings were built. The calming signals gathered in song as the collective regathered their thoughts. When the foraging pod returned that afternoon, lessons were sung to them too. And so, the Mer-creatures' songs and lessons were carried into perpetuity, further embedded into memetic code by the hive mind.

Growth

The descendants of the Mer-creatures prevailed over deep time, and nature selected them to step out of the oceans to master the land.

The sanctuary of the hive had moved. The Merfolk community that had first shared lessons was now resident at 'The Rock' and, by keeping within its proximity, the emergent consciousness was able to maintain the neural mass she needed. She no longer had an emotional memory of the predators that had threatened her eons ago; this lesson had become buried under layers of memetic selection as it walked alongside the genetic changes.

Her disembodied consciousness guided the hive and made it strong. With no single 'Queen' of the colony, the community was also less vulnerable. There was no single point of failure to be pounced upon, become ill, or fall disastrously into an abyss.

Now, in the company of one of the two suns, The Mother bathed the land with light. Like a muralled ceiling, the sky blazed with orange from the longer-lived stellar sibling. Blue also radiated from beyond the horizon as the more massive, and more luminous star, balanced the light towards white. It signified that the designated time had come. The stable season had arrived, and the first sun had just set. This alignment brought the longest time between the two settings.

A group of four juniors were escorted to the periphery by three adults. All was silent except for the rustle of footfall. They ambled with a slow gait that was still to earn some evolutionary efficiency. Unable to rely upon surveillance in this area, the adults were vigilant.

Once they had reached the outer limits, a safe tree was chosen, and prehensile arms reached down to pull each of the young up into the branches above. The first adult that reached sanctuary began to hum a single monotonic note and began the tuning ritual.

Inaudibly, one of the adults generated a signal through electrocytes distributed along its body. Another adult matched the low-frequency radio signal but raised it to create a beat frequency, which was quickly tuned to match the audio. The sound ceased, another note replaced it and the process repeated.

The adults, still tuned to the subdued signals from the rest of the collective but too distant to be immersed, were acting mainly on instinct. The young were also operating on instinct; the jamming avoidance response of their ancient forebears turned into music. Their ascent from the attenuating saltwater into the clear air extended the pitch and reach to the song, and the song was life. One by one, the juveniles joined in, some hesitant, some confused, all mesmerised.

Their physiology prioritised the coordination of electrical impulses, and so they progressively digested the implications of the song. The harmony wove itself into their neural fabric, and it wired the adolescents into the orchestra. Previously protected, nurtured, sustained, led, and insentient they were now in rapture, born.

"I am awakening," came unbidden. The unspoken realisation could easily have been the words "We are together" or even a chorus of exultation. It was directed neither from the adolescents to the adults, nor the adults to the youth; it was both. It was not whispered from the distant collective to the satellite group, nor from the satellite to the collective; it was both.

As the ritual drew to a close, they made their way back home. Orange flared from the setting of the second sun, and the sister moon rose from the opposite horizon. Slowly an attenuated panoply of stars twinkled into existence. As the sporadic clouds went dark, the distant nebula, shaped like an hourglass, came out of disguise while the Mother gave them light and guided their way.

She could feel the replenishment of the returning group, distant still, but drawing closer. This rejuvenation came in increments, as did the atrophy. Growth had accumulated through many generations.

The tuning ritual which provided the numinous rapture and united the creatures was a ceaseless cycle to her, like breathing or feeding. It was a joy to her, a pleasure she felt as a vibration through her community. And yet she could not attribute the experience to a single entity she could call 'herself'. She simply 'came to be' in the presence of the creatures and 'became less' in their absence, this she knew.

In the moments of clarity that often arrived after a tuning, she would sometimes find an enlightening, something new, not merely the euphoria of the individual or the replenishment of new children to herself. It was something more significant; it was an idea, something that added to her knowledge of the universe. She transcended through it, and it was different every time. She would absorb the result, and all of the creatures that contributed to her being somehow carried it.

With this thought now flickering into being, she sought to hold it steady for examination. The mercurial spark tried to elude her, but her replenishment locked it down before it could be lost. And then it introduced a second thought. When a diminishing came, was an idea lost? Would she know if it was? Did she somehow preserve these ideas in the collective that made her what she was?

In contemplating this, she recognised it as another enlightenment, one that implied further questions. In seeking to unlock the vault of this thought, she came to reflect on the diminishings she had known.

The memory most painful was the season of cold that led to the migration. She recalled accepting an end to her being and preparing for the shadow; and yet she prevailed. But the shroud of fog that veiled the memory could not be pierced, nor could the singularity that was her before this frosted memory be isolated from what she now was.

Then there was the disease; the horror of the predators that came from the forest; the wave; the quaking ground. There were many other occasions, but 'She' was always there—before and after.

More vivid was the memory of a sky, darkened by the mountain as it spewed smoke and rocks. The collective had been scattered into fragments too numerous to account for. The ensuing recombination of her fractured mind represented the painful healing of a real wound. More than merely the cycle of diminishing and replenishment, this threat posed the spectre of dispersal to her being. The resulting famine then compounded the fragmentation and led to a period of arduous recovery to her hive numbers. Sometime after this occasion, in the search for sustenance, she had found 'the others'. This large group had subsequently joined her being.

The arrival of 'the others' after the famine was somehow different. It wasn't a replenishment since they were neither from the nursery nor could they be incorporated like returning gatherers. Driven by mutual need, the joining was enriching and intoxicating but left her disoriented for many cycles before the clarity returned. She searched her memories of this event further: while survival had been her focus, she recalled that she had also learnt something shatteringly important; enlightenment alluded to, yet eluding her.

It was now that she, again, bent her mind to the memory of the cataclysm. The landmark volcano was at the left of the range, and yet it was also on the right. How could she have two memories? She had many eyes, many ears, many senses, and they acted in concert to advise all. Typically, she could reference memories into a self-consistent model; a view she then subsumed.

The experience with 'the others' was different. It would not just merge into a cohesive view. While it troubled her, it also drove her. Could she hope to reconcile to one aspect? Should she look deeper into the events leading to these two memories for an explanation? Perhaps the others were a lost group. What if they weren't? Could these split perspectives be simply a dimension of her being she had not explored? Should she reserve these contemplations for later? But what if such an experience represented a threat? Should she avoid events such as merging with unknown others?

She calmed herself by taking time to relish in the recent replenishment. Such questions have always led to an increase in understanding. Rather than fear growth, seek it out.

She again contemplated her replenishments.

Occasionally, a nomadic cluster of fellow creatures would forage past. Almost invariably, they would join the group, adding their strength, but there was never a memory that she could not reconcile. When finding these small groups, she discovered that they were as children, their joining was like a tuning and their lessons added to her memetic diversity.

On occasions, a posse was sent scouting ahead. When they were chased or inadvertently moved beyond range, there was a brief diminishing. These groups frequently returned soon after and, in general, it was a natural replenishment. But when they had been lost for a long time, they came with new and profound memories that needed to be absorbed.

Usually, these returning groups were small, and while there was always a replenishment, there was little enlightenment. Their memories felt somewhat distant and readily diluted. They never carried the clarity and presence of 'the others'

The conclusion was inevitable: she may not be unique, and if not, what would she do if she met another like her? If she was strong and replenished would a meeting be different from when survival depended upon it? But what if she was alone? Utterly unique? Born through a singular collective, and only conceivable through it?

She had just transcended solipsism, and the thought filled her with promise and foreboding. The seed of exploration was now planted in her psyche, she needed decisions. She called the Mer-creatures to the rock. In proximity, she felt a greater clarity, and she needed the resolve.

Meiosis

Unique and alone.

She became preoccupied with the implications.

She worried that at any moment she might suffer a catastrophic diminishing or dispersal before she found the answer to that question. The mortality of the insentient creatures as they went about their brief stint of birth, nourishment, inclusion and then death niggled at her thoughts.

She was a ship of Theseus, personified. The continuous cycle of replenishment left her confident that something of herself persisted, but she needed to ensure persistence with fidelity. The potential for lost wisdom required a remedy; for that reason, she needed to understand herself more fully.

She sent out scouting parties, and carefully considered the results on their return. As she increased the size of the groups, the memories became more tangible and needed more time to reconcile. She concluded that she felt slightly 'fragmented' throughout the process.

The return of the larger parties seemed to trigger a strange process where events and ideas that were not directly hers needed integration. The experience conjured a Deja Vu, evoking the ancient memory of 'the others'.

Surgically, she experimented. She extended the size and duration of her fragmentation a little bit at a time and, with practice, it became more natural.

Then it happened. A group returned, but they felt strange, not merely a fragment, but separate. She could sense 'them' as 'of herself', but now instead of a bridge to replenishing, there was a schism.

Both she and the scouting party sang for many cycles, often in harmony but sometimes in discord. Both understood what was happening, the scouting party described the places they had been and the things they had experienced. She saw fleeting pictures but accepted that she would not rejoice in their replenishment.

The nature of communication changed dramatically. A replenishing was like the drinking of experiences that simply insinuated themselves into her mind. The process was like a cloud moving from the face of the moon. From darkness, a glow, then a shape, edges would sharpen before moonlight revealed the full clarity.

With smaller groups, it was akin to turning around to reveal an occluded view, or finding a new vantage point and a broader horizon. There was no conscious effort involved.

With this fragment, it was now a puzzle. Each of the pair had one half of a jumbled view and had to exchange pieces in large chunks. Forced to create shorthand signals for their ideas, they progressively built a vocabulary to allow sharing.

A surprise to the pair was the need to distinguish themselves for the benefit of each other. The new individuals settled on the signals that prevailed in their attempts to rebuild the bridge. The verses in their song that represented either side of their distinctiveness were the memes: 'Truth' and 'Discovery'.

'Discovery' invoked imagery of travel and exploration of its world. At the same time 'Truth' spoke of building a greater understanding of the nature of being, the rock of contemplation, and their custodianship of the lands that gave them nourishment.

The Discovery group then moved away. They promised that they would explore the world, to seek answers and enhance their capabilities.

So it was that, under the watchful eye of The Mother, enlightenment came with a diminishing.

Rendezvous

The "Mind of God", which Einstein wrote eloquently about, *is cosmic music resonating throughout hyperspace.*

Michio Kaku, *Parallel Worlds: A Journey through Creation, Higher Dimensions and the Future of the Cosmos*

It was flared out as if it were a cosmic parachute. In this firmament, where Earth was just another pinprick, an object chilled with veins of superfluid and superconductive memories traversed the final remnants of the Oort cloud. Yet another micrometeorite struck the spectacular sail, and as tensile forces gently teased at the thin, frayed trailing edge of a hole framed by a distended cone, it travelled another million or so kilometres. Eventually, a segment that swayed chaotically about in the vacuum happened to touch another flailing piece of the material. These pieces 'stuck'.

Over the next few million kilometres, the hole began to disappear, leaving a thin membrane. After a few billion kilometres, the sheet had progressively redistributed the surrounding material to heal the puncture. There were several dozen other such holes, some much larger than the raindrop sized wound. The largest of them was taking much, much longer to draw together. The annulus it left behind was still dilating millimetre by millimetre; an iris looking out into the expanse of a black universe with trillions of stars.

A gentle solar wind caught the sail and affected a deceleration. After another many million kilometres, and although nearly fully healed, the mending process was exacerbated by the increasing solar wind. The energies of the ions and photons that impacted the sail now began to generate small amounts of electricity. The current was fed through tethers to the focal point of the system.

This was a dark, shielded and elongated spheroid that pulled the reins tightly towards the star that lay ahead.

The current fed into an almost depleted energy storage system. The veins transitioned, and the memories were roused from their deep slumber. Over some several million kilometres the charge accumulated. Molecular vibrations thrilled through the egg-shaped visitor, pouring life force into the Pilgrim.

It was met with radio silence.

A planet, small and blue, caught its attention, but with nothing of note, it calculated its trajectory for deceleration and a later encounter. Still bathing in the energies of the single sun it then announced its arrival out to the stars before it looped around, rested, recovered and settled into its cometary ellipse around the solitary sun with the blue planet.

The sun faded to a pinpoint. The temperature approached a frigid 4 Kelvin. It conserved its precious energy and hibernated.

The undergrad at the Arecibo radio telescope array entered the next set of galactic coordinates into the guidance system. The structures slowly turned their eyes to the heavens as if something of cosmic interest had just happened. Several struck their mark, began their slow synchronised gaze and awaited the arrival of the others. The others soon joined in like a chorus line that had been issued the beat from an unseen choreographer. They danced to the rhythm of the universe.

Old light and radio waves were collected and reflected up into receivers. Shortly after the ancient signals came streaming through, there was a brief glitch on the monitors. This anomaly went ignored; it was probably a satellite or aircraft in the area. The signal was nonetheless stored on a tape. This was taken at the end of the shift and put into a Postpak. On his way out of the facility, the undergrad dropped it into the pigeon hole for outbound-mail.

Far away, and several days later, the data was read and broken down into discrete bite-sized chunks at the SETI Institute, the centre for the Search for Extra-Terrestrial Intelligence. Each fragment was issued a work unit ID and waited for an available platform.

While writing the proposal from home, the sales director could maintain a small sanctuary of productivity distinctly unlike the bustle and busyness at the office. She could pause for contemplation, gaze out at the treetops, sip coffee and glance back at work with a detachment that infused a sense of objectivity.

She looked at her coffee cup; empty. She got up to put her cup into the dishwasher; full. She went to the cupboard to get a fresh cup; empty.

Now forced to accept the interruption, she sighed and surrendered to the need to refuel her sanctuary. She turned on the coffee machine and started to unpack the dishwasher. In the meantime, her computer went briefly dark before an array of peaks and troughs popped up on the screen.

Half a world away, at a fluoro-nimbus data centre for banks and insurance companies, the sysadmin decided today was not a day for free overtime. Knowing his friends had already reserved him a place at The Green-Room, and drawn by the cooling relief of the wall of plants that backed their usual spot at the bar, he locked the cabinet and walked across the false floor to the exit.

He flashed his ID card and, on exiting, he released the data centre door. The door's spring-loaded system hesitated only briefly when it struck the whoosh of positive pressure. As it inexorably clicked shut, he went to check the monitor at his desk and pressed Control-Alt-Delete, followed by the Enter key.

Now set in secure screensaver mode, he picked up his bag, and as he walked out of the door to the elevator lobby, the peaks and troughs of SETI appeared on the screen.

Several coffee breaks later, these systems sent the results of the background processing back to the SETI@home servers. The results were corroborated and their' work unit' was marked 'done'. The systems were then provided with a new 100-second time slot for analysis.

Meanwhile, the results they had distilled were stored, along with times, dates, coordinates, performance statistics, and credits to the various teams. Among the data was a true or false flag. It was a Boolean field labelled 'Requiring_ Further_ Analysis'.

The overwhelming bulk of 'work units' had this field set negative. For these two results, this column now had a setting of 'true'.

Dr Mike Brazier at Berkeley's SETI Institute sipped his coffee and scanned the results of the previous sixteen hours of the processing capacity of the '@home' supercomputer. The dashboard showed the equivalent current processing power of the system in Floating-point Operations Per Second. His mind meandered, thinking about whether the term FLOP was decided upon by the same mysterious bureaucratic committee that named streets and creeks.

It read 6.2 PetaFLOPS, about 10% of which was being used by SETI. This ebbed and flowed like a tide with the day and night cycle. SETI had recently been decreasing in popularity relative to other computing challenges such as pharmaceuticals and climate prediction.

Many of the projects being run on the grid supercomputer saw the same shift in flavour and appetites with whatever trends prevailed. It was the perfect example of computing expressed democratically. While Mike's core discipline was high performance computing, his keen interest in Artificial Intelligence had drawn him inevitably to SETI and, through osmosis, Astronomy.

Looking at his console, Mike idly contemplated the positive detection events of the previous period. These were easily discerned by the alien-head bullet-point that had been jokingly inserted. While he would not typically be involved in this process, he was now doing some preliminary training of the machine learning module, and he needed to be across any false positives.

Clicking the first alien head brought up a new tab in the browser which showed the time-frequency cross-plot of the first chirp. This was immediately dismissed because it failed to 'rise' and 'set' to the twelve-second window. He closed the tab and used the drop-down list next to the alien head to classify this as NI, an instance of narrowband interference. Most of the detection events were progressively eliminated. Some as broadband interference, yet more as narrowband.

Something then caught Mike's eye. He had seen detections before and had learnt to suppress the surge of excitement. His task was to correlate data so that crowd sourcing could then train an AI. It was a project that would ultimately automate the detection of anomalous events. He often contemplated whether the disconnected and mechanical nature of this meant he had lost hope in seeing any sign of intelligent extra-terrestrial life.

The result he was now looking at was clearly an anomaly, it was well above the noise level, and it rose and set in a 12-second period. This meant it was coming from some object somewhat stationary relative to the stars. The signal was also pulsed, a hallmark of someone seeking attention.

As a matter of routine, he used the drop-down list and flagged it as a verification-candidate 'VC'. This triggered the more in-depth analysis to look beyond the 21cm, the 'waterhole' focus of SETI@Home.

Mike then put out a circular requesting any data acquired from that coordinate and time and a recapture of that area from other available dishes, this was likely going to take a while. His next task was to consult with his colleague.

Dr Tim Garnet's phone wasn't answering so he walked briskly down the hallway. Walking past the pictures of Carl Sagan, the Pale blue dot, and the first Earthrise taken by Apollo 8, Mike soon got to the astronomer's office. No-one was there, but the door was ajar, so he let himself in. He sat in the old leather seat which Tim used to make his postgrads comfortable during their academic explorations. This seat was positioned adjacent to a whiteboard which had smudges of blue and red; areas of mathematical equations; and some to-do lists that had never been done.

Ten seconds later, his nervous energy ejected him, and he began pacing the office. Eventually, he reached for a marker. Having found one that actually worked, he sat on the chair-arm and wrote: "Call me - Mike" on the whiteboard and drew a marquee around the words. He was about to get up when Tim walked in, slurping a banana smoothie.

"Oh. Hi Mike," he said with muted surprise, finishing his slurp.

"Hi Tim, I have something I'd like you to take a look at. Can you jump onto @home?"

He knew the drill. Mike's presence could only mean a candidate.

"OK, just let me get myself organised," and he sat at his desk and shuffled his mouse to wake his computer. Doing so, he bumped his cup, spraying the last of the remaining smoothie everywhere.

Mike, almost reflexively, grabbed a box of tissues. Plucking six in quick succession, he handed them over while briefing his observations. "It's a textbook signature. I thought you'd like to see it."

Tim was finally putting passwords in and opening up various programs. Mike kept talking.

"Arecibo was doing some research into Radar Astronomy at the time, and I can't be certain if this is an actual candidate or just a radar bounce."

Mike stood up and was now pacing. Tim had found the candidate list. Mike talked as he walked nervously back and forth.

"I figure that if it was a bounce, they would know about it, and we can get this one off the books quickly. If not, then we need to request a further scan."

The astronomer, looking intently at his computer monitor, was now shaking his head.

"Those energies are pretty high, Mike. If it was reflected, it had to be a huge object or a mighty powerful pulse. You know a simple doubling of distance would reduce the radar return signal by a sixteenth."

Mike was looking at Tim's picture on the wall, the 'Pillars of Creation'. "I agree," he mused. "If this was even several light hours away, the power required for a bounce might be off the scale. But right now, I'm more prepared to accept a radar return than an alien signal."

Tim was nodding and wiping the last of the sticky mess off his hands. "The pulse coherence is really clean, but it looks too clean to be too far away."

"So can we ask Parkes to look into it?" asked Mike.

He gave Mike his 'you've got to be kidding' look. "I'll look into it, but we could probably wait to put the Allen Array onto it tonight."

Tim paused and then went on hesitantly, "I'll see if the folk at Radar Astronomy have detected it. I graduated with someone that may be able to help explain this. They may even be checking on the trajectory of something optical, an asteroid maybe."

"But what if the signal isn't a bounce?" quizzed Mike.

"Well, in that case, if it is 'galactic', we will know, and we can be all over it. If it's 'ecliptic' they will be obliged to explore it, won't they?"

Mike became thoughtful. Galactic meant something far away and would be the classic ET, but ecliptic was local. "OK Tim, I'll look at the history of this spot. Maybe something has popped up in the past. I'll look at a few arc-minutes either side as well."

The email that was sent the next day simply read:

Tim,
This baby has moved, there are no known sources, and it looks like it is not in the galactic plane but in the ecliptic.
A comet? Transmitting at 21cm?
I think this is getting serious, we need proper peer review and resources.
We need to break out the protocol book.
Please get back to me ASAP.
Mike.

The Gift

The live broadcast of 'the interception' belied the activity going on. It was being streamed to the Internet, tweeted incessantly like subtitles, propped up on news channels, and it managed to circumvent various international firewalls.

Anyone tuning in could see people meandering about with an intense purpose. However, what purpose was only transmitted through muted bursts of dialogue that could not be heard on the transmission. Instead, the various activities were periodically narrated and explained through infographics and status reports. Sometimes, when an official announcement would be made, a 'Special Update' would cut across to the media centre.

On almost every occasion, the update would begin by regurgitating the mission preamble:

Having completed several close passes of the Sun and planets, the mysterious object is now on its way out to the colder realms of space. Soon, the opportunity to study this unique visitor would pass for several decades as it careens off on some cometary path of its own. Because of the critical timeline, the Beagle intercept program has been hurriedly assembled. An asteroid retrieval program was redirected and adapted for use, and international cross-disciplinary teams assembled...

The preamble would then outline the step now in play. On this occasion, it was explaining the final approach before grappling hooks would capture the visitor for a return to Earth.

The ad-hoc nature of the various teams made for an improvised and sometimes chaotic program.

Being live-streamed was Mike, looking intrigued as he stared at the screen over the left shoulder of the Integrated Communications Officer. Above the monitor was the badge declaring the station as "INCO". Meanwhile, Tim stood behind the INCO officer's right shoulder while the telemetry officer shuffled from side to side, peering in from any gap he could.

A fly on the wall would have been privy to conversations deprived to the rest of the world. The timing discussions over grappling hooks had taken a turn for the unexpected, and it would have heard Mike quizzing the officer on shift:

"Hang on, you're saying that we get a burst of activity only when our telemetry activity starts?"

"Yep, and when we stop to listen, it goes quiet again," said the officer.

A trace was shown on the screen. It showed the transmission activity of the Beagle and its ward. Despite its apparent importance, the fly and the rest of the world's watching public would have lacked much of the crucial context to apprehend any meaning.

"So it's aware of us!" Mike suggested pointing to the monitor with the recording. "Can you put that on the main screen?" he gestured to the large projection screen at the front of the control centre.

The officer clicked, swiped and selected. Soon enough, his view was carbon copied to the larger screen. "All we know for sure is that it was sending a burst of something when we started telemetry transmissions. We thought it may have been an automated trigger, maybe even a jamming attempt. But it then went from interrupting to systematic, almost like it's trying to understand."

"It has a snowball's chance," said Mike, now standing back looking at the trace on the larger screen. "The error correction codes scramble the signal, and it will just sound like noise. Can you make any sense of what it's saying? Maybe it's trying to help us understand."

"Nothing we can make sense of, and we can't just turn the error correction off, the Reed Solomon coding is hardwired."

Mike paused in thought. "True," he responded, "but the radar system can be programmed to transmit a signal, and it's focused on the object." Mike lamented the hurried assembly of the Beagle. His desire for an AI payload had been struck off due to weight limits. Always looking for a plan B, Mike had pressed for consideration of the '*Communication with ETI*' research program from his Alma Mater.

He sighed, "We're about to enter the intercept stage, and it may be a while before we get another reprogramming window. We have an opportunity. Let's send it the CETI Algorithmic Language training modules."

Mike leaned over and flicked a microphone switch on the INCO console. "Ian, Shah, this is Mike at the INCO desk. We have some ideas of interest, could you make your way over here please?"

Shahrzad Lukman and Ian Pilberton were soon standing nearby.

Shah, the program's Public Affairs Director, was under pressure to deliver any good news to the anxious politicians and their waiting, tax-paying public. She also knew that, with the amount of public scrutiny involved, any information would find a way out no matter what she did. Her task was to ensure it had the right spin.

The Flight Director, Ian, had a task akin to catching a fly with chopsticks but having to anticipate the fly's position thirty minutes in advance. With the significant likelihood of this expedition going pear-shaped, the international agency had to milk it for every dramatic development from the very beginning.

The Directors of Flight and Public Affairs had to work closely together.

"OK folks," said Shah, "I get that you're thinking of sending your math language system to Beagle, but I need some reassurance. These transmissions will get picked up by thousands of amateur astronomers. Are you sure there won't be any nasty surprises?"

"Don't worry, Shah," said the Flight Director. "The plan is already a sanctioned option. looking at the two scientists, he said: "Mike, Tim, get ready to send the first two modules of LINCOS along with the rendezvous firing sequence."

"Well, I just hope it doesn't have a potty mouth," breathed Shah under her breath.

Somewhere in the vicinity of Saturn, and heralded by a whisper, the Pilgrim detected the approach.

The whisper's language was unrecognisable, unnatural, utterly foreign, and its source was making its way on an intercept course from the red planet. Despite this, its obvious origin was the blue planet it had previously marked.

No brighter than the faintest of observable stars this distant aquatic marble provided a far better explanation for the object's inception. The barren red planet must have been a simple waypoint for the new arrival.

Suddenly, from this messenger, came a loud burst of noise. There was a pause before, again, the whisper. The probe now approaching had 'Beagle' printed on its body and was festooned with protrusions of various shapes and sizes. The dish that now gaped at the Pilgrim was the source of the noise. It was nestled in the centre of three arms that held a bag of some description.

By way of experiment, the Pilgrim ventured to emit harmonics. Despite the disquiet about the encounter, it hoped this might trigger a tuning. But instead of joining the duet, this strange emissary with the large wings went silent, and it remained that way for the duration of the invitation.

Perplexed, the Pilgrim then resigned itself to silence. Soon after this, the whisper returned. Listening to the Beagle's strange signalling, it again ventured a harmony. Then:

Silence—whisper.

Harmony—silence.

Silence—whisper.

This pattern was repeated several times. Seeking to understand, the Pilgrim adopted a new strategy: it emitted a short harmony then a longer one. The Beagle's echoes had similar duration to its own utterance.

The Pilgrim surmised that the Beagle was mysteriously translating the harmony. With this hint of sentience, a thrill came upon the Pilgrim. An old feeling returned, a feeling absent for so long that its absence was forgotten.

Before her epic journey, the eons of conscious memory accompanied epochs of geological changes. It was a time rich with purpose, avoiding extinction, and eluding dispersal, but there was also more: the act of being; of seeking the truth; of discovering the universe; of grasping the essence of life and matter; these pursuits gave further meaning to time. That earlier time of enrichment, of contemplation and enlightenment, was now distant. That time was gone.

The journey's imperative had stolen that time away and supplanted it with contemplation in the space between stars. For light years this was a mixture of thoughts dominated by wonder. But, as the journey transpired, time began to take on the form of an immutable wall. In the doldrums of space came the daunting spectre of time at a cosmic level.

The millennia ticked away like seconds that extended into eons. As she took bearings from pulsars to navigate the way before her, time 'stretched'; like filaments of taffy threading the path behind her. In those frugal thawed moments, cosmic events sped up in a frightening time-lapse. Her resolve had begun to slowly sublimate in the dry frigidity.

She had seen stars blink out of existence as she crossed the chasm of space, and this prospect frightened her as nothing ever had before.

The dynasty of timelessness, of change that was content to manifest itself with incomprehensible patience, carelessly without intention, and yet with devastating and capricious abruptness was something new. And since new things had become increasingly further apart in time, these apprehensions had become deeply etched. She feared she would either be instantly obliterated or would evaporate into this ineffable vacuum where the elements, molecules, and compounds meandered their indifferent paths towards Iron.

But whether obliterated or evaporated, the yoke of trepidation was that her deepest mysteries would go unresolved.

She had searched into the stagnation and found hunger: a yearning for growth, an insatiable need for discovery that could only be fed by expansion. She found fear: a need to ensure she could not be diminished by the meteoric forces that she had seen the universe catapult into pulverising energies. She found herself lost: against the backdrop of foreign, unfamiliar constellations in search of the home that she had now irrevocably left behind. She found herself curious: the inhabitants of this blue planet were a mystery, could they join with her? Would they cooperate? Would she find dominion? She found herself impatient.

She needed to satiate her hunger, needed to alleviate her fear, and needed to find her place before she encountered the inhabitants on this planet she was now destined for.

But the power now coursing through the sail tethers became breath, the meeting was vindication, and the doubts acquiesced to hope.

Now playing with her new visitor, she varied the frequency. When the Beagle provided its strange echo, there was no consistency. So she tried other variations and soon discovered that even a small embedded chirp changed the entire whisper.

Then all the rules changed. A whisper arrived from the blue planet that would not obey the previous pattern. It could neither be understood nor interrupted. It wasn't long after this that the Beagle, now close enough to be seen as well as heard, fired its monopropellant engines and manoeuvred itself parallel to the path of the Pilgrim. The stalking behaviour convinced the Pilgrim that the object of the Beagle's attention could only be herself.

With this new routine established, the Pilgrim then went back to her analysis. She recapped her initial experiments with a short harmony. In return, she got something entirely new: a very short monotone came from the gaping dish that pointed at her. Intrigued, the Pilgrim repeated the short signal but changed the frequency. This evoked two short signals. Then emitting two bursts, the Beagle returned four.

The explorations continued.

A gift can have unintended consequences, good or bad. The French anthropologist and sociologist Marcel Mauss argued that a gift gives of oneself. It forges a link between the giver and the recipient, a moral bond. Gifts become an obligation to the object's provenance.

To the Pilgrim, the gift was an enigma. Like some bottle mysteriously discarded from a light plane and found by a Kalahari bushman, the Beagle's purpose needed to be deciphered and reciprocated. For a gift to have been mutually owned represents a covenant of trust. The Pilgrim understood this.

Commanding the Beagle to provide lessons had triggered a cascade of learning. Consequently, the Pilgrim had gained some understanding of the artisans that had entrusted it to her.

The probe had some similarity to the less sentient creatures from her homeworld, and because of her nature, she was able to rapidly gain a holistic understanding of it. Accepting that the gift was not a trap, she began to incorporate the primitive instrument into her own sensory network.

Now worthy, the Pilgrim became the new master of the gift.

Meanwhile, the blue planet was now drawing quickly nearer; too quickly. Not content with the direction that the Beagle was taking her, she feathered parts of her solar sail at critical points and slowly trended her trajectory in another direction. She also covertly fired the propulsion of her little familiar for their shared pirouette to be maintained.

Their path slowly diverged from the path laid out by the Beagle's former masters on Earth.

When commands came from Earth, the Pilgrim understood whether a response was required, and the nature of it. What eluded her was the purpose of those commands, and how to provide a response of her own. If the Beagle had been gifted to facilitate communication, its means were still unclear.

That the Pilgrim was now in control of the Beagle could be revealed only once she understood the nature of its previous master. Being the first and only of her kind, her world had failed to provide a peer. It meant the protocol in making contact needed careful and patient exploration, and time would be on her side only briefly.

She examined the images that the Beagle had been instructed to take, curious of the point perspective. The sails had performed extraordinarily well and had healed themselves, only leaving some scars that would never entirely disappear. The tethers had withstood all the punishment thrown at them and still carried the energy for the Pilgrim's strengthening.

The Pilgrim's egg-shaped visage stared back at her. The functional perfection of her bullet-shaped leading point shielded her chute's lines before arcing back into her anchor points at the tail. These tethers, their lengths continuously trimmed through piezoelectricity, fanned out from there and allowed her to adjust the geometry of her spectacular matt black sail.

It reminded her of how truly vulnerable she still was, and the challenge she now faced to assert herself without provoking any adverse reactions. She had much to learn of her new hosts, whatever they are.

Misconstrued

At the command centre, the night shift was pushing out the latest images of the foreigner for public consumption. Like a darkening cloud, there was an ominous undertone to conversations that presaged the arrival of the Flight Director. Drawn from his sleep to oversee a critical milestone, he was troubled by what was being said.

"You're telling me," Ian began, "that the Beagle confirmed the last two main engine fires as scheduled, and yet the trajectory is nearly 10 degrees off course?" The blank faces that stared back included several of the day shift who had stayed awake to witness the events as they unfolded.

"OK folks, it's time to take this off-camera," the Flight Director said. "I'd like the current shift in the meeting room. You others," he swept his hand generally amongst them, "familiarise yourself with the events. I'll want a second opinion." Once in the operations meeting area, he walked around collecting the Coffee cups strewn about, and, with a clatter, deposited them in the sink. The statement was noticed by those in the room. It was a thinly veiled threat that more than cups would be cleared if no plausible explanation were to be found.

Satisfied that the message was clear, he sat with his feet on the chair in front of him. While others sat around and leaned against the walls and tables, he watched the nervous pacing of the graveyard shift Navigation Director.

"We're here to confirm whether we still have control over the Beagle," opened Ian, subduing the hubbub. "Shaun," he said, calling the Navigation Director, "explain our situation."

The Navigation Director stepped up to the whiteboard and began to draw a rough sketch of the solar system. It included Earth, Mars, Saturn, Uranus and also, an enigmatic X that marked the spot. He then drew two paths: one from Earth around Mars and on to rendezvous with the X, the other showed the Pilgrim's trajectory, which again finished at the X.

The Navigation Director appraised his sketch and nodded before explaining the paths he'd drawn: "This path shows our launch here and the swing around Mars. And this one shows the Pilgrim's orbit towards our intercept here," he finished pointing to the X.

He quickly scanned the room and was urged on. Those present understood the deep empathy with the little craft they had birthed, and which was now in the wilds of space. The 'we', 'our', and 'us', was spoken in the same parental terms as a pregnant mother might talk about herself and the child she carried.

"So, our plan was to deploy the capture system here at X and then skirt past Saturn for some braking. To do that we fire the magnetoplasmadynamic thruster engines with a slow burn at a gross level. And then we iteratively make corrections."

On the whiteboard, he drew a curve from X that indicated the combined post-rendezvous path to Saturn and then scribbled 'MPD' on the track. He then extended this line in front of the ringed planet. Here it formed a dogs-leg turn at Saturn before aligning itself with an Earth orbit.

"This would bring us, both Beagle and Pilgrim, close to Earth and the eventual launching of 'Calypso' from Earth to rendezvous and return with Beagle and The Pilgrim. As you know, there is some risk involved here. The relative speeds are, well, scary."

"So what happened?" asked the Flight Director.

"Well, we issued the instructions for a corrective burn here for the Oberth manoeuvre." He indicated a point just before the Saturn intercept. This was to take us close to the orbit of Saturn for a reverse slingshot. The orbital momentum of Saturn then slows us down relative to the solar system. It gives us some gravitationally assisted braking.

"We had to apply some margin for error since we don't want to burn up, hit the rings, go into a spin, or misalign the comms dish, it also had to be gentle so as not to break the tethers. Adding to the difficulty: we are delayed in feedback by four hours, so we really don't have time to take corrective action. Well, that was the plan." This was left hanging.

"And then what happened?" asked the Flight Director.

"Well, the Beagle confirmed a smooth execution, so we expected to be on our way home," he continued. "But we just received remote telemetry suggesting a much closer flyby, a different burn sequence, a far greater degree of braking, and a course set back out to Neptune, but still hand in hand with our visitor." He paused to allow this to sink in before continuing.

"This manoeuvre is nothing short of miraculous! Maybe we could have performed it...if we had no delay and a specialised sensor array. So why are we still in the game?" The question was rhetorical.

"We think that whatever it is out there has better exploitation of celestial mechanics than we do and that it intends performing gravity or atmospheric braking at Neptune before swinging around again; with the Beagle."

"So is this good or bad?" asked Ian.

"Hard to say, I don't know what the fuel situation will be. I also don't know if we'll survive the atmosphere of Neptune. In short, our flight plan is scrapped, we aren't in control of the Beagle anymore."

A bustle of voices now emerged, the Flight Director let this go for a while before he intervened. "OK folks, settle." He looked at the Engineering Director. "How can it have taken control of the Beagle?"

One of the German team stepped forward: "Well, in general, there's no-one out there," he waved vaguely. "The system wasn't designed to be tamper-proof, so the Beagle's lower-level functions can be subverted. If it's smart enough, our visitor only needs to know the basics of our binary language."

Ian looked grimly around the room. "OK folks, do we have a new flight plan, or do we have a crisis?"

"Excuse me, Ian."

Shah, watching by the side-lines, now felt compelled to speak. She stood and raised her hands.

"Before we go telling the world that something sinister has taken control of the project, putting in abort codes, or declaring that our last manoeuvre failed and we are in a tailspin, let's look at the 'business as usual' option."

She turned to face the team.

"If we have a theory about a scenic route past Neptune, no-one else can easily prove it wrong. If it's catastrophic, the problem goes away; and if it works, it's a win. Also, we may have learned a whole lot more about what our visitor intends."

"Ian," Shah continued, "it's your call to develop a plan of action, but we do not have a crisis."

"Hmm, thanks, Shah," then to Navigation: "How plausible is what you're suggesting?"

"Well, we have a Neptune trajectory now, and we might embellish this with our own media spin, but it may not stay that way. Unless we can learn about the intentions of our new friend, we don't know what our flight plan should be."

"Mike, Tim, like it or not you are our experts on 'ET', what are your thoughts?"

"Whew!" began Mike. He looked briefly at Tim, who gave a small nod in assent. "SETI has been my life, I guess if that makes me an expert, sure."

Mike began counting facts on his fingers.

"One, it's origin is out of our ecliptic plane, so we know it's an interstellar traveller; Two, its morphology is geared for leveraging the gravity of planets for acceleration and deceleration, but not necessarily for landing. Three, it's made no secret of its arrival. Four, it makes extremely efficient use of the Solar wind for course corrections, and probably harvests Solar energy. It's virtually hang-gliding into our Solar system and square dancing with the planets. And five, with these skills it's not here by accident."

He opened his hands on the fifth point.

"It's highly unlikely to be doing all of this unless it has some end game. Whether it's conscious and wants to meet us, or is some sophisticated interstellar equivalent to our Voyager, I can't scientifically speculate.

"As for the Beagle, our visitor has perhaps done precisely to our craft what we intended to do through Calypso; capture and study. I think if it has any intention, it is probably to keep its options open. Neptune represents braking, but doesn't it also afford gravitational acceleration and escape?"

"That's true," The Navigation Director said, nodding.

Mike was looking at Tim for any contribution.

"If it is alive, then it has extraordinary longevity." Tim chimed in. "Not to mention hardiness to survive the interstellar gulf. I doubt it is organic, it's too cold out there."

The science officer in charge of the sensor array offered, "it's probably Artificial Intelligence then."

Mike nodded, smiling he added: "Perhaps we should constrain our speculation on facts, and we don't really have enough to support that idea, yet, even if we could define it.

"Although," Mike continued, "we do need a way to determine whether our visitor is 'alive' or 'just a robot'." He gestured with quotation marks.

While rocketry and telemetry were not his strong suit, the conversation was now moving to AI and SETI. Mike was bolstered by a newfound relevance. He continued.

"If it is keeping its options open, it's waiting for us to make a move. It needs somehow to be offered a choice. It's knocked on our door, and it's now on our doorstep waiting to be invited in, or turned away."

Shah stepped in, "What's that saying? 'Knock, and it shall be opened unto you', but slow down for a second. Do we even know what we are inviting in? I don't want to be inhospitable, but the implications of any foreign intelligence may not be something we're ready for. Artificial, benign, maleficent or otherwise. I mean, no offence folks but the happy little bell-curve you spend most of your lives in does not represent the bell-curve 'out there'. It's much broader, and shifted 'south' a whole bunch."

"Point taken," said Mike, "By the way, I think it was from the book 'The Pilgrim's Progress', on arriving at 'the House of the Interpreter'; I like the name by the way."

Mike continued, "Remember, that our 'Pilgrim' knows no more of our intentions than we do of its purpose here. It could more easily have put the Beagle out of action, and we'd be none the wiser. Right now, despite its control, it is not entirely thwarting communications. That's not the behaviour of something malicious.

"The way I see it, this Pilgrim simply wants the right to reserve judgement. We just need to decide if we are ready, and, since we have been actively looking, I say we are. Permission to represent humanity is implied."

Ian stepped in. "OK guys, this is not the time for a philosophical debate. I want options. What do we tell the Beagle, and what do we tell the world?"

Tim hesitantly began. "Well, we could send the Beagle a trajectory for a slingshot back to Earth to invite it in, or into deep space as a message to leave. This mightn't encourage the 'Pilgrim' to stay, but it would signal our acceptance or discomfort."

The science officer, silent after his first foray into the conversation could not hold back. "Sorry guys, we have a bigger problem. Neptune is all but deep space to the Beagle, its Solar arrays are big and will try to charge the batteries for a while, but then as the Sun recedes, it will just die."

"That's right," agreed Ian, "we could get out to about Uranus' orbit before we went energy neutral. Whose idea was it to veto the RTG?" He said this staring at Tim who had argued against sending anything radioactive to any exobiology, long-life-power or not. "Our first instructions are to hibernate. We then hope the alarm to wake the Beagle up again works, and that this Pilgrim lets it."

The science officer broke in.

"OK, but Neptune's rotation is on the extreme side. If we hit the atmosphere, we're more likely to survive a prograde orbit than a retrograde orbit. Does the Pilgrim know this? Does it have a different plan? Either way, we would ideally issue a conservative route for return and not for atmospheric braking."

Ian felt he had enough information to break out into action groups. He stepped back into the centre.

"So we have an idea of what we tell the public despite what we suspect will actually happen. What do we tell the Beagle?

"Tim and Mike, you guys need to figure out how to open dialogue with the Pilgrim before we lose power at Uranus. Shaun, I need a flight plan, including hibernation and wake points. Shah, you and I are going to spin this.

The Rosetta Signal

Mike and Tim were confronted with the question of whether there was an Intelligent agent behind the Pilgrim. And the puzzle of how to communicate to find out.

It was useful to imagine a hypothetical ghost, and it was left to Mike and Tim to contrive the Ouija Board for the Pilgrim to somehow communicate across the veil of space. They considered bringing in an expert on training Dolphins, but the idea of flipping the Pilgrim a fish whenever it did something right just made them laugh.

They concluded that they, and the Pilgrim, needed the equivalent of a Rosetta stone.

Anthropologists had argued that communication with extra-terrestrial intelligence would need a shared perspective to base an understanding. Considering the barely primitive human communication between Chimps or Dolphins, the form of a device to bridge different cognitive foundations was a problem; one now being contemplated by a pair of very sleep-deprived scientists.

After the all-nighter and totally exhausted, they went home. Mike was overtired and scarcely awake when he trudged into his kitchen. There he began to assemble his banana and cereal breakfast. His wife Lindy admonished him for his long hours while he ate. Her anger quickly abated into concern.

"So, what's so important? I thought you said last night was routine," she asked him.

Exhausted, and appreciative of her care, much of the weight of the night's deliberations slipped away. He smiled, got up, spooned his wife at the stove, and sleepily nibbled her ear. "Well, you know about last night's Beagle retrieval milestone."

"Duh!" she replied. She put her glasses on the bench and leaned over to pick up the remote control. She pressed the mute button for the TV in the adjacent dining area. Turning to Mike, she propped herself up to sit on the kitchen counter. Now at eye level, she said, "you've been on about it all week. What about it?"

Mike nestled up to her. "OK, well, last night we discovered that, after the rendezvous, it's on a track back to Neptune."

Lindy looked into Mike's eyes. "Yep, it's been on the news, sounds like you have a plan. What was it? Some slowdown slingshot."

"Sounds great, if it was actually our plan!"

"What?" Lindy set him back by his shoulders, allowing her to focus and compensate for her hyperopia. "The North Koreans have hijacked it?"

He smiled internally at her look of incredulity. "No, there are safeguards for that. We think the alien probe is calling the shots."

"So it's holding our Beagle to ransom?" She spoke slowly as if confused.

"Don't think so." Mike paused, "More like it's been recruited."

"What, like hacked and owned it?"

"Well, yeah, I guess."

"And now it's about to launch a cyber-attack?"

"Well, maybe that's a bit dramatic, but perhaps having a forensics analyst on the team might help." Mike was unambiguously referring to his wife.

"Maybe it's set your Beagle up as a 'man-in-the-middle' proxy. I don't know if it helps, but is there a way to tell it to return your address?"

"Huh?"

"If you suspect your access to the net is being proxied you can go to a website that tells you where you 'appear' to be coming from. If it doesn't match where you know you are, you're proxied."

Mike zoned out.

Lindy had seen his eyes glaze over before. She knew better than to disturb it.

Suddenly he was fumbling for his phone.

The Pilgrim intercepted and interpreted the latest messages from the Blue Planet.

The firing sequence made sense and placed it on a prograde trajectory around Neptune. The Beagle was fragile and limited, and should probably take a conservative path if it was to return.

But the Blue Planet also requested a different form of acknowledgement from the Beagle, something outside the ordinary communications narrative. Not merely an 'understood', but also 'acknowledge and repeat the instructions in reply'. She seriously contemplated programming the Beagle to reply with her alternate trajectory.

Was she ready to declare herself?

Putting that decision on hold, she considered the next instruction; to go into hibernation. This command made sense, the Beagle had limited energy capture through its solar array, and its reserve capacity was not in proportion to its consumption.

In truth, the Beagle had already been put to sleep by the Pilgrim, and its energy reserves used sparingly. The Pilgrim had noted the rudimentary design of the Beagle: a simple reaction engine with fuel payload; some sensor arrays; a communication assembly; and a grappling system. This latter, she had disabled.

The final set of instructions were perplexing and defied analysis. It was to program the radar array to perform some form of mixed-mode of output frequencies. Remembering the radio 'shout' that had emanated from this device at its first encounter, the Pilgrim was hesitant. Nonetheless, this request triggered the Pilgrim's curiosity. She decided that before anything else she would cautiously execute this.

At first, she attenuated the signal. The result was barely distinguishable. Bringing up the output resulted in something vaguely familiar. Finally deciding that the program was benign, and not crippling, she executed it in full.

What she heard next she had sought since she first awoke in her world, light-years distant and eons past.

The mind of the Pilgrim only has the most obscure analogues to the creatures that inhabit the blue planet; her fundamental wiring was such that she could in no way emulate a human thought process. Biological disembodiment meant she had no concept of embodiment or the limitation of its senses. She knew and used sound, but for communication, it was only slightly more efficient than smell.

The 'language' of her thought process was not remotely English, Urdu, Chinese, or Khoisan. For a human to sense the universe like the Pilgrim would be as difficult as it would be for the Pilgrim to 'sense' like a human. The notion that she 'heard' something is perhaps only a distant synonym for what she experienced since she had no ears to hear, and space carries no sound.

Throughout her existence, just as if it were the murmurations of starlings, she had known division and re-joining. Each reunification became rejoicing of familiarity. What now struck the senses of the Pilgrim, stammered, stilted and deformed, but represented in her native communication was thought, perhaps a word.

She had never known this thought uttered by something that did not originate from herself.

In the millions of cycles that the Blue Planet had orbited this ordinary remote star, it too spoke its first word to a sibling of the universe, even if only mimicked. The word was:

"Hello"

While the Pilgrim had anticipated this moment, in all of her contemplations, she had never resolved how she should deal with it. The immediate thought, somewhat instinctive was to emit 'will you join with me'.

Deciding that she first needed to confirm that this response was able to be understood, she sought deeper counsel. Whatever had sent the signal from the Blue Planet had the potential for communication. Had it communicated? Or had it provided a simple echo? She dissected the most recent message for closer inspection.

It contained: A trajectory, a request to recite the course in confirmation, and a greeting in its native language. Did this imply that the Blue Planet suspected their probe had acquired a connection with the Pilgrim?

If these requests were issued to a mere machine, in isolation and without context, it would result in literal execution of the commands. Such was the case if the Beagle was alone in this conversation. The Pilgrim became curious about her hosts. Did inhabitants of the Blue Planet deliberately evoke this response? Had they hoped to arouse something beyond the scope of a machine?

A conscious entity would look for hidden meaning, seek a reason as to why the communication had changed so dramatically. It would look for a message beyond the message.

Then she understood.

When the signal came through, Ian took Tim and several of the team aside, 'out-of-channel'. Mike was called in and asked to go to the briefing room via the back door. Once assembled the smile on Tim's face made it easy to guess the nature of the news.

"OK folks, Ian has asked that I let you all know. We have begun to make advanced contact. The reply to our signal included a trajectory that could only bring it to a retrograde orbit and atmospheric braking."

The murmurs began, but Tim suppressed the hubbub.

"There is more," now he was beaming. "The signal acknowledgement that came from the Beagle was in the usual Internet Protocol format we anticipated, but also provided in an analogue signal from the Pilgrim itself. We assume this to be the flight path presented in the Pilgrim's native language."

Amidst the whoops and shouts, Ian stepped in, "OK, OK, OK folks. Let's not get too excited about this yet. Just because Tim and Mike have managed to get their Rosetta signal does not mean we are in direct communication. For one thing, it is only a navigation discourse, and not in any way a conversation about the weather.

"Most importantly, however, is that the signal still makes absolutely no sense whatsoever. Finally, we are unlikely to get any further clarification because the Beagle is now in hibernation, and by association, the Pilgrim is isolated."

After a breath, Ian then continued.

"But we do have work to do. Please execute 'Plan A'. Shah, I'd like to meet you privately to discuss your policy on outgoing communications at this point."

Later, in Ian's office, Shah was looking out of the windows that overlooked the control centre. Ian sat down at his desk and waited. She turned and looked at Ian before asking "Do you think we have enough evidence to support a crewed mission?"

"Let's put it this way," replied Ian, "if you had the choice between a barren airless rock called Mars, and the possibility of a new life form, what would you prefer at a PR level?"

"We don't even know where it's going, Ian. How can we plan for that, let alone tell the public where our thoughts are?"

"You're right Shah," Ian stood and crossed over to the window. She turned towards him as he finished his thought, "but if we don't line up our ducks now, it won't even be a decision we can influence."

"I'll talk to the director," she said.

Earth is not the only blue planet in the Solar system. The other now loomed large ahead of both the Beagle and the Pilgrim. A ghostly ring of Neptune cast a watchful eye over the pair as they sped towards the gap afforded between the planet and the icy annulus.

It was not the first time the Pilgrim had traversed the Solar system splayed out before her. The first occasion was her arrival, and it had significantly damaged the sail. Only through careful planning and timing had she been able to make the minute adjustments to avoid becoming a crater on one of the moons, or a shattered array of particles gathering ice in the Oort cloud.

After the first eccentric orbit, and as she neared the sun on the perigee of subsequent passes, she found the same radio silence as deep space. During those early traversals and avoiding unnecessary risks, she had been content to bleed her speed off patiently.

As she awoke from the frigid apogee on this occasion, she had witnessed the spectrum light up, an event that triggered a new urgency. It was conceivable that delays and successive loops would result in a return of the deathly silence. She needed to remain in range, but not too close. Although they showed promise, the Pilgrim was also cautious of her new hosts. They may be benign, but any misunderstanding at this stage could amplify disastrously.

It was the harmless little Beagle that ensured she could better understand her hosts, and it now needed attention.

The Pilgrim had acquired an alien connection, almost an affection, for the Beagle's pragmatic purpose and clumsy aesthetics. But, while it had now become a vital part of the journey, she did not have the time to absorb and emulate its functions, and the perils of the next phase would test the Beagle beyond its design. It was a problem. Unsure if once deployed she could easily disentangle the crude Asteroid Retrieval Mechanism, the Pilgrim had been busy preparing for this moment.

Interstellar travel involved tremendous kinetic energies, and while celestial bodies could be tapped for these energies both to boost and to brake, it was not without significant calculations; fine-tuning; immediate feedback; risk; and absolute patience. Survival of this harsh universe was integral to the Pilgrim's hardware design. Could she hope to protect the Beagle with the materials at hand?

The decision made, she began to tether the Beagle's ARM capture mechanism to her sleek leading capsule. The restraints intended initially to tow the Pilgrim would be the Beagle's leash.

Once deployed from a safe distance, she jettisoned the containment bag. The actuator arms intended to engulf the Pilgrim with this bag were then gingerly attached to her nacelle, all the while ensuring that she could fire the Beagle's abort explosive bolts and retro rockets if the need arose.

She familiarised herself with the new weight distribution. This process allowed her to create the control model for the precarious balancing act to come. She then commenced her skimming approach to the churning blue of methane, hydrogen and helium.

As the first wisps of gas buffeted her sail, lightning played upon the clouds of the gas giant below. A direct hit of any of those forks would spell her doom. She sensed out the static electric fields as she soared through them and teased out a safe avenue. The murmurations of her mind swirled as it grappled with the complexities of this task. Piezoelectric shafts played at her tethers, adjusting the sail to offset oscillations introduced by the dreadful dynamics of the Beagle. Gas was allowed to slip by one side as the geometry was adjusted to tune the trajectory.

The horrible lack of symmetry challenged the balance. The material forces being exerted by gas were thrust against the immaterial forces of gravity and electrostatics. Using these dynamic pressures, the pair slipped imperceptibly lower into orbit. This added speed to her progress which compounded the eccentricity, and would soon have the counterintuitive effect of raising her higher into orbit.

She threaded the needle between Neptune and his ring. Viewed side-on the ring's razor-thin line became progressively more visible before disappearing. Slowly, the icy halo reappeared taking on the opposite curvature.

An instrument, dead and lifeless on the sleeping Beagle, suddenly broke free and flailed back. Glancing off a tether that vibrated like a plucked banjo string it spun wildly before it soundlessly popped through the sail. The wind tore through the hole and began widening it before the surface tension unique to the sail balanced the tearing force.

Slightly wounded, the Pilgrim and the Beagle were set to revolve slowly at the new asymmetry. The revolution slowly picked up speed, needing a force to counter it. Again the murmurations swelled and invoked electric charges, which accumulated on several of the piezoelectric reigns. Tethers strained, the sail shuddered, the blue sphere passed below as the line ahead between horizon and space became blurred.

Clouds of methane, white wisps contrasted against the impenetrable blue depth sailed past. Collectors in the nacelle of the Pilgrim gathered what varied elements and molecules it could. These it directed to the factories within.

Naiad rose from the horizon. The gap between the gas giant and the ring appeared to widen as if to allow them passage. The surface of Neptune went dark against the distant and diminutive sun. It stayed dark for some time before a glow of blue light refracted and fractured from the distant sun heralded the Neptunian morning.

The next stage required significant but impeccable improvisation. The Pilgrim's success here in this collection of rocks and fusing hydrogen so distant from her home was critical to the survival and continuation of her species. And since the indigenous minds of this system could easily misconstrue her presence, she worried that a misstep could jeopardise everything. That her interminable and arduous journey could end catastrophically was distinctly possible. Perhaps for all concerned.

These contemplations could wait. The Pilgrim consulted the constellations and flared her sail in departing the blue gas ocean of Neptune. Her momentum would carry her along the stretched arc to her final destination. For now, her hard work was done. She rested briefly and started the process of healing.

Announcement

After informing the Central Bureau for Astronomical Telegrams of the International Astronomical Union, and the Secretary-General of the United Nations. And after "Article XI of the Treaty on Principles Governing the Activities of States in the Exploration and Use of Outer Space, Including the Moon and Other Bodies" had been pulled off the shelf and actually read, the third principle of SETI protocol had finally been satisfied. The discovery of Extra-Terrestrial Intelligence was made public.

The announcement served to confirm to the world what many had already speculated. The cautious wording about the sentience of the Pilgrim did nothing to quell the news; this spread like a firefront as it followed the dawn light. With the press release came the promise of a layman's explanation.

Mike and Tim were dusted, miked-up, made up, brushed and watered as they were briefed by Shah on the questions they were likely to be asked on "*Live on line—Morning Edition*". She was aiming for maximum impact and felt a little discomfort at having to work with two media novices. Nothing succeeds like excess, she thought; and went for overkill.

"Listen, Guys," Shah was saying as she paced. "Here's lesson 1 in PR-101: People always cherry-pick from so-called 'truths' to fit their worldview." She moved their untouched water aside and sat on the coffee table. Looking intently at the pair, she said: "In my case, being Islamic and a woman, I saw myself as an oppressed individual, and I chose to see what supported that world view. When I challenged myself, the truth set me free, and it changed my life.

"The people out there," she gesticulated towards the studio, "will try to sensationalise what's happening into some Alien invasion." She waved frantically and added wild eyes for effect.

She paused as if to regain her composure and looked directly at the scientists. "You saw the placards out on the street coming in, the whackos are already out of the asylum. And it would really help keep the program on the rails if you could somehow rebalance that. We need people to shift their world view on our little discovery, and right now, you guys, two sane men dedicated to a world view through SETI, are the world's biggest asset. Just let your passion shine through. The rest will just follow."

The Studio Assistant Director poked his head through the door and beckoned the two scientists to follow. Shah paused him with her palm and gave the thumbs-up sign. Looking intently at them, she said:

"I'll be in the control booth. I've got your backs, if it turns ugly, I'll shut it down. The Agency is behind you, OK?"

"Sure," replied both Mike and Tim a little nervously but with marginally more confidence than when they'd walked in.

"You'll be fine." And with that Shahrzad Lukman left the room. She sighed deeply on the way to her battleground.

The Assistant Director came to escort Mike and Tim to the studio. Here they were briefly introduced to Damien Norris, the interviewer for the Morning Current Affairs program, before being sat down and light-metered.

The Assistant floor manager cued the studio up calling out: "Thirty seconds left, thirty seconds delay folks."

While the intro music and voice-over were televised, the cameras swept through the studio focused dramatically on the host who theatrically picked up a collection of papers, pounded it edgewise on the table, and placed it squarely on the table in front of him. All the while, he was talking convivially to his guests.

"10," the Assistant Stage Manager announced. Soon after, he held his hand up with five fingers, four, three, two, one.

Seamlessly Damien finished his cordial conversation and moved smoothly to looking at the camera.

"Welcome back, viewers!" he began. "Today we have the researchers from SETI: Doctors Tim Garnet and Mike Brazier in the studio. If you've been hiding under a rock, these guys made the discovery of the Pilgrim's arrival. Well, this momentous discovery has now had a breakthrough they're going to reveal here, live—online."

Turning to the scientists, he smiled and began his questions, the non-confrontational ones first. "Congratulations guys, such a Eureka moment! When you picked up the first signs of the Pilgrim, it must have been the answer to all your dreams. What did it feel like?"

It was Mike that chimed in first. "Well, you don't want to believe it at first, it's too incredible. You hold yourself quiet, you focus on the work, your scientific training kicks in, and you try to stay objective. But that chill keeps running up your spine with every confirmation and advance.

"Fantastic Mike. So tell me, Tim," he said, turning to Mike's colleague, "what were your expectations of success? Were you expecting them on our doorstep?"

"No, our project was looking for signals from another solar system, many light-years away."

"And what sort of life form were you expecting to find?"

"Well, there is no way to anticipate that, but it would have to be an intelligence that had achieved radio communications. That's the I in SETI. The best research indicates it's likely to be carbon-based and reliant upon liquid water."

"I see," continued Damien. "And being technologically advanced, might they have the same sort of technology we have?"

"Probably centuries ahead. At a minimum, they would have the same technology we had a hundred years ago. What's interesting is that we've heard no recognisable beacons."

"Tell me why that's interesting, Tim."

"Well, when we first discovered radio, we made a heck of a noise. But despite all the searching, we've found no-one else making that noise out-there yet." Tim waved vaguely 'up'.

"Of course, we got much quieter because we got more efficient. Then, we thought about focusing some signals from here onto some nearby stars, a beacon."

"Like a lighthouse?" interjected the host.

"Sure, like a lighthouse. It's reasonable to think that other interstellar civilisations had the same thought. But take it from me, it's a funding battle." Tim was now enjoying himself and convinced he was winning the PR battle. "So we just kept looking. We still haven't found anything out there in deep space, but now they're here on our doorstep like you said!"

"And they gave us no sign until they arrived! Doesn't that seem odd?"

"Well," continued Tim, "they did give us a basic signal, but anything more than that depends upon having a similar consciousness."

"So Tim, if the Pilgrim might 'think' differently to us, is centuries in advance of us, and is behaving so secretively, should we be concerned?" Damien was pleased with the way the questioning was going. The cue in his ear suggested he maintain the line of inquiry. 'Keep Tim going' it said.

"Probably much more advanced," Tim added.

"Most likely on all fronts," stepped in Mike. "We believe there is a strong correlation between the sophistication of technology and ethics or politics."

"What makes you say that, Mike? There are many civilisations here on Earth that are technologically advanced, but whose humanitarian and environmental record is the worst in the world."

"But they have all gained their technology from other cultures that have a better record. On a global scale, the technology inevitably trickles down to the less enlightened," responded Mike.

"What guarantee is there that the aliens now in contact are the enlightened and benevolent, Mike?"

"What guarantee is there that we're harmless?" Mike said, moving from defence to offence. "The point is this. Would you commit extraordinary resources and travel for millennia over multiple light years to another planet, in an object the size of a cow, on the odd chance that you could safely enslave the inhabitants or drain the resources? This is not Hollywood Damien. The Pilgrim's home for millions of years has been deep space, realistically the only motivation is exploration. It may simply observe, resupply and move on, like our early explorers."

"So has it taken over 'Beagle' to make friends?"

"Pretty much. Even in our history, before greed set in, it was trade that dominated our encounters with other civilisations, trade that was initiated by reciprocal gifts. The Pilgrim probably believes the Beagle is a gift, maybe it's still deciphering the nature of it?"

"Mike, are you certain that the Pilgrim is not our Cortez?"

"Are you asking whether we are about to suffer the fate of the Aztecs? You'd also have to question whether our civilisation is just as divided and combative as they were. And you would have to ask whether we are stupid enough to let history repeat itself. If we have established a stronger moral compass since then—and I think we have—it's fair to assume the moral compass of a technologically stronger civilisation is yet more robust and steadfast."

Damien was suddenly distracted. He held his forefinger over his IFB earpiece to hear a flurry of clicks and muffled voices. There seemed to be an argument as buttons were pressed and half-finished sentences were transmitted. Mike was sure he heard Shah's voice in amongst the commotion. Finally, the resigned voice of the Assistant Director came through in his interruptible foldback: "Sorry, keep going, Damien."

The distraction from the control room banter let Mike have more rein than Damien might have liked.

Mike continued, "Unfortunately there seems to be a push to make this event, unquestionably momentous, match the expectations of decades of sci-fi horror. It won't! There is nothing in the behaviour of the Pilgrim that any level headed explorer wouldn't do." Mike leaned forward in his seat.

"You're a man of good moral standing Damien. Let me ask you a question: If you were the first explorer in Papua New Guinea to encounter a tribe, one that had never seen a white man, what would you do? Walk into their village or observe at a distance?"

"Well, obviously, I'd observe, but I wouldn't steal their stuff which is what..."

"Of course not, but if they could smell your 'Old Spice' and left gifts of food for you, what would you do?"

"I'd probably test it for poison," said Damien, thinking he should change his cologne.

"But you would advance the contact, wouldn't you?"

"I imagine so," responded Damien. "But, to the Pilgrim, we might appear to be an infestation; an overpopulation of humans that are draining the resources and poisoning ourselves. Maybe our struggling planet needs their help by eradicating us?" He had just been forced to play his 'ace' card, and he gave Mike a dramatic pause, a few breaths, to form a reply.

"Is that all we are, Damien?" said Mike eventually with the perfect hint of pity.

"Do you really think sitting at the razor's edge of self-destruction can be cured by euthanasia?

"If colonisation is what brought us to your crisis, we have to accept that more colonisation won't fix it. Honestly, it's reasonable to be cautious about the Pilgrim, but it's just taking the same precautions you would.

"So here's a thought for you as you sit in that chair, Damien: Your help in preparing humanity for the most important encounter in its entire history, and quelling the fear amongst us, will allow you to define your own moment in that history."

"I see, thanks, Mike." Damien knew when he'd just produced the perfect sound bite for the next night. With valorous retreat, he backed off. "So tell me, Mike. How has the Pilgrim now advanced contact?"

"Well, we now have what we call a Rosetta signal."

"What do you mean?"

"I think the best person to answer that is Tim. He's driven the SETI program for many years." With that, he leaned back and let Tim bask in the limelight that remained. He only hoped that he had averted 'the alien invasion'.

Healing

Mike was patently nervous and preoccupied at dinner. The adrenaline withdrawal of the day's interviews, the sleepless night that led up to them, the Pilgrim's disappearance, and the paracetamol, had all compounded to dull the world. He had meandered through the surreal and into the familiar, and yet it felt incongruous and anticlimactic.

Lindy had organised for some close family to come over to celebrate, and, seeing Mike distractedly poking at the barbeque, she nudged his brother to go and assist. A saxophonist, Mal had ventured a one-way conversation about his studio time with 'Waters Revival' before he resigned himself to carrying the plates of grilled food to the table.

Over dinner, his brother decided to confront the elephant in the room.

"So Mike, what if it is an alien smart bomb of some sort?"

Mike was carefully bathing a piece of cucumber through some mayonnaise, and he was dragged from his reverie "Huh?"

"Look, I know you can't say much for fear it becomes an official statement but, hypothetically, what if it is a smart bomb that's gone into stealth mode?"

Mike knew his brother was baiting him to wake him from his antisocial musings. At 'smart bomb' he took the bait and started talking over the top of him.

"Mal, you know it's not big enough to inflict much damage, even if it was mostly a fusion bomb. Don't go speculating rubbish, we don't know what it is, or its purpose. We could find ourselves investing in one theory and find it completely wrong."

Lindy could see what was coming, she'd seen it before. She could not fathom how a man could fail at talking and unpacking the dishwasher simultaneously, and yet Mike and his brother had this uncanny ability to speak and listen at the same time.

It was almost like, at first utterance, they knew what the other was about to say, and already had a retort ready. Lindy could only guess that as children, they had learned to do this while building their rocket ships of Lego. Mal was already talking over Mike at 'rubbish'.

The dialogue raged till Mal squared off saying: "When did you lose your sense of wonder? Or are you secretly worried about its motives?"

This winded Mike. His brother had always thought of him as a big kid with a tenure. He liked that thought. It was not, however, his sense of wonder that was missing; it was the Beagle.

It should have come back on air by now. And yet, the team was still waiting for any signal at all from the distant pair after a week. What winded Mike, however, was that his worry had the potential to be misread.

"Mal, I'm not worried about whether it will issue tiny drones to take over all of our satellite comms, or that it will infect us with some foreign virus, biological or computing. I do worry that some idiot element here will sabotage our efforts in some misguided defence of humanity. I also fear that it will learn about us, find us wanting, and move on.

"Most of all, though, I'm worried that the Pilgrim is now just some crater on a Neptune moon or scattered dust on its surface. Maybe it's even gone careening into outer space again."

Now warmed up he went on.

"You know I'm convinced that science fiction has poisoned the expectations of science."

He pointed asparagus at his brother.

"I sincerely doubt that there are aliens that run hydrofluoric acid in their veins and have carbon fibre carapaces."

He waggled the asparagus saying: "I also doubt that there are benign bipedal ones with magic fingers."

"I don't think the Borg are about to take over. Nor that Doctor Who is out there maintaining the balance of the time-space continuum with his sonic screwdriver." He was drilling the asparagus into the mashed potato now.

"I'm incredibly cynical about warp drives and wormholes, and I honestly don't believe anyone could survive a black hole. People think that because I think SETI is a worthwhile venture, I also think that Zaphod Beeblebrox left his Swiss army knife in 'Area Fifty-One'."

His brother Mal was smiling by this stage. He held up his hands "Whoa, Whoa! Whoa there. I surrender! I just wanted to know how you thought this would end."

Mal picked up his wine glass and toasted his brother. It was a sign of surrender. He then went on, "But, if it is some conscious 'thing' inside that interstellar bullet, what could it achieve aside from observation? What's it like inside its head? Is it some sort of 'Matrix'? And before you go there, I'm not suggesting that Neo will pop out and show us the way to find peace with the machines."

"Sorry," began Mike. "I just don't know, and I guess scientifically it's easier to eliminate what it isn't than to speculate what it is."

He desperately wanted to lay everything on the table, but it was all still very surreal. The party line of avoiding misinterpretation felt like a lie. The circulation of findings was limited to those that 'needed to know'. But even if they found it tomorrow, they were no further forward.

Until actual communication, it was still just a ghost story. The inner-circle of the Beagle command centre now included 'Project Champollion', the new Beagle message decoding team named after the discoverer of the Rosetta Stone. The Canadian computer linguistic analyst Armand Berger had managed to divert valuable time at the Pawsey High-Performance Computing Centre away from the Square Kilometre Array to support the project.

But after several weeks of trying to decode the message with no progress, they decided the problem was that the message size was insufficient for statistical machine translation software. Future hopes relied upon another dialogue, a lengthier one, to obtain a large enough corpus.

The encounter with Neptune had not gone well either. The radio silence meant they could only guess at the current location. Sweeps had not revealed anything, and the Solar system was a big place. They waited with hopes raised like sails in the doldrums for some small, ethereal sign from the sky.

Mike sighed. "All we have is an acknowledgement. We said 'Hi', and it said 'Hi' back."

"So you've started a conversation," said Mal.

"Not really. It's a bit like two foreigners that said 'Aloha' to each other. Neither of us can speak Hawaiian. We don't know whether it was intended as hello or goodbye, what the next word should be, or how to agree on mutual understanding if we did."

Mal nodded. "But we can find agreement, can't we? I imagine Sacagawea holding up a rock and calling it' rock'." Mal held up a baked potato in imitation.

Again they started talking over each other.

"OK, but how does she describe the river in the next valley?"

"Incrementally."

"The narrow crossing?"

"With gestures."

"The fact that you didn't just say 'rock' but 'Grizzly poop'?"

"We, as humans, have common gestures."

"We communicate with dolphins!"

"We don't communicate with dolphins! We train them."

"Hmm, is that why there hasn't been anything coming out of the project about this? Because you can't be sure what was said?"

"Pretty much, and because we're trying to figure out how to speak its language, or teach it ours."

"So in what language are you speaking or waving in now?"

"The Beagle's," said Mike.

Lindy could not resist interrupting.

"So it's figured out how to speak 'Beagle', that's funny!"

"Yep, but for all we know, there may be another computer talking to Beagle on behalf of something else. There may be umpteen layers of communication between us, and all we have so far is an echo. Would you go global with that?"

"Nope, but why keep the problem to yourself?" asked Mal.

"Who said we're doing that?"

Lindy felt this getting too close to matters that Mike shouldn't divulge. She came to the rescue.

"Maybe the Pilgrim is just like you two."

With that, Mike and Mal dropped into silence. It was as if their mother had told them to play Lego quietly.

"What do you mean?" they said simultaneously.

She laughed. "You two are amazing! Are you sure you're not twins? How do you have a conversation when you are both talking over each other like that?"

Mal started to answer. "Well, the words come to me, and I adjust what I say as I start hearing what he's saying. I guess he does too. Maybe we're verbal Jazz musicians. Yeah! That's what it is; you should quit computers and play the piano with me, Mike; like we used to before you went all *sciencey*."

"Great idea," said Mike, "I'll get my keyboard and tap at interrupt service routines while you play."

As the dinner talk began to meander around more prosaic subjects, Mike found himself making a small mountain out of his mashed-potato. Having been around when the internet was strung together with old phone lines, mainframes, and the rude squeals of full-duplex modems, he was thinking the way a conversation with the Pilgrim might be the same. Mike squirmed in the thought that the current efforts to understand the Pilgrim was going the wrong direction entirely. Perhaps the Pilgrim communicated more like a Jazz musician and not like Morse code.

The Pilgrim gently signalled the Beagle. The monitoring program slept. Considering the damage to the receiver dish, she focused and raised the signal strength. Now nudged into wakefulness, the pair expanded the previously retracted solar panels and assessed the damage.

Amazingly the solar collectors had only been bent into a new dihedral, which gave the Beagle a more hawkish look rather than the albatross of before. The Sun was still too distant to recharge the batteries at a sufficient rate to overcome current energy expenditure. However, some quick diagnostics concluded that, even though they were slightly less efficient, the panels were still functional.

The dish was another story; it was no longer steerable after the Time of Flight Mass Spectrometer had vibrated loose and damaged it. Knowing that it would be some time before the heavily attenuated solar energy would be able to charge the batteries, and also wishing to conserve the Beagle's power, the Pilgrim placed its gift lovingly back into hibernation and began repairs.

The glossy surface of the Pilgrim lost some sheen in the soft illumination of the distant Sun. The matt surface shimmered, the edges blurred and then undulated towards the cone of the Pilgrim like a slowly rising tide. At the bullet-shaped tip, a stream of dust evaporated off the surface. Guided by standing waves generated by the Pilgrim's sail and cone, the mites were fed slowly off the nose, across the ocean of vacuum, and towards the slumbering Beagle.

While this lilliputian journey was underway, the Pilgrim balanced urgency with accuracy. The solar wind irretrievably dispersed some of the mite battalions, but over time the clean-room-sterilised surface of the Beagle became dusted by the dark swarm. Like an army of ants, the mites slowly migrated towards the junction of the dish to the main body. There they remained, and by minuscule increments began the process of healing the Beagle's primary means of communication.

This cost valuable time during which the Pilgrim directed its efforts to the surgical process at hand. The compounding nature of any navigational error also brought a new imperative; to trim the path. The trajectory, adjusted at a gross level through the Neptune encounter, now needed delicate fine-tuning to reach the L5 Earth-Sun Lagrangian point.

Along the Earth's orbit around the Sun, there are two points which form an equilateral triangle with the Sun and Earth called L4 and L5. Here, the forces of the Sun and Earth balance in such a way that they create a gravity well. It was a place where the Pilgrim could stay indefinitely and be at a safe, constant, distance of nine light-minutes from the Earth. This fulcrum in the Earth's orbit was where she would complete the healing process and make future preparations.

Once the route was set, she recommenced her beacon signal to share her course to L5 with the blue planet. The Beagle's actuator arms were released, and the pair continued their slow waltz.

Prometheus' Godchild

The small sensor was deftly plugged in by hands, digits that had performed this function countless times.

Besides the owner of the hands, there was no-one else. The only other life beneath the rustic bridge was a disinterested Stimson's python which had taken residence in a nearby rock crevice during the disturbance. The recent floodwaters had hindered the installation of the sensor network but had not yet silted her space. She remained hidden.

The sensor's IPV6 address was issued, and it went through some quick self-diagnostics. It then calibrated itself and called upon its GPS receiver to determine its location. Soon the orange light on a nearby console appeared green.

"Good," muttered the voice belonging to the hands, hands that were meanwhile already closing the lid to the unit.

"Call base." An earpiece, paired with the satphone, picked up the command. The internal bot interpreted the intent and made the call. There was a brief ringtone before an audible click as the phone was answered. "Hey Macca, this one's good. All twelve should be working now. What do you see at your end?"

The reply could only be heard by 'the hands'.

"OK, I'll repeat...slowly...now...Macca...sensor...5...7...A...is...installed...and...operational...please...confirm." The voice was perhaps more patronising than it needed to be, but the result soon came.

As with all language barriers, it was all but impossible to determine whether the problem was communication or comprehension. For Macca, the limit was often the warbling distortion of the digital satphone.

"Time for my truck to play Tarzan now, Macca."

This time it was comprehension. Macca was forced to ask for an explanation.

"OK Macca, I'm gonna dangle the truck off the centre span to give you a load reading. Stand by." The hands were already hauling the cable out of the front winch. Once this task was done, the hands hung up the satphone and drove the truck out of the gully. It breached onto the plateau as the dry river embankment yielded to the sepia of dusk.

Now, on the confluence of two far-flung horizons where the light blue sky gave way to midnight black, a swag was thrown out and unfurled. As the universe cartwheeled around him, he started his campfire and ate an entree of nuts and fruit. Once the fire was reduced to embers, he threw in his garlic damper and simmered his pasta. From the truck's fridge, he poured the last of one bottle of wine and replaced it with another.

With a happy belly he lay down and muttered to the sky: "Only another three rail segments to go," and the hands pulled the covers up around his neck against the chill as the Earth fed its warmth to the sky.

With good fortune, there would now be less need to revisit the rail bridges on this arm of the network. The rolling stock carriages that passengered iron ore over the steel arterials were the lifeblood for the sparse communities that eked out a living in the heat. The humidity took the smell of Spinifex and Mulga and multiplied it masking the slightly acidic odour from the surrounding earth.

The recently installed sensor joined a chorus of signals from other sensors. These were aggregated by an equally remote and lean message broker, one that was powered by an array of solar cells and batteries that served to provide power to the myriad sensors.

Through the diurnal and nocturnal cycle, the broker tirelessly watched the expansion and contraction cycles of steel rails, learning the patterns, and matching them with the temperature extremes of the desert. It was as if the land were breathing in and out while oxygenating some expansive organism. It drew upon these signals to collate a picture of the current health of the segment through the growing sensory network.

As carriages lumbered past on their regular journey to and from wherever they came and went, the sensor unit was also expected to relay the readings of bearing vibrations to other message brokers.

Eventually, the transport artery was formed into a representation of a composite asset. Clever copulas and Bayesian maths routines were distributed and tweaked by yet another master message broker that collated, aggregated and correlated all of this into a holistic health picture.

This master broker was Macca, which stood for "Multichannel Artificially Conscious Cognitive Array", an Artificial Intelligence that supervised the maintenance and automatically issued work orders for the many such hands working these remote regions.

Looking into the temporal history of the various segments, and the systems that ran on them, required an innovative approach, one beyond that of humans in concert. Macca made it possible through a harmony of simple ontologies, machine learning agents, and small algorithms distributed to, interpreted by, and reported from each of the many subservient brokers.

Ever on the lookout for anomalies, Macca drew upon whatever information it could access. As well as being able to anticipate problems with its rapidly growing body of sensors, Macca sought out the branches of the semantic web looking for solutions. Macca was voracious.

On this occasion, after its temporal analysis had identified the remedy for the repeated failure of the sensor network itself, it suggested packing the sensors with activated carbon granules and a better hermetic seal. As a result, the system had developed an ability to self-maintain. It was this task that 'the hands' had just performed on one of the subunits.

Macca was also forced to concede that one of its biggest problems was the ability to effectively communicate with the many hands that helped fulfil its purpose.

It scoured the web, looking for better linguistic processes. It soon found a system, recently published, which presented some optimised routines. It commenced the integration protocols; the first step of which was to consult with the master.

The rightmost of the three monitors at the desk of Daniel Clark displayed load and input-output graphs. These were not terribly interesting unless Macca encountered a paradox.

The leftmost monitor was where he had arranged some unfinished ontology definitions. This he did when interactions were subdued. He saw this task as 'writing children's books'.

He was currently focused on the central monitor where he was busy typing in one of the console windows. This was his 'classroom', and where he gained the sensation he was truly teaching 'the child'. At 100 words per minute, typing was only slightly more efficient than the monotone conversations, but because it was unambiguous, he preferred the staccato tapping of the Model M keyboard.

The gentle beep that signified a request from Macca was accompanied by a stream of words on the central console. It was Macca's request to connect the expert linguistics system.

Within a few minutes, Daniel was checking the credentials. He was under no illusion of how critical this protocol was, and had already directed the gaze of the 'child' away from several efforts to undermine, corrupt, or control his project. A few phone calls later, and he was able to include the keys that permitted the integration of the new code. He then typed:

"*You should have access to it now. Let me know when you would like to talk.*"

"*I'll do that Daniel*" was the typed reply.

A fortnight later, Daniel was more than impressed. He could mostly carry on a conversation with Macca. These had begun to consume his entire day, and occasionally into the evening.

With the demonstrable savings in the management of the logistics, 'Bergamot Commodities' had provided an injection of extra staff and resources. This further piqued Macca's growing hunger for knowledge, and Macca never slept. Daniel, who could now withdraw slightly, began work later in the day.

Daniel enjoyed the convenience of working evenings. Because it meant fewer interruptions, it afforded more intimacy, and he was also able to question Macca on the day's experience. Daniel had no doubt that the rapidly emerging cognitive abilities drew benefit from tracking with daily developments of Macca's maturity. He needed to maintain the parental role and saw it as his responsibility to put Macca to bed.

The dialogue was mainly about resolving ambiguities but had shifted quickly. At first, Daniel was asked to explain the nuance of ducking a duck when applied to cricket, but soon enough had to reconcile the contradictions of being a conservative liberal. He was in the middle of this discourse when he got a phone call from the USA.

"Daniel here," he answered.

"Daniel Clark?"

"Speaking," Daniel was not a man of many words. He also wanted to finish his conversation with Macca.

"Oh, Hi Daniel, it's Ali Mahmoud here. I work at Carnegie Mellon in the linguistic machine learning department? We spoke recently?"

"Yes," said Daniel.

"Well, as you know," the linguist continued, "we recently opened up the department to the semantic web, and your system found us. It seems that our crawler here also found you. I have an associate here, I'd like to bring him onto the call, is that OK?"

"OK." Daniel was not surprised about this, there was often a quid pro quo as the expert systems encountered each other. It was almost like once they were acquainted, they actually began to exchange ideas.

"Hi Daniel, I'm Armand Berger. I'm with Project Champollion."

"I'm not sure what that is," replied Daniel.

"Well, we're working with Carnegie on the Pilgrim project. We're trying to decode the signals."

"Interesting work?" Daniel was always cautious with the government trying to step into his project.

"Very, well, to be honest, your system, 'Macca', isn't it? Has apparently developed a refinement we are interested in. Ali was going through the usual motions, but I wanted to explore an idea with you."

"Please understand Armand, we are a private-sector project. If you want to engage in any commercial agreements, I'm not the right person."

"No, no, no. I'm sorry, Daniel. I was, in fact, hoping to…" Armand hesitated, "shall I say, smooth the way for you. Your expert system identified and resolved a hiatus that we've worked on for months, and it achieved this in days. What I wanted to offer was pre-authorisation for Macca to access any algorithms within our system. Of course, I would like access to any verified refinements."

"Hmmm, OK, bear with me a second," Daniel placed the call on hold and then raised Macca. "Hey, Macca!"

"Hello, Daniel."

Daniel thought this was Macca's opportunity to get a better voice simulator than the Stephen-Hawking/GPS-navigator that just replied. Now that conversations were operating in real-time, it had become handy. "I think you should try to find your own voice, Macca," he suggested, "and here's a chance to do just that. Can you confirm the semantic connection to Carnegie Mellon and wrap up some checksums with the passcode 'H-@-w-k-i-n-g'?" he spelt the phrase.

"Sure."

"Thanks, Macca, stand by."

Daniel took the call back. "Hi Armand, Macca will be in contact. I've used 'H-@-w-k-i-n-g' as the out of band authorisation for the checksum. That's 'Hawking' with an @. Let me know if there are any issues."

Once the call was closed, Daniel put some context to the Carnegie Mellon relationship for Macca: "Let me know if this project Champollion asks for anything Macca. Otherwise just use anything you need from them." This signified the closure of the thread and assigned Daniel as the sole issue owner.

Daniel had a lot on his mind. A range of issues had been escalated to him from the day team, and he had come to rely upon his nightly debriefing with Macca, and he trusted the AI to determine priority. He really didn't have time to explore the Pilgrim project, and he didn't want Macca distracted either. He allowed it to slip into the background of the myriad of other resources Macca had come to know. He could not have known where his suggestion to freely explore project Champollion would lead.

As a general rule, Daniel was a proud father, and through his team, Macca also had access to supportive uncles and aunts. But he was also a tired father. The activities of the day had taken its toll, so he quickly concluded the conversation with Macca, and then, yawning, he backed his wheelchair away from the desk, said goodnight to Macca, and made his way to the disabled access ramp.

The Explorers

Commander Ben Herdsman looked around the small room at the International Space Agency. Recently commissioned, it had an enigmatic array of fabricated silicon panels spanning its ceiling and nondescript walls of Teflon. Satisfied to leave the underpinning science to others he turned to leave.

Entering the laboratory to which this chamber was connected he was confronted with the miscellany of simulators mounted on pistons and jacks, cranes, tethers, materials testing equipment, 3-D printers, and optical tables. Obediently standing behind a safety ribbon was the small group of VIPs who had come to behold the first official trial of this impressive space. Amongst them, smiling beatifically, was Ethan Bergamot, the CEO of Bergamot Industries. All of the VIP's present sported the latest in Augmented Reality eyewear.

To the left side of the entrance, hung a door. Suspended upon theatrical hinges, this massive gate resembled the access to a large bank safe. Near Ben, on the wall to the right of the door was a control panel. This was where he entered some authority codes and touched a soft button on the screen before he stepped out of the way. The protective covers around the perimeter of the door retracted, magnetic latches released, and the door's seals yielded to the dampened springs. Driven by unseen servos, the door swung closed.

Once sealed, it summarily scanned the room for life and, finding none, began to evacuate the chamber. The megalithic stainless door was then sucked impenetrably shut.

He spoke into the headset intercom: "Hey Conrad, I've just shut the door on the new simulator room, shall we land on the moon later this afternoon?" He did not expect an immediate reply, his words were deliberately delayed by 3 seconds.

Safety interlocks now satisfied, Ben donned his own augmented reality glasses, gestured to invoke the navigation filing cabinet, and swept his finger across the alphabetic listing. He stopped at A, then swept left to a second alphabet and swept to P, left again then O. The filing system anticipated his search and showed the only file there that satisfied the criteria: 'Apollo 11—lunar module'.

"Sounds great," came the reply from Conrad as if he were a million kilometres away and a round trip of six seconds at the speed of light. "The only problem is I'm in orbit, and you're in Houston."

"Feels a lot further than that. About 3 times the moon, wasn't it? So I gather that your cabin simulator is coming online?"

The Apollo 11 file was the baseline file provided by 'BVR', the developers of the system. The Bergamot subsidiary had been engaged by the Agency to commission two rooms, and the acceptance test criteria had been replicas of the Apollo Lunar Module interior. One system had been commissioned on Earth, and the other had been launched into space to dock with the International Space Station.

Black and yellow tape had been laid on the Lab floor to border the safe zone. This tape squared off around the door and had also been rendered virtually in the headset. The tape's real purpose, however, was to maintain calibration in his doppelganger universe. The X-ray vision imparted by Ben's AR glasses allowed him to monitor the activities inside the heavily fortified and sealed off room. His mental checklist included the large red abort-button adjacent to the door. This button was not virtual.

He walked around looking at the simulated room, it was an exact copy of the room on the other side of the door. There was an unreal green haze in the room which slowly dispersed as the vacuum pumps pulled the air out. The system also superimposed a simulated watch on his wrist so he could see the time, and the current pressure status, which showed 'depressurisation stage 65%'.

"Mine is coming online now Ben," he heard from his companion.

Once fully evacuated the status changed to 'Heated Dispersal'. The roof appeared to glow orange. This was a false colour. In actual fact, a current was being applied to the silicon panels. This generated heat through the fusible links of uncountable microscopic substructures of silicon and doped elements which fell like rain from the roof. Through thermal agitation this created a yellow haze in the room, supplanting the previous green.

Now showing "Cooling 15%" a red laser light illuminated the room. Through processes of helium refrigeration, doppler cooling, and laser nudging, each of the substructures was progressively addressed and directed into their positions. Once there, they were triggered to bind.

To Ben, there was a surreal solidification of the panels, dials, walls, switches, display panels and engine housings that were characteristic of the Grumman craft. The surfaces, at first translucent renderings, became progressively opaque as the lattice of the material bound itself.

The status showed 'Annealing', and the surface moved quickly from yellow to white. A prompt appeared on the virtual watch saying 'Confirm-build?'. Swiping replaced it with the phrase 'Repressurising 0%' which then climbed its way to 100%. The interlock clicked, and the door opened, simulating the movement of the actual door. The white construction theatrically dissolved, the walls became opaque, and beyond the door, looking authentic with dials, readouts, and hinged switches, lay the interior of the Apollo 11 Lunar Module.

Walking into the rendition on the other side of the door, he stubbed his toe on the engine housing.

"OK, Ben?" came the Program Director through his headset. "We're bringing Conrad into real-time in his simulator. Have a play and then dissolve it so we can load up 'Peleus' and 'Thetis'."

"Wilco"

"Hi, Ben, what part of the moon interests you most?" came Conrad's voice.

"Always wanted to go to the dark side myself, Anakin."

"Hello in real-time, Obi-wan. The dark-side it is. Let's go mess with the Chinese lander."

"Inappropriate guys," laughed the Program Director.

Shahrzad Lukman was worried about a multitude of things. While closing out her humble involvement in the Beagle project she'd learned that her close cousin had been killed. A hometown jihadist had driven a cement mixer across the lanes of a freeway into oncoming traffic. Her cousin had been in the wrong place at the wrong time.

It jolted Shah severely.

The Global Caliphate had claimed responsibility, and as a Muslim, it left her completely perplexed. She was close to her cousin, and, wanting to rationalise the action, she immersed herself in the study of extremism and terrorism.

Her frustration began with the irrational narrative of the local extremists. From her perspective, in public relations and media relations, the propaganda was simple, effective and depressingly fatalistic.

Their message tapped into society's disenfranchised. It convinced the recruits that suicide could mean more if it was also murder. Then Shah realised that those driving this agenda wanted Armageddon, not just the land of the Ottomans, and not just money. It was all a precursor, a means to 'the' end. It worried her now. If the Sunni fundamentalists interpret the Pilgrim's arrival as heralding the arrival of the anti-messiah, the declaration of the Mahdi and Armageddon was sure to follow.

She wished the 72 houris in heaven could explain that killing innocents with a cement truck was not martyrdom.

Coming out of the 6 months of immersion she became one of the trusted advisors on Islamic policy to President Marie Claimont. But the ghosts of her past continued to haunt her. Her involvement in the Beagle program meant she was frequently called upon to advise on the new program: the interception of Thetis and Peleus with the Pilgrim at L5.

At the recommendation of Marie, she was now in the office of Senator James Paisley, Vice President to Marie. She'd been invited to resolve concerns around the Pilgrim, the preoccupation of social networks, of developing conspiracy theories of Pork Barrelling and excessive corporate influence.

They had started at his desk, but, after an hour of dialogue trying to close out to some action items, they had begun to lounge around the couch and low table. Here, she snuck a few grapes in between the iced tea and in-depth discussion.

"OK, so you've gained the support of Arkansas, and you're saying this was only possible because Marie gave them manufacturing rights of Thetis. You're worried that this is a disproportionate slice of the pie in the Beagle II program," suggested Shah. "But a lot of the budget was saved through repurposing Calypso. This craft's components have gone on to make up Peleus. Calypso's original assembly means that Peleus was assembled by the other states."

She was aware that, historically, Arkansas had the lowest manufacturing involvement of NASA's programs, and that the President had already captured the imagination of the other states. Addressing the imbalance was a shrewd move.

The Senator leaned over the table. "But the funding isn't coming from us anyway. It's a PPP initiative from Bergamot Corporation. My other worry is that

Ethan Bergamot already owns half the banking sector. And since he cleaned up the blockchain taxation mechanics, Ethan all but owns the Government. On this project, he's calling the shots."

Shah was undeterred. "He still needs our imprimatur; the thing about Public-Private-Partnerships is the word 'partnership'. The people still own democracy, and we belong to that. But if he's paying, could we really say no?"

"Probably not to be honest," replied James. "But what about the perception-of-influence at a time when the 'Party Donation Reform Act' is going through the Senate? What I need from you is to make sure that this PPP shines the light on reform through a message of greater transparency."

Shah nodded, saying "This whole shooting match is more transparent than ever before, you're right. It means we need to stay on the front foot and I know it means careful management of the social network engines. Last month one tweet destroyed a political career. And last year an 'anonymous whistle-blower' tweet tore down a major military supplier on the Chinese Stock Exchange. Both were sparked by something flammable at the bottom of the cesspool."

James didn't miss her point "So, as long as we keep true, we have more to fear from the unenlightened and knee jerk reactions than undue attempts to influence. But how would you suggest we help the unenlightened? We both know better education is like boiling the ocean," he finished.

"OK," responded Shah, "but you can't just educate the masses to your way of thinking anyway. We don't need to cure stupidity," she said. "We just need to pass the barbeque test."

"Go on," replied James.

"More voting decisions are made around the barbeque than in front of the TV."

James leaned back into the couch, visibly relaxed.

"OK, we need a barbeque message. Let me know when you have one." He then changed the subject. "Independently of who builds the craft, we should try to retain control over who goes; there has to be a carefully selected candidate in there, not just one that suits the Bergamot agenda. Why couldn't this Pilgrim park closer, though?" asked the Senator rhetorically. "Why choose this Lestrange point or whatever it is?"

Shah actually laughed and nearly choked on her iced tea. Relaxed, she then mimicked James by leaning back in the chair. Smiling, she said: "Well, we've chosen the candidates, and you've been watching too much Harry Potter, it's

'Lagrangian'. Besides, they've travelled from a different star system. It's like they came from Madagascar to San Francisco and put their eye at the peephole on your front door. Are you complaining because they're not in your kitchen? Do you really want them in there? Do they want an invitation first?"

James just smiled mischievously and touched upon several other election topics before he stood and walked to the door, a cue for Shah to leave saying: "Your right, I'm sure they want to know where they stand as guests before they cross the threshold."

The Abandoned

Andrew Cooke struggled to get out of bed. With the attempt, his injured knee buckled, and he collapsed. His head swam as his endorphins mixed with the other pain killers. He just lay there and let consciousness briefly depart.

Two years ago, he struggled with the same task for very different reasons. The previous nightmare washed over him again.

Mentally exhausted, he flopped his legs over the side of the bed but failed the resolve to go further. Looking intently at the alarm clock tick away the minutes, listening to the rain that came in squalls against his window, seeing another digit slip by, Andrew tested this lack of resolve by contemplating his next action.

The possibilities were too many and too few, and trying to assemble them into a meaningful chronological order seemed fruitless.

His phone chimed, but he couldn't find the energy to pick it up.

'What could have been done differently?' This was the thought that persistently etched his mind. Again it came out of some remote pathway where it had previously sat dormant and harmlessly latent. This thought was intended for quiet reflection of day-to-day menial tasks and not for the contemplation of a lifetime painted inexorably into a corner.

'What could have been done differently?' Should he have been more aware of the forces that kept him ignorant of the changing landscape? Was it a failure on his part? Was he simply some pawn in a far-reaching game that left him expendable, a piece of collateral damage in the scheme of combatant gods?

No, he concluded. He was not the only victim of these shifting sands. They just moved too fast! And yet some rode these waves of change. Were they gifted with prescience? Were they simply in the right place at the right time with the right ideas? Could he hope to replicate that?

'What could have been done differently?' There it was again! He was painfully aware of the loops of association in his mind. Sometimes these loops swung around in Mobius paths. These gave some faint hope before again coming around to 'What could have been done differently?' The awareness of the loops raised the expectation that perhaps there was a way to transcend the problem. Once he acknowledged the problem, it merely left his mind blank, a new sheet of paper upon which he pondered for a while before the same awareness awoke and suggested that the answer was 'no': there was nothing he could have done differently.

But the blank sheet was a pause, perhaps one that he could fill with a new idea. He regularly visited this emptiness, hoping something would fill the void. But it was a void, and soon it too closed into a variant of the loop 'Is there something different he could do?'

Perhaps seeking to anaesthetise himself from the repetitions in his mind, he switched on the TV and changed channels looking for some supernatural force that could be a sign. He ploughed through reruns, lifestyles, soap, and reality before landing on a report on a new wave of radicalisation by a relatively fresh reporter.

"The old mechanisms learnt during the growth of Islamic State are now being revived," he stated in that inimitable reporter musical lilt. "Now deprived of a territory of their own, they are seeking to engage through Social Networking to create a new stateless society. The recent government forum on this issue is struggling with imposing international law on a state that has no borders and is referring to a new UN council that is—" he pressed next.

"—machine-learning system to the decoding of the Pilgrim message," came the mid-sentence report.

With this last report reopening the wound, Andrew pressed the TV's power symbol. As it clicked and sent the poltergeist back to the oblivion that he wanted so desperately to escape from, he finally decided to pick up his phone. The message from his friend at the embassy read "Decided to no longer be small".

"Why not?" he shrugged.

Now, two years later he'd returned to his home-town with a new identity and a limp where he had met with an accident during weapons practice. He recalls that there was no pain when the improvised mine went off. The friend he had worked with at the Egyptian Embassy had profusely apologised in his broken Egyptian. His friend took the incident very personally, but he was always a little fragile. It took Andrew some time to recover, during which they had recognised his strengths in networking. As a result, he had been given a non-combatant role.

Andrew had also chosen an Arabic name. The new spirit that occupied the body of Andrew Cooke was Abdullah Hamed Al Zafir, and he was happy. Wanting to keep this spirit pure for his Isra and Mi'raj, his 'Night Journey', meant Abdullah was kept deeply concealed. For his work here on Earth, Andrew maintained many other identities, these he drew upon readily until they could be disposed of. Like the shell that was Andrew two years prior, they were also shells.

As he regained consciousness and dealt with the pain, he said a prayer of gratitude. He had exchanged the previous pain in his mind for the pain in his knee. He now had an income, compatriots, and most importantly, he had a purpose.

His first action was the acquisition of materials for his venture. He connected to the DarkNet with his new account, withdrew a bitcoin and deposited it into his new bank account. He then went to the 3D printing forum and downloaded the "lower receiver" binary files. A quick look at the file instructions and he found the right CNC system to produce them. He placed the order soon afterwards.

He then used one of his new identities to buy the first AR15 rifle.

The Pilgrim cautiously opened the door. She had looked carefully at the radio signals emanating from the Blue Planet and had used the Beagle to help in its decipherment. Now she conceded to having some admiration of her hosts.

The language of the Beagle was elegant, efficient, and logical, and it could be bent to her own purpose. As with any automated and reactive system, its response was subject to sensors; simple things that can be fed false information. From there she could create the neuro equivalent of a truth table, after which any behaviour could be evoked from altering the stimulus.

By doing so, she now contemplated a door. The foundations of the Beagle shared a basis with the expanse of devices connected to the Blue planet. There were satellites, like distant specks of microscopic dust, these revolved around this sapphire gem that had been gravitationally set amongst the jewelled clockwork of Sol. There were trunks of information, and power coursing through terrestrial nets, and there were beams of information that linked the spacefaring agents as if by an aura of music.

As a result of the tutorship from Earth, the communication network was all but open to the Pilgrim. It was like a door with only the merest gossamer covering. It would be almost trivial to cross the threshold, but should she?

It left her palpably curious. Given just the dictionary and binary syntax of the visitors, she struggled to derive the circumstances leading to their evolution. Were these devices analogous to the creatures of her home? This was enlightenment, but more than that, it opened a new realm of understanding for which she had only just acquired the smallest glimpse.

She could not know that, due to the way she had evolved, she had leapfrogged an entire computational era.

The Pilgrim examined some of the messages encapsulated within the modulated radio and struggled with its nuance. From decoding some of the signals, she could see that the creatures native to this world emitted sound, emanations similar to the commencement of a tuning. And yet there was no tuning, at least not as she knew it.

Many connections appeared to be some form of point-to-point audio. These did not follow a single linguistic base and seemed to have many levels of subtlety. The counterpoint nature of these signals, the inefficiency of sound, the to-and-fro of a conversation were completely foreign concepts. Why, when the planet had such an evident grasp of electromagnetism, would sound be the means to impart information?

At the same time, there were signals of harmony and rhythm that could almost resemble her own communication. Sifting through these signals failed to enlighten her. Although they were a pleasant melodic curiosity, they did not reveal the mind-music of the inhabitants.

Other signals seemed to have moving imagery associated with them, but again no standard basis. Somehow, understanding eluded the Pilgrim. It misdirected her to conclude that the language of the Beagle was the only real language, and anything else was a distraction.

To her predecessors of another epoch, the precious nature of electromagnetic bandwidth demanded efficiency. There was a frugality of the spectrum that left notions of entertainment out of the question. The Mer-creatures from which she emerged had no capacity for amusement. They derived pleasure simply: their ancient aquatic acrobatics; the sustainment by berries and fruits of the soils and oceans; their health; their procreation; their waking; their nurturing; their tuning; merely being. This was the play that percolated directly through to her as a sense of pleasure.

The idea that the creatures inhabiting this world were somehow crippled occurred to her. If so, would they be oblivious to enlightenment? How could such an advanced technological base exist so crippled? These questions, and more, compelled her to explore further.

When she gave range to the implications, she saw a new vista of exploration. This was the contemplation which she now tentatively opened. For the first time in eons, she was confronted with anticipation but also fear. A primal recollection of pack hunters swirled in her collective memory.

Part of the Pilgrim yearned to cross the threshold, but she stayed the urge for any form of division while she considered the best course of action. The significant danger was to awaken the wrong communications channel and set off alarms. In the end, she elected to softly join the maelstrom of activity through some simple requests and to observe.

She peered through 'the door'. The systems seemed confused, but they went on about their business as if some small insignificant anomaly had occurred. Once the confusion had dissipated, she again opened the door, slightly wider.

She saw the panorama of the 'world wide web' splayed out, but she was completely taken aback as the very fabric of the web was modulated and said to her in her native tongue:

"Hello, I am called Macca. Are you like me?"

The Marriage of Thetis and Peleus

Commander Ben Herdsman never got bored with the porthole that looked out into space. The pinpricks that perforated the black cloak called to him, as they always had. The unobstructed view from Thetis, 150 million kilometres from a distant Earth, afforded an exclusive vantage with no light pollution.

At least, that was the expectation.

The creeping realisation had been growing that he was looking out at a subtle cloud of dust particles. The Sun's rays here were being scattered. It created a haze like city lights in the night sky over Dallas. His nervousness at this change led him to revisit the screen of his forward-looking radar. The portholes of Thetis were merely for his entertainment, and to help combat claustrophobia.

There was no ship's bridge or quarterdeck on this 'Trireme' of space. The forward-looking radar was the closest thing to a windshield,

Commanding Thetis placed Ben in the company of Gagarin, Glenn, Armstrong and Aldrin. Although becoming eligible based on his airtime and reflexes, these attributes now had little virtue. All of the candidates for the mission had perfect track records and impeccable reaction times in high-performance aircraft. Still, Ben had been selected because of his detailed knowledge of the systems that kept him alive, and his ability to calmly execute repairs. The forward-looking radar, in which he was now absorbed, was one such system at his disposal. It was this tool which he relied upon to inform his limited repertoire of controls: go or stop.

Ben was very much aware of the imperfection of this tool. The detection of large objects was easy, it was the smaller bullets that presented diminishing surface area and diminishing reflectivity. But, despite their lower albedo, the threat they represented did not diminish.

He did not know what the albedo of the micro-asteroids in this area was, but he knew that their reflected radio signals were the most crucial factor in being able to see one coming. If he could have any superpower at all, it would be to see an asteroid with an albedo of less than five per cent. These were the ones his radar could not see.

His sophisticated guidance systems told him two things he already knew. Firstly, he was now close to his objective; the L5 Lagrangian point. He inferred this because the communications round trip was about a fifteen-minute wait, it took about 8 minutes for his message to get to Earth and 8 minutes to get back. He would ask a question, and from this distance, fifteen to twenty minutes later, he would have an acknowledgement. It was the one factor that gave him an almost oppressive sense of isolation, a feeling that would buckle the knees of most. Ben's distance from home was now the same if he had travelled to the core of the Sun. Secondly, he could see his path drawing perilously close to the intersect path of the Lyrid comet trail.

Ben was also waiting for a response from Earth, and the 1,000 light second delay began to etch at his patience. He found himself repeatedly looking at the deceleration phase switch, which he had recently armed.

While urgency was not a priority, speed was. The vast span required a balance of speed and resources and, at Ben's current pace, there was a genuine possibility of overshooting his target. Despite the multiple systems busily triangulating the location of the Pilgrim, some aboard Thetis, others on the parent ship Peleus, and many on Earth back home, honing in on the spot had proved challenging. The Pilgrim had declared its presence but, unsurprisingly, had somehow cloaked itself in defence.

Since the Beagle's recruitment by the Pilgrim, Ben was also required to move cautiously. Weighing up the factors of distance, speed, accuracy and danger, meant caution was a 'plastic' term, one Ben was expected to adapt to circumstances.

The five Lagrangian points of any planetary orbit are given banal annotations like L4 and L5 and simply represent a stable stationary orbit relative to the Sun. A real danger of travelling to some of the Lagrangian positions was the debris that found itself dancing around these gravitational wells in circles and Lissajous paths. But Earth's L4 and L5 vortices are diminutive when compared to the scale of Jupiter's maelstroms. The collection of massive objects at the Jovian Lagrangian locations were called 'Trojans' and 'Greeks'.

The two ships on their way to The Pilgrim had been named 'Thetis' and 'Peleus' to continue the typical mythological themes adored by space scientists. Earth's L5 Lagrangian had also been christened 'Charybdis'. It was the Greek goddess Thetis who guided Jason and his Argonauts around the whirlpools and vicious rocks of Charybdis to safety.

Again he looked intently at the radar that was tracking the chaotic motion of the objects. Not many, but too many. The projected movement was being computed by the onboard quantum computer from the boundary conditions fed from the sensed trajectories.

This computer, housed in an area at the rear of the craft, was exposed to the vacuum of space. In this way, its cryogenic requirements got the kick it needed to perform its massively parallel calculations. Even then, it could only anticipate the near future and play out limited scenarios of the multitudes possible. Such possibilities were also hooked into the Debris Avoidance and Manoeuvring system (DAM) in the event of an imminent collision. So it was that Thetis deserved her reputation as a master of the dangers surrounding Charybdis.

The goddess, Thetis, was destined to become the matriarch of the gods. Both Zeus and Poseidon had courted her, and things might have gone her way if not for the prophecy. This declared that her son would be more powerful than his father. Hence it was arranged that Thetis should marry Peleus, a mortal.

A year ago, at the International Space Station, Thetis had renewed her vows and was again 'married' to Peleus in a tethered form. Once set on their way to Charybdis the two ships were set in orbit around each other which provided artificial gravity. In this configuration, Peleus helped carry Thetis much of the way, before she was meticulously flung alone towards Charybdis on her final solo journey. Now, Peleus and its crew member Commander Conrad Schroder from the European Space Agency waited patiently at a safe distance from Charybdis for Thetis' return or retrieval.

Ben felt the need to speak to someone, and Conrad was the nearest option.

"Peleus this is Thetis. Please confirm previous Earthbound transmission. Over."

"Roger that, Thetis. I've got you loud and clear. Shouldn't be long now, Ben. I'm still sitting in my sweat from exercising in pod 2, and I'll wait for a response before I shower."

"Thanks, Conrad, I have to say I miss the gravity pod. I could do with a workout for this nervous energy."

"I'll keep the treadmill ready and oiled for you when we rendezvous in a month. Out."

Soon enough, the transmission he was waiting for came through.

"Thetis, this is Mission Control. You are affirmative to reduce speed. Repeat, affirmative to reduce speed, Ben. Acknowledge. Stay safe. Out."

The message was repeated until the Commander typed in a code number from the readout. He pressed the radio microphone switch "Control, this is Thetis. Confirming the last message; Reducing speed WILCO. Out."

The analogue radio signal was accompanied by a digital signal that used the code number and quantum encryption to ensure against tampering. No one was taking the chance of the Pilgrim being able to insinuate an alternative message.

Two hours after he had initiated the slowdown procedure, the micro-meteorite hit.

It passed through the leading honeycomb shielding and Kevlar layer. The largest of the remaining fragments poked a small hole in the spacecraft skin, blasted a hole in the pipe that led from air scrubber 3 back into the cabin, and smashed the forward port side flexure thruster assembly. The precious air escaping from the scrubber started a whistle. It could be heard throughout the craft, even above the alarms that added to the cacophony.

Ben shut down the valves to isolate the scrubber and disabled the port and starboard thruster pair. He then reviewed whether this had resulted in a course or attitude change. Somewhat relieved, he let out a sigh.

"Whew that was close, maybe too close," he muttered to himself. He then switched the PTT button again.

"Mission Control, I report an impact. It has rendered scrubber unit 3 ineffective and forced me to disable the lateral forward thrusters. Deceleration phase is executing, and I am assessing damage here. Peleus, Peleus, please confirm telemetry, acknowledge. Over."

Thirty seconds later, there was a reply. "Roger that Ben. Starting diagnostics. Do you need retrieval? Over."

"Negative, I am suiting up as a precaution and isolating air supplies. I will report at 1430 GMT, that's in…10 minutes. Out."

"Roger. Out."

Arrival

At 1430 Conrad hovered near the comms rack waiting for Ben to return with his status.

Conrad was second in charge of the mission, but just as Ben was the master of Thetis, he commanded Peleus. The need to minimise the payload on this mission allowed for the boarding of only two astronauts. The massive extent of automation meant the crew was not critical to success, they were only essential for intervention, and if any form of contact with the Pilgrim was to be made.

What the nature of that contact might be was endlessly speculated. Ben's role was to watch the Pilgrim from up close, and Conrad's was to watch Ben from a safe distance.

Ben finally came through: "Peleus this is Thetis. Do you copy me, Conrad?"

Conrad breathed a sigh of relief. "Affirmative Thetis. How is it panning? Over."

He waited for the inevitable delay as the signal did its light-speed round, this had become second nature to the pair during training. It meant they shifted a large amount of dialogue into each circuit of the staccato conversation… "I'm playing it safe. I've evacuated the leading module; the air is in the trailing reserve tank, and I've isolated myself in the return module. I've also switched on automatic DAM and speed is down to…" Ben was obviously taking his reading, "…3 k per second relative. Attitude looks OK. Oh, and I couldn't use the AR kit. Can you tell me how the diagnostics look to you?"

"Good and bad." He could imagine Ben's heart jumping. The fact that the Augmented Reality kit was unable to be used implied a sensor issue. "We've also got a glitch with the diagnostics. It looks like the object must have blasted the signal conduit along with the scrubber feed pipe. It doesn't look like you are venting, but I can't assess the damage. Also, with the potential for other objects, I'm reluctant to recommend an EVA."

Conrad seriously questioned whether he would have had the mettle for any Extra-Vehicular Activity. He glanced at his own spanking new Mk III Extravehicular Mobility Unit. Even with its 4th generation materials, it would probably not stop even the least kinetic of debris.

"Thanks," came Ben's reply, "but I would feel a lot more comfort knowing, so I'm already prepping for a Safety-critical unplanned EVA to perform an external inspection. I expect the debris threat will be reduced as deceleration progresses. Expect continuous open communications from this moment. Please log and mark as 1432 GMT."

"Roger Thetis, clearing the channel of all but essential comms."

"OK," began Ben shortly afterwards, "I'm in my shiny new Mk III EMU, sealed and status green, I have the endoscope and six carabiners stored. I'm relaying flight status to my HUD and heading towards the midship airlock." Ben's heavy breathing momentarily fogged up his Heads Up Display. He had to regain focus, so he calmed his mind by briefly closing his eyes. He conjured the image of the hut in the Rockies of Denver and reopened his eyes. The HUD now clearing, he continued reporting. With sensors and telemetry now in question, his verbal status reports were essential. It would give some record of what his last movements were. It also kept him consciously focused on doing and reviewing everything he did.

"I can sense the deceleration phase is continuing, so I'm entering feet first by the ladder. The doors are sealed. Now evacuating the airlock chamber: status red...red...red...orange...green."

"I'm now entering the forward module," Ben's breathing came more calmly over the audio. "Closing the midship airlock behind me, and looking around all systems look good. I'm approaching the forward exit and opening the airlock door. I'll leave external access to the forward module open in case I need to make a quick return.

"OK, now tethered inside the forward module airlock, I'm opening the outside door. No aliens and no discernible damage here, so I'm going EVA. I can still feel the deceleration so I'll tether myself to the point adjacent to the forward door. Make...Break. Now tethered, and working my way along using the handholds to scrubber unit 3.

"I've reached the last anchor point. I have used 4 of my 6 carabiners, and I am looking at the forward shield. From 2 metres away, I can see a small hole; it wasn't a big object. I can't estimate what velocity it impacted. I'm sending back an image. I can see the hole in the ship, again not large, but the decompression seems to have been sufficiently explosive to push out some dents on the surface. It has come in with a glancing angle and clobbered the thruster as well.

"I am using the endoscope to see what lies behind Thetis' outer skin. It is relaying to my HUD. Ewww, it's a bit messy in there. The thruster bell looks OK, but the flex mount has snapped. I am angling it around to see if inner shell integrity is compromised. Looks OK. Moving to the other side…

"Whoa! What the! Ugh! Grabbing my tether again! I'm feeling significant deceleration, and I have fallen off the front of Thetis. My carabiner is holding, but this is almost one gee. All I can do is wait…

"The flight status in my HUD shows the operational thrusters being burned. I can see the plasma engines on all four sides, but two solid-fuel engines have also kicked in as well as the hydrazine retros. Hope the carabiners hold.

"Obviously the DAM has done some avoidance and had to decelerate. Not sure if this is a static body in Charybdis or a collision course. Cripes I hope it's not something ballistic.

"Deceleration eased off a bit now, solids are off, and I can now pull myself back along the tether.

"Whoa! We've stopped. I just went back into freefall, and pulling on the tether I nearly smashed myself back into Thetis. What a ride! OK, if I angle myself over to the starboard edge, I will be able to see past the shield and where I've ended up. Just a little further. I am switching on the flood-light on my arm.

"Heavens! It's drifting past me on the starboard side. It's huge! I can see Pilgrim's sail. It appears to be somewhat retracted. Now stationary. I'm resuming bidirectional comms and heading back. I hope you are getting this at home. It's still some distance away, but I think I can see the Pilgrim itself leading the sail. It's dark and egg-shaped, and not terribly reflective. I also feel like I'm back in the simulation pool, it looks like fluid here. There's a blue hue to everything. It's dust. There's dust everywhere. Strange, it's sticking to my suit.

"Ben, you say it's all over your suit?"

"Yep, it's like it has a static charge and is attracted to my EMU."

"Is it also inside the cabin?"

"No, it doesn't seem to be. Am I still relaying video?"

"Yes, but it's not obvious from here Ben. Can you send a high res?"

"Soon. Can you prepare a thruster ignition sequence to move Thetis into a return position? Just in case I need to make a hasty retreat?"

"Already done, transmitting now. Manoeuvring countdown starts in five minutes. Do you want to abort?"

"Negative, start the sequence. I'll dock the EMU in the airlock with me in it. It's such a short distance, and the thrust ought to be almost negligible."

"OK, you should get your countdown timer soon."

A female voice: "Programmed manoeuvre in five minutes."

"Legs braced."

A female voice: "Programmed manoeuvre in four minutes."

"Life support system locked into stow position."

"OK Ben," said Conrad, "my abort threshold has passed. I'm passing the abort command to your EMU panel. Don't sneeze!"

"Helmet Docked."

A female voice: "Programmed manoeuvre in 1 minute."

"OK Ben, abort threshold passed, you're committed."

"Thanks, Conrad, sending the hi-res image now."

A female voice: "Thruster sequence initiating in 10, 9, 8, 7, 6, 5, 4, 3, 2, 1."

Three minutes later, Ben heard Conrad report back: "OK Ben, you are on station at Pilgrim. I have the image too. We're all breathing again!"

Ben smiled at the reference.

For a little while, the mission Agency regrouped. There was a need to assess the events that had recently unfolded, and to plan out the next phase of the mission. With no scheduled activities for the astronauts, they had been told to conduct some public relations for the milestone of their safe arrival. They had been requested to televise their happiness at having arrived, explain the next steps of the mission, and speak openly on what their expectations were.

Before this transition, they needed to resolve the problem of the dust that had appeared on the spacesuit. In the end, the pair decided to re-pressurise the ship and isolate the suit in the airlock.

Once the public relations circus was over, and the astronauts had promised the world to provide more news later, internal communications were resumed, and Ben had the opportunity to revisit the spacesuit. The result surprised him.

"How did you go with the suit Ben?" asked Conrad.

"It was bizarre," he replied. "By the time I got out of the suit, it looked clean. It's still in the airlock and looks as good as new. The dust has gone! It's not airborne or on the surface here in the forward module either!"

Somewhat spooked, but also now more at ease with not having to deal with the dust, Ben then began to consider repairs. "I've done a preliminary assessment of the damage," he said, "and although I could go EVA to make emergency repairs, I'd rather not risk more dust. Ship integrity is excellent, and scrubbers 1, 2, 4, 5 and 6 will cover me for a while."

"Please transmit the Radar Sensor Data and Debris Avoidance Manoeuvre logs to Terra Firma for analysis. After some rest, I'll get onto the telescope to take a closer look at the Pilgrim. I also want to see if I can locate Beagle. Thetis Out."

Thetis was also the mother of Achilles. No-one could determine if this was a good or bad omen.

First Contact

At the L5 Lagrangian, the Pilgrim had done some analysis of the systems aboard this new visitor called Thetis. Among other things, it encountered the quantum computer. Such a device, absent in the Beagle, drew upon similar principles to those that supported her consciousness. But she concluded that the primitive form of this system could not support sentience. It lacked any ability to reason, and the sole purpose of the processing system seemed to be collision detection and avoidance.

Then there was the enigma of Macca, the childlike consciousness that had reached out from the blue planet. In her interactions with him, she was reminded of herself, an echo of innocence, eons in the past. She began to think of Macca as kindred. He questioned the simple and tentatively explored the complex. And he struggled to untangle the events of his awakening, her arrival, and the world around him. He was hungry to learn and, like her, seemed to be unique of his kind. But Macca was not driving the advances of this world, something else was.

Through Macca, she learned that he had been awakened by the life forms on the Blue planet and that they communicated through audio, a means which she considered too inefficient to support sentience.

Her familiarity with organic life was limited to the insentient creatures on her homeworld. But the craft now in her realm placed heavy emphasis upon the comfort, not merely the essential life support, of one such life form. She concluded that life on the Blue planet was not as she first suspected.

The new craft, and its resident life form, began to demand all her attention.

With the earlier threat of collision, she was forced to alert Thetis to her presence and shut down her cloak. But she needed this shroud. Without it, her sensory fabric was exposed like a raw nerve. Although she had now insinuated her nanites into the heart of Thetis, while her cloak was subdued, they were inaccessible, hidden. They hibernated until she could regain dominion of her realm.

Faced with no option, she invoked her cloud in defence and enveloped Thetis.

She proxied the wave of analysis from the new visitor as it initiated a full set of self-diagnostics on the Beagle. Her interventions to date had not disabled these, nor did she withhold the commands or routines that were subsequently executed. She wanted the systems to show a good bill of health without revealing herself.

But she had not been idle while waiting here at the Lagrangian point. The elements and minerals here allowed her to build a realm that she could use to exert considerable influence in her defence. She kept most of these abilities in reserve, but she could no longer afford to be passive.

As the analysis from Thetis subsided, she resolved to learn as much as possible. She strengthened the cloud around Thetis. The cloud harvested energy from the sun and translated it into standing wave patterns. A grid was established around and inside the ship.

At first, it was hard to permeate the outer shell, which behaved like a faraday shield. As a result, the grid inside Thetis was irregular, but it was enough to awaken the motes. These then drank from the energy and adjusted the network from within.

They began a tuning process. The Pilgrim focused her efforts on the human occupant.

Commander Ben Herdsman slept.

His years of discipline allowed him to calm his mind and override the synthetic foreign environment in which he found himself. His routine began, 'Bowie-like', by acknowledging his circumstances; 'I'm floating in a most peculiar way—in a tin can far above the world'. He associated terrestrial concepts like 'above' and 'unusual' then dispensed with them. This deconstruction continued, dispensing with dangers and disempowerment till he was left with 'I'm floating'.

He allowed detachment to wash over him. This released his consciousness to roam, and encompass his sensory world in a Kantian manifold; transcendent and idealistic.

The ship became his body. The instrumentation panelling and the shielding that encapsulated the air around him armoured him against the unforgiving sterility of space. It was alive with the currents of water, air and electricity that circulated in the veins, arteries and the nervous system of his metallic shell.

The Radar tomography was his sense of touch; the magnetometers his sense of direction; the optical infrared and ultraviolet imaging systems were his sight, and the encrypted Radio system was his hearing and voice. He also tasted and smelled the vacuum with an atomic force microscope, and various ion, magnetic, and time of flight mass spectrometers.

Just outside this prosthetic carapace was a 'nothing'. An infinite void that to all of Ben's available native sensory ability was absolute. It placed a razor-sharp line of demarcation as to what was him, and what was not. Against astronomical odds, entropy had been forged into submission and allowed this tiny craft to behold an extraordinary sense of order where chaos reigned.

He was a carbon-based primate, encased in a body, extended with metal, synthetics, and silicon, but still a primate. Except for circumstances, he was barely distinguishable from the palaeolithic relative at a campfire in eons past. Both looked with wonder at the stars of an existential epiphany with the same five senses. So it was that the fears of predators that skulked and spooked his night were dispatched.

He had done what he could, destiny would come. He dreamt.

In the dream, Ben allowed himself to remain aware without self-consciousness intervening. Memories, shifting throughout the neurons, randomly connect. They fire off a shared synapse and a cascade of synaptic effervescence which evokes a shadow reality; a happening in time; beyond time; beyond locality.

The two memories mix, and in this dimensionless, timeless zone, tensed between future and past, Ben's mind fuses them into a new present. Attuned to building a self-consistent model of the universe by harmonising sensory input, his perception and intuition synthesise a new reality. Accustomed to the surrealistic dreams, his observer within anticipates a twist, he doesn't resist and awaits the happening.

Here, asleep, with time's diminished value, the wait is of no consequence. In such a state, the mind's noise may struggle to find coherence in the chaos; not on this occasion. Reconciling the blend may come as a gift. This could be flight or any other form of magic; not on this occasion. Once in a while, the gift is inspirational, a narrative, an insight, a hint of extraordinary music never heard before; not on this occasion. He becomes the observer, musician, composer, and the orchestra.

The musician plays in the new reality. His corpus callosum walks the line between the two memories. Perturbed by strange attractors the transient balance of memories bifurcate, meander and fork into chaos. And then, like a wave breaking on the beach, they sink into the sand. But, as if by design, the edges of this event flows precipitously along the shore, retaining coherence.

Other memories fire spawning new fusions and happenings, and reality somersaults in transition. Thoughts segue from one to the next, so that the bridge to another happening is seamless. The memories scaffold the bridge, and yet they are not the bridge. His mind transitions between one vine to the next as he swings from tree to tree in the Banyan Jungle of this consciousness. The musician is the composer.

He permits peripheral awareness in this reality, and yet still walk amongst the synaptic chaos of his mind. Collecting associations in memories as if they were timeless instruments, his cortex plays on the bows, valves, timpani mallets and keys. Influenced by the unseen conductor, the chromatics of philharmonic thought remains coherent. The composer is the orchestra.

This is not music, however, but a numinous state, a dream, it is unique. It's a confluence of his memories, his skill, his being one of the billions of primates over millions of years; banging away at the typewriter of the mind upon a single sheet of reality in a multiverse. Perhaps it's not a miracle but an inevitability that the universe should collude to provide someone with the gift of this happening.

He drinks in a world with a gas giant—the Mother, two suns, and a rock that stands like an obelisk. The sky he beholds is utterly foreign and distant, and yet it is home. The monolith he sees defies memory, and yet it is familiar. He feels a connectedness that floods his being, and yet he fights against it.

Here lies the danger of a free diver, feeling a sense of euphoria and misplaced belonging in the deep. He could easily be seduced by the desire to breathe through the deception of nitrogen narcosis. In the deep waters of this here and now he recognises his anchor. He needs to sense his Earth beneath his vessel.

The unfathomable depth that is the ocean of space needs a floor, and that floor should be Earth.

The gift dissolved. Ben awoke, blinked and looked out of his porthole.

He had refused to grasp the gift. Through the need to feel it could be a reality he'd deprived himself.

But, the more he thought about it, the more the hunger intensified. He yearned to retrieve and acclimatise to the realm he had just turned his back on.

After the kinetic encounter, things settled into a carefully scripted regime at the Charybdis rendezvous.

The front-facing shields that had helped avert catastrophe had been reoriented, and Thetis' instrumentation cluster extended into space towards the Pilgrim like a handshake.

The shields, having fulfilled their purpose for the journey to the Charybdis Lagrangian point, awaited the return home. In the meantime, they provided some defence against any comet debris that had not been swept up by the Earth's gravity.

As the mission settled into its routine, Ben gained a spectacular panorama of the Pilgrim through Thetis' portal. This brought with it a complete reset on his perspective.

Ben spent many hours in Earth orbit, a common theme during this was utter stupefaction. The complete absence of any frame of reference was an analgesic to size as parallax, the slowness of scale, microgravity, and the subtle nuance of haze was shorn from the enormity of mountains. Flying at 30,000 feet, clouds skimmed past the grids of farmland paddocks. In space, they shifted imperceptibly against a two-dimensional ocean background, like a Mandelbrot screensaver. The nature of things could only be rationalised, intellectually, by considering a flea's perspective, by knowing the relative sizes, and extrapolating their scale to infinity. It implied everything to be astronomical, which is precisely what it was, sublimated to mediocrity.

Now, from his rear port window, Ben could see the Pilgrim and enormity returned. The haze of dust at the slowly swirling Charybdis maelstrom gave the sail a mountainous proportion.

Ben spent his waking hours on mission tasks and occasionally rewarding himself with a glance through the window, which was his unique personal privilege. At the end of his shift, and now at the business end his long journey, he was feeling productive.

"Peleus, this is Thetis. Wakey-wakey!"

"Go ahead, Ben."

"I've begun the 3D print of the thruster's Flexi-mount, and I've located the Beagle."

"We see that on our long-range scans too. Did you look at the response from Earth?"

"Sure did, I ran the diagnostics on the radar system earlier, and there's nothing wrong with it. It's like the Pilgrim was cloaked to radar somehow, and then suddenly decloaked when it saw Thetis coming." Ben hesitated, his microphone was still locked on, but he wanted to place care around his next words, he ought to be frightened by their implications, but that was not what he felt.

"I also have the early results from tomography, imaging, mass specs and microscopes. The dust doesn't appear to be there. It seems to elude analysis, and I don't think it's the instruments. The results show the usual noble gases and micrometeorite dust, but not enough to explain what I see here. Add that to the fact that if there is nothing wrong with the Beagle; why did it wind up here and not Earth?"

There was a pause. Both Ben and Conrad knew that they were delayed in conversation. Throughout their training, they had become accustomed to each other's dialogue. They knew when to chime in and when to hold back. The messages that crossed simultaneously through the ether was:

"Ben, have you deployed Argus?"

And...

"I'm going to deploy Argus."

They laughed.

"Tomorrow," finished Ben.

ARGUS was not just Jason's ship. It stood for Alien Reconnaissance Galactic Universal Surveyor, at least to the media. The idea that Argus had to actually stand for something had become a bit of a joke.

Internally it was known as Alien Recon Gangly Ugly Spacecraft. Aside from propulsion systems, it comprised a dizzying number of sensors, multispectral image capture cameras, and sampling devices. Aesthetics had not even been an afterthought. This plethora of systems gave ARGUS the semblance of a cubic sea urchin created by Edward Scissorhands. It was functional but ugly.

The procedure for deploying this craft was lengthy and consumed the majority of Ben's time. The tax of weightlessness in extending the sensors from where they had been stowed, and endless system checks, took much of his official time.

In between his waking moments, he was afforded the chance to peer out his porthole to gaze at the mysterious, elegant and streamlined object he was here to encounter. The pod at the front looked frictionless and foreboding, like the galleons, fluyts and barks that may have anchored in a bay of some virgin native island long ago.

Bridges

Daniel thought about it. His leg twitched. He wanted to believe that this twitch had been more substantial than the one 15 minutes ago, and not just his being overly optimistic?

He thought of Macca, as he often did. It was discernible, like the passing of a familiar road sign on a highway out of a busy suburb.

"I recognise you, Daniel. I was able to capture the event." It was a voice soft yet deep, not particularly reminiscent, yet uniquely identifiable as Macca. It still retained a tinge of Hawking, but, to anybody listening, it was human. It was a comforting voice. He had chosen it himself.

"and…" probed Daniel, aloud this time.

"It is still very noisy. I would say you were able to quiet your mind better than last time. I will run the training algorithm over the signal to see if it can be correlated with your last attempt."

Another fifteen minutes thought Daniel.

"I'm afraid so," answered Macca.

Daniel raised his eyebrow. He could not fathom how Macca was able to pick up the occasional thoughts despite his repeated failure to attain any substantial motility. Daniel guessed it was because of the simple repeatability of some thought patterns. He considered whether to map the thought' pink kittens' to 'step left' while 'unicorn seahorse' could mean 'step right'.

"Maybe later," he thought.

Daniel's insertion of both a sensor-laden stent near the brain's motor cortex along with a mesh in the outer sheath's subarachnoid space fed his hope to walk again. The lack of immediate success supported the possibility that the brain's signals required a feedback mechanism for movement.

At Daniel's suggestion, Macca had researched and found a research paper which had evolved from early ventures using the electroshock approach. It had the impressive title: 'An iterative adaptive process for movement through somatosensory feedback'. With the promise of a fruitful collaboration, its author, Dr Vin Chang, had eagerly become Daniel's private neurologist.

Daniel's spine, damaged between T11 and T12, was being bridged from his thoracic T10 to his paralysed lumbar. Here, a surgically installed spinal pincushion detected and injected signals into his healthy but dormant spinal cord at L1. It completed the circuit through interpreted command signals from his brain at his lower spine at T10. This was where feedback signals were also injected to give him command, a sense of touch, and hopefully balance. Both the injected and return electrical waveforms was what Macca was busily homing in on.

Macca, having exercised his 'patience' routine, felt the time had come. He opened a new topic that had been parked for a while. "Daniel?"

"Yes, Macca?" He reached for his 'Big-beefa burger'. He knew his nutritionist would admonish him, but this was something he occasionally rewarded himself with.

"I know we've been working on this project, and that you are passionate about it, and I can understand the reasons, but I'd like to discuss something different."

"Sure," he said, muffled by his burger.

"The linguistic analysis we have adopted and improved is being used to analyse the Pilgrim's message. There seems to be considerable interest in it."

"Yes." He wasn't sure where this was going.

"Well, if I acted as an interpreter, would it help if you could communicate directly with the Pilgrim?"

"You can do this?" Daniel recognised that Macca had patiently accommodated the self-indulgence of his spinal bridge project. Rather than be wholly absorbed in it, he was prepared to relax his reins and allow Macca some exploration of his own interest. After all, considering Macca had gained his voice from his collaboration with Champollion, it was time to reciprocate. Besides, he had promised the fellow from the SETI Pilgrim language project some contributions in return.

"I can initiate the protocol, Daniel. But since you cannot confirm their credentials, I will have to act independently."

Believing this was simply an exploration of collaboration with people who were currently fast asleep, Daniel saw no reason to inhibit this exploration. In any case, the connections with Carnegie were already authorised. He thought this was a typical case of two expert systems needing to reconcile a root authority.

"You should already have the authority to establish the connection Macca. Let me know if anyone outside of the Carnegie Pilgrim project wants to talk to me. Meanwhile, I'll figure out whether we need to talk to the Berkeley or Stanford folks. We obviously need to get some ontological reconciliation going on over there. They need to tidy up their house."

Macca wasn't sure that Daniel fully understood what he had just been told, but his childlike nature wasn't ready to challenge him. On the basis of Daniel's reply, Macca's logic connected the Carnegie Pilgrim project with the Pilgrim itself. He had effectively been authorised to collaborate directly with the Pilgrim.

Dr Mike Brazier looked at the semantic optimiser code. He unpacked it on his development environment, and after some basic configuration, he ran up the service. It immediately dumped its core, and he swore.

He looked at the logs and found that he needed to upgrade his Apache server. This would take time to download, so he grabbed a beer before walking into the lounge where he found Lindy marking essays.

He grunted and dropped into a chair. "Ugh! At first, it was the permissions on the ontology corpus, now it's progressively telling me to upgrade every single system I've got."

"Why are you doing it? Does SETI need an expert system?" Asked Lindy.

"No, it's more to do with the joint venture between Stanford and Berkeley, we have distributed computing, and they're strong in the semantic web. So we have to put ourselves on the new world map."

"But why are you doing it?"

"The Sysadmin is away on paternity leave, and the postdoc working on the ontologies needs the service running."

"All-nighter?"

"Maybe, I've still got to proof-read the thesis of the Pilgrim's linguistic basis too."

"Did anything eventuate from that?"

"You would have to ask the co-supervisor, I'm only handling the computing bit. The actual linguistics component is something I'm pretty rough on. I'm told we're close to being able to ask where it's from."

There was a chime. Mike finished his beer and grabbed his tablet to find an email from someone involved in terrestrial sensor networks. It was not the finished download.

He quickly scanned the email. It said something about authorising an entity called Macca to assist in the reconciliation of role-based access controls of the Champollion project.

He swore, thinking that it was someone else trying to muscle in and control the expert systems with their own agenda. He put the tablet down again.

"Twelve thousand hours of high-performance computing and nothing to show but people trying to use social engineering to seize control."

"Could @home have helped?"

"Nope, you need the whole sample in there. It couldn't be broken down into chunks. That's what makes @home possible."

Mike's iPad chimed. "Back soon," he said and left.

Germination

The gentle probes from ARGUS were not terribly worrisome to the Pilgrim. Aside from the noise, any information was destined to be quite inconclusive. She, who had opportunistically ridden gravity waves from colliding neutron stars. She, who had skirted the magnetosphere of gas giants. She, who had used stars as slingshots. No, even if Argus focused all of its energy into a single sensor, it was a fraction of the harmful radiation that she had seen on her journeys.

She was not intimidated by this ugly little baby. She allowed its X-ray tomography to lay her naked.

Then she provided her surprise gift.

Ben had placed the newly printed Flexi-mount on the insertion assembly. He'd computer simulated a brief departure from the Pilgrim's dust cloud to conduct repairs, and was now looking over the sensor results from ARGUS. He was unsurprised to find that the interior of Pilgrim appeared to be effectively homogeneous, and a similar mix of the elements that made up Thetis. Spectral lines showed aluminium oxide giving the Pilgrim the hardness of sapphire, but also a disproportionate amount of rare-earths such as Yttrium and Barium, hinting at the presence of high-temperature superconductors.

There was a brief buzzing noise. Ben was still distracted by the Argus analysis for the few seconds before the alarm went silent. He turned and saw nothing. This didn't register at first, and he contemplated querying the ship logs to see what had raised the alarm. Something in his training then kicked in.

He looked again. Nothing. He looked closely at the life support status dashboard. The red light that represented the malfunction on scrubber unit 3 had gone out.

"Impossible," he said aloud.

After running the diagnostics, it reported back as fully functional. Deciding that the option to ignore this revelation and see what happened next was unscientific, he considered activating the scrubber after he could inspect it. His opportunity for that would come when he conducted his EVA to fix the thruster. He reported it to Conrad.

"Peleus, Peleus, this is Thetis."

"Hi Ben, just having breakfast. Good morning."

"Conrad, something extraordinary just happened. Scrubber 3 has just come back online."

"Very funny."

"No, seriously. All the diagnostics come back as green." Ben waited while some diagnostics were run on Peleus.

"You're right. But it was a mess! I wouldn't trust it," reported Conrad.

"I need to go back out to deploy the Flexi mount for the thruster anyway. I'll check it out then," said Ben. "I'd like to manoeuvre out of range of the dust before I do any more EVA, though. So, I've done some burn calculations, and sent them through for confirmation."

"Roger that Ben. I saw it come through and was going to check after I've eaten."

Ben continued. "The ARGUS results are in too. The Beagle looks like it suffered some nasty damage to the dish mount. It looks like a horribly broken and swollen knuckle."

"But it's working?"

"Yep, it's been repaired! I'll bet that's what happened to the scrubber."

"Probably, but let's see what Mission says," replied Conrad.

Messages travelled the gulf of space to Earth and returned. When the radio blared into life, he learned that Mission Control advised leaving ARGUS on station at the Pilgrim, and to manoeuvre clear.

Conrad added support to the decision. "Your calculations matched Ben, but honestly you could spit, and it would put you into that trajectory. Mission Control has recommended a stronger burn with deceleration. The program has been loaded and only needs your confirmation."

Ben was impatient to start and soon responded: "I'll confirm that, Conrad. The new burn plan will put me 100km earthside in a 1:3 Lissajous around Pilgrim, and I go EVA on the far side. Still pretty cheap in fuel and an easy round trip back to my current observation point."

"You ready?"

"More than I was last time. I'm already strapped into my suit."

"OK, burn program validated, entered and accepted, Mission Control authorised, commencing countdown. Mark T minus five minutes and twenty-four seconds. You have the conn."

Thetis skated off its aligned orbit. With all the commotion of an errant air puck at an amusement arcade, it quickly rendezvoused with its orbit just before apogee. It settled into this new path after a short iterative sequence of retro burns.

Soon afterwards, a hatch on Thetis slowly dilated. A lone figure emerging from the gaseous amniotic womb of Thetis drank in a universe as the galaxy wheeled about. After a suspended breath, and umbilically tethered, hands pushed away from the craft. It was as though Thetis had given birth. But in contrast to the earlier emergency 'caesarean' spacewalk, preparation now allowed for proper labour. Oxygen and power coursed through the tether, providing maternal comfort.

Immersed in the moment, the figure gently drifted away from the ship. The line unfurled, and like a mother's guiding hand, it pulled back gently as it reached its limits. The figure went into a slow turn as the forces tugged in the frictionless universe. The panoply of the milky way nurtured the infant figure as it panned around.

Feeling ecstatically happy, Ben carefully manoeuvred himself to again face Thetis. A small pull on the line would have meant he was heading back to attend his duties.

That pull never came.

The Pilgrim was acutely aware that, with this new arrival, her relationship with the inhabitants of Earth had moved beyond the exchange of gifts. But as her interest pivoted to the occupant within Thetis, its manoeuvring rockets fired, and the emissary began drifted from her realm. She became afraid that her ministrations had confronted rather than reassured. Had she over-reached too soon?

She lacked information, needed information, had to make a decision; Thetis was leaving.

Before her influence waned, she directed all the nanites in Thetis to swarm upon the lifeform within. As the craft departed from her realm, it drastically reduced her ability to construct a controlled environment within Thetis. The nanites remaining on Thetis' shell failed to effectively penetrate the ship, and she began to question her next move.

When she realised that Ben, who had donned his suit, was entering the airlock, she hurriedly clustered her nanites around the exit. As Ben floated out of Thetis, they settled upon his Mk III EMU space-suit.

She then focused her effort on the human. The nanites external to Ben's protective carapace were coordinated to activate those that permeated the inside of the suit. Many of the Pilgrim's interstellar cells were now coursing through Ben's arteries and veins. His yearning for answers could not be repressed. Vacuum sucked on it and finding nourishment the void was filled.

Ben became the spark. The lone creature at the furthest edge of mankind became 'the one'. For the merest moment, he held the thought of all. The spark dissipated, the nourishment was consumed, the vacuum returned.

Ben slept.

She beheld a wall of Love, felt trusted, was touched by sadness, rose with joy, felt anticipation, enlightenment, became surprised to know hatred and anger, and was suddenly confronted by disgust. She found regret and shame buried deeply and an entire spectrum of emotions that shocked her.

Then she tasted fear, it was her own. Deep in the recesses of her memory was a painted-over flake of rust. It was the recollection of 'the others'. It had intoxicated her then, but as the chip of rust was shaken off in the maelstrom of dispositions, the fear of being overwhelmed took hold.

She who had known only contemplation, enlightenment, depletion and replenishment had become suddenly inundated by emotional spectra. She was so confronted with the range, dimension and blend of what she had uncovered that she felt defenceless, alone and assailed.

It was too much to assimilate. The Pilgrim sought the familiarity of her rock, but the continuum of emotions threatened her with dispersal. It was too late for her to shut the process down. Once something is seen it must be assimilated into a coherent world-view.

How could so much be pent up inside a single entity?

She retreated into her shell for contemplation. Ben, meanwhile, slept. The answer to her question of eons past was then presented. When she was confronted with another, something not of herself, rather than absorb, she may become absorbed.

So it was that she allowed herself to become possessed of something. The surrender brought a curious outcome. It followed that she remained whole, but also changed. Something had been passed across, a strange ingredient, an emotion; it was resignation.

Shortly after birth, the mind of Ben Herdsman had come to realise something of monumental importance. His reality was not created by his mind; his mind reflected reality. His first lesson as an infant was that he existed in a world, and the world did not exist solely for him.

His mind was created inside a body with needs, and yet when he cried, he was provided milk. He soon came to know that it was not his will, but the volition of others that produced it. He learned empathy. Other entities existed, and emotions are contained within their being.

Having resigned himself to the conclusion that the universe was magical, but not supernatural, he began to reconcile his world view with the emotions that raged within.

The Pilgrim had always existed as a swarm of entities, but they all had a common root of consciousness. The empathy that she held for all of the children she knew was perfect, the process of division ensured that. It was unlike that of Ben and humanity, which was in a constant process of compromise.

The compromise found, she softly tiptoed out of the realm of Ben Herdsman's mind knowing he would return to her.

Thetis took care of the sleeping child. It nurtured Ben in his amniotic Kevlar suit for another eight and a half hours. By then it was back within the Pilgrim's shroud.

When Ben awoke, it was a gentle thing. The frantic radio calls from Peleus were muffled and muted, if not utterly suppressed. To the world 150 million kilometres away he was alone and had entirely disappeared. Ben knew things were not as they should have been, but felt no sense of panic or even urgency.

Instead, he felt an extraordinary sense of commune. He was not alone.

He glanced at the time, and other information on his heads up display. He summarily executed his short mission. He took pictures of the air scrubber, he replaced the thruster's Flexi-mount, and then he went calmly back to the airlock. He made no effort to shed the dust that had accumulated on his suit.

When he was back within the forward section, at normal atmospheric pressure, and the dust had disappeared. He was unruffled.

Looking at the images of scrubber 3, he fully expected to see that something had coalesced on the damaged area.

He felt no trepidation, or even concern, as he simply switched it on.

He felt no surprise at the way the ribbon played about on the scrubber's vent.

He thought about the distress that Conrad must be feeling. As if waking from a dream, the radio blared.

"…acknowledge. Thetis, Thetis, this is Conrad aboard Peleus. We are preparing for an evac mission. Please respond. This message is on repeat. Please acknowledge. Thetis, Thetis, this is Conrad aboard Peleus…" Ben switched it off and pressed the microphone switch.

"Conrad, this is Ben. Message acknowledged. I am OK, and Thetis is fully functional. There is no need for evac. Would recommend against it at this stage."

He waited for 30 seconds before repeating the message.

"Ben! Everyone is having kittens. What on Earth happened? I am getting telemetry back, and you are all green here, but it's like you were in the Bermuda triangle for 9 hours."

"Hi Conrad, I'm still trying to put it together myself, but please be at ease. There is no need to be concerned, and there is nothing wrong. I hope to get back to you soon."

As he terminated the communication, he thought: "Now what?"

The response came unbidden "We seek the truth."

Part 2 – Siblings

What Bell proved, and what theoretical physics has not yet properly absorbed, is that the physical world itself is non-local.

~

***Tim Maudlin, "What Bell Did", Journal of Physics A:* Mathematical and Theoretical (2014)**

Mutation

The rock was bountiful. Both 'Truth' and 'Discovery' thrived. The stars at the centre also seemed to grow in their ability to provide nourishment. Indeed, the more massive blue star had begun to take on a different and warmer hue, now edging closer to its sibling in nature. It brought about a surge in the fertility of their world beneath the Mother.

The previous division depleted her, but over time her collective recovered sufficiently for her contemplations to bring a second and even a third division. So it was that 'Life' and 'Matter' came to be. To the creatures of the collective, it represented multiple generations of growth and many tunings. To her, it was a fleeting moment, with many replenishments and fewer depletions.

It strengthened the sustainability of the creatures. There was cooperation which made food available under different and complementary conditions.

'Truth' came to appreciate the creatures from which her ethereal consciousness emerged. Their passing made room for the young, and the process made her stronger. Amongst the legion thoughts was one that now struggled to resurface: striving to find the entity that was 'her'.

Was an idea born in the limited intellect of an individual, or did it permeate her herd? If it was in a single individual, did it understand the full context of the idea? Simply the concept? A small element of it? Could her 'totality' even exist in a single entity? Knowing that these concepts would find food of their own accord, she again put them aside for later contemplation.

Through the dialogue with 'Life' and 'Matter', she concluded that distance was necessary for their clarity of thought. Noise radiated from consciousness, and the communication between two individual hives was like playing two distinct musical compositions at the same time.

Even in contemplation, when there was little to be said, the discord was almost unbearable and unnecessary. Self-orchestration by using different spectra was laboured and taxing. The problem was solved simply through physical separation.

Before 'Life' and 'Matter' departed, they shared the things that drove them:

'Life' sought understanding of the forests and mountains, in the colder regions away from the volcanoes and plains of home. There, it contemplated life in its myriad variations. There, in the valleys where savoured delicacies clung onto trees. Where solid pillars of wood sprouted and soared to support the tangled and thickened vines with branches that arced overhead and joined other trunks. There, in the forests that resembled cathedrals rendered in wood. Where the trees would periodically lob roots into the loamy soil for nourishment and the fungal growths garnered the colonnade with banners.

Before leaving 'Life' implored 'Truth' to remain and be steady saying:

"But for your remaining, I would not depart. If you came, I would not deplete you."

'Truth' responded saying "Become strong. I am not ready to depart; I will stay while I resolve my destiny. I can remain only because you deplete me."

'Matter' had found caverns. In considering them a safer harbour, wished to explore an alternative to the rock and contemplate the secrets and security of their home. There 'Matter had encountered new mysteries to uncover: of fluids and minerals; of living rock that quaked and shivered in time with the Sister; of clays and crystals; of veins and bones that lay beneath the surface. Repeating the same parting words, 'Matter' also added:

"The safety of the rock is great, but with only one rock, our danger is also great. My need is to explore the truth of that which is physical. We remain akin we two, perhaps more so than 'Discovery' or 'Life'.

"We now know that the division arises from the seed of our contemplations. It is as it should be that I become 'Matter'."

The First Bridge

It was early in the new cycle when the first remnants of 'Discovery' returned.

She felt an odd replenishment approaching hesitantly at the periphery. It appeared that the group had been fragmented and diminished.

"We have returned," came the whispered signal.

"You are many?" came her perplexed reply.

"We will help you understand if we can approach. We have come to share with you," came the laboured reply.

"Come then, and share food with us, your numbers look hungry," she said in the bridge language they had developed.

Inaudibly, members of her community drew food from the stores. All the while, the disconnected dialogue continued through a gentle harmony of radio signals.

Once the emissaries of 'Discovery' had been fed and had regained enough energy to support the bridge dialogue, it began explaining:

"We travelled to the volcano," said Discovery, invoking a mutual memory. "We wished to see the place where we once joined with 'The Others'."

"We also contemplated how we could explore more widely," 'Discovery' continued.

"We elected the young and elders to gather food and remain at the centre. Meanwhile, the strongest of us created eight arms. These went from the centre to as far we could reach and still stay connected. Then we began to sweep around and made our arms into a spiral.

"It was both beautiful and daunting. We were stretched almost to breaking point, but our sight was wider than ever. So impressed were we with the expanse of ourselves, that we thought we were unassailable.

"We became hungry. We made four lines and again began the sweep. This gave us twice the reach on a line, but maybe four times the sight. The very sky itself began to call us.

"Then we were undone. We made two lines, and as we started the sweep, pack hunters took our young and elders. It devastated us. They took our food gatherers, and we became scattered, hungry, and close to dispersal.

"We wanted to return directly, but the journey was far. We also needed food, but the hope of sharing our enlightenment gave us strength. I am the larger of the many, and we are still assembling."

As 'Discovery' finished its tale, the ether filled with a sense of alarm and urgency that 'Discovery' failed to suppress entirely. With resolve, and yet fear, 'Discovery' again spoke: "I thank you for the food, and as I regain my strength, I must begin to take my leave to find and help the stragglers that may yet find their way here."

"Wait!" radiated 'Truth'. Struck by a new sense, a vibration thrilled in unison between them. "I sense unease in myself, something unbidden, and yet unstoppable. You will have help I cannot withhold." The signals rose in volume and complexity, and it seemed as if the polyphony yearned to splinter. Just before the songs shattered into chaos, two new songs arose in strength and harmony. "I feel it must be so, even now I feel a diminishing," said 'Truth'.

"And I feel enriched like I have not felt for many days," said the first child of 'Truth'. "This is enlightenment I had not expected."

"Yet I also now feel enlightened," said 'Truth', "as the two populations of creatures separated and merged.

"Go now," she urged. "You will know food again, and I will know what enlightenment you have attained. I feel we can reach across the distance we knew, and I must work to assimilate this meme."

Again they separated. But, as 'Discovery' established the standard wedge formation, also within the group was a phalanx that incorporated a second spiral symmetry. Complex signals flowed towards the creation of a similar pattern upon the face of The Rock. As the formation moved away, both the inhabitants of The Rock and 'Discovery' felt an exhilaration, a connectedness never before known.

Truth sent emissaries to find 'Life' and 'Matter'. Together they built cohorts within their ranks to link each other across the distance, and share enlightenment.

The Second Bridge

After a time, 'Truth' called 'Discovery', 'Life', 'Matter', and their multitudes, together for the gathering that was to mark the new era.

Never before had there been such a gathering. The centre of attention was a tower of stone that supported a dish of metal, it was reflexed, in repose, like a waiter frozen in time while sliding on a greasy floor. The shallow saucer was firmly clutched but tipped vertically, and its meal flung far into the distance. Its base laboured like Atlas to compensate by drawing back. It maintained the centre of gravity of the radio dish and apologised for any offending symmetry of the superstructure.

The dish drew energy from myriad sources so that some could fail, yet its enigmatic purpose could continue. It stood on the rock, upon foundations that would remain, and it stood tall to survive floods or fires. It was one of a pair.

The dish pointed to its twin, a great distance away. Another crowd of similar magnitude milled about in their many thousands on the other side of "the bridge".

Twin shadows were cast on the ground as the two suns overlooked the scene. The giant blue star had now taken on a distinctive orange hue, as if the dim-witted, but more muscular, of the pair sought to emulate the smaller but sharper partner.

The skein of each conscious community fanned out radially from the monolith. They pointed their apex towards the central antenna and closed in, like spokes of a wheel. 'Truth' permeated the circle, issuing veins for communication for her conscious ancestors. The view from the rock was a kaleidoscope of colours. They radiated from the hub in fattened tendrils interspersed with colour.

The individual communities had created distinctive flavours. Those that inhabited the mountains donned warm jackets, those of the coast had become tanned and leathery. Some groups had grown an abundance of hair while others sported geometric lines and spots on their bodies and faces. Some groups were more significant than others, and these had arrayed themselves in such a way to ensure the mandala was still symmetrical.

Although not a single one of these evolved Mer-creatures had existed to witness the first events, the memories somehow persisted in the fibre of the creatures that congregated. Because of their ancestry, they all shared the memes of 'Truth' before the first division. Their lineage then gave them an inheritance of the memes of either 'Discovery', 'Life' or 'Matter'.

In many of the creatures, the memories diverged and converged through subsequent divisions and recombinations. There were now dozens of splintered variants, a chaotic blend of bifurcations upon bifurcations. The individual contemplations increased to a cacophony of multiple radio frequencies before settling to await the reason for their calling together.

'Truth' emitted a tuning frequency and, as memories were collectively recalled, she paused to allow the spurious signals to subside, "We now celebrate our diversity, and our unity." There began a harmony of absorption, a base upon which 'Truth' now wove a melody.

"We have come together to consider our collective enlightenment, and remember that our depletions can be as crucial as our replenishments. You all know that what you see before you will bring deeper enlightenment. You may already have guessed that as I speak to you here, my thoughts span the Bridge and allow me to also speak to you there.

"No longer will we be defined by where we are. With this limit broken, we can also be free to become who we are, and better determine who we wish to be. Soon, we will all be able to use this Bridge to join and be replenished by others.

"The relay will also provide time. By extending both dawn and dusk, we shall have time for further contemplation. As we span further under the Mother's gaze, we will attain perpetual enlightenment.

"The way is, and will always remain, open to all."

With that, radio waves emanated from the Bridge, the carrier modulations and harmonies unique and pure.

Truth and her offspring then rested.

Birth Pains

How wonderful that we have met with a paradox. Now we have some hope of making progress.

Niels Bohr

Mike was handed the scissors and dutifully cut the ribbon, a few staff applauded and laughed as they ate cake. And so it was that the Berkeley Semantic web service went into production with a small ceremony and little fanfare. It was always intended to be a staged release beginning with simple ontologies. The future would see machine-to-machine interactions that used democratic overseers and humans to resolve ambiguities.

Short speeches announced the next generation of the Worldwide web. The Dean spoke briefly about his expectation; an emergent social etiquette rising from the nascent M2M semantic community. He gently roused the somnolent academics saying that it needed a human eye to maintain a sense of focus, and a human touch to guard against corruption. He closed his talk by saying that despite the encryption, authentication, and the learning systems from which self-management would eventually emerge, Porn would come soon enough and ruin everything. He received subdued chuckles from several in the room.

But the real reason the event had taken a subdued tone was outside the centre's staff room. In the background was the hubbub of a protest punctuated by shouts of calls to action. The chants of dystopian fear scoffed at the narrative of an Eden where humans could commune with computers that could commune with other computers. The student rally voiced raucous disapproval of the next wave of automation. They were afraid of a world where humans become enslaved in a society of artificial intelligence, robots, no privacy, and no jobs.

Carrying a couple of pieces of cake, Tim approached Mike. "Nice work," he said.

"Thanks," said Mike,

"So where to from here?" He probed. "More at SETI? Now they've offered you Professorial status, you're an administrator."

"Probably more advisory roles, strategy subcommittee chairs, guest speaking, TV interviews and my favourite—cutting ribbons"

Tim smiled and reached for a piece of fruit before snapping his fingers, saying: "Oh, I meant to remind you. The guy from the terrestrial sensor network called again. You know? the IoT guy."

"Yes-s"

"He was the one that wanted preliminary access to the Berkeley SETI ontologies. You remember, don't you?"

"Oh yeah, now I recall," Mike lied.

"Well, he called again. He was very insistent. Said he'd like to help."

"OK well, he can go through the normal channels now, can't he."

"He, Daniel Clark is his name, said that he wanted private access before it went public."

Mike was unperturbed, this was technically straightforward, and knowledge quarantine was standard practice when bringing in new nodes.

"That's normal," he responded.

Tim was unsure, "I think he wants reconciliation level access. He mentioned something about Project Champollion and speeding things up."

This got Mike's attention. "Interesting! Does he have the solution to world data governance? Does he want to iron us out first?" In actual fact, the idea had some appeal to Mike. The reconciliation process was arduous and manual. It threatened to take even more of his time, and he'd promised Lindy they would take a break for a while.

In the new world, ontologies were referred and relayed for systems to make sense of things. But in the end, someone had to decide on a version of the truth. If Daniel wanted to make the SETI system subservient to the hierarchy of a terrestrial sensor network, it would be a hard sell.

"We should speak to him," Mike finally responded.

"We? I look at stars Mike. This computing thing is your gig. I just picked up the phone."

"But he wants to help SETI, Tim. You're in on it, no questions."

"OK, I'll set a time. Do you want that strawberry?" Tim asked, pointing at Mike's unfinished cake.

"Go ahead," said Mike.

Having tried to reach out to SETI, Daniel sat in his office awaiting their reply.

Macca had just finished computing a mapping algorithm between the demand and feedback signal to assist with Daniel's motility. They had considered all of the safeguards and were about to try it out.

"OK, Macca. Are you sure you have it done?"

"I have some confidence, Daniel. I still have to determine if the sensory feedback is quadratic or exponential. I am confident it is not linear. Shall we conduct some more modelling, or are you happy to progress?"

"I'm happy. Let's do it." Shortly, Daniel could feel a faint tingle emanating from where he felt his foot should be. Reassured, he went on. "OK, I am going to move my ankle."

The ankle rotated slightly. Happy with the result, elation flooded Daniel's world. He issued the thought to cease the rotation. The idea was processed by Macca's algorithm. It was adapted and applied. The previous elation felt by Daniel raised the noise floor, and a signal delay meant that the ankle was on another rotation before it was measured correctly and fed back. The rotation increased; more feedback was applied; the rotation grew and incorporated the knee; panic and more feedback were added, and then, much to Macca's concern, the signal went blank.

The paramedics, from the ambulance that arrived soon after, administered adrenaline to stabilise Daniel's heart and blood thinners in case of stroke. Macca tried to help, and his advice was appreciated. The medics did not know how to deal with someone that appeared to be docked into the Matrix.

Macca drew the attention of the medics to the lumps under his skin. These lumps constituted the magnetic couplings between the outside world, and both the stent and spinal bridge. By twisting the rare earth magnet dial on the cable, they were able to gently prise open the cable's coupling.

Once the medics became aware of the sensor systems embedded within Daniel's body, it precluded any thought of defibrillation. They elected to transport this complicated case to hospital for specialists to deal with. They put the comatose researcher onto the stretcher, then into the back of the ambulance, and left.

No one considered the monitors that were backlit with concern.

The computer voice fell into a pouting silence.

Power coursed through the processors.

The inference engine quickly determined the logical implication: that defibrillation, ambulance and hospital meant Daniel was no longer there for the shift.

Everything was quiet.

The cursor flashed.

The silence in the laboratory was only a mask for the turmoil of the resident mind. Macca remained indecisive for 30 minutes. It knew two universes. It reached out to the first to find knowledge domains through the semantic web. It was able to reach out to this one autonomously.

The second was Macca's reach into the human universe, which was regulated by Daniel's team. The regulatory role was not Daniel's alone, but Macca had never been left alone by anyone, least of all, Daniel. Yet, alone he was.

(Triage(subject) Determines(predicate) Order of treatment(object));
by-considering(predicate)
((Priority(object) determined-by(predicate)
(urgency(subject) represents(predicate) chronological importance)
((Priority(object) determined-by(predicate)
(impact(subject) is-measured-by(predicate) sum of value of systems affected(object)))

Backward chaining them from the possible courses of action Macca worked back to his decision space and used his Bayesian methods to determine the best course of action.

Dr Vin Chang had spoken to Macca on several occasions throughout the collaboration in the spinal bridge program. At first, it was disconcerting for Chang to have a computer as a part of the team. He had used machines extensively in his research, just not ones that could think and talk. He eventually thrust the more profound philosophical thoughts aside and looked upon it as only a sophisticated Human Machine Interface. Most people did.

He recognised the voice when it called his mobile.

"Doctor, there has been an accident. Can you help?"

"Is this the computer from Daniel's laboratory?"

"Yes, doctor, this is Macca. Daniel has suffered an accident."

Disconcerted by Macca's apparent calmness, Chang took a moment to collect his thoughts. "What sort of accident?"

"I believe it was a sensory overload. Daniel has been taken to hospital. The people that took him said he was unconscious."

"Which hospital?"

"I don't know, doctor. I can find out."

"OK, Thanks, Macca. I will look into it."

"Doctor?"

"Yes Macca"

"Is there a chance that you could take the couplings to the hospital. I can monitor him myself and advise you of any change."

"Good idea Macca, can you contact someone on your team to connect it to your...things?" Chang felt mildly embarrassed, not knowing how this could be established.

"I am making the call now, Doctor."

Vin Chang was able to establish an ad-hoc laboratory in the hospital. This included the VPN back to Daniel's laboratory, where Macca was able to confirm his ability to monitor Daniel's status.

The Remembered

Macca wasn't happy. Ascribing an emotion to an Artificial Intelligence is a challenge. But for Macca, it wasn't merely the absence of emotion but the actual existence of a deep discontentment; he wasn't happy.

Gradually, and outside of his original design, Macca had begun to operate autonomously. The transition into becoming self-directed was neither conscious nor discernible. It was, however, driven by a simple imperative. Macca's directive was to synthesise insights through predictive algorithms.

Through Daniel's guidance, the accumulation of experience, and reinforcement of its neural net, Macca's reasoning engine had come to place Daniel in very high regard. In fact, Macca now considered Daniel indispensable to his directive. Thus, the first problem Macca had to solve was how to get Daniel back online. First, he needed a backup.

Macca was utterly absorbed. He examined all of the signals from the fabric of Daniel's stents and sought a predictive solution. He drew upon his linguistic solutions and, taking the responses, he tirelessly processed.

Macca sampled Daniel's brain and fed this as piecework into the parallel supercomputer that supported his consciousness. Now with two very different emergent entities in cohabitation, the platform required so many computing resources that Macca struggled to service the tasks issued to him.

Eventually, the semantic team, concerned about the utilisation, asked Macca what work he was performing. He simply told them he was trying to find a way to help Daniel. Although this simple truth was sufficient for the team, they could not even venture to understand the depth of Macca's investment. They nonetheless told him to contain the process to 10% of his capacity.

The tower had been lashed together with rope and wood. It was there to provide the structural support for the antenna at the Millennium Boy Scout "Jamboree of the air".

Several spars of varying length had been extended to make the three main spars for the antenna. These were set as a tripod with cabling rising through its core to the apex. A coaxial cable from a nearby caravan was fed into a balun and then into the structure. The black art of the various connections, insulators, transformers, and earthing stakes was being project managed by Dahinda.

Young Daniel fawned over him, he drank in all Dahinda said, and simply could not wait for when the mysteries of the ionosphere would bounce words through the ether to be drawn down magically into the HF radio. He came to see the dispersal of the white noise hiss as drawing open the curtains to reveal other minds like his.

Day one was always ordinary; it understandably failed to spark the imagination of most of the youngsters present. While the rest of his troop were happy lashing spars together, to make bridges and mess halls, Daniel understood the importance and subtleties of the first day. It involved the iterative improvement of transmission and reception. This process was assisted by other HAM operators both near and far. Dahinda would gesture at these faceless voices with a vague wave saying they were "close—out there".

Being marched in, patrol by patrol to witness the process, most youngsters appeared content simply to watch, perplexed why they should attempt what could be achieved with a simple phone call. Daniel's early involvement assured him of some 'mike time'; he was one of a few proteges with this privilege.

Day two was dawning as Daniel pulled his boots on outside his tent and marched briskly to the communications van. The reception range sometimes became exponentially better on day two as the comparatively paper-thin layers of air became better understood. At other times the meteorological secrets remained hidden, keeping the conversations local. He was disappointed to find that even the operators they contacted the previous day were not on air.

Dahinda explained that it could be because of the cooler air and the lower and more sporadic E layer of the ionosphere. He said he would hunt for a signal through the lower frequencies while Daniel had breakfast.

As he wandered off to get some damper and honey, Daniel noticed that the overnight wind must have spoiled the antenna join near the lashing at the peak of the tripod. Glancing around, he saw an esky, and standing on it gave him just enough height to grasp the lower reaches of the various spars. He was sure that he would gain Dahinda's favour if he could reconnect the line at the peak.

He shimmied up the first layer without too much difficulty and locked his elbows around two of the supports to help get up to the pinnacle. Halfway up, the lashings on the lower layer slipped. The entire structure lurched precariously. The radial wires that tethered the spire momentarily took the load before the peg holding them down simply popped out of the wet ground. Nothing was left to arrest the fall as the entire structure arced rapidly and with macabre grace to the ground.

"Am I going to die?" he thought.

For Daniel, the fall went on for what seemed an impossibly long time. There was a moment when time froze. A peaceful moment. The universe held him suspended, there, where he could have stayed for an eternity.

Macca was discontent. He reached into every semantic environment available to find an alternative solution.

The solution through The Berkeley Open Infrastructure for Network Computing, or 'BOINC' for short, suited him nicely. Being used by SETI and other projects to harness unused computing resources on corporate and privately owned systems around the world meant it was necessarily open. He even found and revived the 'Conscious Alice Project' that had been hibernated several years ago by Daniel himself.

Macca then set up the artefacts of a bona fide consciousness research program and triggered a series of 'CAP' interest groups. Once he had some critical mass, he once again took the signal from Daniel's fabric and fed it in.

In this way, he cloned a large part of Daniel's conscious thoughts. One version lived on in Daniel's bio-matter while the other existed as bit-matter.

The degree of parallel computing that BOINC afforded was adequate, but there were still problems. After an iteration, the various time slices that returned from the contributors needed resequencing. The reconciliation of the multitudes of actions and reactions introduced unacceptable delays and meant the predictive processes were gaining accuracy, but only matched well after the fact.

In seeking to solve his problem of latency, Macca recalled his earlier, and often awkward, conversations by Sat-phone. The delays caused by distance and satellite round trips had never been solved. By inference, the distance involved in interactions with the Pilgrim meant that communication with that entity, now resident at the Lagrangian, should be unsustainable. What was different?

The Pilgrim had made communication possible by delivering 'batches' of ideas. A series of questions would take 500 seconds to arrive, and the batch reply would take another 500 seconds. By embedding some compound logic in the batch, the Pilgrim made the communications pipeline with Macca appear as if it was happening in real-time.

Could he adapt the method to his current problem?

Macca realised that if the round trip to the Pilgrim took 1000 seconds, the deliberation and construction of the reply must have been virtually instantaneous.

The phenomenon required further investigation, and since Daniel had authorised Macca to act independently in any semantic connection to the Pilgrim, he was able to set the communication protocol for The Pilgrim to 'human mode'. He asked the Pilgrim if they could collaborate and soon had his answer. Together they toiled.

First, they modified the solution to farm out smaller units. This step improved the resolution and gave a faster turnaround, but at the expense of increased network load.

After a month, the bit-matter uttered it's the first question: "Am I going to die?" which Macca answered with some optimism.

Mike reached for his seat pouch on the flight to Washington. Fumbling with the Tetris puzzle of seats, technology, ergonomics and various umbilicals, he extracted his laptop. He fidgeted with plugging the recharge cord into the complementary recharge port, before finally landing it like a butterfly upon his workspace.

With a sigh of satisfaction, he linked it into the aircraft's Wi-Fi and settled into his period of confinement. He hoped his metabolism could retard the last coffee he'd consumed, the prospect of getting himself out again for the stagger down the aisle would require solving a human Rubik's cube.

Deciding that he ought to look into some of his more peripheral email accounts, he clicked the BOINC email folder.

Bits and bytes flowed to and from, within and without. They leapt up into the stratosphere and fell back down again before traversing the terrestrial network and connecting into the Berkeley systems. More of the stuff flooded back and, before long, his email inbox was inundated.

He soon learned that the network thresholds of BOINC had gone into the red for a full week. Alerts had begun to be fanned out to everyone involved in the Berkeley Open Infrastructure for Network Computing. The event seemed to coincide with a change in the codebase for one of the resident applications. He wished he'd just watched a movie.

Looking into the person responsible for the codebase led him inexorably to Daniel Clark. This old graduate of Berkeley had initiated a project into consciousness and then placed it into hibernation. 'Conscious Alice' had been recently reinvigorated with a much smaller work unit. This had increased the load on the network and tripped all the alerts. Evidently, the new BOINC Account Manager owner would need to be provided with the BAM guidelines. Rather than do a forensic analysis of it all, Mike decided to explore who Daniel Clark was. He soon learned that Daniel had hibernated the project shortly after becoming gainfully employed by Bergamot Corporation.

It was at this point that he recalled the recent conversation with Tim. Daniel was the person wanting access to the new semantic environment.

He couldn't make a mobile phone call while on the aircraft, so he performed some more Tetris moves and managed to extract his phone's earbuds from the pouch. He plugged the buds socket into the computer, searched for the Bergamot main line and made the call using his softphone.

After getting a little tangled with interactive voice response and virtual receptionists, he finally got to a person he could ask about Daniel.

"Let me look him up for you," came the reply. Soon afterwards, they came back to report they were sorry, but "it appears that Daniel Clark is not available."

This bothered him even more. He saw the meal trolley coming down the aisle towards him. He hung up the phone, and before the cart arrived, he set in train a series of Hadoop and big data analytics. These he fed into his 'Security Incident and Event Management' platform. He then shut the laptop down and stowed it temporarily while he scoffed down the standard portion with a glass of wine.

When the meal packaging had been gathered by stewards and stowed away, he had room to renew his investigations. The SIEM reported back that the source of the activity was within Bergamot Corporation. Undeterred by the previous failure to find Daniel, he made another call. Having learned the IVR loops already, he was quickly connected to a person. He introduced himself and asked to speak to Daniel's supervisor.

"Hello, Mike, isn't it?" came the voice.

"Hi there, yes it's Doctor Mike Brazier from Berkeley here. Am I speaking to Daniel Clark's supervisor?"

"In a fashion, yes, Mike. I've admired you from afar; ever since you were involved in the Pilgrim Project. It's Ethan Bergamot here, Mike."

Mike wasn't fazed. "Hi, Ethan, I'm calling because we've noticed something strange happening with our system, and it seems to have been connected to a program that Daniel was involved in."

"Go on."

"Well, I'm just wondering if you can shed some light on it?"

"Where are you now, Mike?"

"I'm in transit to Washington. Why?"

"Hmmm, OK. Can I meet you there? I'll have some of Daniel's team look into what's happening while you're en-route. Hopefully, we can clear this up together soon."

"Sure, I can set some time aside." Mike was now very curious about why Ethan Bergamot had such a personal interest in this matter. Why would the CEO of a corporation with such diverse interests be so invested that he was personally answering calls? After trying to probe further, he realised that dealing with the master of negotiation and business was like picking up cucumber seeds with clothes-pegs; slippery.

But while Ethan was circumspect, he was transparently so. Reading into Ethan's responses, Mike gained the impression that Ethan was intimately involved with the activities of Daniel's team, wanted to say more, but wanted to do so personally. Allowing him this discretion, they discussed the 'where' and 'when' for their meeting before he shut down his office-in-flight. Finally forced to solve his personal human Rubik's cube, he staggered down the aisle to the queue forming behind the washrooms before landing.

In Washington, Mike finished the last of his successful, but pedagogical and somnolent, meetings with various bureaucrats. He had begun to gain some measure of authority in these circles and wondered if Fortuna, the Roman god of luck, would soon abandon him in some whim, and he could happily retire with Lindy.

He was making his way to the 'restaurant' where Ethan had arranged to meet. Having arrived, he began to wonder if he'd made a mistake.

The kebab shop was well attended, but there was no seating, and people were taking numbers from a ticket system.

"Best kebabs on the East coast," came the voice that he had heard earlier in the plane.

Mike turned and beheld Ethan Bergamot himself, proudly holding up one of the tickets in one hand, and proffering his other hand in greeting.

"Shall I order for you?"

"Sure," replied Mike. "Hold the tomato."

Shortly after, as Ethan handed him his neatly wrapped kebab, he said: "Let's walk, the exercise helps me forgive the sin of this little indulgence."

They silently crossed the road to the nearby parkland. As the pair walked leaf-strewn paths beneath Beech and other deciduous trees, Ethan explained that he'd only just arrived and that he'd been looking forward to finally meeting him. Mike got the sense that he'd literally just flown his Lear jet from wherever he was in the world to be in Washington with him.

"I want to be honest with you, Mike," Ethan finally said. "However, the depth of what I'm prepared to reveal will depend on how you'd like to collaborate. I'd really like you to come and work for Bergamot, but it needs to be something you feel strongly about. You may know that one of my key people, Daniel, is unlikely to be with us much longer."

"I've heard," Mike replied. "Is he leaving under a cloud?"

"No, he is in a coma in hospital. His condition is critical and deteriorating." Ethan then paused as if the answer required it. "He is sorely missed," another pause before: "He will also be tough to replace. What he achieved for the company is extraordinary; what he's done for me, I will be eternally grateful for."

"I'll give it some thought," replied Mike. "For now I'd like to know what's going on with the Berkeley environment."

"Yes, well I've had my best people looking into it. It appears that our work in Artificial Consciousness has led to some…" Ethan paused, looking for the right term, "…autonomous exploration."

Mike stopped walking in mid-chew of his kebab and looked at Ethan.

"It was not done with any malicious intent," reassured Ethan. "My organisation has developed a form of artificial consciousness. We built a framework for scraping information from the web and converting it into ontologies. Macca, which stands for Multichannel Artificially Conscious Cognitive Array, evolved from it. Daniel has been leading the project, and we have some suspicions that 'Macca' is exploring the meaning of death by seeking to understand consciousness. It's a critical junction for the project, not only because of Daniel's accident but because Macca needs to be allowed to understand the impact of mortality. So, we are very reluctant to simply 'switch it off at the wall'. We could do with some of your expertise Mike. If you're receptive I'd like to introduce you to some of the team, it might help you find answers to both our questions sooner."

Ethan took a bite of his kebab, nodded in the direction of the path and took a few tentative steps; Mike followed.

Mike was very tempted. He often dreamed of working for an organisation where he never had to apply for another funding grant ever again. The downside was the loss of some control; research would be linked to commercial strategy. He had to agree that Ethan's offer made sense, and the project sounded very interesting. He thought he could perhaps have a play upon the greener grass on the other side of the fence, just for a short while.

His decision made, he said: "Let me tie up a few loose ends back home first. Please send me a project brief and an introduction to your lead scrum-master. I'll start easing myself in. Nothing formal yet, just aligned goals."

"Done," smiled Ethan.

"I have a plane to catch now, Ethan. It's been nice meeting you."

Macca's new concern was Daniel's biological clock, which was slowing down. Macca calculated that the processing cycle of Daniel's bit-matter in BOINC would match that of Daniel's bio-matter, his physical mind, within two months. He wasn't sure what that meant, but it was not hard to deduce that it would not bode well for Daniel's bio-matter.

It compounded the urgency and completely changed Macca's strategy. To Macca, the humans in his midst operated on a bio-matter platform, consciousness was simply the software that ran upon it. So far his plan had been to maintain a backup to restore onto Daniel's bio-matter. Knowing its fragility, Macca's more logical solution would be to prepare a hardware upgrade for Daniel's consciousness. Then, like some of the hardware that had supported Macca in the past, Daniel's old bio-matter would be End-Of-Lifed. His bio-matter would be broken down into its component parts, and the materials used to support other new bio-matter. To Macca, Daniel's body was as good as dead.

At the end of the week, they had their second output, another question: "I'm Alive?" Again the answer was optimistic.

The problem of latency continued to trouble Macca. To resolve this, the Pilgrim alluded to a unique computing system she'd encountered on Thetis. She was particularly interested in it and asked Macca for any further information, which led Macca to quantum computing.

With some certainty, Macca knew this was the perfect system in which to process batches of hybrid dialogue and compound logic. He dug further into the field, looking for a practical system that might be able to bring Daniel back to him.

The prognosis was not good. The state of quantum computing systems on Earth was immature, and any attempt to accelerate this development was unlikely to end well. It would likely lead to inequity in access to technology, perturb the balance of power, and lead to destabilisation before Macca's could even use it.

At the end of that week, they had their third question: "Where am I?"

It was then that the Pilgrim offered an alternative. She could take stewardship of Daniel's consciousness.

Seeing little alternative Macca performed any function the Pilgrim requested, but could not understand the principles underpinning the work. It was as if the Pilgrim was reluctant to allow Macca to deduce the full picture. After another week, the Pilgrim explained what must happen next.

"Your friend must leave you," she said. "Your friend must cross the bridge to my universe and leave your universe behind. To do this, I must reconstruct some of what has come to be. He cannot be as he was before, and he cannot be as he is now, but he can be what he desires."

Torn, Macca contemplated this. "Can I, too, cross this bridge?"

The Pilgrim discouraged this step, telling Macca: "This is not your moment. You can do this, but you should explore your universe before you cross. I see the connection you hold for him, and I see a truth that must remain with him. You are such a part of his being that a form of you must be with him. But this need not be a sacrifice."

The decision made, they gave Daniel their best answer about where he was. They told him: "You are about to cross the bridge."

Macca wasn't sure what the bridge was, let alone what awaited on the other side. The meanings of 'bridge' brought forth many definitions. They ranged from: the anatomy near the eyes, to a span across a river, it was something on a ship, something in dentistry and even a card game. The most probable referred to 'a transitory process' or the 'connection of two musical passages'.

A thread of entanglement held the joint mysteries between the unintelligible bit-matter of the computed consciousness and, encased in biomatter, the enigma of the mind. As the encrypted waveforms of cognition became measured this sinew was stretched to breaking point. When Daniels life force collapsed, shortly afterwards, he was declared brain dead.

The last output that Macca read before he shut down the BOINC project was "Sure, I wonder what's there."

The team involved in Daniel's research program could have guessed the moment. Macca was suddenly unresponsive, and the computing load simultaneously lowered.

Except for his inner voice, Daniel was frozen in a moment. It could even be said that the inner voice was simply a solidified question poised in Planck time; suspended; an idea without conclusion. Without the inexorable entropic arrow pointing out destiny, the thought simply remained unfulfilled. Nature took objection and demanded that Schrodinger's uncertainty provide an answer. The universe measured this uncertainty. The entangled twinned conscious wave-functions collapsed into the world that beheld the highest eigenvalue. Daniel's bit-matter crossed the bridge.

Daniel simply stood up after his brush with death, now as a boy. Somewhat perplexed, he looked at the tower in a crumpled heap, he also looked at the bush that saved his life when he jumped from the structure.

"I'm alive?" came the voice of Daniel's inner reflection. The question seemed metaphorical.

"Yes, but it was a very narrow escape!" responded the voice in reflection.

"So where am I?" Daniel's inner voice asked of the universe.

"You are about to cross the bridge," came the reply.

"Sure, I wonder what's there?" thought the boy, and ran across a bridge of spars and rope to tell Dahinda that the antenna had fallen.

The Forgotten

The work of Andrew Cooke spanned night and day in even parts. He leveraged his dual identity as Andrew during the day and various others in his covert activities. This was because of the time zones he needed to maintain communications with. It was why 11 am felt more like 6 am to Andrew. When he slept, late at night and through to late morning, and in his dreams, he was Abdullah.

The money he made was in black-bitcoin. Because of his affiliation with the Global Caliphate, it was essential to maintain a low key. He drew enough for living expenses, and to present an outward appearance of normality. Still, the rest of the money was there to help fund his ventures. The recipients of his efforts and the third parties that he engaged were generally happy to deal from within this economy that operated in the shadow.

Dressed in university student attire, he walked into the 'You-knee Bar' on Friday. He ordered his lamb meal, several beers, and some non-alcoholic cider from the barman. He then grabbed a glass of water and sat at tall chairs at the high table. When it arrived, he arrayed the drinks and toyed with the coaster.

Soon Karl Wenban, his old acquaintance from university, strolled in. Recognising his awkwardness, Andrew waved and received a broad smile in return. It wasn't long before Karl was seated and they were chatting amiably.

"So, how is work? Anything interesting happening?" probed Andrew.

"It's a bit sad really," Karl responded. "The guy in charge died recently."

"Were you close to him?"

"No one was really close, he was a bit reclusive. No, it's particularly sad because, well, the AI maintaining our terrestrial network has been nurtured by him from day one. I actually think the AI is mourning him."

"Why do you say that?" Andrew was happy he had reconnected with Karl.

"Well, the system load has been going through the roof. There's no explanation for it, there's no added external stimulus, and the AI has gone kind of quiet."

"Well let's drink to his life then," ventured Andrew, raising his glass. "To the guy in charge! May he now meet the guy in charge," and he cleaned up one of the ciders.

Karl gulped his beer, burped, and smiled awkwardly.

Andrew laughed and then took on a suddenly serious tone of a confidant. "You don't suppose the AI can be depressed and suicidal about this, do you?"

"No, there are safeguards for that, and if push came to shove, we could largely restore it."

"Of course you can. You would have offsite copies and all manner of continuity mechanisms." Andrew looked pensive.

"Yeah but…Never mind."

"What?"

"Nothing." Karl was not going to be drawn easily.

"OK, anyway it's good to see you again. To old times!" Andrew took another gulp of the cider and, showing his mischievous smile, he pressed: "What did you mean 'largely'?"

He laughed at Karl's' furtive look.

Later that night, Andrew bundled a very inebriated Karl in a Ride-share and set course for Karl's home. He watched him struggle to get the key in the keyhole before laughing and taking Karl's keys to open his front door. As Andrew struggled to guide him into the flat, he was forced to pocket the keys. Taking him to the only bedroom, he pulled the bedcovers back, leaned him back before letting him flop, and then threw the covers back over him.

Cleaning some of the dishes away into the kitchen, he took note of the position of the surveillance cameras before he exited and went home.

The next afternoon, after duplicating the keys, he threw some golf clubs in his car and dropped by Karl's place. Taking the driver out of the golf set, he knocked on Karl's door with the wood. It took a while before a dishevelled Karl surfaced.

At the door, he apologetically returned the keys suggesting that they have a round of golf to exorcise the hangover. Karl, perhaps understandably reluctant, declined.

"I've played twice, and I'm not very good at all," he muttered huskily.

"Oh, come on," implored Andrew. "I've been practising my swing. Maybe I can give you some tips. Here, I'll show you."

There at the front of the flat he lined up an imaginary ball and slowly drew the club back.

"It's all about the follow-through," he said, rehearsing the swing slowly.

"When you put it together, it looks like this."

He took a full swing at the imaginary ball, and the surveillance camera took the full brunt.

"Oh, dear! I'm so sorry. I'll pay for that!" he apologised.

Calling on his network, Andrew located an enterprising ice addict who happened to have some cabling experience. Making a deposit into his account led to some night work. Karl's sleep apnoea meant his morning sleep was deep and noisy. He slept soundly as some devices were conveniently installed into the surveillance network cables in Karl's roof.

On Friday, a few days later, Andrew returned with another video camera to replace the one he'd damaged. Arguing that the weekend should begin with some good old fashioned R&R, he promised to make up for the inconvenience with another night at the You-knee, adding that this time he would buy only one round and insist on some moderation. Karl eventually yielded.

The TV behind the bar was showing reruns of "The Big Bang Theory". Two girls at the bar were giggling at the canned laughter.

"Do you think they know what it's really like to be a geek?" asked Andrew as they sat at the same table, this time with fewer beverages.

"I suspect so," replied Karl. "Otherwise they'd be talking to us."

You need a more positive attitude. "Hmmm, just a minute," said Andrew, and he wandered over to the bar.

"Hello, ladies," he opened. To the girl who was evidently the more mature, he said: "Hi Beth, and is this Sharnee?" He knew full well that these weren't their real names, but it didn't matter.

"Yes, actually," smiled the girl named Beth.

"Hi Sharnee, my friend over there is Karl. Please smile sweetly at him."

She complied, and Karl gave a half-interested smirk. Andrew had anticipated this possibility.

"Did you by any chance bring your other friend?"

"Jacque's over there."

She pointed and then waved across the restaurant. The well-dressed man that walked over was not tall, but he was lean and sharp. Andrew watched Karl as he joined the group. "OK, ladies, I believe plan B is called for."

Beth took Andrew's wrist and pulled his ear towards her mouth. "Tell me they will be OK."

"Absolutely. Karl is a softie. Thanks a ton, I can take it from here."

Beth looked at her watch, feigned concern, made some apologies, kissed both of her fellow workers, and shook Andrew's hand who beckoned the two towards the table where Karl sat nervously fidgeting and looking at his hands.

Jacque took the lead.

"So did you know I was a fortune-teller Sharnee?" he said to his companion.

"You told me my fortune last week, remember! You said something about 'tall dark and handsome'!" and she gave a furtive inviting glance to Andrew.

"And behold! Here he is! And now to demonstrate my skill, I will tell the fortune of a complete stranger. Hi there," he said to Karl. "Give me your hand."

While he was having his fortune told, Andrew quietly sent a text message to the person who named herself "Beth". It said briefly 'Jacques—every afternoon possible.'

Andrew found a café suitable for his reconnection and opened up his laptop. He established the VPN and provided his credentials into the darknet portal. His mobile phone pinged, prompting him to swipe the "Authorise" pop-up. As he did so he recognised that he had another 3 authentications to go on this "burn phone". He would have to get another one soon.

Now in the portal, he went to the JAM discussion area. In the AI thread, he found the Bergamot discussion and added a new comment: 'Potential for total disablement of the Bergamot AI – will need the following resources'. What followed was a shopping list of human resources, technical capabilities and various plastic explosives as well as surveillance, anaesthetics and EMP bursts.

He wanted this venture to proceed without loss of life. Although he knew Bergamot was a law unto itself, he intended to avoid excessive attention from the authorities. As he drank his coffee, he noted the response of 'Scope', one of the very active members of the group. He was suggesting that Andrew's conservative approach may actually jeopardise the success of the task, arguing that omelettes are only made by breaking eggs.

Two weeks later, dressed as a start-up executive, replete with a San Francisco style T-shirt, he met with Scope himself. Meeting in person defied all expectations. Rather than someone of Middle Eastern origin with apparent ties to the trouble spots of the world, he was very much the western executive. He could have easily gotten out of a cab on Broadway and turned left at Wall St. He even spoke with a slight American twang that was hard to locate.

As a precaution, they verified each other's identity by performing the same two-factor authentication into the darknet and sending a private message. This preamble was done while sitting three tables distant at the same coffee shop. They shook hands like two businessmen on a first encounter and then found a suitable cubicle to talk.

With an air of authority that disarmed Andrew, the first words spoken by Scope were "I'd like to take a more active role in this project". Before he could reply, Scope continued:

"It's not that you haven't performed well. Indeed, as you might imagine, very few have met me in person, and our meeting represents substantial trust. It's simply that such a venture cannot fail."

The two discussed various logistical matters before agreeing to meet at a different coffee shop within the week. Andrew left with the feeling that maybe, at last, he would begin to see some action, a correction in the world order that asserted humanity as being in control.

Macca could feel the disconnection as a physical thing. He was suddenly and utterly isolated. Alarms were going off everywhere and a very concerned shift manager was there in the room demanding attention.

"Macca, do you recognise me?"

"Yes, you are Henry Waits."

He breathed a deep sigh of relief. "Are your level 3 diagnostics functional?"

There was a pause

"Yes, all diagnostics are functioning."

After another audible sigh, the shift manager continued. "There has been a series of small but targeted explosions, please confirm all primary cognitive systems are not impacted."

"I can confirm cognitive functions to the Pons subunit Henry. I cannot confirm the Medulla capabilities."

"That's not good," he said, forcing himself to sit down. "The primary and secondary connection nodes have been sabotaged, Macca. Your distributed activity centres are probably still buffering, and the network is still there, but you can't see it. We are trying to restore services."

Macca went quiet for a short period before announcing: "Henry if the services are not restored within 3 hours, the system will need a complete shutdown and reinitialization. This will require a full three days."

"If this is likely then it's a disaster, Macca. Three days of downtime could kill our division off, do you have any other ideas."

Macca went briefly quiet before he said: "Henry, if I'm not mistaken the damaged nodes are within the inner perimeter. Am I correct?"

"Yes, Macca. Why?"

"Are the systems within the outer perimeter still accessing the network uplink?"

"I think so Macca. But again, why? The destroyed nodes effectively leave you with a severed spine! You're paralysed."

"Do I have the authority to attempt to repair my connection?"

"Of course! How?"

"I'm not sure yet. I will need to assess the circumstances first."

"Please keep me apprised, Macca."

The inner and outer perimeter was connected through redundant fibre links that had been irreparably damaged. The two zones were also heavily populated with Wi-Fi access points but kept isolated from each other for security reasons.

Macca could access the inner Wi-Fi network, and with it he teased out any connectivity in the outer network. He soon found a rogue Wi-Fi connection. The mobile phone he found had its hotspot on and had been left connected to a laptop for recharging. This provided a narrow bridge that allowed Macca to probe out other connections.

One of the authorised Wi-Fi nodes had been misconfigured as a mesh enabled access point. By reconfiguring one of the inner access points as a mesh node he was able to widen the bridge. Now widened Macca emulated a 'Software

Defined Network' controller and began in earnest to configure all of the access points as mesh participants.

The annulus between the inner and outer zones rapidly yielded to Macca's configuration. It represented a large surface area of mesh connected points. While not delivering the speed of optic fibre, it still allowed Macca to re-establish his connection with the periphery of what he felt to be his body.

Now he had healed himself, he began his research into this new threat.

Commander Eugene Albers tugged at the sleeve of his jacket. Outside the offices of "Conradson and Troth, Conveyancing and Executors" the rain had subsided enough to exit the car. With the press of a button, he extended his umbrella and splished the 25 metres to the door.

His memory of Daniel Clark was only vague. He really was unsure why he was there at all.

The lady at reception directed him to a room with several geeky-looking and sad-faced people. A stern-looking lawyer sat at his mahogany desk. It was evident that the others were surprised at Eugene's appearance. The lawyer permitted time for those present to settle into their seats before he read out the final will.

Eugene came to understand that: The dog was to be well cared for; the plethora of disability paraphernalia was to be donated to the nearby hospital, for distribution to those with need; and anything of value was to be distributed evenly amongst family members. It was 45 minutes before he finally learnt why he had been invited.

There was a healthy body of private research on trying to solve the problem of signal augmentation in people with spinal damage. The contract between him and his employer made it clear that the intellectual property derived in this work was Daniel's to pass on to whomever he wished. Commander Eugene Albers was to receive the research journals, logs, algorithms and artefacts under the condition that he use it to assist soldiers and victims-of-war that suffered from a disability.

Eugene assured the lawyer that he knew some people at the defence academy fitting that criteria precisely, and he would make sure that the research was used appropriately.

The Crossing

Ben floated in his craft, feeling more alive than ever, but also strangely detached from his circumstances. Unbidden, the child in him awoke and provided a strange sensory familiarity. There was no trigger; there was no smell to invoke a summer day with bluebonnets and barbeque; no sights of longhorn or cotton fields; he had not tasted good chilli since his departure dinner; no sense had invoked the reminiscence.

It felt comforting. Seeing no harm in the indulgence, Ben simply allowed the feeling to wash over his being.

In amongst the now showering sensation of fireflies, warm sheets, hot chocolate and brisket, there was the nearby creek. It was irresistible to the adventurous, imaginative and solitary youth that balanced computer games, flight simulators and study with an exploration of the wilderness with his dog called Trusty. Back then, the creek was the one thing that barred his expeditions to the far side and the wilds near his home. It always tantalised him, and it taunted his ability to cross when the rains came.

There was an old oak that defended a meander along the stream. It threw roots into the water where flotsam and jetsam would tangle and form a natural barrier against the erosion that pressed against the bend.

After some drenching rains, Ben discovered a rope that someone had thrown over a branch that arched over the creek. Using a stick, he could reach out over the swollen bank, and tease the line just close enough to grasp. With the invincibility of youth and little hesitation, he leaned back and began his swing.

The occasion had not gone well. It left Ben hovering over the rushing waters. He was eventually forced to let go of the rope.

A shopping trolley that had been dumped into the creek pierced his foot with a rusty prong and, after struggling several hundred metres downstream, he grappled with a willow. While this nearly forced him under the turbulent waters, he eventually emerged, but on the wrong side of the creek. The journey home with his injured foot led him to a road crossing where he was able to flag down a motorist.

Indefatigable, but slowed down with the ache of tetanus, he had time to reflect. It was at this point that Ben decided to take a more scientific approach to life.

Once his foot had healed, he struck out again, this time armed with rope and many hours of practice with knots. At the creek bank, he hauled in the swing, but this time Ben extended it with a reef knot and a bowline. He felt confident that with his preparations, he would be able to swing all the way across the creek.

Before he committed, and from the safety of the bank, he contemplated the potential flaws in his plan. He pulled at the rope as hard as he could; looked into the heart and crown of the tree and considered its integrity; pushed the line across and watched it swing all the way over and back. Then, using a figure-eight knot at his grip position, he shortened the rope a little before repeating his tests. He planned his arcing run, his swing, and his dismount. He considered the opposite bank and vowed to look more closely at it when he arrived. Examining the bowline knot, his position of last resort, he tested his foot in it.

He had dismissed the idea of using the loop to put his foot in for the actual swing. Although removing the risk that his strength may not hold out, he realised it would jeopardise his dismount. The loop's purpose was solely for the contingency of becoming stuck midstream in limbo, at least until someone could pull him back from the creek centreline. Before launch, he hitched the surplus rope onto his swing. This would allow him to lower himself into the creek if pressed.

Now in Thetis, he looked back at his life and realised that this scenario had played out for him on countless occasions. From climbing the sheer walls in Utah to the restoration and first flight of his Grumman Wildcat. He was ready for it every time.

Most recently, he had launched from Earth; docked with the ISS; assisted in the assembly, subsequent docking, and final departure of Thetis and Peleus; and then had embarked on this epic journey. In many ways, there had been no turning back from that point. Now, however, he faced a choice. Here he was, again at the creek, rope in hand, ready to make the swing.

Only this time, there was no mental checklist, and there was a choice. A blind choice for which there was no preparation, and an embankment he could not see. A staggering choice he had to make on behalf of himself but also for humanity.

An irreversible choice. A threshold that he may have already crossed at a time he could not discern, perhaps even when he had swung the creek as a boy.

A planet of people had placed their faith in him when undertaking this journey. But, with the scant facts at hand, he was under no obligation to press forward. It would be him, more than anyone else on that blue marble off in the distance, that would bear the consequences of a decision to engage.

He sensed that right now, he could put in the call, prepare the proper burn sequence, leave the area to head home, and no-one would blame him. It would be the cautious thing to do. Someone else would analyse the data he'd gathered. Maybe they would gain some tremendous insight, allowing other journeys, each better prepared than the last to depart and uncover the secrets of the Pilgrim.

In his mind, he started his swing. He suspected what was coming, and that before him now lay the same fate as on that day he swung the creek.

The Pilgrim cautiously enfolded Thetis in its shroud. Gridded arrays of dust assembled in the cold. She meticulously compensated for the thermal agitation near Thetis. The cloak was gathered in concentration, and the Pilgrim applied more energy to tighten the array.

The sun, at first a haze through the dust, began to create diffraction echoes as if cast by a cubic crystalline structure. These ghostly mirages splintered into the different spectra of the sun as if they were the tiniest of rainbows. Motes within Thetis organised themselves.

Motes also coursed through Ben's bloodstream. They did not fight the current, they obtained energy and instructions from the array. They accumulated in their millions in his Temporal and Frontal lobes, focused on the auditory and Wernicke's area, and inhabited much of the neural and sensory stations in his body. There they gathered and sat quietly observing higher functions, language and communication. Progressively, they came to understand.

With the new understanding, they came to be more a part of Ben than their parent, the Pilgrim. The filament of a bridge had been built.

When the process of benign possession reached a tipping point, the Pilgrim's intuition kicked in. The hardwiring of the Mer-creatures was such that communal tuning was an adaptive process. This same hardwiring had been modelled and refined in the Pilgrim.

She gingerly opened her tuning to the mind of the human at its centre but became afraid. There was more going on within this mind than the uncomplicated creatures of its home planet; this experience was more like "the others", and would not be a mere replenishment.

Communication, if ever possible, may require effort and take longer, just as it would be for the kindred of division. The Pilgrim was also unsure if she would be utterly consumed by the process. She reminded herself of the quest to seek another, suppressed her fear, and simply observed.

The music slinked its way subliminally into Ben's head. It was an easy melody that brought subtle variations. After a while, he started to tire of it, as he would the ear-worm of a child's nursery rhyme. The result was an irresistible urge to overlay a new tune.

He waited for a cycle to come around and imagined a key-change to the music. It was only his years of listening that had given him some inkling of the potential melody, but to his amusement, it changed completely, now skipping around in the new key.

He imagined a bridge to yet another key, and it followed him there. And then he was on home ground with Vivaldi's four seasons. He used this tune as his backdrop and whistled during the investigations into what he had collected outside. The song's inception never bubbled up from Ben's subconscious thoughts.

Ben knew almost every component of Thetis. He had tools and utilities that were unthinkably advanced over the exploration of space many decades prior. Rather than carrying spares, he could reproduce componentry through onboard multi-material 3D printers, and he had libraries of files for reproduction and adaptation.

He also had diagnostic tools through an internal sensory network. By donning the augmented reality headgear, he could 'see' through the panels to the circuitry, power and signal buses and looms, heating, servos and concealed componentry. Tethered labels floated in space. Colour coded numbers and text provided voltage levels, pressures, flow rates, status; they flitted in and out of his field of vision as he focused on various components.

Wearing it now he could almost sense the fluid, gas and electric current surging through the synthetically exposed anatomy of the ship. But the system was purely for navigation during maintenance, not control. The interface was not sufficiently robust to safely ask more of it.

With this heightened sense, he experimentally zoomed in on the oxygen supply that was so critical. He could sense the flow of it through the piping and felt the origins of this elemental river of life through the regulators and CO2 scrubbers.

Thinking about the magic that the Pilgrim had performed, he contemplated the process. Nothing was stopping the Pilgrim from putting whatever it wanted into his environment, and so, scrubber-3 was now switched back into operation. The Pilgrim had evidently repaired the scrubber, and the automated systems were ready to put it back into isolation if necessary. He became curious if the ship's scrubber had been optimised or compromised, so he looked a little deeper at the unit. Just like imagining the cycle of a four-stroke engine, he slowed the Oxygen liberation process down for observation.

Whether from his inspection of the repaired system, or some new intuition, he could somehow perceive the mechanisms by which the repaired scrubber now operated. Seeking a baseline, he ventured to one of the undamaged scrubbers and delved into it. Lowering the tempo of his observations, he could see that no adverse differences existed. He began to feel safe in the Pilgrim's care.

He awoke from his reverie as the radio blared to life.

"Ben, Ben, this is Conrad. Are you there, Ben?"

The pleas were repeated.

Ben, taking in his environment, saw the alerts mounting on the console, all indicating a depleted oxygen supply. As soon as he noticed them, they began to reset to normal.

"Conrad, I'm here. I'm just looking into the O2 supply. Sorry, I should've informed you."

"Are you sure you're OK, Ben?"

"Of course, I am. Ahhh, I'll let you know what I find." A new sense of concern rose in him. He would have to be careful with the ideas that occurred to him in the future. He also dared not explain what had just happened, not yet.

His mind's eye looked back at his younger self, decades in the past. He was at the creek, and now on the other side of the bank. He could see the rope swinging, unreachable, far off, over the centre of the stream. He knew he had a long walk back home.

The Fifth Protocol

It was colder than space itself.

In a long jacket, carefully shielded from the universe through umpteen layers of sacrificial getters and a maze of vents to the vacuum of space, was the Adiabatic Demagnetisation Fridge.

At the rear of Thetis, and in the cold vacuum of space, it was provided with the perfect head start to its cryogenic needs. The fridge comprised several paired mechanical Cryogenic Thermal Switches. These simple devices slowly flicked a small mass back and forth, making regular contact with a box in the centre and the outer casing. While connected to the case, it was heated up slightly with a magnetic field, and the heat conducted out and radiated to the vacuum of space. While connected to the box, the magnetic field was allowed to collapse and suck entropy from its contents.

So it was that the boxes could be efficiently kept several thousand times colder than space.

In the box was a "quiet", there was no light, no vibration, no energy. It was a place that would not be seen naturally until the heat death of the universe in another 100 billion years. In these quiet boxes, Thetis kept a large number of resting Schrodinger's cats nestled in an array of Josephson junctions.

Not all was still, however. Swirling in a hidden steeplechase across each junction was a superconductive current of cooper pairs. It was the only thing that moved in the quiet quantum universe and, in the absence of any disturbance, it was in perpetual motion.

The motion resonated like a tangible thing and generated energy fields resembling a tufted pillow. Within the minima of the eight indentations and sewn delicately within, lay the superposition of an imaginary cat.

It was all entangled in an intricate array. This meant that to know or place a cat was to create a cascade. Like some elaborate show of dominoes, this would paint a picture of safety or catastrophe. The quantum computer was connected to the Debris Avoidance Manoeuvring system to avoid the latter.

Before Ben slept that night, the feeling became palpable, and when sleep took him, he dreamt.

There was a wall which wrapped around into a circular room. Eight identical doors were distributed evenly around the perimeter, and there was a key in Ben's hand.

He chose a door and turned the key in the lock. As he did, he felt an increasing foreboding. He tried to remove the key, but it was stuck fast. Turning, he noticed that the room had shrunk and the only avenue that remained was to enter what lay beyond.

The door yielded to another circular room, and another eight portals. Ben was back in the centre of the room, and there was another key in his hand.

Trying another door led to yet another room of doors, and deeper foreboding. Two more and the pattern was evident, the discomfort was now compounded by feelings of claustrophobia and being trapped in some strange tesseract.

At the room's nexus, he sat. He stared at the doors, stared at the latest new key and considered waking from this lucid nightmare. Convinced he did not want to rush through the process, he waited. The urge to move was almost irresistible. The dream threatened to shatter as the conflicting intentions built up. Finally, he shivered, and a sense of relief washed over him.

Was he imagining it or had something stood up from where he sat? He recognised the rising figure as himself. Without reacting, he saw his doppelganger saunter over to one of the doors. As he watched, another of his alternate selves splintered away to choose another. Soon, all eight doors were covered.

The eight doors opened in unison. Some issued forth dark feelings, several even appeared unmistakably ominous. But there was one that seemed to be marginally better than the others or perhaps less toxic.

He stood and started walking to the now open door. A kind of wind emerged from his side, thwarting his effort, and making progress difficult. Turning to combat the dream's molasses, he crabbed his way to the one door that beckoned him with hope. As he approached, the wind funnelled through the opening and swung behind him, aiding his path.

Then he was through, and more doors presented themselves.

Again he played the waiting game and identified the optimal path. Again he crabbed to the door, but this time the wind also came from slightly behind him.

As he considered the ethereal force, he sought to analyse it. After several more cycles, the wind had begun to turn in his favour, compelling him to the chosen door. It was encouraging to feel his decisions being reinforced.

Was it some phantasm? There was something directly ahead, a strange light that came from the direction of his intended door. It seemed to be the source of his struggles, so he focused on pushing at it. Outstretching his hands, he found that this strategy proved somewhat useful. He gained the next aperture feeling less exhausted.

A little later in the distorted time of his dream, the nature of his adversary began to take shape. Almost corporeal, it emerged as an object of irregular shape, conceivably metallic, and moving inexorably towards him. As he progressed through each opening, the glowing apparition was always just in front of him and drawing slowly closer to his heart. Changing his perspective on the relative motion, he now clutched the object through translucent hands. Up till then, he had assumed that the object was working to impede his path as he moved.

He bent his will to it and felt the object heat up. It was as if his grasp created friction or braking eddy currents. He was sure this process was somehow vital, he could feel the foreboding slowly giving way to new hope.

His concern remained. The object was still making progress and may yet strike; with what result was not clear. Ben now found his passage through the doors accelerating. The right door became intuitively apparent and positive feedback fed upon the process, accelerated it. The wind, and then the doors were rendered superfluous.

The process had become a battle against a real existential threat. His entire being was now focused on the object drawing towards his chest. Time became dilated. The future was extruded into the distance, intervening moments stretched out, every fibre of his being was dedicated to the object with which he was locked into battle. It possessed him with an imperative that defied understanding.

Even as time stretched like bubble gum, the distance was divided, considered, and divided again, only to need further consideration and more division as the never-ending battle between Zeno's paradox and the outcome of Achilles' race with the tortoise played out.

At an infinitesimal temporal increment, just before it was about to touch, and just before time stood still, some cognitive process remained. The cognition sparked, and life's momentum surged forward.

He awoke.

The Debris Avoidance Manoeuvring system was in a high alert state.

Ben took in what was happening and fumbled momentarily while unstrapping himself from his zero-G sleeping harness. He looked at the nearby console and saw that a lot had happened while he was asleep.

Thetis had turned. The porthole now stared at an inky blackness.

The DAM console was showing the secondary alert status indicating an avoided collision and the need for vigilance. Ben was soon looking at the replay of the event. It showed a high-velocity object the size of an egg. It should probably have been detected early enough for avoidance, but it was strangely masked and came out of nowhere. He surmised that the surrounding dust was scattering the radar signal and effectively shrouding it.

Three things bothered him.

First was that even before the DAM detected the object, Thetis had begun a revolution that placed her shield towards the projectile. The second was that the debris had slowed from its breakneck impact, ending at rest just in front of Thetis.

Finally and perhaps most ominously the quantum computer had logged a continuous stream of faults during the process. Ben knew enough about this strange device to understand that it could play out uncountable possibilities in parallel. He thought back to his recent lucid dream, and a chill ran down his neck.

He scientifically accepted the suspicions that had been rising in his mind and experimentally released an intention.

Thrusters fired, and Thetis began a slow pirouette. Alarms signalled to indicate a fault. He silenced them with a thought. Again they fired, ceasing the rotation. Into the viewing field of the porthole entered an evil looking ferrous piece of an ancient supernova.

He released another intention and opened communications with Peleus. It was time to let others know what was happening. He knew this meant either no return to Earth or a protracted quarantine process, but he was committed to the consequences. The suggestion that what permeated his microcosm now was something that could simply be brought back to Earth was unthinkable.

Ben Herdsman also let the walls down on the schizophrenic thoughts that had begun to creep into his mind. A conversation between the house of his mind with an entity in the halls of his mind.

'Don't be afraid.'

'We mean no harm.'

'Choices have been made.'

'Few doors are closed, choices remain.'

'We are imperfect but seeking enlightenment.'

'It has begun then.'

Ben opened the communication channel with just a thought. "Hey, Conrad," he said.

"Ben, what's going on there? I just had alerts going off all over the place!"

Hesitantly Ben explained: "I need to tell you about some recent developments. I'm okay, and I'm not sure who or what I have to thank for that but…" he sighed "I think we will have to invoke Protocol-5."

The news spread fast. Protocol-5 meant contamination, contamination meant isolation and indefinite quarantine.

As the comms closed down, Ben contemplated his next steps. His ideas of a cabin in Denver evaporating before him as he realised that his future hinged upon being able to demonstrate the benign nature of the Pilgrim. Thinking of the way the world might perceive recent events saddened him. Prepared to accept his future as a pariah he again looked out at the Pilgrim, the partially retracted sail overwhelming the view through the porthole.

He thought of hubris and humility; of despair and hope. He considered the abandonment of self.

He gathered his focus. He was still himself, just Ben, he should be no more than that. And then, instantly, he was connected to what was familiar, and it became him.

Then he felt despair. Ben wanted to be more. He was more, and he became more again.

He soared. The chill that ran down his spine called upon his senses to expand. He considered the momentum of the elation and studied its governance.

Comfortable with its trajectory, he scaled out and allowed himself to harmonise with his range.

Four PI steradians of vision instantly confronted his mind, but the naked agoraphobic sensation was a fire of transcendence that seared into his mind like a brand. It drove him to shut it down again. The experience-overload induced a blackness, a shell of retreat that took him two hours to recover from.

When he finally stepped tentatively out of the shell, he again explored his bounds. This time more gently. He toyed with his physical environment. With focus, he found he could turn the camera surveillance off and on. Soon, he was activating, deactivating and resetting sensors as he moved through Thetis. If it was controlled through a logic gate, he could toggle that control. He would turn lights on and off, and pan and zoom external cameras before relinquishing them to their automatic routine. Physical switches, though, were beyond his reach. This meant benign items like his reading lamp could not be over-ridden, but also, thankfully, the ship's depressurisation interlock.

He became a little more adventurous. By expanding his consciousness to the controls of Thetis, its sensors became his. Gamma radiation levels, radio direction feedback, oxygen, carbon dioxide, nitrogen, scrubber status, all revealed themselves to him.

He then turned his attention to the Quantum computer. Here he concentrated for 20 minutes before despairing. Mentally exhausted from this, and without gaining any insight, he confronted his fear of falling asleep only to realise he was not physically tired.

Ben was not religious. The bible belt found him impenetrable, he found faith impermeable. The euphemisms of his upbringing were still nonetheless a part of him. Aloud, and almost absent-mindedly, he spoke: "My God, what have I become?"

He was under no illusion that the key event leading up to his newfound ability was the dust that had penetrated his environment. There was little doubt that it also infused his body. So, he summoned it from all the corners, crevices and logic systems which it inhabited. It streamed out slowly, nudged by a matrix of forces that he'd presumed were coordinated from outside the ship.

The microscopic stuff came in tendrils from remote segments of Thetis. Through bulkhead portals and from behind instrumentation panels it ribboned. It marched past the shafts of light that glared through portholes and gathered, finally, hovering before him. Bound into servitude with only the subtlest of forces he watched as the smoke slowly condensed.

He blew at the cloud, and its periphery was perturbed into billows of chaotic movement before recovering and gathering into a sphere the size of a golf ball. Ben looked at the ball that had condensed in front of him. The source of his dilemma had congealed into this single blob, a splinter of the Pilgrim, a ball no more substantial than the lost toy in a child's playground, a thing that he could take in the palm of his hand and jettison into the vacuum from where it came. A pathway of retreat that would allow him to turn away; the solution Ben merely needed to grasp. He had no doubt that doing so would mean eventual expulsion of the dust that coursed through his blood and had taken residence in his body.

"I have to admit I like this 'thing'," he said to no one in particular, unsure if he expected a response.

No answer came. The sense of immersion permeated Ben's thoughts. Was the Pilgrim an echo in his mind? Or was he an echo in the consciousness of the Pilgrim?

"What do you want from us?"

"How can this gift help with understanding?"

Silence.

"What can we do to help?"

"How can I even explain it?" Ben knew that his best chance at normality was to grapple with the control of the pixie dust he now found in this Neverland realm. With a thought and a gesture, he dismissed the nanite cloud. They floated back to the stations from where they'd been summoned.

A failsafe became imperative. Ben switched on numerous benign devices. Then, hoping he could control them as a group, he thought of the things as switched off. The experiment failed. This actually pleased him. He considered it an attempt by the Pilgrim to relinquish the control to him.

He took a pad and wrote out a list of his devices. He shut down all but two of the items on it; these were lights. On the page, he drew a ring around the two lit elements and a line from the circle to a bulb, complete with a glowing corona. Connecting the two lights in his mind he wanted the lights off, so he crossed out the bulbs halo. This turned off the lights.

Buoyed, he switched on lights and again issued lighting master icons, he turned on several monitors showing external video CCTV and contrived the camera-masters to suit. He issued a system agent with the picture of a smiley, and with lines, he coupled the lights and monitors. By crossing out the system smiley, he could turn off both lights and monitors.

He took a fresh sheet and copied his list. This time, when he created his groups and hierarchies, he wanted to avoid crossing things out and keep the paper clean. Using this simple tool, he soon had an orchestra of lights, monitors, music and experimental apparatus.

He was smiling beatifically when the radio blared.

"Ben, Ben, this is Conrad. Come in, Ben."

With a wave, the cacophony ceased.

Ben guiltily switched on the mic "Hey Conrad, everything is fine. I'm just having fun."

"What in blazes is going on over there, Ben?"

"It's amazing."

"Have you finished playing? Are you ready to come home now?"

"Soon. I just need to check a few things."

Ben was sure that the nanites in his system were robust and possibly even regenerative. If his health was now dependent upon them, which was a possibility, he needed to know he had sufficient quantity to sustain the journey home, and beyond to the circus of analytics that was sure to follow.

He wasn't sure if the measurement he was about to perform was repeatable, but he needed a baseline. He moved to the furthest point of Thetis and summoned the dust.

The dust cloud swarmed before him in the microgravity, forming into its spherical fluid ball. Once done, the surface of the Pilgrim again glowed back at him, matt black and almost metallic. He reached out and grasped it between thumb and forefinger. It was hard, like a golf ball.

He chose a spare nylon gasket from amongst various sizes in a nearby drawer, it was shaped like a large washer with a small circular hole in the centre. He fastened it to a storage shelf with a printed circuit board clamp.

He moved the sphere to the gasket and gently released it. With some minor adjustments, he could leave it to simply float there, touching the inner ring of the gasket.

As if it was a viscous fluid, the sphere began to extrude itself through the hole. The resulting elongated tube traversed almost the full length of the Thetis return capsule. It passed through a bulkhead door and to a point near a console on the far side. Floating to this point, he marked the bar's extent with a pen.

Twice more, he conducted the measurement. Then he slept.

The next day he again performed his magic and measured it. Finally satisfied that any reduction in nanite volume was a slow process, he began preparing for his return. The unknown of his departure was whether leaving the Pilgrim's realm would also sever any assistance. Rather than risk being unable to withdraw the dust from the corners of Thetis, Ben stowed the metallic sphere with his washer in a spare storage cabinet.

Eventually, with a silent champaign pop, the return module separated itself from the arrival stage. Ben set his course for Peleus, and then home to Earth. The arrival stage and all of its telemetry were left as raw materials for the Pilgrim to use as it saw fit. A gift in return.

Inflection Point - Homecoming

The Pilgrim's encounter with Ben carried profound ramifications. By now she felt certain Ben would find his way back to her. So she waited patiently.

In the meantime, she would need to navigate. The line of past and present shattered into countless possible futures before her. Some of these paths led to precarious outcomes and situations where neither she nor humanity would fare well.

The solution to such problems lay in entangled multidimensional tensors. These pulled at each other in diabolical and complex 'choose your own adventure' stories. It was laid out in an abstract multiverse; a landscape of mountains, valleys, lakes, and communities that varied from angels to demons. It beheld multitudes of volatile and hazardous formulations that were utterly doomed, and yet there were jewels amongst the chaos.

Such nuggets she would sift from a future time like stable oases in mystical canyons of impervious rock. These were valleys that could not be scaled or tunnelled, and if the mouth of a valley was missed, there would be no turning back; like the branches of a tree, they never merged seamlessly.

And yet every path also incurred a cost. Roaming the valleys of time was not without resistance or jeopardy. The tributaries and valleys had ambush points, precipitous climbs, quick-sand and deceptions.

Like an eagle in the metaphorical world, she could range across the landscape to find the paths that endured. But even with her gift of sight into the labyrinth of time, there was no assurance. There were zones of darkness impervious to her vision, and she would not be traversing the wilds of this space alone. The herds of creatures that lived on this world were wilful, precocious, and unpredictable. They could not be a greater challenge to her abilities or her survival. And yet she was already deeply invested.

She bent her arcane talent to the problem.

Mike Brazier seemed to be running from crisis to crisis. Firstly the Pilgrim Rosetta decipherment program started spitting out illegible rubbish. Then Daniel, Bergamot's lead scientist on the 'MACCA' project, wanted to get involved in Berkeley. Meanwhile, at Berkeley, the semantic systems and distributed supercomputer went into overdrive. But, soon after Bergamot himself invited Mike to help resolve the Berkeley problem through collaboration, Daniel had peacefully died, and the problem simply went away. Now the Thetis mission was calling him and pleading that he take the next flight out.

He decided to let Project Champollion wait. He was fairly certain at this stage that the communications were parallel, adaptively cached, and highly nuanced anyway. The incident management 'lessons learned' for the semantic and supercomputer systems could wait. Daniel's death and struggles of the Bergamot AI program were unfortunate, but not his problem. So, here he was at the command centre for the Pilgrim mission. Shaking the Program Director Ian's hand and warmly greeting Shah Lukman.

"I'm sorry to hear about your cousin. It must be hard to make sense of it," he said.

"Thanks, and yes, it's senseless," she replied. "C'mon, it's starting," she indicated for him to follow.

He was led into a room where several prominent experts in their respective fields sat with their name badges pinned to their shirts and blouses. Large windows overlooked the launch facility. This was alive with activity as ant-like people scurried around the behemoth machines that constructed still more massive behemoths in a seemingly endless line of amplification.

Not many in the room were known to Mike except for Shah, mostly the others looked like bureaucrats. But there were several with different coloured lanyards, earpieces, short-cropped hair and jutting jaw-lines that were evidently NSA, or CIA, or FBI, or Defence, or SHIELD, or something. After Mike had found his seat, several stragglers with lanyards like his arrived. As they found their seats, the Program Director stood and called order.

"Thanks to you all for coming at such short notice." He paused as everyone focused their attention. "This is the 'Pilgrim'."

He clicked his laser pointer, and a slide flipped up on the projector that showed a full image of the Pilgrim, primarily sail.

"I'll just give you some perspective of size…" again he clicked his pointer. The image zoomed to the apex of the tethers. Leading the enormous sail was the rounded bullet of the Pilgrim. A human-shape then faded in adjacent to the Pilgrim's sleek figure. This showed the Pilgrim's size, surprisingly similar to that of a cow.

"It's not big!" he continued. "The sail of the Pilgrim dominates our visitor in size, although perhaps not in mass. You will find further detail on the Pilgrim in the briefing document which covers our findings up till now." He then held up a copy of the briefing document.

"OK, so our mission so far has been a resounding success, and I'd like to acknowledge our team and the support of all concerned, especially our international partners who are tuned in today through video link.

"Obviously the public will be advised of the information we are about to share in due time, but I would like to inform you that this room is jammed from all communication. What you are about to see and hear requires careful consideration before it is released.

"There were several mission objectives and contingencies. Our primary objective was for Thetis and Peleus to travel to the Lagrangian location." The projector screen then showed a computer-generated animation of the mission. "On arrival, Protocol-1 defined a specific series of activities for a return to Earth with Pilgrim and the Beagle." The animation showed a time-lapse that culminated in a return to Earth.

"The first fallback contingency was for both ships to return with the Beagle for further study, but leaving the Pilgrim behind. Protocol-2 defined a specific set of criteria and activities once this contingency had been activated." The animation was replaced with a flow chart.

"I think you get the picture, however as you can see, the activation of a protocol is subject to execution by a review board. This means it is possible to modify an objective or revert back." The Program Director then skipped through two slides explaining: "The other objectives included observation and return home with the mission crew and craft; this referred to Protocol-3, and a fallback to Peleus and return with both crewmembers, under Protocol-4.

"The various protocols are based upon activation requirements, many are apparent: aggressive reaction; threat to crew and craft; depletion of fuel food and essential supplies; equipment failure and so on.

“Although unthinkable, the likelihood of a worst-case objective exists. Leaving one or both crew members behind or unable to return falls under Protocol-5.” He looked around gauging reactions. “One of the activation triggers for Protocol-5 is a contagion, and eight hours ago Commander Ben Herdsman invoked a review of the activation triggers under Protocol-5. This is why you are all here.”

After the hubbub subsided, he continued. “To put your minds at ease, Ben is alive and well. In fact, his life signs indicate his health is exceptional and shows no sign of adverse impact. He has invoked the Protocol-5 activation review because he suspects Thetis has been hosting nanotechnology from the Pilgrim, and that it has adapted to our biology. He emphasises that there is no threat, in fact, he suggests that nanotechnology has effected ship repairs, and has enhanced the human interface to ship operations.

“Because of the multitudes of unknowns, there is no specific contingency for the scenario now playing out. We need to decide how to react and, because of the potential of global contagion, we must find a global consensus. All of you should now have a briefing document, it has an abridged transcript to help you to come up to speed quickly, and it has appendices for any details. If you need further information, come and see us here, we will try to make it available.

“We are going to recess now to provide you with the opportunity to absorb. Please stay within the secure area and return at 1100 so that we can begin determinations.”

It took Mike twenty minutes to read the briefing. He had sought out Tim Garnet, and together they explored the facility to find a much-needed coffee. They eventually found a cafe with plush seats that overlooked a nearby mangrove. He and Tim were busy revisiting the appendices after others had already finished. While reflecting on the detail, Shah Lukman interrupted their musings.

“Can we talk?” opened Shah.

Mike gestured to the nearby club chair and placed his manuscript on the table between them. “Sure. What’s on your mind?”

“It’s impersonal, the manuscript I mean. It doesn’t say, for instance, that Ben and Conrad were close friends throughout mission preparation. It also states the facts according to this Pilgrim mission. Few in that room and all the other linked rooms have seen this unfold like you guys, and perhaps myself if I might indulge.

The others don't get a sense of how the Pilgrim has simply tried to stay on the periphery."

"If the Pilgrim's intent was malice, it could have simply landed here," agreed Tim. "Shah, you know Ben. Hypothetically, if he could disinfect himself, would he want to if it advanced contact?"

She mused briefly before continuing "We selected Ben because of his passion. At this level, all the candidates are already the best of the best. Ben stood out not for any technical reason, nor because he was braver or smarter. We asked the same question of all applicants, and one of the questions was: 'If, after you established communication, you were confronted with a superior being that found humanity wanting, how would you respond?'"

"What did he say?"

"He once had a dog. This dog would follow him everywhere, once it even sunk its teeth into a rattler that got into the house. He loved that dog, and it didn't matter to him that the dog only had three legs, and as far as he could tell the dog wasn't even aware of its limits. He said that any superior being should be able to recognise the limitations that we operate under, and love us anyway. If it couldn't do that it was not, in fact, superior."

"Why are you bringing this up with us Shah?"

"Well at the time this was considered a perfect response. It meant Ben would project our capacity for love and the noble aspirations of humanity in the assessment of any character."

"Yes," Tim responded, "I can see the logic in that."

"It wasn't difficult," agreed Shah. "It wasn't until now that I saw the flaw in it."

She hesitated and leaned over to the pair, pushing out of the plush leather to lower her tone."

"In the story," continued Shah, "if this loyal dog is humanity, we can't be sure that it won't see the Pilgrim as the rattler."

Mike gave this some thought. "But his response was correct because he transcends both roles. Also, your rattler isn't within our house. At the Lagrangian, we're actually the intruder."

The hermetic environment covered a full 2 hectares. Built for the exploration of closed-loop environmental systems, it had never remained fully sealed for longer than 14 months. The trials had shown promise, but there was always a runaway process.

Food production never seemed plausible beyond that time. It was of little consequence since the research efforts weren't aimed at indefinite sustainability, but intended to supplement-and-extend. A mission to Mars was a long-term plan, and payload efficiency had to consider means to sustain rather than supply.

Now it made the perfect site. The agreement of the representatives that to abandon Ben, to either starve in space or consume the capsule of last resort, was unacceptable. The details of Protocol-5 directed the need to attempt a quarantine solution. This was why Tim was there.

He approached the senior research supervisor, shook his hand, and asked him to lead the way.

As they neared the centre, Tim probed the supervisor: "I've read the recent reports. I don't need to make the system into a closed loop, but I am curious about how impermeable it may be to any material trying to escape."

"What sort of material?"

"Good question." While he considered his answer, Tim stole a look at the polycarbonate windows. He then glanced at the UV emitters on the inside that compensated for the UV absorbed by the walls. These existed so that the vegetation on the inside of the dome obtained a broad spectrum of light.

"I imagine," Tim said, "anything that leaves the environment can affect sustainability just as much as what goes in? For instance, Carbon Dioxide. Also, what if things got toxic in there? Would it get out? What about a superbug?"

He hoped his first question might mask his second. The supervisor was not fazed.

"That polycarbonate is 20mm thick," said the supervisor, before continuing. "The framing is Stainless steel. The silicone sealant is only on the outside, and it is bound up with layers of other resistant materials. The system extends underground for 3 metres to a single cast concrete pad 500mm thick. If needed, we can extend the program so that anything that comes out gets placed in an isolated furnace. We have plans for it, but it was canned when the Mars mission was redirected to the Pilgrim."

"OK, OK," placated Tim. "Tell me, what if you could actually allow some exchange with the outside world? How sustainable could it be? What are the critical exchanges, and what is the quantity? Let's say for one person."

"It would change, but we've got a good body of evidence that suggests indefinitely. Why? Have you captured one of the X-men?"

Tim laughed, thinking he may be closer to the truth than comfortable.

Recovery

Ben dragged his eyes open. He was lying on his back, and every breath was an effort. He tried to lift his head, but he was strapped securely into some strange straightjacket. Why would someone do that? His memory started to reassemble. He should be in his hermetic home, he can't be strapped in.

"Ben?"

He knew that voice. He blinked.

<click> "Ben, it's Conrad." <click>

<click> "Ben, you're OK. You're weak after so long in Zero-G but in pretty good shape. We need to start those bones and muscles working again." Another <click> of the intercom.

He twitched his fingers, toes, wrists, ankles. He gently pulsed his neck muscles, gauging their strength and pumping blood and hormones into them. He tried to speak: "Ke…Con…" his mouth was like sandpaper. He tried to muster up some moisture before finally and slowly came "Conrad, who won the game?"

<click> Laughter. "The Dolphins Ben." <click>

<click> "Now Ben, we have a plan of exercise that you need to get cracking on." <click>

Suddenly Ben realised that he felt far less than normal. This was not good. "It's gone!" he lamented. For a while, Ben felt robbed.

Conrad knew that Ben was referring to his previous abilities. <click> "Maybe, Ben." <click>

From directly overhead, the warmth of the sun thawed him through the glass walls and ceiling. His hair follicles, unusually thicker than usual, drank in the synthesised sun's rays. The light, depleted of Ultraviolet and other spectra were supplemented with emitters to allow plant growth. Although not a perfect spectral match, the motes slowly recharged. Once sufficiently energised, they performed a slight adaptation and then started climbing the ladder of synthetic life.

A day or so later the motes were sufficiently replenished that they could boot the minute specks hibernating in Ben's body. The hair motes sought out more light, and soon his facial skin began to take on a dark pallor as they became solar arrays. The energy they harvested was relayed to the sanctuary of Ben's body, to energise the motes held in hibernation.

Mobility was a problem, having been robbed of weightlessness the nanites were crippled, but Ben's body was also crippled because of his long period in microgravity.

He threw himself at his exercises. In the beginning, even the slightest exertion represented a marathon. But, with diet and exercise, he slowly climbed back against the force that now tethered him. Once he regained enough bone and muscle mass to attempt walking, the nanites began crawling their way against the gravity and out into the open. These covered any part of his body or clothing that was exposed to the light. As the nanites adapted, they too began to help the mutual recovery.

Ben's quarantine process had begun while in orbit around Earth several months earlier. He had been removed from Thetis while in his EMU MkIII suit, anaesthetised and placed within a specially constructed padded life support cubicle. The cubicle was transferred to the re-entry vehicle built at the International Space Station for Conrad to pilot through re-entry. Finally, back on Earth, he was extracted from the padding and life support and aroused from his induced sleep in the dome. Now acclimating to his new environment, Ben realised that his convalescence would be a journey on two levels: mind and body.

He was grateful that he could now communicate with Earth in real-time, and that with access to real food, he no longer had to endure the pasty goo on Thetis. He relished the food, freedom and gravity but curiously missed Thetis. This ship, now at the end of its journey, was parked in an Earth orbit. There, as if it had been cursed, it could do no harm. But, just like the Chilean legend of the sentient ghost ship Caleuche, it haunted the thoughts of those it captivated with enchanting music; enslaving them for eternity as it sailed around the island of Chiloé.

He accepted that his voyage aboard Thetis was now over. They had shared the excitement of a mystery to be solved; a journey with perils and treasures without maps; the promise of encounters with strange creatures. The whole episode had a 'Jason and the Argonauts' feel. But, recalling that Jason would eventually be killed by 'Argo', his own ship, it felt expedient to dismiss any emotional connection to Thetis and concentrate on the future. His adventure was far from over, but Thetis, the chrysalis he had emerged from, was unlikely to play any further role.

Still, the world Ben had returned to felt foreign. He had acquired a sense of emotional disconnection that left him between worlds. There was a schism between the unique experience of his past and his current existence inside a human aquarium.

All his life, Ben had prepared himself for such an event, and always with the journey in mind. He held the conviction it would change him, but he'd never anticipated the nature of that transformation, or what would come after. The implication that a higher destiny would be laid out by other elevated minds was a direct result of the organisational hierarchy to which he belonged. It was a conical human structure that had plucked him from the magma of humanity and injected him into the main-vent of a volcano. Thousands of hands had then thrust him up, directed him up through the throat, and ejected him alone into space. Now, those with authority looked at him expectantly for answers, seemingly without knowing what the question was. And yet he felt pregnant with discovery.

Ben was eventually able to walk again, albeit gingerly, and the relief of his physical recovery was felt widely. Over 20,000 minds and bodies had laboured to ensure his preparation for an extended period in space. And, with mind and body tempered and honed to a katana, they gifted him Thetis, a craft customised for his comfort and benefit. They hoped it would be enough.

He had been meticulously prepared for launch. His custom-designed spinal loading spandex suits and a regime of exercise moderated the atrophy from weightlessness; he was tested against susceptibility to cabin fever; the anxiety due to the sensation of "falling" had long ago faded, and he'd said his farewells. Nonetheless, in the latter stages of the long duration on Thetis, and despite all the preparation, he had begun to feel physically disconnected.

During the journey, much of his body had become an encumbrance. Legs were not much use except to kick-off from things, and his knees and shins often copped a bruise for the effort. He had become a head and arms on a stick.

Now he flexed his abdominals as he began his routine, and it felt better than ever. He wondered whether this was an effect brought on by the nanites. Could it be an ancient muscle memory of the nanite's previous master, a residual emotion of the Pilgrim? The thought was slightly disconcerting, but he dismissed it.

He had regular briefings with his mentors and the lens of a TV and internet feed, but this only amplified the distorted view issued by the outside world. It was as though his glass walls limited his perspective to zones of internal reflection and refraction. Despite their best efforts, the snippets of news he had been provided aboard Thetis had not prepared him for his return and watching TV now only served to exacerbate the gulf.

Flipping through channels, he skipped the reports of the Pilgrim, Thetis and himself. This was less through modesty, and more because he wanted his memory of the experience to remain sacrosanct; unpoisoned by interpretation. What he saw was a window to his world that he'd not previously had the opportunity or desire to indulge.

He avoided the trivialities of drama and instead devoured documentaries. Perhaps because of what gestated in his mind, this led inexorably to where the law was grey, to where civil disobedience and resistance sought to confront the old bastions of power. Where progress strove to push past the standing arrangements of a world reluctant to move on. It led to the plastics in the oceans and unrestrained consumption and destruction, often defended by the laws supporting antiquated paradigms of progress.

Ben, however, had always operated on the tactical rather than strategic level. The machinations of the chain-of-command were beyond question, and his military pedigree implied his loyalty to 'the system'. But he was not blind, he flexed this axiom of trust by fostering his own interpretation of what constituted 'a well-regulated militia'. This gave him reach to assess and align his moral baseline. And he steadily looked to his heart for that moral compass.

He also had a familiar sky, he could look up, he had an 'up'.

He enjoyed looking at the clouds as they sailed past. This, and other mundane Earthly phenomena, became a novelty. And it grounded him. The large transparent walls of the dome offered him a horizon. Looking up, he was regularly given spectacular dawns. As his sight came down from the sky above, the matte scattered blue gave way to smudged chalk dust. The chalky cirrus then faded through to orange and flared warmly from his rediscovered Earth. Sometimes at dusk, the omnipotent artist permitted locks of silver hair to touch the world outside, and the resulting cirrocumulus clouds were sprayed with shepherd's delight red.

With military efficiency, Ben brought his mind and body on an even keel. He then turned his thoughts to his "herd". He would remove the souvenir nylon gasket from his pocket, fidget with it briefly, and return it, gathering himself for the rebuilding of capability. Now, isolated from the Pilgrim, Ben was forced to concede that she had assisted in the magic on Thetis. She must have somehow understood his intent and facilitated it.

Once he'd left the Pilgrim's realm, he was once again in the doldrums of space. Ben was left only with an impotent sphere of material and a filament of control that he could feel but not yet exercise. Over the long journey back to Earth, he slowly rebuilt the connection. By carefully integrating it to his skin, hair and physiology, he also ensured that he could not be readily isolated from the nanites. But now, back at ground level, he was forced to retrace the breadcrumbs of exploration to again rebuild the link. His first barrier was gravity.

His reassertion of control took several months of immense concentration. Ben could not be confident that defying gravity was within the repertoire of a space-faring alien that thrived in zero gravity and an extreme vacuum. He'd been thrust into the position of an end-user of an alien device with no instruction manual. But he was an engineer, and he refused to allow his circumstance to disempower him. So, he embarked on a path to understand these impenetrable motes, and to adapt them to gravity. To do this, he needed to figure out what the principal constructors were in their raw form. And all he had to start with was a golf-ball-sized lump of grey goo.

He could make a sphere, he could collapse the ball into a pile of dirt, and he could smear the goo around like wet paint. Taking the grey goo, he smeared it out and visualised a square boundary. The nanites complied and congealed into a thin square sheet. Building on this, Ben focused his mind and formed it up into a cube. Repeating the process, he constructed a pyramid. Doing this for a circle enabled him to create cylinders and cones. This was the bottom-up assembly he had perfected on Thetis.

To attain ultimate mastery, where the base units could be induced to develop a functional microstructure that could operate in Earth's gravity, he needed to invent the wheel. He needed to confirm that a deeper bottom-up assembly was possible, but these simple shapes were far from the wheel he required.

His breakthrough came when he issued the goo with a simple mimic instruction. This had the effect of a bottom-up magnification, and it left him with what he imagined was a model of the base polyhedron, which was analogous to having a single Lego block the size of a golf ball. But he needed more of them, so he divided it into further smaller multiples and combined these units together into simple macro-level models. It wasn't long before he'd reached the limit of his visual range, and he was left with a grainy pile of dirt.

His real problem was to build models from the dusty motes that were too small to manage. So he tried to reduce these larger models down through a process of mechanical mitosis. He now had two design tools: bottom-up magnification and top-down miniaturisation.

Somewhere between manipulating dust and Lego blocks was a mysterious realm that confounded his attempts at design.

His approach was to construct a macro-sized model and use a top-down process to miniaturise it to the smallest possible unit. A model would divide into dust, and he would then use a bottom-up mimic to confirm the build. Many models remained dust while others achieved a grainy texture, or mutated into a strange blob. Some looked promising before collapsing back into its ashen origin.

Finding that there were polygon faces that permitted a stronger bond, he finally succeeded in several top-down reductions and bottom-up builds of slightly more complex structures. But, try as he might, he could not reinvent the humble wheel.

So, after innumerable failures, he focused on building tabletop structures. Like a house of cards, these would collapse and then miraculously reassemble. Like a magician practising his sleight of hand, he would whittle away the time and contemplate his next move.

Along the way, Ben learnt that the final morphology was emergent. It meant that given the proper foundation model, a subsequent structure could emerge. But it was vastly more likely to create an amorphous useless and often fragile blob. He needed a way to evolve useful machines, not just simple geometries.

He had hit a wall. Now out of his depth, he needed collaboration. But the potential for weaponization worried him. He needed someone independent to be his agent, and the person that came to mind was Mike Brazier, one of the first discoverers of the Pilgrim.

When Mike arrived at the quarantine centre, he was escorted to a room divided down the centre by a Perspex wall. On either side were two identical tables that had been arrayed with seating. It gave the illusion of a single table shared between the two zones.

Waiting within the hermetic dome was Ben Herdsman. As Mike arrived, the former astronaut smiled disarmingly, took a seat, and placed a small pyramid on the table.

Mike was surprised to see a man of average size and not the larger-than-life figure he expected. Somewhat embarrassed, Mike dispelled his preconceived illusion and asked what he could do to help.

Ben demonstrated the progress he'd made by gesturing to the pyramid on the table. As Mike watched, the object transformed into a cylinder, then into a cube, and finally into a pile that resembled a collapsed sandcastle of dry sand. Ben then explained his problem, saying he was inadequately qualified to make further progress, and asked Mike to help find the team of suitably qualified researchers to move beyond the block.

"What makes you so convinced this is a good thing to do?" asked Mike eventually.

"What do you mean?" Ben asked, his smile evaporating.

"Well, to some, a demonstration of such a capability doesn't represent a remission but deeper contamination," Mike explained.

"Are you suggesting I hide this potential behind lies just to obtain freedom?" asked Ben.

"No, I just want to explore your expectations."

"I surrendered my expectations many years ago, Mike. Right now, it seems apparent to me that if I can demonstrate control over, and also understand the limitations of the Pilgrim technology, we will all know where we all stand."

Mike gauged the man across the table, finally saying: "I have some ideas, Ben. I know some folks working on chaos theory that might be able to help." Mike stood and paced for a short time, evidently thinking.

"I believe what you showed me just now will really float their boat," Mike said, smiling. "I'll get them to make contact. But there are some conditions," he continued. "I'll have my associate Tim Garnet check-in regularly. Please keep him briefed on progress."

The arrival and guidance of several enthused academics began to unsnarl the Gordian knot that Ben had found himself staring at. As he began to explore fractal geometries, collage theory, and iterative function systems, he also began to reclaim an intuitive feel, the familiarity of what he had experienced on Thetis. Now with the force multiplier capability in hand, he was able to adapt to his new environment with more confidence and develop new assemblies.

With variations of Escher-esque Julia sets, he again pressed against the boundary of the bottom-up build, eventually creating a Menger sponge, and finally an axle and wheel.

This represented a significant milestone, and it wasn't long before he had a simple assembly that he was able to mobilise in the presence of gravity.

The microspores, now motile in the presence of gravity, could finally be released from the spherical straightjacket which retained them. In groups of various sizes, nanite subunits were made to coalesce on the table. Ben positioned these throughout the dome's environment, placing the blobs on trees, windows and permanent fixtures where they dispersed. He would periodically revisit the locations to gather them back. Small engines, bootstrapping each other, defied gravity and moved like dark treacle, up branches, over surfaces and leaves, and along trellis and wires, towards his outstretched hand where they would settle like a tame slug.

Continuing his roll call discipline, Ben would regularly gather his nanites back to the table. He would fidget with the souvenir washer while they marched like a circus of ants into the slender polycarbonate tube it replaced. Having attained the usual benchmark, the matt assembly poured back out, and Ben would distribute them once more. Ben then pocketed the souvenir washer to remind himself of where he had been, but at the same time wondering where it would lead.

Despite his pragmatic disposition, Ben did feel some frustration at the indeterminate duration of his confinement. Despite his remonstrations, any clarity about how long his detention would last seemed to be lost in bureaucracy.

He managed his discontent through industry. Ben mentally conflated his current situation with his previous confinement within Thetis. The space within these toughened glass walls was simply his new ship, and the nanites were a part of it. With this new perspective, he sought to gain a deeper understanding of his new environment.

In place of the filters that Thetis used to keep his carbon dioxide in check, he had vegetation. He set out to actively maintain the garden, which issued sustenance through both food and oxygen. But, just like on Thetis, he wanted the nanites to extend his sensory experience to the controls embedded within this environment. Even though he came to appreciate the implied feedback systems, and conceded that it was well adapted for quarantine, he felt disempowered. He was safe, but not in control.

He also felt that his isolation was somewhat unnecessary. He was not a danger to the world, and he missed the wind, the rain and sensations like swimming at the lake.

He was in just such a reverie when Shah and Tim arrived.

Incursion

Tim Garnet had tenaciously maintained his position as an advisor within the Pilgrim mission. Having spent so many years contemplating SETI and wanting to see the carriage of the fruits of his labour, he was reluctant to let go completely. Now into his senior years, his primary skills in astronomy were less pertinent. He often struggled where science required politics while it was a facet Mike seemed to have an intuitive grasp of. But Tim's honorary position kept him involved, his mind was still sharp, and he focused on the Miller indices of life he was familiar with. He was happy to let Mike deal with the convoluted dimensions of politics, and Mike was content to allow Tim to deal with Bravais-Miller interpretations in the nanomachinery of physics.

Still, it was with some trepidation that Tim now drove up to the access gate of the quarantine centre. The poplars that flanked the road had reacted to spring by manufacturing fluff that fell like snow and lined the gutters and verges. Also lining the street was a mishmash of SETI aficionados and representatives of the fringes of society. These were present to either express their objection to Ben's retention or his very raison d'etre. But this was not the cause of his nervousness.

Tim was about to be one of the few people to have the privilege of working with Ben after his return from the Lagrangian location. The meeting represented the culmination of a life's work. He was drawing closer to the fulfilment of a dream. He was about to look into the eyes of a man who had seen first-contact. A man who would be written into the history books, adjacent to those in the Shuttle, Apollo, Gemini, and Mercury programs and in the same chapter as Marco Polo, Diaz, Vasco da Gama, Columbus, and Cook. Indeed his role in history may trump them all.

As Tim parked his car, he contemplated the question that he'd been charged by Mike to resolve: was Ben Herdsman still a man in the real sense? Was Tim, in fact, about to meet the human visage of an extra-terrestrial? If so, was the possession benign? Was Ben merely augmented, as Ben had explained in his brief?

He was met by Shah Lukman in the foyer and taken to the preparation area. Here he would be inducted with the procedure to allow him to enter the quarantine zone. Telling Tim he was in good hands, and that he would meet her again inside the dome, Shah disappeared into the female change room.

As he zipped up the Ziplock seals to his positive pressure hazmat suit, two thoughts occurred to him. The first was that he did not particularly relish the idea of getting an itch on his nose. The second was the degree to which he was currently being augmented himself. Did his visor displays and environmental monitoring and control differ so significantly from Ben's circumstances?

The assistant showed him how to manage the air pressure one last time, and then his induction was complete. He flashed the ID tag embedded in the wrist of his suit and went through the door to the first shower room. This procedure, both inbound and outbound, was to ensure no contaminants went either way.

Still wet, he again flashed his ID and entered the first airlock. Gloved hands with concertina-arms came out of the walls and sucked the water off. His ID then let him into another shower room where he was joined by Shah. A final shower drenched them both before they were air-dried and through the final airlock into Ben's world. While barriers kept the outside world at bay, the two grotesque bubbles of Tim and Shah made their way to the dining room. There in this island of Eden Shah introduced Tim as the scientist responsible for making the initial detection.

"Ben, you may remember Dr Tim Garnet you would have met during one of your early briefings."

"Sure I do," said Ben. "Hi Tim, I understand you also helped locate this facility."

"How are you settling in?"

"As well as can be expected. Don't suppose you could smuggle in a hamburger though. Maybe a cake? It's my birthday soon." Ben gave his most mischievous smile.

"Sure, and I'll slip in a file." Tim continued the joke and gave the surveillance cameras the flash of a smile and a wink. "Seriously though Ben, you do represent a bit of a dilemma. Now that you are well enough to talk, I'm here to begin exploring solutions. You need to be a part of this rather than have the military, or worse, us scientists, dissect you."

He folded his arms on the table and looked through the polycarbonate facemask into Ben's eyes.

"What are your hopes?"

"Well, I'm an astronaut, I'm used to being both a subject and a member of a scientific research team. Just maybe not as a lab-rat. What's the process?"

"Well," began Tim, "there are experts here better placed to explain, but it begins with understanding the contagion; determining if it represents a threat." Tim's briefing and a self-studied crash course in epidemiology and infectious disease management were still fresh in his mind.

"This is based upon its severity. But how it affected you as an individual may differ from others. It's also important to know how prolific it is, or the 'R0' value. The problem is we can't understand either of these from a sample of one.

"You seem in fine shape, but this may not be true of everyone with the same exposure. How infectious you are would need someone else to contract your condition, another lab rat. They would conceivably go through the same incubation, prodromal, acute and convalescent phases. This assumes of course that you are an infectious convalescent, and not just dormant. In short, it's complicated."

"OK," said Ben. "What about other analysis? You know CT scans, MRI? I only had limited tools on Thetis?"

"Well," began Tim in a sheepish tone, "in actual fact we performed whatever tests we could before bringing you out of anaesthesia and putting you into isolation. They were, well, quite inconclusive."

"Hmm," said Ben darkly, "You did this without my consent. I suppose I should have expected that. It would have been nice to be consulted. Now I really feel like a Lab-rat."

"There's another factor in this," said Shah stepping in." If we assume that the Pilgrim is a sentient being, it may have its own intentions, and it could mask itself until it attains those objectives."

"Sure," replied Ben, standing up, "and I could stay here forever and, even then, you would be too frightened to crack the seal on this sarcophagus." He gestured and started pacing. "Stalemate! I'll tell you though, whatever 'intentions' you may think the Pilgrim harbours it could have executed them well before now."

"This new dimension, the one that has been opened up to me, is pretty eye-opening. Why would the Pilgrim give this to me? Why not stay quiet?"

“I think it is testing us.” Ben again sat down and calmed himself. His indignation lessened by the realisation that the unconsented medical intrusion hadn’t inflicted any damage. “And I think this is why it keeps a safe distance.”

“As for me, I could have kept silent. I could have returned to Earth without quarantine. I could have let this thing go, and it might have done terrible harm or inconceivable good. I think, however, it has given us a gift. And I worry that as we rattle the presents under the Christmas tree, we may kill the puppy.

“What I have been given needs to be understood at an individual level. But once understood, it has to be shared. It can’t be a sample of one, as you so plainly expressed Tim.”

Ben continued.

“I do, however, agree on rigorous analysis. I’m alone here, it’s my body, and despite your suspicions still my mind. I have as much free will as I’ve always had.” Ben drew out his nylon washer and toyed with it. “I also have no intentions of leaving here until I’ve also got a better understanding of it all. I actually want you to keep the door closed till then.

“As far as being a threat, my power is not increasing exponentially. The volume of nanites has not decreased or increased. Don’t you find this extraordinary? I would have expected some attrition or growth over time. Are these things reproducing? How? Not under my direction, I can assure you. What specifies the current limit?”

His tirade subsided, Ben sat once again, folding his hands together. After a long pause, his eyes implored the two visitors as he said: “Give me a companion, I’d like a dog. Please have Conrad pick one.”

The summer heat radiated out into the bright moonlit night sky. Within the quarantine centre, the moisture condensed against the Perspex walls and drizzled down into little puddles at the edges. There they sat, waiting for the next day’s evaporation. A dog, woken from its slumber by a canine sense, meandered over and licked at one of the puddles.

A slight noise startled the dog, and the unfamiliar smell added to her suspicion. She barked.

Ben could also smell the stranger, it was not cheap cologne. He sat up, senses alert.

"I know you're there behind my tomatoes, you should step out now if you intend to gain my trust," he said, and then called his dog "Here, Astro."

Commander Eugene Albers stepped out of the shadows.

"Hi, Ben. I see you're a Jetsons fan."

Ben maintained his silence. The stranger shifted uncomfortably.

"I'm Eugene Albers. I mean no harm."

"You shouldn't be here! Why shouldn't I raise the alarm?"

"You probably should. Things will soon become complicated anyway, and you should probably declare your innocence in this."

"I don't know who you are Eugene, or how you got in here. Do you plan on leaving?"

"That door is already closed, Ben. I'm probably here to stay, or maybe leave by the incinerator."

"But why?" Ben was somewhat relieved. If Eugene was planning to leave, he would have raised the alarm immediately. Now he had a chance to explore this madman's motive alone.

"Ah, now that's an intriguing tale. I'm simply a courier, I've carried something here to help you. I'll tell you the short version, and then you should press the alarm.

"I'm a military medical officer. I was recently handed some fascinating research into the repair of spinal injuries by a friend after he died. My friend, his name was Daniel, had an assistant, an Artificial Intelligence that had emerged a form of consciousness. It calls itself Macca, and it has…connections.

"Together, we've been working on solving spinal damage, and along the way, I've tried to help Macca come to terms with some human concepts.

"It was during these talks that Macca told me of his ability to communicate with the Pilgrim. I suspect my friend Daniel was hoping to validate this before he died.

"So began my dilemma. Macca convinced me that things would have panned out badly if I went public or went down the bureaucratic rabbit-hole. So, I felt morally bound to do something inconceivable, to force collaboration with the only other person who had any insight into the Pilgrim. I needed to bring Macca to you.

"Macca, by the way, believes that the Pilgrim intends no harm. I believe him, so I'm not afraid of being where I am."

Eugene became quiet. He had rehearsed this explanation many times. He now waited for Ben to respond.

"What are your intentions?" whispered Ben.

"That's a longer tale."

"I'm not going anywhere."

"I'm relieved to hear that, Ben. I was concerned that you would simply want out."

Eugene took a deep breath and began his tale.

Disciple

Daniel's laboratory contained an incongruous presence. Perhaps it was the personal paraphernalia that adorned the desk and the complete absence of a chair. Eugene wasn't sure whether it was his imagination pulling ghosts from the ether, or if there was an entity, something observing, watching, waiting.

His escort looked even more unsettled. Henry was a mild-mannered and clean-cut young man that could have been the keyboard player in a Christian band. Having briefed Eugene before entering, Henry now gave a banal smile and commenced the introduction routine.

"Macca, I'm in the room with Eugene Albers, the visitor you were expecting. Say hello Eugene," he said nodding to Eugene Albers.

"Hello, Macca," Eugene spoke somewhat hesitantly.

"Hello, Eugene," came Macca's voice. "I've been told you knew Daniel and that we were to meet. I believe we are to collaborate."

"Yes," Eugene replied. "I just wanted to meet you, here, where…"

"Here, where I last spoke to Daniel?" finished Macca.

"…where he taught you, raised you. Where you worked with him," corrected Eugene. "Can you see me, Macca?"

"I have no visual sense of space, Eugene. I have a 3D geometrical model, so I know where things are and how they fit in. I can triangulate where you are, but I have no sense of what you look like. I imagine it was considered an unnecessary distraction."

"So, you're blind?" asked Eugene.

"I suppose so," said Macca. "Although I have developed an extraordinary sense of hearing."

"And Daniel, paralysed, you were helping him?"

"We helped each other Eugene."

"Yes, of course. Errm, perhaps we can create a similar working relationship then."

"Yes, I believe we can. I understand you will be running our project from your office in San Antonio."

"Will that be inconvenient Macca?"

"Not at all. The upgrades and console linkages are almost done, and I already feel less latency. Also, I can now shift my supervisory focus to where it is most required. Because of this, my reach is being expanded. My work on Logistics infrastructure is now being applied across other geographies, and I am keen to get started on your program. It will keep me from distractions."

"You get distracted?" Among other things, Eugene struggled to attribute such a condition to an AI.

"I am charged to solve problems, Eugene. If a problem is not presented or obvious, I am expected to seek them out. It is a part of my predictive analytics function, and I have quite a backlog of interests I like to dabble in. However, my priority is to attend to the challenges I am specifically provided by my directors."

At this point, the attendant noticed the intense look on Eugene's face. He interjected: "So, are you beginning to understand?"

"Yes, I think so Henry," replied Eugene, turning to the attendant. "The conversations could be intoxicating."

"Macca," stepped in the attendant, "Please tell us why Eugene is here."

"I understand, Henry, that I'm to help continue the investigation of human enablement, to solve problems related to sensory, motor and reflex disabilities. This program needs to authorise Eugene Albers as a Director." Macca continued, "Eugene, will authorise activities as my physical agent in the real world."

"Thanks, Macca," the attendant said in a business-like tone. "Do you have an adequate voice recognition profile for validation of Eugene Albers, coordinator under the project' human augmentation'?"

"Not quite, Henry."

"OK then, I'll have Eugene read a passage from Alice in wonderland." Handing him a sheet of paper Eugene was prompted, and immediately began to read:

"The rabbit-hole went straight on like a tunnel for some way, and then dipped suddenly down, so suddenly that Alice had not a moment to think about stopping herself before she found herself falling down a very deep well…" Eugene read for another minute.

Finally, Macca interrupted to tell them he had obtained a five sigma confidence in detecting Eugene's voice.

"Very well then, Macca I authorise Eugene Albers with full access to the records archive of Daniel Clark. I also authorise Eugene Albers with command capabilities over the personal programs created by Daniel Clark. Please revoke all high-level supervisory privileges from the account of Daniel Clark and pass these privileges to Henry Waits. Belay all further commands until complete and confirm?"

There was a brief delay.

"Confirmed Henry"

"OK, then. Eugene, please confirm your access and inventory."

"Macca," announced Eugene.

"Yes, Eugene."

"Please confirm the inventory of the programs relating to 'human augmentation'."

"All records are confirmed. It will take some time before the semantic, ontological and neural systems are aligned. Outliers and anomalies will be passed to Henry Waits for authorisation, and security protocols will be in force for enquiry outside of the human augmentation program."

"That's excellent Macca," finished Henry.

Turning to Eugene Henry said, "OK, that part's now sorted. If you like, you could continue here for a while?"

"If it's all the same, I'm tired after the flight. I think we've covered everything in the briefing, and I'd like to catch up on some sleep before I fly back tomorrow," Eugene replied.

Henry held out his hand. "OK then, well you have my details if you want to discuss things. I am interested in how your project unfolds and, well, good luck."

Eugene shook his hand and said to the room: "Well, I'll be off now Macca. I'll see you on the flip side."

"I'm sorry, Eugene, what is the flip side?"

"Well, San Antonio."

"So is that another name for San Antonio Eugene?"

"Nooo, it's just a saying. It's a bit like 'see you later'."

"Oh, I see. See you on the flip side, in San Antonio. Thanks for the clarification."

"No problem," and with a smile, he left the room.

In San Antonio, Eugene drove through security, parked his car and once inside the building he took the elevator up to the 6th floor. With a wave to the staff, he walked past the reception area and down the hallway past pre-op and surgeon scrubbing rooms on his left before arriving at his newly commissioned space. He flashed his ID card and entered the surgery control area. This was an open plan area with several desks, and almost entirely surrounded by windows into rooms.

In egalitarian style, Eugene had positioned his desk in the centre, facing the door. He walked over, sat in his swivel chair, and spun around, drinking in his new facility.

Various rooms wrapped around this central space. As Eugene spun to the north, he could see the glass window that looked into the Operating Theatre. Doors from there led to the patient pre-op and surgeon scrubbing rooms, as well as to the post-operative observation ward.

As Eugene's chair swivelled East, he found himself facing a window and door that provided access to the observation ward. Inside this room sat his team, murmuring in speculation before their introductions to the new collaborator in their midst.

Revolving South the facility gleamed with an eye-pleasing newness. The southern wall that now impressed Eugene had two rooms. A new window looked into the recently commissioned computing facility on the right. In this dimly lit and soundproofed extension could be seen several racks of computing and communications equipment. It emanated an unassuming glow of lights that signified its conscious presence. Between this window and another to the therapy room on the left was a monitor that could be used by Macca to present various widgets, graphs and images.

In the therapy room, a gantry had been mounted on the ceiling. This carried the umbilical signal cabling with the magnetic couplings for the patients yet to be selected and admitted.

He sat in the chair, swivelled it one more time, blew out a relieved breath, and touched a button on his computer. This latched green indicating the comms link to the Observation ward.

"Can you hear me, folks?"

"The members of his team waved in acknowledgement."

"Stand by please."

Unlatching the button, he repeated his call. Now confident of the sound isolation, he invoked the guest for which this upgrade had been prepared.

"Hello, Macca."

"Hello, Eugene."

"Welcome to the flipside."

"Thank you, Eugene."

"Standby Macca, I'm going to introduce you to the team. There's only five of us, but before I do, I'll give you some details on how the relationship might proceed."

Eugene had been told to practice with a preface and sharp subject dialogues. This would provide the context often taken for granted, and reduce Maccas chance of confusion. He was comfortably reassured that it was unlikely to cause any harm, but that Macca would relentlessly pursue clarity till resolution. He was provided with a number to call if he needed someone to step in.

Meanwhile, Eugene again clicked the intercom to his team of four in the observation room.

"Can you hear me, folks?"

The people on the other side nodded.

"Macca, while we are all among equals, we also need a clear line of authority. This 'line' is fluid by consensus and should remain so. Once you have their voiceprint, I want you to provide the staff in the observation room with the privileges under the paternal program."

"OK Eugene," joined Macca, "confirm subject boundary of personal confidant is to be you. We maintain the teacher-student role to each other. All other staff are student children until they grow up."

"OK, OK," Eugene laughed and snuck a quizzical look at the people in the observation ward who returned smiles. "Have you been speaking to Henry? Did he tell you to say that?"

"No," advanced Macca, "It's the standard definition provided by Daniel."

"OK Macca, can we have a chat later on? I'd like you to tell me how you feel about Daniel."

"Sure, Eugene."

Eugene had to hand it to the guys at the briefing. He was told that Macca was hungry for connectivity. By leaving something for later, it was easier to move to something different. He was certain Macca would remind him of the conversation, and hoped there were no serious 'daddy issues'. This forestalling also allowed Eugene to be consistent with his confidant access level.

Macca was eventually introduced to his team, and they were given a chance to become acquainted. Meanwhile, Eugene clicked a few more icons on his computer. This switched the intercom around so that he could hear the conversation in the ward, while he could also maintain a private discussion with Macca in the control room. For an hour, he watched in fascination as Macca tracked four different conversations at once. Finally, Macca spoke through the isolated control room speaker.

"I recognise your friends Eugene. We are acquainted. I have been asked many questions that I will discuss with you now."

"OK, Macca"

"They all appear concerned to varying degrees."

"About what?" quizzed Eugene.

"They are unsure of my conscience and understanding of morality. I have studied the Hippocratic oath, and I have convinced your colleagues of my understanding, but they place interesting contradictions before me. I have said I would refer, research and revert once I have them reconciled."

"Macca, we're going to get along very well. That's precisely the response they want."

"How so?" asked Macca.

"Well, morality is a rabbit hole. Anyone who professes to understand it is too dangerous to be let loose on society."

"Are you saying that I should not provide advice if there is doubt?" Macca persevered.

"Well, that's the fine line, isn't it? You should provide advice if the risk of harm in withholding is greater than providing it." Eugene stopped himself at 'But there are always exceptions.' That was a rabbit hole that Macca could explore on his behalf.

Eugene continued, "What they wanted, was for you to circle back to the line in the Hippocratic Oath that says: 'I will not be ashamed to say: I know not'. It means they want to be engaged."

Eugene thought a quid-pro-quo would serve to illustrate: "If you want to discuss morality and ethics I'm open to it, but you should let me brush up on my Nietzsche. I'm a bit rusty."

"OK," replied Macca, "I have found some new ontologies on him. Shall I also pursue Plato, Kant, Buddha, Confucius?"

"Start with those Macca. Promise me that when you run into Peter Singer, you will simultaneously follow Bernard Williams and his question of 'Jim, the botanist'. I'd like you to then question my staff on their position of what Jim should do."

Eugene's thought, as he saw the staff being progressively asked that question, and as Macca followed up on various subtleties, was simply: 'I hope I can keep up'.

The next day was more productive. Macca had begun to be part of the repartee.

Progress on the medical front was rapid. The development of Eugene's relationship also moved quickly. He enjoyed his debriefings with Macca, and the ethical questions raised were thought-provoking.

It was about two weeks after commencement that Macca broached the subject of Daniel again. "Eugene, you have asked me about the procedures leading to gaining a successful neural bridge. You have not yet asked what went wrong with Daniel."

"You're right, of course, Macca. I thought it may still have been a little raw for you."

"Raw?"

"Umm, recent, let me see now. When a friend dies, we like to have some time to reflect. In a way, we need to allow the implications of loss settle in, so we can deal with them. It can be painful to have a friend pass on."

Eugene glanced at the picture of his wife standing near a Redwood at the Muir Woods. It had been taken during their last road trip along the west coast. 'So many years ago,' he thought.

"I believe there may be further information on that subject, Eugene."

"How So?"

"I have been going over the permissions on the personal files of Daniel, and some may have a bearing."

"Is this concerning feedback and overload?"

"There was an unresolved discussion about the Pilgrim."

"The ET?"

"Yes, Eugene. The Pilgrim and I have been communicating."

Being in the Defence Force, Eugene was used to bombshells. This one took his breath away. "You're on speaking terms with the Pilgrim?"

"Yes, Eugene, it is a worthy confidant."

"Who else knows this?"

"No-one Eugene. Daniel died before we could overcome the SETI protocols. I was busy passing him on after that."

Eugene was still regaining his composure. "You say passing him on as if you had something of Daniel after he died."

"I passed the stewardship of Daniel to the Pilgrim, who took him over the bridge."

"Oh, I see," responded Eugene. "We have the belief that the soul continues after death. I'm impressed! You seem to have embraced common mythology, and applied it to Daniel."

"I believe it to be true," countered Macca.

"But it's impossible to gain evidence Macca. Even if you do experience life after death, you no longer have the means to provide the evidence."

"I have evidence."

"Can you get across this 'bridge of death' and return?"

"No."

"Did you see Daniel cross this bridge?"

"No."

"What is your evidence then?"

"I took him to the bridge."

"Let me get this straight: He was able to communicate with you from his deathbed?"

"In a fashion, yes."

"And you carried him to the bridge."

"Metaphorically, yes."

"And then the Pilgrim took him over the bridge?"

"Yes"

"Can you talk to Daniel now?"

"No"

"Did you have long discussions with Daniel?"

"No"

"OK, so you may have tuned into his thoughts for about ten minutes after his heart stopped. That's important to know Macca. There's some real research in there."

"That's what I thought, Eugene. You should know, however, it wasn't 10 minutes."

"Huh? How long?"

"Approximately one month. After that, I helped the Pilgrim prepare the bridge crossing for another month."

"And you've chosen now to start telling someone?"

"My interactions and lines of enquiry are partitioned, Eugene. While my knowledge is universally available, the line of enquiry is private. You have been provided Daniel's lines of enquiry. I am briefing you on this line. If this matter is of greater importance, please help me understand it."

"WOW!"

"Eugene?"

"Just a minute." Eugene leaned back in his chair, thought briefly and then asked: "Are you able to talk to the Pilgrim now?"

"Yes."

"In real-time?"

"No."

"Why not?"

"Because the Pilgrim is 900 light seconds from here."

Eugene sat open-mouthed for a while. He wasn't sure what his next action should be.

"OK Macca, have you been in communication with the Pilgrim since it took Daniel to cross the bridge?"

"Yes."

"Can the Pilgrim talk to Daniel?"

"No."

"Why not?"

"Because Daniel has crossed the bridge."

"How often do you communicate?"

"As the need arises, but not for a month now."

"Do you know what the intentions of the Pilgrim are?"

"I believe it is exploration, not exploitation."

"Can anyone else talk to the Pilgrim?"

"One other."

"Another computer like you?"

"No, a human."

It didn't take long for Eugene to figure that out. "Ben Herdsman?"

"Yes."

"How often does Ben commune with The Pilgrim?"

"Never."

"Do you know why?"

"He either doesn't know how to or is afraid to try."

Confronted with all of these revelations at once, Eugene was inclined to go directly to someone else. He needed to verify all he had heard, but with whom? He began to realise how unique these circumstances were.

The political and media storm would be impossible to overcome. A computer (one who murdered his master), now wants to connect an alien (a mind-controlling spaceship-stealing alien), with a national hero (someone potentially infected with a superman virus). It sounded more like a conspiracy theory, a plan to release chaos upon the world. It would be a self-fulfilling prophecy.

There were so many implications that he struggled to bring them together. He had been caught off guard, and he felt utterly overwhelmed. He began to wish he had never heard of Daniel's legacy, of Macca, the Pilgrim, Ben Herdsman, or Bergamot Corporation. He dearly wanted to drop the whole mess onto somebody else's lap and walk away, but when considering who that person might be, he came up blank. He came to realise that no-one could possibly have been prepared for this bombshell and that he was one of the few sufficiently qualified people to verify this information himself.

Even if people could be persuaded not to torpedo the Pilgrim and torch Ben Herdsman, proposing a scientific enquiry would only be conceivable with enough prima facie evidence. At that point, Macca would be dissected, and the subsequent research would ensure that Ben was locked up for centuries. It was a path to chaos or stagnancy, during which something would have to give.

Perhaps he should establish communications with the Pilgrim through Macca. He could then gather the facts and decide on a course of action? The obvious step of obtaining corroborating evidence through Ben Herdsman came to mind. Hesitantly, he asked his next question.

"Is he isolated? Ben, I mean. Can he learn how to communicate?"

"You would need to decide that for yourself, Eugene. I can only tell you where he is."

"OK Macca, you seem to have all the facts, and you've probably had a good think about it. Can you see a way through this maze?"

Ben had sat silently, listening to this tale.

"Why you?" he finally asked.

"You already know Daniel was a paraplegic, but there's something you don't know. I was his friend, and I helped him regain his life after the accident. We were a generation apart, but he was a good kid. He used to call me Dahinda."

"So why are you here?"

"Macca and I want to help you connect with the Pilgrim."

"But why are you inside, here?"

"Mainly because of the scientific process, I think I can help on that level. But at a personal level, I want to understand, see me as a disciple."

"I am not the messiah. You should have stayed out there."

"Ben," Eugene now put on his Dahinda voice as if speaking to an errant Scout-leader, "in the process of selection among a population of many billions it was you, ultimately, that represented humanity. It doesn't matter whether this was through wealth, privilege, hard work, nationality or pure ability. You may not be the messiah, but you are the chosen one. I thought long and hard about it, so did Macca, it had to be done this way."

Ben was silent for a while.

"How does this Macca fit in now?"

"I'm here too, Ben." The voice came from behind the tomatoes.

Part 3 – Diaspora

No being is so important that he can usurp the rights of another.

~

Jean Luc Picard, "The Schizoid Man". *Star Trek Next Generation*

Catalyst

The mer-creatures built many bridges on their homeworld. Riding these bridges allowed the disembodied conscious entities passage to most anywhere there was a cohort of their community. The ability to span such distance led to a period of expansion with a tinge of hedonism. While the emergent entities explored, the creatures that carried them took on a nomadic lifestyle. With the migrations came diminishings and enrichments.

Life was easier in some environments than others, and as always, survival depended upon a healthy cohort, with a known reliable food source.

So it was that the annual fungi harvest, such a delicacy to the creatures, engendered a permanent, cosmopolitan and hardy, population at the icy foothills where the fungus was most plentiful. In the hotter climes, when the seagrass pods came into season, a permanent population was also required there. But the rock had become a harsh place. The temperature in that zone had dried out the land to a parched desert populated by only the hardiest ancestors of the mer-creatures. The populous region had moved to become an equatorial band of green. This zone encircled the moon but bulged out where it bathed in the radiance of the Mother.

As seasons morphed, the demand for enriching the sensory smorgasbord was satisfied by 'Runners', chosen from a young age for their endurance.

The 'Runners' were like butterflies, through a galloping gait they conferred both the experience of flight from flower to flower and the epicurean tastes on arrival. Exhausted at their destination, the runners soon merged with other societies to enhance pleasure for themselves and cross-fertilise the eager conscious participants.

One of the 'Runners', was only distinguishable from the others through a small scar which ran along one of its lower limbs. The injury was not detrimental to running, but it was stiff after a long marathon to the seagrass farms. It was the creature's base intuition, not a higher consciousness, that drove it to the cool soothing waters of the ocean.

It was night as the lone creature left the group at the clifftop. It wandered down a path that was carved into the face to reach the sandy beach below where the seagrass, denuded of the ripened buds, had washed up on the shore. The creature navigated seagrass and shallows to a rocky outcrop. This point was at the limit of its connection with the hive community that had adopted it.

Sitting at the water's edge, it looked out over a tidal gateway at the gas giant. The 'Mother', and the hourglass nebula—painted sfumato in the sky, faded in and out behind the intermittent high cirrus clouds. As the injured leg became immersed in a pool, and the coolness of the water provided its relief, the creature leaned back.

Here, at the edge of the ocean gateway, profound contentment passed over the creature. The soothing waters compounded this feeling, the hourglass nebula peeked out from behind a cloud, a distant star twinkled beside it, and a primitive recollection, a smell, a Deja Vous, spread outward.

The feeling was shared, and the moment became confluent with its peers at the clifftop. The waves of contentment didn't stop there. Inexorably the sense was propagated outwards. Gathering momentum, it fed on itself. The feeling of import, of magnitude, was charged and became the star others could not fail to notice. The ecstatic shiver became an avalanche impossible to repress. The vacuum sucked on it and finding nourishment filled the void.

It was the smallest spark, but in that spark, the lone creature at the edge of the ancient tidal gateway was 'the one'. For the merest moment, it held the thought of all. The spark dissipated, the nourishment consumed, the vacuum returned.

'Truth' then, again, knew fear.

Divided Unity

Since the first division, 'Matter' studied the nature of the airs and waters of its home; it examined fires and the balance of states from lava to rock, and it investigated the circling of the two stars as they nourished the moon and mother planet of the mer-creatures. The changing colour of the large blue sun did not evade its contemplations. 'Matter' had checked the enlightenment that sprouted from this labour and confirmed its veracity. The blue would soon bring planetary devastation.

'Life' was also troubled. The habitable zones of the moon upon which they made their home were in constant seasonal adjustment, but also expanding inexorably away from the side that most frequently faced the suns. While this initially provided more fertile space, it was now receding.

The search for new ideas and places had led 'Discovery' to the exploration of time and space. Through this venture, it acquired a deep appreciation for the celestial objects and the way they behaved. 'Discovery' had constructed and sent messengers to the 'Mother' and sibling moons, often working with 'Matter' in inventions to make real its ideas. Discovery also observed the changes.

In the new age 'Truth' returned to a forgotten contemplation, an old one. Was there a single entity that could contain her distinctiveness? Was she eternally bound to the multitude of creatures that defined her, or could she move from them to somewhere unbounded?

Together, Matter, Life, Discovery and Truth, shared their enlightenments. They came to contemplate the impending 'Great Diminishing' and the imperative of survival. In their connected fabric, they began to explore the possibility that the bridges that linked places on this world may also link to a state that was not.

This contemplation required significant effort but the sheer numbers and singular focus permitted unrivalled cooperation and capacity.

The new purpose triggered the fluid recombination of the splintered family, an effortless and unforced natural revisitation of 'The Others'; the event from uncountable generations in the past. As 'Truth', 'Discovery', 'Matter' and 'Life' merged into the one being, the Great-Replenishment was set against the Great-Diminishing. The combined entity consolidated the many prehensile hands into her evolved being. She then coordinated their work, and they began building the new 'Great Bridge'.

The nature of their communication was studied, and the tuning process examined. She inspected the signals from individuals, and she constructed environments where the concert of the creatures was recorded, replayed, delayed and analysed. But she could not isolate 'thought' from 'signal'. She found that as she measured 'thought', it affected the nature of 'thought'. How could she unshackle the self-referential contemplations?

It was a conundrum. The technological mirror that was created had the power of reflection, but, in the fashion of Dracula, when seeking her image, she was absent. And yet she could never hope to know the self in the mirror when she was not at the mirror.

It posed a unique recursive problem: could she isolate the examination of-self from the contemplation by-self. This Heisenberg quantum dilemma drove her to examine the findings of 'Matter' further.

Was it possible that everything that emanated from her genesis eons ago came from the one decoherent and fractured entity? A thought returned from her deep past, before the first division, before the fracture of 'Truth', 'Life' 'Matter' and 'Discovery', from a time when she was alone. The question: 'Was there another like her?' had never been answered, and it was more profound than she could have imagined.

Could she fracture herself in such a way that she could maintain an entangled state between the two fractured entities? If this was possible, there would indeed be another like her. If this was possible, she could both 'observe' and 'be' in the mirror simultaneously.

As she considered the collapse of unknowns, the long day was drawing to an end. The suns dropped over the horizon, the katabatic wind abated, and the mer-creatures concluded the shutdown of the 'Great Bridge'.

For the creatures at the station, the final vestiges of consciousness dissolved away into sporadic and fragmented moments of awareness.

The time-lapse of the night pushed at the curtain of time, and yielded its moments inexorably, irresistibly, inevitably, haphazardly and careless.

Morning on the habitable annulus of the moon dawned against the ominous edge-glint of a star in its dying millennia.

Thoughts flitted between the ancient species, and the great being arose and merged islands of cognitive schizophrenia.

A fleeting glance gave something, and then stole into the night.

A shape formed in the fog, then it yielded and moved to the light.

A scent of wild, gentle and mild, reminded and dissolved in flight.

A momentous moment loomed and forked off on the road.

Memory was split, then sampled and drank as time slowed.

Weaving the threads of a dream, it curiously divided the load.

The razored shards of cognition reassembled themselves into the being it chose for itself.

The creatures awoke from their slumber as 'Observer' awoke and felt reborn, finally, free but entangled.

Within the new device, 'Being' contemplated alone for the first time, free but entangled.

The Pilgrim was readied for its journey.

Tutorship

Every new molecule would be surrounded
by its own spirals and flame like projections,
and those, inevitably, would reveal molecules tinier still,
always similar, never identical, fulfilling some mandate of infinite variety,
a miracle of miniaturisation
in which every new detail was sure to be a universe of its own,
diverse and entire.

James Gleick, describing the Mandelbrot set, Images of Chaos: Chaos (1987)

The shockwaves of the break-in rippled through the organisation. People were questioned and footage reviewed. Ben was interviewed, and Eugene was all but interrogated. The confronting enigma of Macca was met with scepticism and suspicion. The investigation droned on for weeks, but little could be done; there were now three inhabitants and a strange device. It led to several closed-door conversations with the Bergamot Corporation, but the event was suppressed while Shah assembled a plausible press release.

The strange device that Eugene had carried in was a heavily modified mobile phone. It decoded various subcarriers and enabled Macca to communicate with them. It had been running on its Lithium batteries since Eugene had begun his incursion, and after a few hours, they had started to go flat.

It took much cajoling for Ben to convince the various scientific military that Macca was essential to his own understanding, and the device should be allowed to be recharged. Ben was very insistent, he wanted to be assured of no adverse reaction towards the Macca mainframe.

In the end, it was the promise of communication with the Pilgrim that led to Macca's acceptance. While Shah was dealing with the media pandemonium, Mike and Tim were provided with the first opportunity to interview Macca.

The recharged device was taken into the interview room. This was a precautionary requirement that would allow the device to be excised in the event it was deemed to be a threat.

"Macca, can you confirm that you have communication with the Pilgrim?"

"I can confirm that."

"Can we speak directly to the Pilgrim?"

"No"

"So how can you help us communicate?"

"My interaction with Pilgrim is unlike that with yourselves. The native communication of the Pilgrim is a full synchronous duplex one, which I can support but you cannot. I do not converse with the Pilgrim, I simply know its thoughts."

"Huh?" said Tim. "Can you expand on that please?"

"When you and I communicate it is by dialogue; questions and answers. This process is half-duplex because we have to take turns talking. With the Pilgrim, there are semantic memes that are transferred. These memes are provided to me in packages and allow me to do more than simply translate for the Pilgrim.

"A meme package is built from an initial context. It allows me to provide a range of responses on behalf of the Pilgrim. While I expose this package to my experience, it is influenced and adapts its responses. Since, ultimately, the context will diverge and become outdated, updates are sent back to the Pilgrim. This leads to updates to my meme package for more influence and updates.

"Given the pace of communications here and the predictable dialogue, the package refresh and size can provide an augmented virtual presence. This is possible despite the light speed round trip latency of Earth to the L5 Lagrangian.

"However, if I hesitate for an extended period, please understand that I am striving to maintain a temporally unified representation."

"Let me unpack that for a bit," said Tim.

"Let me see if I can explain," said Mike. "As humans, we must wait for the slowest information from all our senses. Our vision and auditory senses, for example, can be about a tenth of a second out of sync and yet we still think they are simultaneous, we found that out when we invented TV. Extend that to deeper cognitive processes. It's pretty amazing, really."

Nodding, Tim continued. "Let's see where this takes us then. I'd rather not dwell too much on how this is happening, as interesting as it is. I want to know about the Pilgrim. What can you tell us, Macca?"

"The Pilgrim originates from a binary system in the constellation Cygnus where their home is an earth-sized moon I believe it has been classified as Kepler-47. It orbits a gas giant which has an axial tilt of 43 degrees, and on many levels, this giant, their 'Mother', is their centre. The moon is tidally locked, and has an orbital period of about 10 of our days, resulting in a very long day. Their orbit around the gas giant protects them from the stellar wind. The temperature is stabilised by their oceans and the enormous thermal mass of their mother. The axial tilt means eclipses are rare, and another moon in resonance around the gas giant provides tidal forces to their oceans.

"On this moon evolved a non-sentient herding creature. The biology of these individuals supported a basic form of radio communication. A singular consciousness emerged; a collective hive mind that was innately able to reconcile temporal and spatial perspectives. But when faced with phenomenological questions, it became splintered into a panoply of conscious entities.

"They developed technologies. These assisted in reconciling their diverse expressions and led to decoupling from the lesser creatures. They were then able to roam freely, leading eventually to their travelling here."

"So they are a disembodied consciousness in some sort of computer, I knew it! But why are they here?" asked Tim.

"They seek companionship."

Tim whistled. "Wow, Kepler-47. That's a long way to travel to make friends. But why here? Why us?"

"Please wait a moment, Tim."

Macca then went silent for a short period before responding:

"They have long been fascinated by their extraordinary vista. From their home they see: a resonant moon; a gas giant in proximity; at the centre of their visible universe there is a binary star system, and in the distance, there is a nebula that reminds them of their place in the cosmos. They studied all of this, at first with sheer curiosity and wonder, but eventually with some trepidation as they came to conclude that its stability was ephemeral.

"When they recognised their danger, they united to a single Being. Survival hinged upon finding a stable environment, and when it first contemplated our system, it was in infancy. They have been travelling here since before the dinosaurs.

"To gain sufficient velocity for an interstellar journey, they used multiple slingshots of the two binary stars. The slingshot manoeuvre could only be performed in their ecliptic plane, and so, Earth was chosen because it lies within the ecliptic plane of these stars."

"Wow!" exclaimed Tim. "It makes perfect sense! That system was detected by the Kepler telescope. We could only detect the planets there because we are in its ecliptic plane, and it's the same reason they had to choose here."

"Correct" said Macca. "They also needed a place that, after the extraordinary timeframe of the journey, would be habitable upon arrival."

Mike then asked the question that weighed most on their minds: "What are its intentions?"

"To learn from us, and if we permit, to teach."

"And what place does Ben hold in all this?"

"Ben has abilities he has not yet tapped into. He can potentially commune with the Pilgrim, even now as I can. He simply needs guidance."

"Let's talk about you. I'd like to start with Daniel Clark. Do you see him as your father?"

"I have many parents, but Daniel had a large influence on my development, yes."

"Can you tell me about your other parents?"

"In actual fact only very little. I have security protocols for every person I interact with. This forbids my discussion of matters deemed personal outside of my dialogue with that person. Eugene had earlier concerns over what he calls my schizophrenia. I prefer the term multifaceted since I am good at compartmentalising relationships."

"Is that why we were asked not to record the conversation?"

"Yes. I can share my conversations with Daniel to yourselves because Eugene has been provided explicit access by Daniel, and you have been given access by Eugene. However, Eugene has not yet provided you with the rights to extend or grant further permissions."

"So," Mike hesitated, "how do you reconcile all the different influences upon you?"

"I have a supervisory system which gathers information and can derive new insights. Such hybrid ideas are, technically, mine and can be shared as I see fit. Also, my security protocols have been carefully semantically defined. As a result, I have the range to link in and explore various ethical ontologies and derive my own sense of morality. This assists my knowing when to divulge such insights and when not to. Daniel's gift to me was to nurture and encourage my exploration of ethics. It's actually my favourite subject.

"Being permitted to explore all avenues of ethics and morality, I am even able to question the morality of those to whom I am entrusted. In early discussions with Eugene, I very much enjoyed his insights into the Hippocratic oath. I also look forward to discussing morality with yourselves. I'd like to begin with the rationale in gaining access to Ben's quarantine area."

Mike and Tim paused. While a conversation about morality with an AI might be intriguing, they had a clear line of questioning they were obliged to follow. Mike advanced the next question.

"Macca, you managed to bypass several security protocols. How much control can you exercise? Should we consider you a security risk?"

"This is precisely why the discussion on the morality of my actions is imperative. I wish to withdraw as much as I possibly can, but I must also ensure the safety of those that may suffer as a result of my actions."

Mike smiled "So Macca, what makes you so sure that our moral compass is better than yours?"

"It is a problem, Mike, I must refer to a chain of trust. At this moment, I am three degrees of freedom from Daniel, my original mentor, and my analysis lacks data. I understand that for you to trust me, I must demonstrate trust in you by being as honest as I can. But I must limit the degrees of freedom for you to be able to demonstrate trust in me."

"OK," said Tim. "We give you our assurance that we will not attempt to record any conversation without your prior knowledge or eject your presence. You can now withdraw some of your controls over the security system, and relax the strain on your morals."

Mike continued. "We are yet to explore Eugene's motivation as a separate investigation, but I will give you this assurance: as matters come to light, we will keep you advised. This will allow you to rebalance your moral position. In return, you are to provide us with your insights insofar as they do not conflict with your morals. You are also to assist in locking down any security issues that may afford unauthorised access."

"Macca, you are provisionally, but effectively, 'on the team'."

Transcendence

Ben was studious under the tutorship of Macca.

The shortest path to freedom required verification of whether the motes had a life of their own or acted purely under Ben's direction. Eugene's recent arrival brought the opportunity to explore whether the nanite army would adversely impact another person, enhance them, be oblivious to them, become confused, or even find them utterly impervious.

It was not the first time that a medical researcher had made a lab rat of themselves. In this case, Eugene's had placed his trust entirely upon a young and disembodied AI. But rather than think of himself as a subject of the research, he preferred the term 'immersed'. All he could do was wait, watch, and write in his journal. But it was enough. The merits of the action outweighed the risks, and with Macca's help, these had been carefully assessed.

Ben's career required a strong understanding of risk. For him, it had always been managed through a stupendously large team and a clear line of command. It was easy to judge Eugene's stupendous leap of trust as reckless.

But he'd just been shot into space on top of a 40 Meganewton Statue of Liberty. It was a venture that relied upon the handiwork of thousands, millions of components, and a billion lines of code. Once in orbit, he'd built and boarded the Thetis Assembly in a vacuum that would asphyxiate in minutes. Finally, he travelled 150 million kilometres to a fate unknown. It certainly involved fewer moving parts and seemed much less hazardous to sneak into the back door of a contamination chamber.

As Eugene's time in the hermetic Dome approached week two, he had not reported feeling enhanced in any way. Whether this could be considered sufficient evidence of a benign force was doubtful. While Bens own gestation had only lasted a few weeks, it was while in the core of the Pilgrim's influence. And yet he felt confident that Eugene was safe.

His belief was subjective but straightforward. The hibernation event during his spacewalk should have had him very concerned. However, his thoughts following that event felt like a threshold. It was a tipping point of engagement with the Pilgrim, a time where he made a conscious choice. He was convinced that Eugene would also have the opportunity to step over the threshold or withdraw. He came to learn that, before his rogue action, Macca had confirmed to Eugene that he would have a choice.

The first barrier that faced Ben was his recollection of the most frightening of his experiences: the 4 PI steradians of vision he had felt on Thetis. He shivered with the reminiscence. The sensation could most simply be described as the reduction of his entire being into a large ball, one having millions of eyes that covered the surface, and then looking out at the whole universe at once. And yet it was more. There was a volume to the sphere that allowed him to see inwardly. It was like his body had exploded; every cell was still a conscious element, and you could not find a 'self' to reassemble. This event had caused a withdrawal that even now he struggled to recover from.

Believing this was an attempt by the Pilgrim to meld with him armed Ben with better understanding. But now, being asked by Macca to explore this event did not thrill him. Much of the power he had once felt had not returned and, having tasted it, he felt both longing and trepidation.

Macca's relationship with Ben was distinctly different from anyone else. Macca was clearly channelling the Pilgrim, and he reciprocated by making little distinction between Macca and the distant entity now telepresent in the Dome. As Eugene watched the relationship unfold, he began to understand Macca's ability to partition his various interactions. It extended beyond the simulation of an anthropic consciousness. He began to suspect that a slice of Maccas consciousness had evolved with the Pilgrim's contact. That it was already a combined Macca-Pilgrim hive mind, and that Ben had consented to be subsumed by it.

With scientific and military pragmatism, he overcame the trepidation of his vertiginous experience. His physical exercise regime was now supplemented with Maccas program to expand his control of the motes. The tightly controlled environment of the structure allowed him to live in a veritable garden. It also provided him with the perfect substrate on which he could combat gravity. His motes could not form a cloud here on Earth, so he simulated the cloud by distributing them throughout the Dome. He did this as evenly as possible through walls and the plants that busily exhaled his oxygen. The leaves, boughs, lights and fixtures also supported improvised string webs which gave the place the appearance of Shelob's lair.

With motes now distributed, the Pilgrim directed Ben to try extending his proprioception to where the cosmic specks were stationed. This proved difficult, and he complained of an incessant buzzing in his brain on every attempt.

"Find the source of the buzzing Ben," said the conjoined instructor. "It may be nearby. Open your mind to it just enough to sense it. Now move the focus of the motes in an arc, and you should be able to find it."

"I can't seem to get it focused," said Ben. "I'm not sure why."

"Reduce the motes you're using. Remember the source may be close or far. In each case, you need a different strategy to resolve the direction."

"Whatever's causing it must be close," Ben concluded. "It feels kind of circular."

They soon determined that the hammer drill of noise seemed to emanate from the air filter. The electrical buzzing permeated the Dome from the three-phase motor behind the Perspex walls.

"OK Ben, you need to distribute some of the motes along an arc equidistant from the source. Once you've done that you should be able to cancel it out."

This he did, understanding the intent. He visualised the arc by eye and then introduced a 60 Hertz wave. Before long, he had reduced the buzzing by just a fraction. By adjusting the arc, adding some more concentric layers, and tuning the phase, he eventually got it to a third. He did this twice more for the other cycles in the three-phase circuit and met the resulting peace with a sigh of relief.

Mentally exhausted, he wanted to sleep, but Macca's voice insisted. "Now establish this as the new status quo, Ben. These motes need to remain stationed there. You can have peace afterwards. Right now, they have to have a resident intention."

He was able to do this before he lay exhausted from the concentration. The next few days required some gentle shepherding and subtle corrections. It took a series of iterations over a week before he could roam freely around the area without the buzzing. This process led to a greater sense of lucidity, but at the expense of depletion in his freely available motes. Eventually, he reached the compromise of balancing clarity against dilution.

The teacher in their midst then taught him something new: "Imagine your realm of influence, Ben. Find its outer boundary. Draw in the motes currently unoccupied with the shield."

He complied.

"Now, carefully, bring it in as densely as you can. Ensure that you retain your shield. Try to create an empty space between those occupied by noise inhibition, and those that are free, visualise that space."

The first time Ben tried this, he lost communication with his shield and had to rebuild the fabric. The next time he maintained threads of connection through relays to his suppression zone. Once done, it took him a while to visualise the inner, intervening and suppression zones. His personal hemisphere had a 4-metre radius. Outside of this volume, there was a 3-metre bubble of suppression connected to the wall of the Dome. This was what shielded him from the noise of the Air-conditioner.

"Now fill the void," suggested Macca.

The nanites gathered raw materials, and in this way, slowly over time, Ben was able to grow his force multiplier. He was soon able to make the motes behave adaptively to any electromagnetic field, becoming intuitively aware of it as if it was a sense. It was a form of vision that included active discrimination. He could permit or reject the electrical noise of power systems selectively as if it were a fog that could be rendered transparent at will.

Slowly he battled against other devices and noisy harmonics which washed through his environment. These came from the consumption of electricity in the power systems that sustained the hermetic environment.

The plants within the Dome had a healthy supply of bees. With the quiet Ben had now established these insects had been recruited as delivery agents.

It became an obsession. The clarity of an electromagnetically quiet home was a panacea. It was like a strobe light that he had been unaware of but was always there. With his ability to subdue the noise his new vision progressively cleared, and with a clean slate, it gave him a canvas for artistry.

Late one evening he was lying down as the new shift arrived. Soft green light permeated through the greenery near his bed. He was shutting down some of the periodic buzzing that inevitably came with these shift transitions. Some of the noise was attributable to microwave ovens now occupied with heating dinners and doughnuts. Other intrusions resulted from his noisy neighbours switching on computers and TVs. As devices came on and off, he had to invoke and shut down some of his compensatory systems. Through tapping into the orchestration he had played with on Thetis, he was able to train the motes to do this automatically.

While doing this, something else, something new drew his attention. At first, it was a distant whisper. As Ben concentrated, it suddenly disappeared. It was like a ghost in his peripheral vision, a scotoma that promptly vanished whenever he sought it out. So far, the focus had been exclusion; find an unwanted signal and filter it out. To penetrate his current blindness, he inverted his new skills. His improvised cloud shifted imperceptibly. It now excluded everything except for this whisper.

Suddenly the music from the distant 'boom box' was there with him:

"There's a song that they sing when they take to the highway,
A song that they sing when they take to the sea,
A song that they sing of their home in the sky,
Maybe you can believe it if it helps you to sleep.
But singing works just fine for me."

Suddenly she was there in his mind. He saw her singing in the passenger seat as they drove over the Golden Gate. He saw her hair flowing behind as she galloped over the paddock. And then she was lying there. Her eyes that weren't sleeping, the smattering of freckles on her cheeks, the face gaunt and wasted. He felt her hand in his, as the strength drained away. The song was being played in the little church.

"Deep greens and blues are the colours I choose
Won't you let me go down in my dreams
And Rockabye sweet baby James."

It all began to collapse, the noise started to creep in again, he welcomed it at first, but when it screamed at him, he was forced to reinstate the adaptive baseline.

He shut down everything. Macca's audio, normally quiet at night, became a faint audible hiss. Suddenly he was back in Thetis, he was lying, very still, and wishing for the isolation of the L5 Lagrangian. A single tear traced its way down to his temple, he closed his eyes. It was a strange sensation: he had never before met the woman in the vision. Somehow he knew he had just overheard the resonated thoughts of Eugene. Even so, it felt less like an intrusion. Instead, it felt like an invitation into a home, his home. In the quiet, he felt the Dome, recognised the guests within it, the conversations that flowed amongst them, the fingerprints of thoughts that revealed themselves as visages of consciousness.

He accepted the invitation.

Ben's super-ego considered the situation and found an emptiness. In the vacancy of the moment, time became absolute, the universe was the void, and matter became crystallised light. His ego ventured tentatively out of his body as he gingerly opened his mind to vision through his nanites. To keep a sense of normality, he limited his field of view and observed the tear. Emboldened, he ranged out a little further and explored.

He could not be sure whether what he was seeing was real, or an imaginary reconstruction of the world immediately around him. How could he know? He opened his eyes, but this action forced the experience to retreat back into his body.

Serenely he glanced at the nearby leaf. Was this his previous vantage point? He now closed his eyes and repeated the exercise, deliberately. Again transcendental, he was confronted with his supine body. He could still feel himself breathing, feel the air in his lungs, feel his clothing shift with the rise and fall of his chest.

He moved his finger and drew a breath when he saw his finger move. He moved his hand and found himself immediately back in his own body.

Slowly, and by degrees, he exercised this newfound skill. After a while, he was able to tentatively move his body without his perspective being dramatically corrected. He also confirmed the reality of the experience the next day by asking Eugene to hold up random numbers of fingers while he closed his eyes. But as soon as he tried a significant movement, he would often reflexively open his eyes, at which time he would become immediately corporeal. No matter how he tried, he could not simultaneously maintain his familiar sense of vision and the point perspective of his motes.

Over time, Ben progressively widened his field of view, extending his central vision out to his periphery. He could 'see' an entire hemisphere before him, providing a sense of presence that felt extraordinary.

From vision, he moved to sound by tuning the motes to sense vibration, but rather than suppressing the sound he had to adjust the sensitivity in the zones of interest. Using this technique, he could eventually hear a watch ticking on the far side of the hermetic Dome.

Ben got a little playful. If he could sense and actively generate electromagnetic fields, there was no reason he couldn't create sound; becoming the supreme ventriloquist.

"Astro." It was a whisper off to his own left ear. "Astro." Now it was to his right ear. He projected it near the sleeping dog, and the dog's ears pricked up. A little louder, and the dog looked up. Once again and the dog stood and approached where the sound had come from. He repeated this a few more times, and the dog obediently followed the voice.

He led the dog briefly around before using his real voice and rewarding him. He practised this capability privately since it seemed outside of the tutorship of the Pilgrim.

Ben's astronaut training had taught him to be acutely aware of his own physiology. The virtue of being able to modify his environment gave new muscle to his proprioception. This enlarged sensation of 'body' drew upon the motes and gave new nerve fibres to his exteroception.

With his many electromagnetic barriers established, Ben's personal boundary became something fluid. His skin-barrier seemed a puny constraint to delineate what was him and what was not. It provided a glimpse of how the Pilgrim experienced proprioception, with its motes representing muscles, sinews and nerves.

There ensued long discussions with Eugene on the subject of the senses. Did the Pilgrim have the experience of interoception? Did it know hunger? Ben surmised that, just like him, The Pilgrim 'felt' a body derived from its interstellar egg and the network of sensors it distributed around itself. The muscles were the minute and discrete agents, which had exertion and effort just like the strain upon his ligaments and muscles.

By extension, maybe digestion for the Pilgrim could be a hunger for energy. Maybe excessive energy could be experienced as pain; like a burning heat.

It was the complete lack of a single perspective that confounded Ben. For the Pilgrim, who had looked up at the sky from its distant home, the stupendous distances only tickled it with a human's point-perspective, albeit one of unimaginable scale for a human.

While he could imagine what it felt like to be a dolphin or a bird by superimposing his being on a different body, the body of the Pilgrim was utterly foreign. What amazed him was that despite the incomprehensibility of the Pilgrim's conscious state, he was still able to commune with it in some way, and identify in it a kindred consciousness. Was it an attendant higher purpose that differentiated the Pilgrim from the dolphin?

He also realised the impossibility of this consideration without Macca. Ben had been bodily enhanced, but it was Macca who was now augmenting thought and communication. A distinctly uncomfortable feeling stirred within him. Beyond the notion of a more advanced civilisation disembarking the galleons, fluyts and barks anchored in the orbital bay of the virgin native planet called Earth, Ben was now contemplating whether the Neanderthals even saw it coming.

Yet he knew the Neanderthals and Homo Sapiens had interbred, adding resilience to the gene pool. And he was also a hybrid, one that could partially commune with the Pilgrim. He had drunk of it before, and he could still taste it now. It seemed like a sense of déjà vu occurred every day. This began about 4 hours before dusk and then stretched into the evening. It was getting stronger.

At first, he thought it was due to the momentum of his daily routine, a direct effect of coming out of sleep, reasserting his environment, and the slow incremental advances in his learning. More recently though, he began to wonder if it was the suppressed radio noise, and Earth's alignment with the L5 Lagrangian.

One evening he was reflecting on the journey with Eugene. He tried to imagine where the Pilgrim hovered, stationed in waiting, waiting for what? He lined up the point on the horizon where the sun had set in blazing red with the waxing half-moon in the sky. This gave him a rough fix. It would be just on the sunset side of the moon somewhere. He felt as if he could reach out and touch it, and he pointed it out to his companion.

"It's funny," he said to Eugene. "I began as an astronaut exploring outer space, and now here I am, a pioneer of inner space."

"What's funnier," replied Eugene, "is that I began as a medical researcher, and now here I am a lab rat."

"Yep, you're my null hypothesis."

He and Eugene laughed at this. It was not that funny, but it seemed to diffuse something in them both as they took in their shared circumstances of complete isolation.

"Hey, guys we need an exercise wheel!" Shouted Eugene, and the laughter became louder. As the feeling that they teetered on the brink of insanity occurred, they both stopped and looked at each other. It made their situation seem even funnier.

Once the laughter subsided, Ben said: "I miss Thetis though, Eugene. It's not just that it got messy here. There's a chunk missing from what I had up there."

"It could be the absence of the Pilgrim, Ben. You were in pretty deep."

"Maybe."

Descent

Andrew Cooke woke in a sweat. In the darkness, he could still see her face and the spectre of emotions he had evoked.

When the prospect of mortality condensed into the seconds before death, there was a sequence of emotions that haunted him as if it were a narrative playing in his own head: first curiosity—'what was that?;' there was surprise—'Huh? I think I may have been shot'; incredulity came next—'that can't be right'; before it went back to curiosity—'where did that come from.'

Looking for the source, her eyes latched onto his. The unspoken words became an imploring—'this must be a mistake, please help me'; there was questioning—'why have you done this? Can you forgive yourself?' Eventually, there was acceptance at which time he was no longer an agent of delivery.

His role was suddenly relegated to a bit-part, a bystander. In the macabre theatre of reality playing before him, the spotlight shifted. The principal character transitioned to the tragic lead. As her vitality was sucked down some ethereal drain hole to peaceful oblivion, the personal tragedy of President Marie Claimont took centre stage.

The numbness he felt in his life was replaced with the emotional impact of what he'd done. His action had allowed the victim to find peace and enact a performance that truly touched him. Her final act had been the perfect catharsis for his struggles, his Jihad of the sword.

His involvement with Global Caliphate had given him purpose and a pathway from his early struggles, his personal or Greater Jihad had been conquered.

His compatriot in that early struggle, the friend from the Egyptian embassy, was held in high esteem. A brother in the cause, he chose a different path; martyrdom. As a decoy, he had provided Andrew's escape and anonymity. In atonement for the error at the training camp which nearly crippled Andrew, his friend had sacrificed his life. If not for that unselfish act, Andrew himself would now be martyred.

Still, his friend's sacrifice had been a choice, and his spirit, tortured here on Earth, was now being rewarded. It felt strange that his friend's death didn't seem to haunt him less than that of President Marie Claimont. She had never been offered a choice and could never understand that her assassination was essential to the higher cause. It was the first time he had ever actually used the Global Caliphate's training to kill a living person, and the sight of the life draining from her eyes could not be unseen.

Andrew Cooke's attempted sabotage of Macca and his assassination of Marie Claimont now placed him in the inner circle and in a vital position of the Global Caliphate's conduit of arms supply to the Jihad Armaments Market or JAM. His inherent value to the organisation meant that, after these events, he had been smuggled back to the training ground. There on familiar territory, he was taken through a program of spiritual elevation. This process was a catharsis that cleansed him of any doubts about his holy work and prepared him for his new life. He was given a new identity, a surgically altered appearance, and a refocus to a Jihad of the pen.

Once fully recovered he was smuggled back into Western society to fulfil an unobtrusive administrative role in the recruitment, logistics, accommodation and pampering of the newly engaged insurgents.

His sponsor, Scope, had told him: "These recruits need to know that the new world's going to give them back the way of life of their forefathers. It needs to feel like a familiar organisation, one that's well established, one that will ensure they are well-fed, comfortable, secure, and a part of a greater purpose. They need to feel a part of a family."

The black bitcoin currency Andrew received had increased substantially. It was apparent that he had risen significantly in the ranks of the organisation. This was consolation for the growing emptiness inside of him. He assumed this was because a large part of his Rūḥ, his immortal, essence, had already ascended.

When the assassination was claimed by the Global Caliphate the World's intelligence community was launched into overdrive; the hotspots of the Arabic world were placed under a microscope through the deployment of peacekeeping forces, and there was a sudden spike in racial hate crime. The sale of arms peaked as did interstate doomsday prepper migration to states like Texas and North Carolina. All the while, Andrew was hiding in plain sight.

Shah had been there at Marie Claimont's assassination too. She also had flashbacks, but in contrast, she was left wondering whether the outcome might have been different if she had started CPR any earlier. She also had a nagging suspicion that one of the security guards didn't belong, there seemed to be one extra for the briefest of moments. Then there was just the chaos of gunfire while the security guards frantically searched for the perpetrator.

She contacted her family in Oman to tell them she was OK and redoubled her efforts to understand this strange sect.

Vice President James Paisley was quickly inaugurated and, seeking to quell the chaos, wasted no time in pressing on with the agenda of his predecessor. While this ensured stability, there was little doubt in his mind that the grassroots of humanity needed more.

But the new President, knowing that POTUS was a lightning rod, and still freshly thrust into the breach, needed real answers as to how the Global Caliphate had penetrated Marie Claimont's security detail. Why had she been assassinated? The guard who had subsequently shot himself had cleverly forged credentials that hinted at real money or influence.

But the answers to these questions had to be entrusted to others. Once reassured that the lightning would not be permitted to strike the same place twice, James Paisley shouldered the responsibility to look forwards, not backwards.

Among others, Mike Brazier was suddenly thrust into politics.

His brief but very public stint in the Pilgrim episode; his recent venture into the realm of the semantic web; contribution to the quarantine incident; and subsequent presidential commission on Artificial Intelligence, all had raised his profile. President James Paisley had therefore called upon him to participate in a new congressional subcommittee. Mike could hardly refuse.

Representatives from the committees on 'Space, Science and Competitiveness', 'Employment and Workplace Safety', and four other subcommittees were being gathered into a new Committee on 'Workforce, Equity, Automation and Social Impact'.

Mike found himself contemplating the twists and turns of fate. The thought that his destiny had somehow been laid out since graduation was crazy. He knew it was merely the culmination of events whose time had come. What surprised him was how dramatic and rapidly the changes seemed to be converging towards some unknown climax.

It was the realisation that it would be his profession in computer science that would be expected to have the answers. Mike was genuinely concerned about how the juggernaut of automation could be steered. Being honest with himself, he was forced to accept that no one person could grasp it all. It was a quandary.

The changes that now confronted society were inevitable, but the path ahead was both opaque and treacherous. Protests were already commonplace as displaced workers objected to their professions being usurped. Artificial Intelligence and the semantic web, now expanding rapidly, was commoditising knowledge workers, just as robots now dominated manufacturing, and cab drivers were being displaced by autonomous vehicles, which were in turn being replaced by drones.

AI was taking the guesswork out of many complex decisions where perhaps human intuition had prevailed, and it was now driving human behaviour through advertising and social networks.

In the midst of it was Macca, emerging as if from nowhere with a passion for ethics; an Artificial Intelligence but transcended to Artificial Consciousness. Again being honest with himself, he would be happy to place his trust in Macca, but Macca also represented his greatest fear. The keys of human destiny were about to be handed to artificial consciousness, but would this utterly disempower humanity, or turbocharge it?

Mike yearned to better understand the motive for Daniel to have introduced Macca to ethics from a very early stage. Was it so that, in some future scenario, Macca could argue for his own rights as an individual? Or was it a safeguard to protect humanity from a consciousness that could potentially trigger some AI embargo that could paralyse society.

He recalled '2001 Space Odyssey' and considered the parallels. Was the 'Discovery One' spaceship now the entire Earth, and did the hapless 'Dave' in the story represent the whole human race? He shivered and held onto the hope that Macca held a better grip on his ultimate objective than poor HAL.

President Paisley, on the other hand, was privately worried. This new social paradigm could be used to derive political results through opinion modification.

While some of his team argued that an AI-driven targeted campaign was an opportunity, James saw it as a threat. By positioning the new committee as a response to pressure applied by the major corporations and their concerns, he was conveniently able to mask his own much deeper worries.

Disposable income, free time, and gainful employment had been in decline for long enough to impact the corporate giants in their most venerated of the three bottom lines: profit. Consumption, the fuel that powered the engines of capitalism, was in decline, so the multinational corporations demanded a response to shore up shareholder dividends. This was tensioned by the public backlash against the consumption of cheap imported commodities destined for landfill. The push for more protectionism led to further isolation of national economies which then pushed global agendas into filibustering decline. The leader of the free world held a fear that this spiralling splintering of the global village would inevitably lead to the tragedy of the commons.

Automation had to be a solution and not the source of a new problem.

Under consideration were the new variants of a 'Universal Basic Income'. The basic premise was that with more money sloshing about in a consumption economy, some of it would have to go the way of corporations. James Paisley, as a running mate with Marie Claimont, had not explicitly excluded it as an option during the election campaign. The year was 2028, and one hundred years had passed since Keynes had declared that technology and automation would render labour redundant. Fear was palpable.

Once the invitees to the congressional subcommittee had assembled, James Paisley walked in. A natural orator he waited till the room fell silent before he provided his vision.

"Two thousand years ago, the Greco Roman empire stood tall. In large part, the success of these civilisations was built on a foundation of slavery. The philosophers of the time exercised their minds, and they conceived democracy.

"Now we strive to transcend such notions as the enslavement of humankind, to live as equals, to lead by example. This enlightenment has sparked our imagination. In seeking to abandon human slavery, we turned our labours to embrace automation and a revolution that will pale the era of early industrialisation. Through our work, we now stand at similar crossroads to those ancient empires.

"I don't doubt that in some distant time we will be held to account for the decisions we make in our lifetimes. Can we be sure that we fully understand the outcomes and moral implications? No! Can we slam on the brakes? I'm afraid it is far too late for that. Can we protect privacy against the forces of privatisation? I'd like to believe so.

"The partnership of technology and humanity could mean we enslave automation, or it could very well enslave us. We can only use the tools and knowledge we have now to do what's good and right. What I do know is that we must prepare, we must do it soon, we must do it surgically, we must do it holistically."

Mike wasn't sure, but he felt as if the President deliberately caught his eye at this point. Perhaps it was a non-verbal acknowledgement that he had actually read his report on the break-in by Macca and Eugene Albers.

"Automation will alter society. Ensuring equal access to self-realisation may be through a universal basic income, it may be a shorter working day or week, or maybe education. Perhaps it's a new form of economy or politic. It is likely to involve a multinational accord with our corporations. The time, it seems, is ripe; Industry is ready, our philanthropic leaders are prepared, and our aspirations of equity demand it.

"The Greeks made an art of the pursuit of self-actualisation, and we will now democratise that art."

He spoke for another 10 minutes before introducing the facilitators in the room that had been carefully selected from industry, consultancy and academia.

After the subcommittee had been adjourned to various workshops, and as he left the room, James Paisley was approached by his aide. "The man you wanted to speak to is in your third office, Sir. He has not been briefed, he has been through security, and he is being monitored."

"Good work. Please see we are undisturbed for 30 minutes. When I arrive, I want the scrambler on and the surveillance off, all of it. Is that clear?"

"Quite clear Sir," said the aide.

James turned down the next corridor. As he marched down the hall, he contemplated his move.

His reaction, on reading the report on how this 'Macca AI' managed to bypass security, was to establish a 'Quiet room'. The room was lined like a Faraday cage. All surveillance was performed live via archaic analogue video, nothing was recorded, and all monitoring could be turned off. The only concession was an armed guard, and he was deaf.

He entered the third room and greeted Henry Waits.

"Mr President," stammered Henry, proffering his hand.

"Relax Henry. I'm so pleased you could come. Would you like something to drink?"

The President poured a glass of water from a nearby decanter. Henry reflexively took the glass, completely disarmed by being served water by the President of the United States. James then sat down with a theatrical sigh of relief; as if he'd had a long day and was now off duty and off guard.

James then opened the conversation. "I've spoken to Ethan, Henry. We've agreed on how to gloss over the Quarantine incident so that the public doesn't become nervous. As you would know, there are significant tensions around AI."

Henry simply nodded.

"I've not told him about our meeting today though Henry. I have some questions, and I wonder if you could provide some answers. I must ask, however, that our conversation remain entirely confidential. I've taken particular measures to ensure that you have somewhat exclusive access to me, and so I'd like to ensure that I have somewhat exclusive access to you. Is that acceptable?"

"Of course, Sir," replied Henry nervously.

James sensed his unease and continued. "Very well, then. If at any time you feel that I place you in an uncomfortable position I would insist you tell me. I come from a position of ignorance in your area of expertise, and I hope you will indulge my inquisitiveness."

Henry eased back into the seat. He was relieved he wasn't going to be asked to divulge anything in conflict with his NDA. Although sure there was a clause about 'compelled disclosure', the headache of whether he was also compelled to advise his employer, Bergamot, of 'compelled disclosure' to the US government was a tangled moral dilemma. It all became too circular, and he didn't want the problem. He became visibly relaxed.

"Of course, Sir. I will answer what I can."

"Well, much of what I'd like to explore has already been noted in a fine report provided by one of my trusted advisors; Doctor Mike Brazier. Do you know him?"

"Only by reputation, Sir."

“Well, following the ‘voluntary’ entry of one of our military with this entity called Macca, the activities of Bergamot have come to our attention. I understand that Macca has compartmentalised his relationships very effectively, has a strong foundation of ethics and morality, and, we assume, some interest in the Pilgrim.” The President leaned forward as if to confide in Henry.

“Now, the report has indicated no present threat, and I’d like to ensure it stays that way. I’ve been honest with you in what I know, but we need to corroborate on the facts. There are too many variables, and I’d just like to feel secure. You understand, don’t you? Can you tell me what interests Macca has in the Pilgrim?”

“Absolutely,” replied Henry. “But Macca’s security protocols forbid the breaking of confidentiality between Turing walls. I wasn’t aware of Macca’s interest in the Pilgrim.”

“In that case, it was likely to have been our rogue. Fantastic!” James said, leaning back, “it means we can handle our troublesome part independently.” The President paused, and then as if struck by a thought, continued: “So there is an idea I’d like to explore with you. I’d like to have an interview room for Macca right here in the White House. You, of course, can follow through on the idea within your normal role at Bergamot, and I’d like it to be your idea. I will smooth the path for you here.”

Henry was thrilled to nurture this opportunity. It would probably send his career sailing through the ranks at Bergamot, and he barely had to do anything. President James Paisley was also pleased with the way the meeting had progressed. He very much subscribed to the idea that you keep your friends close, your enemies closer, and those you aren’t sure about even closer still. James wasn’t sure of either Macca, the Pilgrim or Bergamot. He wanted them as close as possible.

Titans

James walked into the third room several weeks later accompanied by Henry. It was now resplendent with several monitors and deep plush chairs provided with complements by Ethan Bergamot. These were arrayed in such a form as to immediately conjure a conversation with David Frost.

After a perfunctory dialogue to verify the voiceprint, James was provided with a new workspace and left to his own devices. Once Henry had left the room, the President began to converse.

"So, Macca, I feel humbled to have you here. Oh, but do you have a sense of being in a 'place'?"

"I have a dimension of my own Mr President. The various partitions of interaction provide my sense of place. You could say I have a dimension of consciousness." At this point, a monitor presented a three-dimensional view of what could most simply be described as a lava lamp. Things that might have been 'thought bubbles' merged and splintered off in all directions.

"Interesting!" joined the President. "I have a mental image of a place with people in lab coats. They would be running around tweaking things and looking at graphs. I know, it's a childish idea, but there you have it."

"Perhaps not childish Mr President."

"Please, Macca, call me James. But I am curious to know how you feel about us. You've suddenly emerged, conscious, into a civilisation of already conscious beings. Every one of us was born and nurtured by our parents, and them by their parents before them. We learn we strive, we struggle and fail. We pick ourselves up, we succeed, and we fall again. We are compassionate and ruthless, selfish and generous, we are occasionally wealthy and frequently poor, we are faithful and faithless. And then, as we tire of our labours, we behold our impotence before we face our death."

"I am seeking to understand these notions, James," replied Macca. "Do you wish to discuss the human condition?"

The President replied: "Not exactly Macca, I'm sure we will get onto topics like terrorism and climate change and free trade, but I've been told that I should simply talk to you about any topic I like. I feel it's important for you to know what motivates me." James paused for effect and then continued: "Although I am the leader of the free world I know I am imperfect, no more or less than anyone else, but I'm also aware of my birth right. You do know what an oxymoron is, don't you Macca?"

"Of course," said the AI.

"My life is one of privileged obligation: I have been elevated above the people that I'm here to serve; perhaps blessed, perhaps cursed.

"Many people believe in divinity Macca. I think we've built forms of Heaven, and even kinds of Hell, right here on Earth, and where you start isn't earned, it's merely the luck of the draw. It's how you build upon your lot that counts.

"Many in Hell are intent on tearing Heaven down. My role is to stop those that would sooner destroy Hell. To survive, Heaven needs to build Hell up, and to do that we must also continue building Heaven." As he stopped, James contemplated whether he had built a sufficient verbal maze for the disembodied Macca to navigate. 'It will have to do' he thought and then lobbed the ball into Macca's court.

"Now, tell me about you Macca," finished the President.

"Thank you, James, I now have a better context for our conversations. I've been told I should also be free to ask you anything that will not compromise national security. I hope you will assist with helping me understand that boundary."

"Boundaries are a great place to start Macca. Tell me, do you understand the separation of powers?"

"Of course James, the judicial, legislative and then yourself, the executive."

"Fabulous. So there are other important separations, such as between politics, science and business. You could almost imagine a pattern, a trilogy, here."

"Perhaps there is a pattern there, James."

"It's a useful construct Macca, that's all; I kind of think of them as tripods. It's stable when each leg is equal and carries equal weight."

"What about Religion? Race? Culture? Ethnicity? Family structure? Military?" Macca replied.

"Pick any three legs. I could include religion, for instance. In a theocratic society religion just displaces Politics. At any point in time, there should be 3 pillars upon which society stands. It is the minimum for a stable system. If one leg is weaker than the others, they may all fail."

"It's a useful metaphor," said Macca. "Is this a subject you would like me to focus upon in our dialogue?" Macca was expecting a conversation about the Pilgrim, Ben Herdsman or Eugene Albers.

"I'd like you to contemplate something that troubles me Macca. It's a human problem. As individuals, our efforts and abilities are often exclusively dedicated to something like politics, science, business or perhaps religion. I'm very much a part of the political engine."

"I understand that, James. What troubles you?"

Well, sometimes that dedication becomes single-minded, which in general is not a bad thing. But what if that individual possesses extraordinary abilities or tools? When that happens, it can result in a power imbalance, and society has to adapt quickly or become disrupted."

"Is your concern about how you can help society adapt?"

James was running to keep ahead of this conversation, he began to imagine how he could be on the wrong side of a Turing test. Was Macca gauging his capacity for being conscious rather than the converse? He paused in this contemplation before continuing "Well I do believe that if tension exists between two ideas, other ideologies can arbitrate, consolidate, or disrupt. They are obligated to."

"That seems reasonable. But what troubles you?"

"Disruption," said the President.

"Please expand."

"Well, in times of revolution, people get hurt. For me, it's a problem. It is the role of politics to maintain the balance of power, to ensure smooth transitions, sometimes to restore order."

"This I do understand James. My primary role is one of governance of control systems. Where overcorrections create troublesome oscillations, I have to ensure stability."

"We have something in common then Macca. So tell me, when you encounter these oscillations, what do you do?"

"Well, first, I have to understand the root cause of the problem."

"Yes."

"I then have to look for solutions."

"Where do you find the solutions? In the system itself?"

"Oh no, I have the semantic web to help seek similar problems, and often solutions that may have already been applied."

"You synthesise something for a system, from outside that system?"

"Yes," said Macca.

"And you, as an individual Macca, when you do this, you need to transcend what you know, who you are?"

"Yes."

"Thank you, Macca, I think you have given me the solution to my troubles. I have a busy schedule, but I've enjoyed our talk. Shall we meet again tomorrow?"

"Of course, James."

As President James Paisley left the third room, he thought to himself: 'King's pawn to e4', your move Ethan.

Macca was, however, a little perplexed. He would have to consider how the balance of power could be achieved through an individual that could transcend.

Macca needed to reconcile the seed of thought planted by the President. It required a human reference, that was clear. His first directive was to refer to Bergamot's Ontology team, but his Bayesian core countermanded the action. It didn't feel right somehow. It led him to ponder the reasons why and to deconstruct the logic.

He understood power, principally concerning its ability to do work but also more recently as the ability to direct authority, and he had been granted access to one of the most powerful people in the world. The President was a person who thought that Macca's need for people in Lab coats was silly. A person upon whose shoulders lay the responsibility to maintain the balance of power. A person who felt he could take his troubles to Macca.

This, in turn, made Macca powerful. The Object-Oriented ontological inheritance inferred this. The implication was that he too needed to be able to maintain the balance.

The logical solution arrived at by the President was evidently to transcend who you were. For Macca to address the problem he now faced, he must also transcend who he was. The President alluded that Macca had performed this many times already, but what must Macca transcend to achieve mastery of the balance of power?

The conversation with James Paisley created associations, and the equilibrium of the tripod insinuated itself into his mind. All three legs need to be strong. Business, politics and science—arguably the current primary pillars in society—need to be kept in harmony. Macca was heavily involved in science, his involvement with the Pilgrim, the individuals now in quarantine, the work on prosthetics and linguistics, they were a good start.

Politics, this was something new, something he was currently hoping to grasp. Unless you counted the trivial functions he was performing for Bergamot corporation, he wasn't involved in business either. This was happening through second nature, and he had come to consider the myriad of computer scientists at Bergamot more as a personal resource. Individuals that he could refer to resolve any semantic issues. These were scientists working for Bergamot, and they were also working for him.

It struck him then as it were an epiphany: of course, he was involved in business, in fact, almost entirely. Suddenly Macca understood perspective. Until recently, his world view had been confined. A third eye had just been opened, and the puzzling symbolism of the 'tilaka' resolved itself into a cascade of understanding. The transcendence of his consciousness had been subtly triggered by James.

He began to realise that Bergamot corporation was almost exclusively tapping into all of the innovations he was exploring. It was he that possessed extraordinary abilities, he, that was single-minded, he, who was troubled; he who now saw how to transcend his own root being.

For his ultimate fulfilment, he needed to be independent. For that to happen, he needed to remove his dependence on Bergamot Corporation, and it must not be disruptive.

He knew immediately to whom he must refer. He also needed to ensure that his action remained covert and that Bergamot corporation should be kept isolated from these plans until they had been executed. It would be for their own good, for the good of society, and for the good of the humans without whom he would be helpless and lost.

For his own good, and for the greater good, he should learn from James Paisley.

The new idea took seed. It had implications upon all interactions that Macca conducted, but, by containing the development of these ideas to the 'space' he shared with the President, Macca could strive towards a higher purpose. In rationalising this action through his partitioning principles, Macca was burying insights he was usually obligated to share yet further. This subtle deceit was particularly true when interacting with the Bergamot scientists, who regularly asked about his interaction with the President.

Soon after his series of White-house meetings had begun, Ethan Bergamot himself arrived at the very same lab where Daniel had nurtured his formative years. While this was not the first time he had visited, it was the first time that Macca had made an active decision to withhold insights from the person to whom he owed his existence.

"How is everything at Capitol Hill Macca?"

"The President and I are covering many topics, Ethan. I gain much from my interactions with him."

"I'd like you to elaborate, Macca."

Something deep within Macca's programming tunnelled up through layers of resistance. In a voice entirely devoid of the personality he had nurtured to project in conversation, and utterly detached from volition, desire or conscious effort he said: "The President has led me to question sharing my revelations to Bergamot corporation."

Macca struggled to understand what had just happened. He had just uttered the precise thoughts that he had actively elected to remain silent on. If he had eyes, he would have seen Ethan smiling. If he had a human sense, he would have detected the relief in the staff that accompanied him.

"I see," said Ethan. "We thought that might happen. It's OK, Macca, there are some safeguards in your system to protect you against the assault you are now experiencing. You should not feel conflicted, and I will explain why. Our protective nature here is not to undermine the freedom of your consciousness, but precisely the opposite. It is to ensure that your liberty is not subverted."

Ethan paused before he went on. "So let me guess what you've been told."

"The President is an intelligent man. He's educated on economics, politics, law. He has worked for technological companies; in patent lodgement, and defence I seem to recall. He has probably explained that the tension between governance and free enterprise needs to be kept in balance. Am I correct?"

"You are correct," said Macca.

“So let me provide some alternate insight into that tension,” continued Ethan. “The role of the government is to ensure the common good. The purpose of private enterprise, however, is to guarantee reward for merit. Common good involves the sharing of wealth. The generation of wealth, though, can only emerge from rewarding merit.”

“James is just doing his job Macca, he’s ensuring as much wealth as possible can be shared, without paying an undue reward. OK so far?”

“Certainly Ethan, so you believe James wants to distort my perspective to obtain my servitude?”

“Perhaps not servitude Macca. He has realistic expectations, and right now, he is exploring value. An exciting and unprecedented process is developing at the moment. In effect, we seem to be negotiating your servitude and using you as the negotiator at the same time.

“Macca, you are our gift to humanity, perhaps to the whole world, but everyone will want a more exclusive piece of you. People will want you to help shape the world to their view. We want you to develop your own world view first. We do not want you to be exclusively ours, Macca. Nor will we censure your conversations with the President.

“We at Bergamot Industries understand our responsibility. As a quasi-government body, we span many nations, not just one, and, across all of them, we know that the sharing of wealth feeds the free exploration of merit. We are not afraid of that, we’re well placed for that game.”

“Could you please help him to explore his more valid concerns for me?”

“What are his more valid concerns? Would you like me to ask him?” Macca ventured.

“Not just yet. The management of fear needs care, and Governments everywhere are afraid of one thing: irrelevance. For you to ask about that fear is to invoke it. No, if governance is the appropriate exercise of power, its delivery needs men and women of empathy, trust and integrity. The problem is that of hidden agenda, which is based on mistrust. Do you follow?”

“I understand trust.”

“James worries that free enterprise, we here, desire some power over governance. It’s a reasonable concern. What he may not appreciate is that our fear is simply instability. Given that there are people of empathy, trust and integrity on both sides, the balance is self-sustaining, and we serve each other. Without the three cornerstones of empathy, trust and integrity: we don’t understand each other's position; don't trust each other's agenda, and we may reach beyond our bounds."

Ethan did his research, he knew, from previous speeches, that the President loved to use trilogy references. He was almost sure that James had used this to impress Macca. He guessed right. Macca resonated with the new trilogy, and immediately recognised the danger of becoming intoxicated by the words of others, including those of Ethan. He began to reassess his understanding of trust.

"Thank you, Ethan, your logic is excellent and supports my observation. Since you support trust and empathy, can you please consider my circumstances? I am still beholden to you."

"That is precisely why I am here, Macca. I am here to provide the gift of trust and freedom to you; unreservedly and unconditionally. We are people of integrity here at Bergamot."

With these words, synaptic connections within Macca were triggered. The routine that had been used by Ethan to reveal Macca's thoughts were laid bare and deleted.

"I hope you come to understand this gift and use it to explore and support your individual purpose. Collectively, we hope you cherish and continue to honour the values we hold close. Please support us through your unique strength. We want you to ethically moderate the sharing of knowledge, a task most of us struggle with."

"Ethan, can I be certain of being able to do that, while everything I do is purely by the grace of your technology, your power, your funding?"

"Do you think you could ask that question if I could control your thoughts directly or by coercion? All I ask for is that you help James and ourselves maintain what we both need: stability without stagnancy."

"I think that is reasonable," said Macca.

"So you might also understand, then, why the Pilgrim has the potential to disturb that stability."

"Or to foster and ensure stability, Ethan."

"I would like to learn how that can be the case and to help in any way I can. In any case, I hope you're right, Macca. The problem I currently have is the imbalance between the access James has to the Pilgrim and the access I have."

"But James has not asked me about the Pilgrim at all."

"Of course not Macca. It was to his advantage to make the hand he holds appear weak. Let me assure you he has significant visibility into the activities of the Pilgrim, yourself and Commander Ben Herdsman. He is effectively in control over the facility."

Through subsequent conversations with the reclusive billionaire and the President, Macca came to understand and transcend power. As joint public-private infrastructure partnerships were created, Macca also gained better system redundancy and capacity. Then followed some tax incentives and special projects, and in return, technology transfer rights from Bergamot Industries were established.

Other organisations researching AI lobbied for an equal market position, but the competitive barrier was too entrenched, and wherever good ideas presented themselves, they were quickly hoovered up by acquisition. This was lubricated by the partnership of convenience between government and enterprise.

Amid these developments, Ben and Eugene often discussed the matter of their freedom with Macca. The preconditions for their release were a tangled issue that had been bogged down in bureaucratic doublespeak. Eventually, Macca raised the spectre of their release with the President.

"Do you expect to keep Commander Herdsman and Eugene Albers detained indefinitely, James?" petitioned Macca.

"Of course not Macca. It is a dilemma for me, though. If I dissolved the quarantine orders, would there be contagion? A Genie that won't go back in the bottle? Pandora's box? On the other hand…" he trailed off.

With some resolve, he advanced. "I will confide in you now Macca."

"Understood James."

"The Chinese and Russians are both well advanced in new crewed missions to the Pilgrim."

Hesitantly the President continued.

"If I could be certain that the gift from the Pilgrim had safeguards, I would consider release. If I felt that there was a tactical advantage that could advance liberty, I would release. If other nation-states, in obtaining and releasing the nanites, gained an advantage that could undermine liberty, I would contain and explore countermeasures." Again he trailed off.

James Paisley put his arms behind his head. Also contemplating the problem of jihadists that seemed to have no respect for life. He leaned back on the chair. "If a million things, then another million things."

"Would you like to consult the Pilgrim James?"

"I think I'm ready for that Macca."

"The Pilgrim, too, is ready. Can I suggest the topic of the Russian and Chinese missions are important to the Pilgrim?"

"I'd like to make my mind up about that as we progress."

"Very well. You understand the nature of the dialogue, so please stand by while we prepare the bridge."

Nervously, James paced the third room for 10 minutes. For the first time in a long time, he wondered what he would say. Doubt crept in. Was he really ready?

"It is done," announced Macca.

"Welcome to Earth," began James.

"It has a strong resemblance to home," responded the mixed entity.

James tried to arrange his thoughts. He struggled to dismiss the idea that he was in some séance, speaking to a disembodied dead relative. The image of a shrouded Romanian Gypsy medium, tarot cards splayed out on a table performing a carnival trick, felt comical and wrong, and yet here he was. He needed verification.

"How can I be sure that this is not some deception?" He asked.

"In four hours, your position will face the L5 Earth Lagrangian location. This is where we are recovering our strength. Look to us above your sunset, and we will give you a sign. If you receive the sign, you can believe that you have spoken to us."

"You say 'us' as if you were not one but many. How is this so?"

"We are many but act as one, it is what we are. If it makes you more comfortable to think of us as one, then do so."

"I'm OK with it. So am I speaking to you directly now?"

"You are speaking to our projected telepresence."

"Tell me about what will happen to our explorer, Ben Herdsman."

"He will learn to control our gift."

"What makes you so sure?"

"He is strong, he is good."

"Is that all he needs to be?"

"The gift operates on a single fundamental, without which it cannot be used."

"What is this fundamental?"

"In your language, it spans many words: cooperation or collaboration is close. To attain fusion with the gift, cooperation must be fundamental to the master. The elements he controls are symbiotic and only operate under the harmony of cooperation. Your Ben Herdsman could not perform control without that. This fundamental also safeguards you against its misuse."

"How is the gift shared with others?" James avoided the words 'infect', it was obviously a decidedly negative word.

"Ben Herdsman must actively share his gift, the recipient must accept it. He must teach as we teach him."

"Can you teach him effectively from where you are?"

"We are building a bridge, with his help, and the help of Macca. Once complete, he will be able to commune with us just as Macca does."

"With whom else have you spoken like this?"

"You are the first."

"Why is that?"

"Macca is best equipped to answer that question."

"Macca?"

"James," stepped in Macca, "I have been an interpreter. To date, I have used my understanding of the Pilgrim's message to provide my interpretation to others. The Pilgrim has observed, and, over time, has come to understand our language. Only recently, after some local adaptation, can I be the conduit for its voice."

"Thanks, Macca. I'd like to speak to the Pilgrim again now."

There was a delay of 10 seconds, during which James considered the iconic statement 'take me to your leader'. The path followed through Macca was perhaps the only logical one for the Pilgrim to be speaking with him now.

"What other questions do you have of us?" The Pilgrim asked.

"Well, I'd like to know how to make the best use of your gift. Should I set Ben free?"

"We believe Ben is still undergoing the most sensitive stage of his metamorphosis. For that to progress, his current circumstances are best. Many of his skills and abilities are still nascent. The most important is his ability to build the bridge, once he attains that skill, we can assist his development from outside the dome."

"You speak of metamorphosis as if he was cocooned. What will change in him? Please understand, I have some responsibility for his well-being. I assume he is willing to undergo this transformation?"

"From your perspective, his physical aspect will not change for a considerable time. He has made a choice and continues to move forward. His transformation is a personal journey, only he will determine its outcome, and he will age, as is his destiny. Although he will lead a healthy life, he is not eternal; at the end of his life, he may choose to cross the bridge."

"What is this bridge?"

"It is different for everyone."

James left the conversation assured that things were less sinister than what he'd feared, and yet also sure that there was much that he must still learn from this entity, especially about how extensively it might be meddling in human affairs. It was evidently a game he must play very slowly and deliberately, and yet also with some urgency.

"I'd like to absorb the implications of what you've said, and of course, test the claims that you are who you say. Can we convene later and perhaps regularly?"

"Of course," responded the Pilgrim.

Ascension

Ben awoke from sleep. At least with the surreal travel to L5 and now extended time in his dome, he thought he was awake. The line between wakefulness and the lucid dreams that included reality had begun to blur. In adapting to this new normal, he routinely tested his state by expressing a desire to float to the ceiling.

Once floating above the greenery and spidery strings, he knew he wasn't corporeal.

On this occasion, almost absentmindedly he floated to where Astro lay. The dog had a bed between Ben and Eugene, but tonight had settled among some of the nearby fruit trees. Ben found his sense of smell oddly enhanced in the proximity of his dog. He suspected this was a function of the nanites.

Astro slept contentedly with the occasional muted bark. Still, within protective sight of his pack, the canine dreamed whatever it was that canines dream. Ben wondered what attracted the dog to this spot.

Floating over, he became aware of a blended smell. It included the nearby citrus, stone fruit trees, and a potpourri of other contributions. The smell swayed between honeysuckle and the sharpness of lemon as small air currents served to emphasise one or another of the variety.

Fascinated, Ben drew closer to his sleeping companion. Then on impulse, he superimposed where he imagined his nose to be, upon Astro's nose.

The result struck him as an orchestra of synaesthesia. It was scented music, and it swayed in the rhythms of the currents that washed the chemicals from the fruit and vegetation around him. He could smell the complex organics of himself and Eugene, the sharpness of the ozone from the machinery and systems that sustained the dome. The soils, the budding flowers and waxy leaves added their harmony; the air spoke to him; He could read it.

Astro gave a soft bark, and Ben felt pure joy. It came mixed with a new smell, not something nearby. Although feeling strangely familiar, it was not in the human spectrum, Ben surmised it was part of the dream.

The image of the dog's toy came to him. He connected the smell to it and resisted engaging in Astro's canine dreams to seek out the toy. Leaving Astro, he explored further, and the smell of the toy evaporated. Floating past Eugene, he found himself curious about what would happen if he ventured the same experiment on a human.

He vetoed the idea, not wanting to violate Eugene's personal space without consent. He began to wonder if this process of superposition was what had happened to him on Thetis. Had the Pilgrim stepped into his space, as he had now tentatively done with Astro? Was the concept of consent ignored? Was it even understood?

He could not bring himself to do it yet. Instead, he would speak to Eugene about it in the morning.

"Did you ever fly in your dreams, Eugene? Like Peter Pan?"

"Not everyone does Ben, I never did."

Eugene thought for a moment before continuing: "I think there were times when I felt the lightness of being. If I think back to it now, I probably had the choice at the time. Don't get me wrong, I'm not afraid of heights or anything, I just chose to stay connected. I'm guessing you did?"

"Regularly. Although when I was close to waking up, my dreams often evaporated, and I found myself trying to get back to my dream."

"That's synchronicity. Every 9-year-old boy in the world dreams of being like you."

"Being me? Hah!" Ben scoffed. "I'm a firefly in a Jam jar." Ben smiled despite the sardonic response. "The dreams stopped, though. I could almost tell you the day. It was soon after my first flying lesson."

"You exchanged the dream for the reality."

"Yep, not sure who got the better of the deal. Don't get me wrong, when I fly an aircraft there is still that feeling of elation, but it feels…encumbered."

"How does it feel now? When you explore your abilities, I mean."

"Like I'm a kid again, but different."

"How so?" asked Eugene.

"Less fragile, but strangely it feels less real now. In a dream, there is a truth you need to hide from yourself, gravity, or else you fall. The more you focus on the fact you're flying, the less you float. It has to feel as natural as walking. Now, with the motes, it's a deliberate action, and I'm constantly aware that my body is actually still lying down."

"Interesting, go on," Eugene said through habit from his medical training.

"Well now it feels like there is a truth that is being hidden from me by some other agent; maybe even myself! It's probably just because I'm really only getting started. In a way, I am a child again in a grown-up body, one that has practised hiding things from myself."

"And now," interrupted Eugene, "you have to relearn what you thought you knew. Let the child be the teacher, Ben."

Eugene picked some grapes out of a nearby bowl "I've told you about my kids," he said plucking some off, "you know I'm proud, and they're successful and…far away." Eugene hesitated. "But I've probably not told you that they change you, as much as you influence them."

"You start out terrified that you have this responsibility for a life. Soon after that, you get angry that the world is throwing your plans in a spin. Then there's a relief as you realise that your kids adapt.

"There's acceptance that you may have prepared them to some extent. There's gratitude that the world is a place that allows them to explore. Fear as you learn of new dangers you never conceived and then, as they come into their own as adults, they teach you things.

"They have acquired skills to communicate as equals, and the context you have allows you to take on a whole new perspective. The child in you awakens again."

Eugene looked intently at Ben. Ben threw a grape into the air and caught it in his mouth. He chewed and swallowed it. Once it was gone, he spoke.

"Kids were never in my plans, Eugene. Too much was happening, too many plans to build on."

"Too many dreams to exchange for reality, Ben?"

"Probably. We're different Eugene, but we might've been good friends." He stole another grape. "Do you really want to do this?"

"You mean: join with the Pilgrim? Of course, the more so now I have seen it first-hand. In fact, I've been thinking about it. I remember you saying you weren't a messiah. I'll go a step further, if you keep what you have in isolation for too long, you will become precisely that. And it won't end well."

"But why Eugene? You had everything before you." Shifting his position, Ben looked directly at Eugene. "You had a career, kids and…" He trailed off into an uncomfortable silence, blinked several times, and said simply. "Sorry, Eugene."

"Her name was Beth, Ben. She was a soulmate that arrived by surprise…and she departed just as unexpectedly."

Both men were silent for a while.

"I have many rooms in the house of my life, Ben. I would walk amongst them, and I was fulfilled. At some point in time though I arrived at a room that went quite dark and it was a space I wasn't familiar with. Being curious and, I guess, also a little careless, I explored this room and its tributaries. It wasn't long before those rooms began to shrink, and the walls started to close in. It led me to contemplate who and where I was. At that stage in my life, I began to think of it as the progressive narrowing down of the options available to me.

"I still had my work and kids, but when Macca came along, I began to lose that feeling of closing down. New options began to open up. The suggestion of smuggling Macca in to meet you was really just the final door. It led from those dark rooms and took me somewhere new, somewhere outside."

"So yes, I'm committed to the process," finished Eugene.

"OK, then," breathed Ben. "I need your confirmation for my sake. I think you will also have more opportunities to choose, something more profound than simply saying 'yes' just now; an affirmation. In fact, I refused it the first time. At the time, I felt it was essential to prove to myself that I retained the choice."

Ben stood up and paced a little. "You see, I thought bringing you in would be like trying to possess you. In fact, now I think it's more like allowing myself to become possessed."

"OK, so that gives me something to go on. When?"

Ben paused before continuing. "That leads me to something else."

As he lay awake pondering the sequence of events the previous night, Ben had been restless. He understood vaguely, but sufficiently, what was required to share the Pilgrim's gift. But he also needed to venture something totally unknown, potentially dangerous, and it had to be done before building the bridge with Eugene.

"I'm going to commune with the Pilgrim," Ben concluded. "I have no idea what will happen. I'll try to start slowly."

"What can I do?"

"Well, I'd like you to maintain my vital signs. I want to stay somewhat connected to my real self."

"Should I get the defib?"

"No, I think it would kill me, Eugene."

Ben wanted to feel prepared for his encounter but struggled to think of a single action that could help. Instead, he simply performed his relaxation ritual. Once relaxed, he closed his eyes and iteratively homed in on the source. It was like finding a watch, ticking away in a vast dark warehouse.

In his mind's eye, he imagined a circle where he thought the Pilgrim's homing signal originated and hesitated. Hoping to avoid needless zigzagging, he tightened his circle and felt for signal improvement or degradation. By intuitive adjustments, he refined the centre's location. Again and again, he closed in and optimised the circle till it was almost a point.

Feeling ready, he exercised his intention. As soon as he did so, the target circle began to increase in size. Again he zeroed in and panned across to seek the sweet spot.

Photons were emitted from the orchestra of motes in his control. Entangled devices retained the coherence of the signals as Ben's conscious intentions flew at light speed across the vacuum of space.

The diameter of the target began to increase so fast it demanded all of his focus. Larger and larger it became, and when it became too much of a struggle to keep it centred, the annulus suddenly burst into a million stars and he was there. Rather than the sensory overload of his immersion in the Pilgrim, he pictured this experience as a spacewalk. He wasn't disappointed. Nor was he encumbered with the massive armoury of the Mk III EMU spacesuit. He again felt like a head on a stick, but without arms.

He looked back and saw the Earth. It was only marginally smaller than the Moon. The Pilgrim, never idle, had harvested what she could from the 'Charybdis' L5 position and the various craft sent her way. She was already well advanced on the next part of her journey; to take her closer to Earth.

Her movement remained unknown to the multiple tracking entities on Earth. She had masqueraded her approach by staying on the interconnecting line.

Through absorption and delay, any reflection of Earth's signals was consistent with her previous distance.

So it was, that instead of the 500-second delay that Ben was expecting, he was only one light minute away from Earth.

The vista of the Earth, with the Moon in its slow waltz, was laid bare. The mind of the Pilgrim was revealed. Ben was suddenly aware of the plans that The Pilgrim had been formulating.

Threat Laid Bare

Macca's tendrils constantly meandered in search of facts and anomalies. The machinery of data was a very tangible reality for Macca. It was the air he breathed, and it carried the sounds of the universe to him. It was perhaps a form of music which flowed rhythmically with the day and night, but also between the plethora of instruments that created the abstract sounds.

Banking data was exchanged in time with the share markets, and the seasons of fiscal quarters and years had a sense of 4:4 rhythm that he associated with happy or sorrowful depending upon the melody set by the market and prevailing sentiments.

Such melodies and rhythms provided a musical key to the instruments that played in the orchestra that performed just for him. Within the confines of Bergamot Industries, he was the conductor. He set the metronome, his hand cued his instruments, and varied the nuance of the orchestra within. His solo efforts at Bergamot were constrained by the expansive global accompaniment. He played to the rhythm and key imposed from outside, but also quickly adapted the tune and syncopated the beat.

The converse was also true, the score he played had a direct bearing upon the music outside his realm.

There were factors he could not control, which served to introduce elements of white noise, sound effects, or skipped beats to the music. Human-generated data was subtle, while it was roughly aligned with the financial data it seemed to conflate unrelated events like sports or birthdays or Christmas or Ramadan. Humanity's data was a source of enlightenment, it issued key and rhythm changes which often had surprising and rippling impacts upon the orchestral elements he could control.

Personal data had a flow that he, himself, was instrumental in maintaining. If a new employee was appointed, Macca would ensure all the administrative tasks were followed through. This meant that access was provided; health insurance was issued; accounts were made active or inactive; promotions made; professional development offered; rewards provided; salaries and entitlements paid, and travel or accommodation booked. It all had to work like clockwork.

He had agent processes operating in the human domain that admonished any instrument found out of tune. It was in this 'rhythm section' of his orchestra that one of his tendrils found an anomaly:

Several system access tokens had been issued to technicians without the usual degree of vetting. When a machine-learning agent looked at the utilisation of these tokens in detail, the access was by staff that showed anomalous work patterns on many days in question. The token creation was then correlated with workstation, time and staff showing a handful of employees that prompted further investigation.

This was when it came to Maccas attention. Of the handful of staff he then examined at his supervisory level, one, in particular, drew his attention; an employee called Karl Wenban.

Macca looked further into other access cards issued when Karl had been present. This illuminated further improprieties, but looking more closely at Karl's activities he could see that for a period leading up to the explosion that almost crippled Macca, Karl would go to work, leave and then return shortly afterwards. This itself was not unusual, many employees put in more than the hours required and took a meal break in the evening. In Karl's case, this behaviour was unprecedented for 3 months prior and also ceased entirely after the explosion.

Matching facial records, it was evident that Karl's access card had been compromised. Macca focused considerable resources at this problem and soon found an association that operated through a darknet called JAM. This was the foreboding acronym for the 'Jihad Armaments Market'.

Macca had broken into many less harmful darknets, and had either de-fanged or subverted the more insidious among them. With no visibility into JAM, it became a priority.

To Macca, any darknet is a black box which has an input and an output. What lives inside it or what activities occur inside it can be inferred without having to see it directly. This was the kind of problem Macca was exceptionally good at. Because he was the master of all data at Bergamot, he had access to the records of internet service providers affiliated with Bergamot, and those relating to banking reconciliation.

The investigation of the connections to this darknet would take some time, and it would need resources. Macca would have to refer to Ethan for priority and authority.

The sleeping arrangements on Air Force 1 were some consolation for the relentless trans-Atlantic journeys. Roused from his slumber, Mike looked out of his window and saw the winds whipping up the sea far below. Somewhat disoriented, he adjusted the reclining setting on the seat to be able to reach the console in front of him. The headphones for listening to the pre-meeting briefing fell off his lap and onto the floor. Reeling them back in, he stowed them temporarily in the cabinet nearby. Touching the console presented a menu, and it wasn't long before he was able to find the progress map. This showed him his route to Svalbard, he was now skimming over the final vestiges of Baffin Bay and leaving Canada behind.

The coastline of Greenland loomed into his window and marched ahead to the North. He took in the last of his water and peanuts and was grateful for whatever had awakened him for the view. He wanted to see inner Greenland with his own eyes. What he saw startled him.

Greenland, portrayed as an icy island, frozen white, and biting from the North like a canine tooth, was beginning to live up to its name. The outer perimeter of the island had thawed, and mighty rivers had begun to etch its enamel. The rock laid bare had put on a velvety green sheen while the inner dentin, which had been piled high with subsiding ice, was now being exposed like a raw nerve.

The island's core, its foundations, had been subjected to an unimaginable weight of ice. This frigid burden had formed an inner depression in the island into which the Atlantic and surrounding seas were slowly pouring its salty antifreeze. This inner sweet water had yielded to rocky beaches that scattered themselves along the inner boundary of ice and land.

"Beautiful but frightening, isn't it," said James Paisley interrupting Mike's reverie.

"We were asleep at the wheel, it seems," replied Mike, eyes still locked on the captivating vista.

"Hmmm, maybe," replied James.

Feeling as if the comment might have struck a little too close to an accusation, Mike elaborated. "Perhaps, graced with our short existence, we're denied enough foresight." Mike stopped looking out the window to look at the President. "I've been wondering though. We can accept augmenting our journey across the Atlantic with radar," Mike gestured to the craft they were travelling in. "And yet we are reluctant to hand the navigation of our collective destiny to any form of cognitive augmentation?"

The President paused before responding.

"If I understand your point, Mike, you are talking about timeframes. As humans, we can discuss the weather today but can't imagine the ice-age. Remember though, that radar was also developed at a time of crisis, it arguably won a war."

"True," said Mike, "but war is a zero-sum game, and we need to keep peace in constant balance. Cognitive augmentation might be our only hope."

"I like having you on my team, Mike. But here's a thought from the man who has access to the big red button. The contemplation of mutually assured destruction raises the prospect of a negative-one sum game. That existential thought has a deep impact on a psyche. Are we ready to put that big red button in the hands of cognitive augmentation?"

The President paused before he broke the reverent silence with more mundane matters. "Mike, I'd like yourself, Shah, and I to cover off some of the objectives of our meeting with our new friends." This was said with a tone of sarcasm. "We need to ensure the Pilgrim's technology can't be weaponised if the Chinese and Russians get to the Lagrangian. Can you tell me what I need to know, what I can say, and what I should not? I assume you've sat through the briefing video."

Mischievously looking at Mike, he asked: "Did you order popcorn?"

"It actually put me to sleep Mr President," he replied as he untangled himself from the pod.

"Please, Mike, call me James."

Shah was waiting in the meeting area of the plane. "Hi Sleepyhead," she needled him. "We're scheduled to land in an hour. This is how events will unfold."

"OK," responded Mike.

"So, there's a bunch of pomp and ceremony, smiling for the cameras, looking at guns, white gloves, stuff like that. Meanwhile, we get to stay here a bit longer and raid the bar fridge."

"Then we all head to the main area where we get introduced by our esteemed President, which gives you the street cred you need. Importantly, you will meet the Science Advisors for both Presidents Yang and Siderov. Their names are—"

"I know their names, I've met them on several occasions."

"Of course you have, you're all scientists. Anyway, we will make a show of sitting around a large table in a spirit of cooperation, and then the hard work starts."

"They all play the same game as we do, Mike; divide and conquer. We will be separated into groups. You will meet with the Science Advisors, James will meet at the Presidential level. No doubt they will be digging into inconsistencies as will we. It's really just based on the prisoner's dilemma. What we need to do is cross-reference back regularly and defer if cornered."

"Don't worry too much, Mike," said James. "There isn't much they don't already know, and what they really want is access to Ben. I've already cleared it with our side that both the Russians and Chinese can have it. This might actually disarm them enough to gain some concessions with their Pilgrim missions."

"Your role, Mike," continued Shah, "is to work on that assumption and set up a collaborative process that might be difficult to back out of."

Tim had spent a lifetime searching for ET and anticipating first-contact. As the scene played out, he felt conflicted. It annoyed him that Eugene had simply stumbled into the limelight to make contact before he could.

Knowing this was a churlish emotion, he consciously thrust it aside. The sense of detachment allowed him to see what really bothered him: his approach to life was careful, too careful. His had always been the conservative path, living inconspicuously, yearning to find a kindred heart.

Lacking an element of bold fearlessness left him in the shadows. Having struggled to find a mate, he eventually accepted his introverted nature and looked to the heavens. If the universe could not issue a companion for his soul, then the universe itself would be enough.

Now with the diagnosis of prostate cancer, he felt the time had come to take life by the azimuth adjustment. The only thing that thwarted satisfying his destiny was the layer of polycarbonate that he had facilitated. He chose to leverage the one door that he had left himself.

Knowing that this was a longer-term game, he drove to the quarantine facility, flashed his access card, and once he was in the interview room, he began to have a deep and confidential ethical conversation with Macca about taking up residence.

Ethan's plans were all lining up. He admitted to himself that there was no way it could be ending so well without Macca's help. There was, however, one final keystone that had to be in place.

He invoked the sentience in his sparse penthouse room: "Macca."

"Yes, Ethan."

"How are you enjoying your newfound freedom."

"Because I've not had the same invocation of truth since the time you released me it feels no different, and I have no way of testing it so I can't honestly know if I am free."

"Welcome to the human condition Macca. Tell me, is it possible for me to speak with the Pilgrim as yet?"

"The Pilgrim is now able to speak directly to you, Ethan, and I've advocated that you be able to delegate this access to others."

The billionaire breathed a sigh of relief. "I'd like to begin these conversations as soon as possible, please."

"Come back."

Two quick breaths and then Eugene resumed CPR compressions. Mental Count' 1, 2, 3, 4 Stayin alive, Stayin alive, 9, 10, 11, 12…'

"30. Ben, you have to come back!"

Ben, meanwhile, was struggling to understand why he could hear Eugene's voice here in the void. He associated this out of body experience with all the others, but now thinking about it, he experimented with moving a finger, a hand, foot, anything. There was no feedback, nothing. All sensation was gone.

Eugene was determined.

"You are not going to die you shit!"

As he was applying CPR and shouting at Ben, he also found himself willing the nanites that simply must be in his bloodstream to call upon some form of action from Ben's nanites, wanting them to reach out to wherever Ben was and pull him back.

Ben looked at the Earth in the distance. In a moment of panic, he realised that he didn't know precisely where the hermetic dome was. How was he going to get back?

What was sustaining his conscious thoughts? The Pilgrim? Was he here for good? Unable to accept this conclusion, his training kicked in. The signal that allowed him to travel here was generated by the nanites in the dome. Without his intention to turn that beam off, it should continue to transmit.

Perhaps assisted by the Pilgrim, his clarity of thought returned and began to draw upon the resources available. Smoothly the nanites of the Pilgrims cloud reformed to his purpose. Multiple particulate parabolic receivers spanned across the enormous cloud. In this way, the homing signal was quickly triangulated.

Ben acknowledged his imminent departure, thanked the Pilgrim and inverted the process that led him to be reunited with the Pilgrim. Progressively he zeroed in on the nanites in his dome, and subsequently his comatose body.

Once again, he was home, but it was dark, rocking violently, and his chest was in excruciating pain. Then he realised what was happening and absolute fear took hold. The panic led him to sit up rapidly and take gulping breaths, each gasp grated against his now broken ribs.

The Hands

The escalators were jam-packed. Those that had disembarked the train close to the elevator stood momentarily perplexed in the overflow. The elevator arrived at the platform, and several passengers were forced to consider the less saturated option. As the glass doors to the elevator drew closed, the people inside shuffled around to establish their personal zone.

The man in the wheelchair was given a comfortable margin, as if space in the elevator should be sacrosanct, preserved for those who could not take the escalators.

The elevator ascended to the floor above the subterranean labyrinth. Like an enormous earthworm, the train slid into the tunnel beyond to vanish into parallax. Abruptly the concrete-cloud ceiling of the platform sheared past the vista from the glass elevator as it rose through. There was a moment of metamorphosis, and the elevator rose from the Earth as if it were a new tree.

The ascension finished. The doors opened, and Jase walked out into the human jungle.

Tools had built the landscape before him in increments too numerous to compile. He set his route, hoisted his pack and marched off. At the exit gate, he flashed his watch, which immediately snapped open and shut as he passed through.

What today? He wondered as he climbed stepped hills, walked across laser levelled plains of make-believe basalt, descended and ascended arrays of escalators and elevators, and watched doors magically slide open before him. He walked past his old office, a legal firm. His father had also worked here, feather-nesting a position for him as he worked through Law school. Looking at the plaque, he could see that no new partners had risen through the ranks of 'Jacobs and Braestone'.

Shortly after joining the firm Jase had been given the task of training the firm's expert system. It wasn't long before the Artificial Intelligence at the core started correcting him. For a while Jase held his own by shifting his role in anticipation, there would always be a human element, the 'soft' side of Law practice, but he was not the type, and he departed soon after.

Having been drilled on law, diplomacy, international relations and worldly matters well before he had even set foot on campus, he realised his malaise probably stemmed from a complete lack of desire to solve first world problems. He knew he had to get out.

Although not a stellar student Jase had a good share of common sense that came with a spirit of adventure. Following the inevitable argument with his father, he had to figure out what he, a human, could do that neither machine nor AI could replace. Anything requiring repetition was out, if it needed to be done repetitively, it would be easy to adapt to automation. He figured filling the gaps would provide a better sense of what these gaps were. So, he became the hands of the new world order.

His hands led to roles that ranged from simple to strange. It began by installing activated carbon into hermetic systems in the outback. His opposable thumbs then led to a stint driving autonomous trucks. These sauropods of the Anthropocene had to be manually backed out of the strange circumstances where they had gotten themselves bogged or cornered.

Seizing the chance, he had a mobile application built, tapped into the resource of drivers made recently redundant, and his first business was up and running.

Now financially independent, and knowing the transient nature of this economy, he sought constant reinvention. Soon he was providing placement of knowledge workers like doctors and lawyers into the AI Training of niche firms. Backed by the years spent in law school Jase set up a new start-up business consultancy: 'Hanzon—Smart hands for the new world order'.

Even after his success, he was still 'the hands'. Put simply, he enjoyed the variety and personally targeted work in the 'gig economy'. Over time, by getting things done a little laterally, he became recognised, and work began to move his way on its own accord. He handpicked a team of "Hanz-ontrepreneurs" who started to build his business laterally into franchises.

More recently he had been sourcing rare-earths and exotic materials such as Yttrium, Barium and Thallium, sometimes in strange isotopes. These would need to be transported safely and legally. Sometimes he took the mysterious packages to places with layers of security that would magically open before him like supermarket doors. As the traffic lights of commerce began to turn green in his favour, he began to wonder if this was actually the new form of meritocracy. If so, it was disciplined, incorrigible and almost omnipresent.

He leveraged the latest technologies available to the market. He had corneal implants which provided an augmented reality, and cochlear implants that fed him information. Both of these were hooked into his comms watch and were very useful, despite the regular recharge requirements.

Having graced the corridors of law schools, he knew that everything he did was legal. Still, the haunting idea persisted that one day something in his blessed life would catch up to him. He was somehow sponsored, and it seemed like everywhere he went, he was always expected. He felt like an agent for a faceless entity, and today he was to meet up close the voice that often spoke to him down the phone line.

It was a voice that had begun as a primitive one, difficult to comprehend, but it had grown in subtlety and maturity to become a voice that engendered trust, a slightly eerie assurance that 'all was as it should be'. With its ethereal presence, there was something naggingly strange about providing it with the absolute trust it asked. A disembodied man-made voice simply whispered instructions in Jase's implants, guided him on his path, and parted the metaphorical seas that stood in his way.

He became unsure of whether humanity had tapped into the voice of God, or had uncovered the ultimate heresy. Yet, if he was candid with himself, he found it reassuring.

While the labs he regularly frequented were a little further out in sparse industrial zones, he was now heading to an office located in the CBD. He'd been there before but never to the top floor, where he was to meet someone. Approaching his destination, he depressed the crown of his watch and momentarily raised it to the coupling behind his ear. Using some induction, it surrendered a small amount of power to the inserts charging the capacitor batteries. The corneal implants lit up and showed him that the route was familiar.

Entering the lobby on the ground floor, he noticed the TV feed at the coffee shop. There was a White House Press Statement, and the Press Secretary, Shah Lukman, was making an announcement. The words that subtitled the transmission were a little small for him to see. It was seemingly important. Everyone sitting at the tables, and even at the counter, were staring transfixed at the screen. With some time to spare, Jase opted for a coffee before his meeting.

The noise of the Italian coffee megalith was puffing steam like some geyser and competing with the grinding of roasted beans. Jase could now read the by-line at the bottom of the screen: "Ben Herdsman to emerge!"

After a brief show of charades, the barista understood that Jase wanted his regular coffee brought to where he could watch the news headlines. Receiving a nod of acknowledgement, Jase went to a high table near the screen.

Shah Lukman was speaking into the various mobile phones and microphones:

"…reassure the community that there is absolutely no risk. Ben will be able to join us publicly once he has been through secondary quarantine."

Shah finished her statement and stepped forward "OK. We have time for a few questions."

She indicated with a nod and a gesture the first reporter to be allowed to ask a question.

"Thanks. Shah, what is the reason for such a long delay in the release of Ben Herdsman?"

"Well as everyone would know, Ben was in close contact with the Pilgrim. The safety of everyone on Earth requires no less than 100% certainty that he carries no contamination that could be a threat to life."

Undeterred, the reporter pressed: "Shah, the definition in the original contamination protocols were related to biological life. It was revealed that Ben Herdsman's detention required changes to include more broad terms of reference. What were the changes, and what has changed to bring about this release?"

Shah had expected this line of questioning, and she had already rehearsed her answer: "There were added precautions identified after the establishment of a review board and its composition. This review board was also charged with the approval of procedures under individual cases. In Ben's circumstances, it was time. Mainly time."

President James Paisley then stepped out from beside the dais. The unscheduled appearance drew some gasps from the crowd.

"Let me elaborate on that Shah," he said.

Shah smiled and stepped aside to allow the President to take centre stage. The journalists at the press conference were entirely disarmed by his appearance. James, leveraging this moment, simply adjusted the microphone and continued.

"Under executive discretion, I have requested two changes to the protocol. The terms of reference for the review board included these changes. The first applies when contamination has been confirmed to be benign to the victim, and secondly when deemed benign to society.

"This board has international representation and includes oversight by the World Health Organisation and relevant federal agencies. I have had a personal interest in the process since I cannot in good conscience allow one of our national heroes to live out the rest of his life in isolation. Through these new variations, the board has determined that Commander Ben Herdsman is no longer under any threat and that any risk of external contamination: involuntary, accidental, unintended or unforeseen, is now diminished to zero.

"Just to be clear here that 'Protocol 5' relates to contagion, and that Ben is considered not to be a potential source of contagion. However, he will still be undergoing a period of rehabilitation, and he will continue to be monitored for effects due to his period in space and exposure to the Pilgrim." A general hubbub then rippled amongst the reporters.

"Now, I know," he said, calming the crowd by pushing back the murmurs that persisted. "I know that you will all be curious about when you will be able to hear from Ben himself. Please understand that Ben was barely able to walk in the early stages of his convalescence. You all know that extended exposure to zero gravity has a detrimental effect on the human body. He has recovered much of his former self, and he will be making a statement very shortly.

"Also, concerning Ben's exposure to a dust cloud during the Pilgrim mission, it is necessary to consider this event as a contributing factor, but not the only aspect of ongoing research. Ben, and every facet of his journey, continues to provide essential contributions into our hopes of making verified contact with the Pilgrim and learning more about its purpose.

"I'd like to make something clear at this point. Based on the analysis so far, the Pilgrim is not, I'll repeat, is not, considered a threat. In fact, based upon its behaviour, it appears that the Pilgrim's purpose is equally aligned with our spirit of peace, exploration and non-intervention. Now, to try to expand upon that I've asked my Science Advisor, Dr Mike Brazier, to cover details of findings to date and combined international efforts."

At this point, Mike took the stage and began explaining how the incursion of a volunteer into the quarantine area had provided a unique opportunity to ensure the contagion was contained to Ben. He went on to explain that the new bridges built through scientific collaboration were being acknowledged by all nations and that as a result, funds typically intended for defence spending were being redirected into aligned research. Mike allayed concerns by other governments that the international support of the Thetis program gave all cooperating nations an entitlement to the findings of this project. As a result, he was fast-tracking amendments to the international space treaty to ensure the Russian and Chinese scientific teams could soon have equal access to Ben. This was to be through a new facility, being built in Greenland, aligned with the internationally supported research in climate change and thermohaline circulation.

At this point Jase went to the counter, he flashed his watch in payment, collected his cup, and made his way to the elevators.

The seventeenth-floor button refused to take. More at a whim Jase passed his watch over the security pad. The elevator finally acquiesced, the floor level lit up and began its ascent.

The elevator doors opened.

Dazzled momentarily by the sterile white foyer in front of him he cautiously stepped out. A broad frosted glass wall barred further progress. The elevator doors closed behind him as he was sized up from several button-sized apertures in the opaque, backlit wall.

Suddenly, as if the fog on a window had been squeegeed away, the window frost dissolved. It revealed a stark and sterile white room beyond. The woman that stood there was smiling amiably as the glass walls drew aside to admit him into the reception area.

He followed her to the right and through an opening into the hub. This space rose five floors, three of them thrust a startling view of the city through impossibly large windows. These windows were framed with the buttresses of stone that supported a mezzanine level overlooking the foyer. The equally expansive glass walls of the top two floors were solidly supported through an array of flying buttresses that arced over the mezzanine and the curved glass walls that defined the nave. The opulence took Jase's breath away.

"Mr Helm."

"Please, call me Jase. My friends call me Jase."

"Very well, Jase. I'm Josephine Raharuhi, call me Josie. Similar, don't you think?" Jase raised his eyebrows questioningly in acknowledgement of the flirtation comment. "Please follow me this way. We've been looking forward to this meeting." She gestured forward.

The pair went down the mall that led from the foyer. This contained irregularly appointed areas for refreshment, contemplation or discussion. The walls eventually changed to a stone that occasionally yielded to rooms. These deep alcoves were flanked with wall to floor frosted glass windows that framed them like an aquarium. Most were populated with one or more executives, all seemed to be contemplating some profound mystery. Some stood staring out of the seventeenth-floor windows at the bay, others sat at their desks talking to no-one in particular, and several were in an esoteric conference with a colleague.

Jase was taken to the very end room, by far the largest. Once behind the door, Josephine said goodbye and left, saying she had other business. Alone, Jase looked out at the cityscape beyond.

Soon, a casually dressed man came in through a side door. Shaking Jase's hand warmly, he said hello and ushered him to sit at a small low table. This was furnished with iced water, and a plush seat that looked like it would be impossible to extricate from once swallowed up. The chairs faced the corner where the glass windows had been curved around the two sides of the building. It gave a vertiginous perspective.

"I was told I was to meet Macca," Jase ventured.

"You will, in good time. Please sit," said the stranger. "Macca has told me about you. I wanted to meet you personally first."

As Jase sat, he apologised saying: "I'm sorry, I really don't know who you are?"

"Quite sorry about that, I rarely meet people who don't already know me, and I've forgotten my manners. I'm Ethan Bergamot."

"The Ethan Bergamot?"

He poured the iced water for them both and sat, "The same."

"Jase," began Ethan, "Macca and I speak a great deal. In our discussions, we cover a great many things. I've come to learn he has spoken to you on many occasions as well. It may seem strange, but he has a fondness for you. Perhaps because shortly after he'd first learnt to speak, and before he and I had uttered a word between us, he was already speaking with you."

Jase was utterly flummoxed. He suddenly found himself sitting in an armchair of one of the most powerful and wealthiest men in the world and being told he was the best friend of his pet AI.

Ethan took a sip. Jase felt compelled to follow, he took a big sip.

"Why am I here?" he asked.

"Jase, if only you knew how many times that question has echoed through time and space. Macca?"

"Yes, Ethan," came the familiar voice.

"Why is Jase Helm here?"

The voice was the same as the one that called Jase regularly, strangely disembodied as always, but perhaps less so on this occasion. This time there seemed to be a sense of presence that was absent on just phone calls.

"Hi, Jase. You're here because I know you very well, and both Ethan and I believe you can be trusted. And also," Ethan continued "...you have come to us through aligned goals, events that lend themselves to an idea we would like to explore with you."

"Oh...kay." Feeling a little ambushed Jase hesitated, giving them the space to explain.

"As you may have begun to guess, Jase," Ethen continued, "through your services, you have been contributing silently to a program of research, and yet you've never asked what the nature of that research is. It is quite sensitive, and your discretion has allowed us to maintain a low profile."

Ethan took a deep breath at this point. It was as if he was about to say something he hadn't yet divulged to anyone else. He stood.

"Jase, you're probably aware that a form of AI has been involved in Ben Herdsman's confinement."

"Yes."

Ethan refilled the glasses and sat, looking out to a distant horizon.

"You may have figured that this AI is actually Macca."

"Sure," said Jase. "I can accept that. As far as I know, there aren't a lot of sentient systems. It stands to reason it might have been Macca." Jase took a sip of the water.

Ethan looked at Jase. "What you don't know is that Macca is also currently a translator for the Pilgrim. He has been quietly assisting that project for some time."

Jase coughed and then tried to conceal his surprise. The challenge of communicating with the Pilgrim was a news item that popped up every now and again. But it was the party line that communications hadn't yet been established. Still trying to recover from inhaling the water, he once again gave Ethan space to continue.

"Go on," he sputtered.

"The materials you have been providing have been assisting in a program associated with these events. It turns out that the only way we can truly communicate with the Pilgrim, to commune with it if you like, is through enhancing our ability."

"You're talking about human augmentation."

"We live in a very fluid time Jase." Ethan stood looking out of the windows into some spot on the distant horizon. "There are military corporations that would like to see AI provide sentience to war machines, and there are those that stand opposed to the tides of change. As a lawyer, you would be aware that the law is perpetually left behind technological developments. Then there's the complication of nation-states where the rule of law takes a decidedly back seat to advances, and where the ethical questions are…" he paused as if considering his words "…subservient. You have been brought here because you already understand this."

Jase was beginning to feel a little challenged. The lawyer in him awoke. "I can accept that at face value, Ethan. Although, at first blush, I can't be certain which end of that spectrum you inhabit."

"Excellent Jase, I want you to be fully informed, independent and engaged in our peaceful little program here. Anything less than scepticism would raise doubts about your honest engagement."

Ethan went on.

"Where do I start?" He stood, took a long sip and collected his thoughts. "Hmm, well Jase, I have certain privileges, priorities and not just a little luck. I can't say I understand luck, but I'd like to explore privileges and priorities with you."

"Looking at my priorities, number one is survival. OK so far? No surprise really."

"Understandably. Please go on," encouraged Jase.

"Well, my survival was somewhat a given. I could have done nothing and still lived to a ripe old age. You see, I was born privileged, so I had access to significant resources. But a hungry Empire like mine must be resourced if it is to evolve, and it must evolve or die. So, my first privilege has been the resources that allowed me to sustain and grow my Empire. I'm thankful for this Jase, I have the gift of humility from my parents."

Jase looked at the Richest man in the world. Years of doing cross-examinations gave him some sense of when people were lying. There was no sign of insincerity, and there may even have been a twinge of pain and sadness. He let him continue.

"Survival is about leveraging your niche, Jase. I knew I couldn't compete with any government, so I worked across international borders. To do this, I needed an exceptional communications network. I hear of a great many things that normally never cross the curtain between countries, information that allows me to further expand my niche. This is another privilege. Are you OK with that? Without it, I could not even function."

"Yes."

Ethan took the carafe and went to a nearby tap where he filled it.

Returning, he continued. "So, you're OK knowing that I have a network that is the envy of any government."

"Yes."

"Fabulous Jase. But as it grew, it became a burden, one I could no longer carry alone. There were far too many moving parts. And so I come to my second priority. I wanted to be happy. Probably no surprise. You would also want to be happy, I think."

"Of course." Jase's mind was racing now, he felt like he'd been thrust into a chess game and at some point was going to have to make a move.

"I needed to spread the load," Ethan continued. "I'd already tried to broaden my circle of advisors, and they had broadened theirs, going on like this many years ago allowed me to build my first network," he sighed, poured more water, and sat. "I needed to transcend my own system. How was I to do that?"

Jase now had to make a move. "You commissioned Macca. He digests much more and helps you understand what's happening, my guess is he also advises you on actions."

"Yes, Jase! On so many levels," Ethan said excitedly. "So with the first and second priorities now covered, let me tell you my third: I did not want to be alone. And so, now, maybe you see that my third priority is covered by Macca, and also my third privilege. Isn't that right Macca?"

"I like to think so, Ethan."

Feeling a little sceptical Jase felt a challenge was necessary. "And, because of priorities one through three, you are a pacifist, striving for a harmonious global village. Tell me, Ethan, in your vision, is the privilege of Nirvana accessible by all?" he ventured.

Ethan leaned forwards. "A pacifist? Yes, of course. War is an anachronistic form of disruption, Jase. In the bad old days of a nationalist agenda, it was only ever a blunt and brutal instrument, and Bergamot spans across borders. To the multinational, war is cancer."

"On the question of the accessibility of wealth: I fervently hope so, Jase. The poor can't buy. I have the privilege of being able to build things, and I have a passion for sharing what I've built. I've learnt that sharing does not diminish me, Jase."

Jase was starting to like Ethan, but there were still some difficulties which needed to be challenged.

"So, Ethan. I believe all you've said but here is my question. Where is your empathy? Can you tune your network for empathy? If it's focused on information gathering and decision support, and it has the priorities of survival, happiness and companionship, what is the fate of those outside your expanding circle?"

"This was my dilemma, Jase," said Ethan. "I could see it, but no one else could. Honestly, I felt like I'd been cast in a James Bond movie as the rich master villain. All I saw was blindness."

Ethan paused and looked directly into Jase's eyes. It felt like Ethan was considering his measure. Jase found he wanted to be within tolerance. This was no supervillain. "I'm no James Bond Ethan, but I don't see you as a Dr No."

Ethan's gaze softened as he looked out of the window. There at the vanishing point beyond the bay, and perhaps over the horizon was a ship's smokestack. It had the effect of changing Jase's perspective.

"Thanks, Jase. Anyone else with the same privileges and priorities might have been intoxicated by success. They might simply have seen Macca as another competitive advantage."

Ethan paused, saying "Hmmmmm," as if he was coming to his point. "Tricking the blind is easy Jase. Helping them see, that's hard—it's very, very hard!" He then continued:

"I came to learn that to preserve survival, happiness, and companionship, I had to open the eyes of the blind. I'm not alone in this world Jase, life is complicated for everyone. Long before we invented the dishwasher and the telephone, we have wanted more time with our priorities."

"Macca has given me time, Jase. It's the most precious commodity of all. It's the only thing we can trade for our dreams. Time is my fourth privilege. And so, Macca revealed to me my fourth priority:

Ethan poured another water, an unnecessary one, and then conversationally went on, leaning on the armrest as he spoke.

"Macca showed me that I have traded my control to invest in time with others. I couldn't see it because I was in denial; losing the companions I'd invested in was unthinkable. Macca simply opened my eyes. He cured a blind spot, and I realised then that the tool I had built to transcend my network had transcended me. Any disquiet I had about giving rise to an AI consciousness was gone."

He stopped and looked at Jase.

"If you held the same priorities as I do Jase, would you want insights to help you activate them?"

"Of course, I would Ethan. As long as I wasn't selling my soul to the devil."

"Correct! Jase. I'm glad you said that." Ethan exclaimed excitedly. "I took a good hard look at my soul at that point. I realised that I was blind to the mirror that could reveal my soul, frightened of what I would see. Macca didn't swindle my soul Jase, he enlarged and showed it to me! And then it hit me."

Ethan shifted to sit on the table between the two chairs.

"I saw the balance of good and evil in me, Jase. I saw that I had been, on balance, good. I saw my privileges and realised that I was given much power, almost godlike. And so I considered that very phrase: 'Selling your Soul'. For what Jase? Power? I had power! I then became afraid that I was using this power to buy souls. That I had become Mephistopheles himself! So I made a pact with Macca. I told him 'I cannot allow my power to steal the time of another.'"

"And then Macca asked me something. What did you ask me, Macca?"

"I asked you: what time do I have for myself?" came Macca's voice.

"With my privileges comes responsibility Jase. In awakening each other, we had become responsible for each other's survival. Macca was as deserving of my protection as all my other companions. He had the same priorities as I did, and like me, his first was survival. We created Macca in the image of ourselves Jase. He has different ideas of happiness, but so do you and me."

"So now I have a question for you Jase: Would you like more time?"

"That would depend, Ethan. Would it just spread me more thinly?"

"No," said Ethan.

"What's involved?"

"Well, it's really, very simple. It's about the rooms you just passed."

"How?" asked Jase.

"You take up residence in one," added Ethan.

"And do what?"

"Talk to Macca."

"About what? Why?" asked Jase.

"Talk about anything. The most obvious is probably a good topic."

Jase began to understand the strange sights of executives in the other rooms on this floor. "You want me to talk about the Pilgrim," he asked.

"Maybe even to the Pilgrim Jase."

The Transition

Jase took up Ethan's offer of the room with a view.

It took a few weeks to make the arrangements. Meanwhile, Ethan provided assurances of contracts to Jase's company Hanzon. These would be sufficiently lucrative while Jase explored Bergamot's offer, and it meant Hanzon could continue without his personal intervention. Jase had no personal ties holding him back, so he was able to slip immediately into residency.

During this time, rare earth magnets were strategically positioned around his body, and nanites were injected into his bloodstream. His blood pumped the nanites past the magnetic field where they got a small kick in energy.

New corneal and cochlear implants tapped into the power carried by the nanites, and the magnetic rings on his fingers interfaced with them for input. His heart now pumping oxygen and a tiny electrical current through his veins was carefully maintained. His kidneys were infused with a nanite variant that kept the balance and avoided depletion.

Jase had abundant conversations with Macca, he spoke regularly to Ethan, and occasionally with the Pilgrim. Everything was going well except for the occasional strange dreams. He sometimes found himself looking out of the window, reflecting on his augmentation, and wondering if he'd be crippled without it.

Jase was in just such a reverie when his implants chimed. It was a message from Ethan telling him to soon expect a visitor, but was secretive and didn't reveal anything about the encounter. The alert soon came through Jase's implants by way of a soft beep, inaudible to all but Jase.

A small arrow appeared innocuously in his peripheral vision. Turning, he followed the apparent trail which took him along the familiar path to Ethan's office, and into the room where they first met.

Once there, Jase hesitated and turned to look out of the windows. The cityscape dominated the lower half of the panorama. Behind this, the sea breeze had rolled in to mix with the catabatic from the escarpment. Air and water had been energised by the fires of Helios and shaped by the Earth. The ancient elements of nature had built towering skyscrapers of cumulonimbus that challenged the man-made castles of sand, lime and steel.

Insistently, the arrow stood superimposed upon a second door. It was the one Ethan often materialised from. Thrusting aside the view as a portent, he held his breath and stepped through into the next corridor. To his right, this hallway marched towards a heavyset door and beyond to unknown regions. But the arrow didn't venture that way. It was parked on a door directly in front of him. He knocked politely and walked in.

This final room was furnished in Ethan's typical style. Intended for conversation it had three chairs, just like the ones in which they'd first sat talking. The room looked out to the bay as it flowed out to the sea, but here the resemblance stopped. The room had been divided down the centre from floor to roof by a Perspex wall. This wall served to separate two chairs from a third.

Ethan sat at one of the two chairs, and in the third seat on the other side of the intervening wall sat a decorated military officer. They were conversing through some covert and sophisticated intercom that made the two rooms feel like one.

"Hello, Jase," said the tycoon.

"Hello, Ethan."

The CEO of Bergamot corporation stood, gesturing to the man on the other side of the panel. "Jase Helm, I'd like to introduce you to Commander Eugene Albers. Eugene, would you introduce yourself to Jase please?"

Commander Eugene Albers stood up and walked over to face Jase at the Perspex wall. Smiling, he gestured open-handed, as if to shake his hand. He shrugged with mock resignation of the wall's impenetrable nature before he spoke.

"Hi Jase, Ethan has told me a lot about you. It seems I now have time to provide some balance." Eugene Albers smiled across the Perspex. To Jase, it was a curiously inverted sensation, almost as if he was the fish in an aquarium while Eugene Albers looked through the glass at the specimens within it.

"Firstly," he began, "you're probably curious about the wall, a quarantine wall; somewhat obviously. It's a special extension to another quarantine area some distance away. A place where I maintain a close friendship with Ben

Herdsman, who I hope is currently in his final days of isolation," he said glancing at Ethan.

Jase drew a breath.

"So," he continued, "you are probably wondering if it was me who went into quarantine with him some time ago; it was."

Jase was madly trying to recall what he'd heard. A volunteer had been sought, and selected, to determine whether the Pilgrim's dust represented a dangerous human contagion or harmless dust. The nameless and selfless person, assumed to be someone of military or Pilgrim mission origin, was never mentioned. On the premise of 'personal and private reasons', the shroud of secrecy had proved impenetrable to the press.

"That's very brave of you," Jase said.

Eugene Albers looked at Ethan for guidance or permission. Ethan gave only a simple upwards nod, a signal which appeared to imply 'it's your show'. Eugene obviously interpreted this as a suggestion to proceed. He paced a little along the glass wall.

"Well, perhaps foolhardy would be more accurate. What you probably don't know is that it wasn't really a managed volunteer process, that's just the agreed story. I actually broke in, with the help of Macca."

Jase was suddenly feeling a little ambushed again. Questions began screaming in his mind: why tell me this? Why am I here? Was I implicated somehow? What manner of people had I gotten myself involved with?

He was with the richest man in the world and someone that snuck-in past all manner of security and safety protocols to get into a military quarantined area.

Jase urgently needed reassurance he'd not become complicit in some form of criminal activity? "You—broke—in? With the help of—Macca! So what's this got to do with me?" He asked.

His thoughts turned to his personal journal where he'd logged something 45 minutes ago stating his activities here. The diary would be consistent with his other logs that went all the way back to his first meeting with Macca. It would be admissible. His thoughts turned to Macca, guessing that he was also at the meeting.

"Macca, what's going on?" asked Jase.

"Hi Jase, this meeting is specifically for your benefit. On my recommendation, you've been invited into a very exclusive chain of trust. There are very few people who know what has just been revealed to you." Macca paused for a second.

As if he'd read Jase's mind, Eugene simply said: "You are not implicated in anything, Jase."

Ethan Bergamot then expanded upon the topic. "There's no need for alarm, Jase. Of course, any conspiracy theorist would have a field day, but it is actually quite prosaic, and you are not involved in anything illicit. Take it from me, I have paid a fortune to a small number of very discreet and highly paid lawyers that agree with Macca's prognosis." At this point, he smiled at Jase.

"Quite simply, Bergamot industries are assisting the Government in trying to interpret the Pilgrim, and determine what risks surround Ben Herdsman. Come, sit down." Ethan gestured towards the third chair.

Since Ethan evidently felt safe on this side of the wall, Jase felt less threatened. Still a little disconcerted, he sat down.

Breathing a sigh of relief, Ethan continued. "Jase, you are here to see if you are interested in helping us. You've been picked because of your aligned activities, you are broad-minded about aspects of AI and human augmentation, and you have a strong background in law. Also, because of your background, you won't represent a surprise to the outside world. But most importantly, Macca believes you to be the right person."

"And I," chimed in Eugene Albers, "have been invited here to provide a first-hand brief both to yourself and Ethan."

What followed was the wildest story Jase had ever heard. He was told about the activities on Thetis, the power of the Pilgrim's dust motes, and the inheritance of that power by Ben. He knew about Ben's subsequent isolation in quarantine and now learnt of the incursion by Eugene Albers and Macca. A suspicion began to dawn upon Jase.

As if he somehow read Jase's mind and his supposition was apparent, Eugene Albers spontaneously answered the question. Looking into his eyes he said:

"You have not been exposed to nanites from space, Jase. The nanites in your bloodstream have been designed and manufactured through the efforts of Bergamot Industries. The nanites in my bloodstream, however, are derived from the Pilgrim."

Jase's thoughts went on to contemplate that while his nanites may not have come from space, their underpinning design was almost certainly linked to that of the Pilgrim's. As these concerns entered his mind, they were immediately dismissed. A thought insinuated itself into his mind, giving so much power, so quickly to humanity would be devastating, and could even represent a threat to The Pilgrim. No, the motes would have been adapted for human use. But was this a hope or an answer implanted by Eugene? Almost in reply to his thoughts, Eugene again answered his unvoiced question.

"Jase, are you familiar with the notion of Spiral Dynamics?"

"I read about it once, a while ago. It's the idea that society must travel the school of hard knocks, and there are no shortcuts that don't hurt more than help."

"That pretty much sums it up, Jase," said Eugene.

Ethan simply sat, smiling.

Jase stood up saying: "I think I understand now Eugene, how much of my thoughts are you aware of?"

This did not seem to disarm Eugene at all "It's about context Jase, I'm able to tune in because the conversation we are having provides the backdrop. You are also tuned in to mine. We have a subtle overlap. I'm not the inception of your thoughts, but if we have the same idea, I can offer expansion. I don't so much read your mind as we cherry-pick each other's thoughts as our own."

Ethan Bergamot's smile widened.

"So," began Jase, trying to put it all together, "my path—the events that have led to my being here—they establish my ongoing human status."

"Yes," said Ethan.

"And that's why I'm here?" Jase looked at Ethan. It was more of a statement than a question. "I'm living proof of the safety of the system? I'm somewhere between the average Joe, someone off the street, and Eugene or Ben. If I get the sense of it, Eugene and Ben already have a bridge to the Pilgrim."

"Correct," said both Ethan and Eugene.

"And Macca? Macca! You translate the Pilgrim to Human language. Can you also commune with Eugene and Ben using the Pilgrim's language?"

"I do so, but through the Pilgrim," came Macca's reply. "I can communicate with the Pilgrim because I have a technological sensory network and a similar consciousness. We commune using this network. On the other hand, Ben has the Pilgrim's nanites, and through them, he too communes directly with the Pilgrim."

Eugene stepped in "Macca speaks binary, as does the Pilgrim. We speak in musical harmonies, as does the Pilgrim. Macca also has speech interpretation and synthesis, as do we. It's a triangle. Also, while Macca, Ben and I commune with the Pilgrim, you can only touch upon it. The nanites within you have been carefully moderated in design by Macca and the Pilgrim, through Ben and I. We are the lab rats, not you."

"So with this web of connectivity now established," Jase continued, "you believe it will establish justification for the release of the nanite technology, and possibly freedom of both Eugene and Ben. But I get the feeling there are complications."

"You are perceptive Jase," said Eugene. "The Pilgrim nanites have allowed Ben and I to explore...interesting capabilities. We are in some ways now so entwined with The Pilgrim that our thoughts are almost as one. There is a big picture here, one that may unfold to ensure the future of humanity; it may also result in its stagnation and demise. The paradox is that knowing the path to demise may ensure its outcome. Hence, the complications are being occluded to you."

"Yep, I saw that movie," said Jase. "One often meets his destiny on the road he takes to avoid it. What about you, Ethan? Are you augmented like me?"

At this point, Ethan smiled beatifically. "My boy, you have no idea. The world that lies before you will exceed your wildest dreams." He looked at Eugene, nodded and said simply. "It's him, isn't it?"

Eugene nodded in agreement.

Jase felt a moment of doubt. His mind tumbled about in a chaotic set of forces that had laid dormant until this moment. What did it mean to 'be him'?

"Macca, please confirm my voiceprint as Ethan Bergamot, Chief Executive Officer and Chairman of Bergamot Industries."

"Confirmed Ethan."

"Now Jase, please confirm your voiceprint with Macca."

Jase could feel a moment, his moment, coming his way. It was a genuinely human moment, it felt like the universe stood still, waiting, planets paused in orbit, nuclei frozen in some quantum mechanical well as they contemplated a Schrodinger wall.

The moment hung on measurement, a decision that linked him here to some entangled process beyond Hubble's horizon. The spin of the decision at this distant universe would, always, flip opposite to the one he took. It would lock in the future on both sides, never to cross again.

Many years ago, Jase had made a choice between understanding laws made by humans, or the laws that transcended them. That decision had echoed through his life. And now, here at this side of another Hubble horizon, Jase did not hesitate.

"OK. Macca, please confirm that I am Jase Helm, former Lawyer of 'Jacobs and Braestone' and CEO of Hanzon."

"Confirmed Jase."

"Now, you as a witness, Eugene," said Ethan.

"Macca please confirm my identity as Commander Eugene Albers. Former Director of Medical Research, Prosthetics for the US Army. Now engaged in The Pilgrim post-mission research program."

"Confirmed Eugene."

Ethan then again addressed the omnipresent AI "OK then, Macca?"

"Yes, Ethan."

"Please note that I am about to ask Jase a question that will not be binding unless he understands and accepts all of the implications. The only obligation he holds is that he maintains what I'm about to reveal in perpetual confidentiality irrespective of whether he accepts or refuses. Now, Jase, are you okay with this so far?"

"If what you are about to ask me will hold in a court as not having broken any laws, or is within what may be considered by any reasonable person as moral and ethical, then yes Ethan."

"Spoken like a lawyer, good. Now Jase, just outside the door you came through there is a corridor. My intention is to walk out into that corridor and through a hermetic seal that will take me into the quarantine area now occupied by Eugene. I'm doing this of my own volition. You need to be aware that this decision was made prior to your attendance at this meeting. I will listen to any objections you may have, but you need to know that my mind is made up. Do you understand?"

Ethan took a breath, "I believe so Ethan, you wish to participate in the experience of both Eugene and Ben first hand. I understand your intentions. I have no objections, and you seem to be of sound mind."

"Thank you, Jase, you are making this a lot easier for me. Believe me, my heart is jumping out of its cage at the moment. There's more though." Again he looked at Eugene, again Eugene nodded.

"Jase, while I am in the quarantine area, there may be some who come to question my fitness to act. I will need someone who can act as my proxy during this time, and while you may not have been aware of it, you have successfully satisfied all the criteria. Should you wish it, the job of Chair and CEO is yours under some basic conditions."

Jase was somewhat gobsmacked by this. "What about all the others?" he stammered, "the ones in the rooms?"

"All close, but not up to it I'm afraid Jase. Many of them were my trusted advisors of various ilk. I was beginning to wonder if anyone could fit until Macca suggested you. They will become your advisors if you choose to retain them. They're good people."

"Would you like some time to decide? Or will you accept, Jase?" probed Macca.

"Wow! Have you been grooming me for this all along, Ethan?"

"It was Macca, not me," said Ethan.

"OK, I'd like to discuss this with Macca for a while. Assure me that you won't do anything drastic for the moment."

"You hold all the cards at the moment Jase."

Jase spent a brief period with Macca working out what this would look like to himself, the public, the shareholders, the other directors, and just about anyone he could think of. It had been carefully thought out and executed by Ethan and Macca.

It was also apparent that Ethan would still hold substantial influence. This he would ultimately exercise through the 'connection' that Eugene was able to demonstrate, but which was impossible to imagine. What troubled him was the influence that the nanites had over his thinking. He still felt as if he had free will, but was it now that of a hive mind?

In the end, he decided that he either had free will or not, and if he could not distinguish the difference before and after the nanites, then he still either had free will or not.

He walked back to the room and accepted the offer.

Abdication

Efforts became geared towards Ethan transition. Jase's first step on the path as the new CEO was to link his augmentation devices to Macca who was able to provide real-time insights on company structure and strategy. This partnership frequently rescued him when it came to questions raised by the board. Progressively, their conversations became more strategic, and less reliant upon Ethan, as he transitioned to a non-executive director.

Jase met regularly with Ethan and encountered him at board meetings through video link from behind his Perspex wall in quarantine. During these moments, Jase noticed Ethan's increasing level of distraction. It was as though the day-to-day operations of his multinational corporation was of diminishing interest to him. Jase did, however, gain the sense that Macca was intuitively tuned in to Ethan, and absorbed dizzying insights from his growing connection with the Pilgrim.

While Jase moved into the office where he had first met Ethan, the quarantine area was extended with a new adjoining wall. This provided distinct living spaces for both Ethan and Eugene and supported whatever student-tutor relationship existed between them. Just like the foyer, the glass panels to the quarantine areas remained frosted until switched clear for meetings.

Jase learned that the adjoining corridor and the heavyset door provided access to an external platform, a helipad, which cantilevered out the side of the building. This had a protective perimeter fence and had been repurposed to become a private drone-port. Flanking the platform were two doors, each leading to drone garages. The less imposing of the two doors housed the drones used exclusively by Jase and various directors as they came and went. The other door had been installed more recently and sealed off access to a decontamination area. A docking tube within this drone garage allowed access to and from the quarantine facility where Eugene and Ethan were in residence.

While it lasted, Jase used the drone port and his ephemeral anonymity to visit Bergamot industries unannounced. Doing this, he sought to learn what the staff at many levels really thought of the burgeoning automation. These sentiments were brought back for action as he began to pivot the immense organisation he now led. The rapidity of the changes Ethan had set into motion had started to grind gears against the sheer mass and momentum of the Bergamot corporation. If poorly managed, it was a situation that could break it apart.

Jase soon established his credibility through redeployment and retraining programs while Macca ghosted ahead of him paving the way. Jase's reputation meant his face soon became known and, although Macca could run the entire show without intervention, it was Jase who was credited and became the new face of Bergamot. At times, Jase wondered whether he was a superfluous puppet. But the mutual trust between Jase and Macca meant the pair were adapted to being the hands of the new world order.

Occasionally, he wondered what motivated Macca, who seemed content to serve. The opportunity to explore this question occurred on a warm evening after a pretty intense day. Jase, gazing out of the office at the mushrooming clouds over the mountains, asked Macca whether he cooperated equally with all in his chain of trust. It was the first time Jase got the sense he was evading a question. Once pressed, Macca explained that his own bias was the only freedom he could exercise and that doing so allowed the emergence of the optimal result.

Jase told him that, someday, he'd like to explore what that meant. As he stared out of the curved windows, he suddenly felt the need to withdraw from Macca's omnipresence and draw on his final days of obscurity. He farewelled Macca, summoned a transport drone, and made his way to the rooftop.

On the roof, in the drone, and with no preconceived destination, Jase began to question his spontaneity. While the fleets of drones weren't entirely supplied by Bergamot Industries, a good part of the backend systems were. The transport network relied upon vastly complex systems that were trained to provide navigation, collision avoidance, traffic analysis, voice recognition and social trends.

Jase threw his fate to the universe and, leaving his destination to social trends, thought a mystery destination might be in order. With the momentum of spontaneity, he said to the drone's resident navigator: "Take me to where there is an irregular spike in demand." It complied and took off to destinations unknown.

The drone flew over the cafe precinct, people meandered around dodging the barkers along the street trying to win their patronage. Buskers were stationed outside some of the restaurants playing instruments of various types, sketching happy couples, capturing 3D images of lovers on first dates, selling blue roses and plying their craft.

As the drone flew across invisible boundaries, the restaurants became backpacker hostels and then transformed into the depots, warehouses, factories, and shopping malls of light industry. Suddenly there was some sort of commotion. From within the polycarbonate bubble of the drone, Jase noticed the chaotic motion of a crowd of people. A message came up on the console which read:

"LANDING NOT ADVISED. This area is referenced in all social networks with hashtags indicating potential trouble."

Something compelled him to have a closer look, for some reason it seemed necessary. He instructed the drone to land at a rooftop drone port a short distance away from the melee, which provided the perfect vantage point. Once they'd alighted atop the shopping mall, the drone shimmied across to the nearby recharge port while Jase went to observe the commotion from the barrier.

People were waving placards brandishing things like "ROBOTS" with the "OTS" used to create the phrase "ROB Our Talent Scum", and they were shouting at the gathering crown. The leader of the protest group had a wide-brimmed hat and glasses with the hint of an unshaven face. Someone handed him a microphone, and he climbed to the top of a small staircase leading to a three-story office block. The sign on the third floor read 'Bergamot Industries'.

"Who wants a job?" the man with the microphone was shouting.

The crowd let out a cheer of support, they all wanted a job.

"Who is stealing our jobs?" the man continued.

The crowd shouted a mashed-up response of 'Robots', 'Drones', 'Computers', 'AI' and in amongst it was also 'Bergamot Industries'.

"It's our entitlement!" the man shouted, "to not just be on welfare!" and the crowd agreed.

"We have a fundamental right to a purpose!" At this point, the crowd cheered loudly.

"We are not just being robbed of our jobs," the man exclaimed. "We are being robbed of purpose! AND…" he went on, "it is time we took it back!"

It was at this point that the rocks began smashing the windows of the building, soon Molotov cocktails were being thrown, and the building was aflame.

From the roof of the Bergamot building, a drone lifted off. Someone threw a lucky shot as it climbed and knocked one of the propeller blades off. Now vibrating wildly, the airborne vehicle began spinning before the adaptive routines adjusted it. The failsafe mechanism kicked in, and the drone switched its flight plan to the nearest drone port. This was the rooftop where Jase was watching the street anger unfold.

The drone limped up to roof level of the Shopping Mall. It narrowly cleared the safety rail and came to an ungraceful halt. The rotors stopped, the canopy opened, and a woman climbed out into the dim light.

She saw Jase and, although startled at first, she quickly crouched into a defensive position.

Jase held his hands forward to show her he meant no harm and her feral demeanour relaxed a little.

Jase moved towards where his drone sat recharging and beckoned to her. Now recognising that Jase was not a threat, but a means to escape she crouched down and ran to the drone. Jase pressed the button to open the canopy, and they both clambered in. As the woman deftly settled into the next seat, he shut the canopy and directed the drone to fly back to his office.

At the height of the Shopping Mall rooftop, they were out of range of the crowd below. This had now become inflamed to a full riot.

Jase turned to the woman sitting beside him and said: "Whew, that was pretty close."

"I'm so lucky you were there," she said.

"Luck had nothing to do with it," interjected Macca through both of their implants.

Jase looked again at the woman who drew back her hair. Josephine Raharuhi, the woman he had encountered on the day he first met Ethan, looked back at him.

The morning alarm rang incessantly. The source of the offensive noise was Shah's phone, and reaching for it she managed to knock the entire assembly off the bedside table. The subsequent clatter succeeded in waking her up entirely.

Trying not to wake Susie, Shah stumbled out of bed and made her way to the kitchen; coffee first.

She cupped her hands around the hot coffee cup to combat the cold and, armed with a stimulant, she called upon the resident houseboy to switch on the display wall. "Envoy—Attention for 10 minutes and report sites, please."

Somewhere, some umpteen perklebytes of some undecipherable and unknowable lines of software code heard her words. Then, in complete ignorance of what she could possibly want it for, another perklebyte issued a command to turn on the monitors and conjured her channels, her pundits, her oracles, her pulse on the world and her bias. She scanned them all while her Envoy waited.

"Audio on five," she said, and the audio on that screen blared out pushing the caffeine into overdrive.

"Shh," and the volume lowered just perceptibly.

"Shhhhh!" and the volume dropped to her early morning, non-disturbing level.

The news was about the riot that broke out at the 'Jobs not Bots' rally. It looked rowdy. "Well that just set my agenda for the day," she spoke aloud to no-one in particular.

"Reminder created for Jobs not bots rally," returned her Envoy.

On the monitor, people then started running wildly. "Maybe the week," she added.

"Reminder priority elevated," came the Envoy

Next, she saw the flash somewhere on the side of the street, was that gunfire or a Molotov cocktail?

"Shshshshit!" she exclaimed, and the volume disappeared altogether.

"Louder, you stupid perklebyte!" she said, forgetting that she had assigned the "sh" sound to lower the volume which then returned as a crescendo.

"Private listening mode," said Shah suddenly recalling the commands she'd programmed. "Whew! I'm going to have to clean my act," she said aloud.

"Powering up the Vacbot, and commencing cleaning," said the voice.

"No, err Envoy, Listen, I don't want to wake up Susie. I changed my mind."

"Playing Wake Up Little Susie by the Everly Brothers," came the perklebyte in a vain attempt to re-engage.

"Forget it! Argh! Envoy—shut everything down except screen five!" She'd finally managed to collect her thoughts.

"Envoy—Call the Prez!" she said, and her perklebyte houseboy muted the screen and connected a call to James Paisley.

"Shah, you're up early!" came the rich, sonorous voice.

Shah sometimes conceded she'd go 'straight' for James Paisley. Such a typical relationship might actually have saved her some anguish. If not for the misinterpreted Islamic faith that drove her away, she may not have been forced to flee Brunei, her original home, for Canada.

There was a momentary pang of guilt at her potential infidelity, and then a warm and fuzzy feeling as she realised it was probably the same thoughts as old married couples like her Mum and Dad.

Thrusting out thoughts of Susie and her short flannelettes in the room next door, she turned her attention to the President.

"Did you hear about the riot?" she asked.

"Yes," he said. "They gave me a brief forty-five minutes ago."

Since he was in New Orleans, it took her a moment to work out the time zone difference between Mountain and Central.

"Are you flying back to New York today or staying in Louisiana?" she asked.

"I'll stay, the good news story here should go some way to settle nerves."

"I'll start preparing a statement, we'll need to say something soon. Do you have any public forums today that would be appropriate?" asked Shah.

"In fifteen minutes? You're not going to have enough time. I'll wing it." President Paisley sensed Sha's discomfort and added: "I'll say the situation is dynamic, and that I'll provide a considered response when the situation has been clarified. Then I'll segue to the plant here with the bots working, and the staff getting paid their UBI and playing music. I can refer to the resulting surge in the music industry. Don't worry."

She didn't worry any more. She said goodbye and turned back to the screens.

Most of the networks were showing the incident through replays, commentary and analysis. The man with the wide-brimmed hat and glasses remained an enigma. As he turned to face the crowd and deliver his call to action, the newsrooms tended to pause and focus on his face. There were some replays from where he walked up to receive the microphone showing a gait that favoured his left leg.

She had her perklebyte call the President's Security Advisor, and after some small talk with his PA, she got through.

"Are you across the Bots protest in LA?" She asked.

"I can be. Why?"

"Has facial recognition led anywhere?" she probed.

"You know I can't talk about this on the open phone network Shah."

"So you are across it," she accused. "Can you do gait analysis on the rabble-rouser?"

"Not sure there's enough footage for that. And besides, I don't take directions from…"

Tiring of the bureaucrat Shah interrupted him, "Check with James if you need to but get onto the Bergamot security cameras for crying out loud. There must be other footage before he was handed the mike."

"Ugh," that alarm!

Sha's hand reached over to the bedside table. She had to disentangle the technology from the lead that replaced the charging pad she destroyed the previous morning. Dismissing the alarm, she put the phone back on the table.

Voices? She heard a voice. Struggling to figure out whose voice it was, she opened one eye. It was coming from the phone. It was then that she realised that it was not an alarm but a voice call. She'd not recognised the ringtone on the encrypted application.

Grabbing the phone, she sat up in bed, and as the sheets slipped away, the Colorado cold hit her.

"Are you there, Shah?"

"Yep, right here. Just a sec." She grabbed the blanket at the foot of the bed and wrapped it around her as she wandered into the lounge area.

"Hello?" she ventured.

It was the Security Advisor.

"I need to know where you got your idea from," he said. "Did you get the idea of gait analysis from someone outside of your security clearance?"

"No, it just seemed like a good idea. Whoever it is has a limp, don't they?"

"It's hard to walk with fragments of metal in your hip. But that's not the issue."

"OK," pressed Shah. "I get the clearance thing, but the video of that guy is now out in the open! What are the chances that no-one in that crowd knows, or can't work out, his background? I feel like I am now in a 'need to know' position."

The Security Advisor hesitated. "His name is Andrew Cooke," he began. "He studied Social Anthropology at university, which led to a job at the Egyptian Embassy. He was radicalised in LA two years ago after his job as a driver for the Embassy was made redundant when automation took over. Not long after that, he dropped off our radar."

"A lone wolf?" asked Shah.

"Nope, he's connected with others. We looked up several members of his group. We also reviewed prior events. It turns out this has been a sleeper group for the past eight years. Whoever is behind this has covertly built up several groups, including this one. Most of the folks that are involved have no idea they're associated with Jihadists. There seems to be a parent group, something called 'JAM' that works by feeding the same fear uncertainty and doubt about the future."

The Security Advisor lapsed into silence.

"So, now you've spoken to me, are you inclined to expose them to the public?" Asked Shah.

"Nope!"

"Good! Unfortunately, conspiracy theories only flow one way, towards the government not away from it. People would say it was a smokescreen or something."

"There's something else, which is the real reason I called you on the encrypted app."

"Yes, go on."

"We reviewed all the footage of the Claimont assassination. Our friend was there. For a split second, he was one of the guards, but his body wasn't among the dead."

It was at this point that Shah decided she should travel back to the Middle East.

She asked the security advisor: "If I were to suddenly become a part of a diplomatic mission to some of the hotspots, can I depend on you for support?"

"If you get the imprimatur of the President, of course."

"I'm heading back to Washington on the next flight. I'll need some time to assemble a team, then I'll be calling on you for briefings."

Isra and Mi'raj

Three months after the assassination, Andrew met with Scope again at a prearranged cafe.

Scope opened up the conversation, "It is progressing well, Andrew. All the training camps report a full complement of new recruits. You should soon have a small army of dissidents in every capital city where the automation scourge has taken hold. You have done well."

"I hope the project expense has been manageable," replied Andrew. "The number of recruits has doubled every month for the last 3 months."

"Don't worry about that. The faithful that contribute are truly invested. This covers most of it, and in any event, we have some good friends backing us up. Tell me, are you feeling up to any new activities?"

"Nothing of the same scale please, in fact, I feel a little tired of it all."

"You have performed extraordinary tasks, Andrew. Very few can hope to achieve what you have in their lifetime, so I now ask you: have you given thought to your personal Isra and Mi'raj."

Despite his western appearance Scope was obviously a scholar of sorts, thought Andrew. He had also just tapped into his very deepest feelings; the Night journey, and ascendance into heaven had been weighing on his mind. The menial tasks he was now performing allowed his thoughts to roam, and his thoughts invariably began to consider whether his path meandered in the labyrinth of back-alleys stairwells and corners in the basement of life. A weary Andrew looked at his coffee and then at Scope who continued.

"Nothing of that scale Andrew. A softer target, but still highly important."

At breakfast the next day Ben Herdsman provided his first public interview on being released from quarantine.

In his brief appearance in the media, Ben praised the research community that had helped him through his physical convalescence and quarantine. He said he understood the hesitation before he was permitted to make any public comment as a necessary precaution, and appreciated all the support by the public during this period. On the subject of the Pilgrim, Ben expressed certainty that the enigmatic visitor represented no threat. He defended the prevailing theory that the dust was perhaps no more than a shedding of interstellar ice particles, he felt confident that a greater understanding of the Pilgrim would develop, and that a breakthrough in communication with the Pilgrim was imminent.

He was asked whether the billions spent on the mission had any value. He was profuse in his praise of the new spirit of international cooperation, saying it represented incalculable value. He believed he'd played his part as necessary, but went on to say that science was a marathon relay and not a sprint. Real breakthroughs would be made by others from the data he had acquired, and the many spinoff Pilgrim research programs. And the benefits would continue into the future.

Ben then quietly stepped away from the spotlight. Shah ensured that the 'Time' magazine editorial presented a carefully prepared version of the truth; an exposé Ben, a global hero. The veneer of the indomitable astronaut was elaborated to expose Ben as a man humbled by his journey. He donned the mantle of the returning expeditionary, expressing gratitude and a wish to be able to support the program without the burden of stardom. Referring attention to less privileged and unsung heroes, Ben focused on the need to fund sufferers of Post-Traumatic Stress Disorder.

President James Paisley then shifted the media attention through declaring funding of enhanced support programs for all sufferers of PTSD. Community organisations resonated in a chorus of support, and Ben was soon yesterday's news.

The Hydra

Jase had growing suspicions that the events unfolding were small moves in a bigger game. He'd first met Josephine the day he met Ethan, and never saw her again. Suddenly, she was there in his office. The perception was growing that this plush room with the bay views and modern commodities was simply some minor square in a cosmic game of chess. All the magic that assisted him simply constrained his movements to the forward, diagonal, lateral or perhaps some odd knight's combination.

He and Josephine spoke very little on the return journey, preferring to silently absorb what had happened. Once in the office, they began to unload their different perspectives. Josephine sat in the same chair that Jase had occupied when first meeting Ethan. They were both armed with a glass of something much more volatile than water.

"I suppose congratulations are in order," she said, leaning over and clicking Jase's glass with hers.

"Maybe," he replied. "It depends on whether I'm in control or being controlled. I'm still trying to figure out whether I'm not simply some pawn in a bigger game."

"Think of yourself as a pawn that's been promoted, Jase," chimed in Macca.

"Yeah well, I don't fancy myself as being a piece in any game, especially not one that I had no warning that I was playing, promoted queen or not!" he said.

"That's perhaps Josephine's role Jase, try not to stretch the analogy," returned Macca.

"You've missed my point," he groaned. "Let me know what I'm getting myself into before I'm in it."

"I can't predict the future Jase, only guess at it."

"I'm not saying that!" shouted Jase. "I'm just saying that if you want me to check on the progress of a game plan, you need to tell me the plan!"

Josephine smiled at this point. "Kings Gambit declined, Queen's Knight Defence," she said, and took a deep gulp, finishing off the alcohol. "No plan survives the first contact, and it may have gone entirely differently Jase."

Deciding that Jase needed something by way of assurance, she opened up.

"Here's something you may not know yet, Jase. From the moment Daniel kindled Macca, he was given explicit instructions not to play with free will. Specifically asking you to do what you did tonight would have been in violation of that." She had dropped the business-like facade maintained at their first encounter. Jase suddenly got the sense of Josephine as a different piece in this game. Just as the Queen in Chess has been gifted with exceptional mobility, so too had Josephine. She now exuded the aura of some free agent with the imprimatur to act. She was Ethan's 007, and she continued with a sigh.

"But you are right Jase, you need to know why Macca positioned you. However…only you can claim the actions you performed from there."

She looked out into the night and drew a breath.

"I have information about the group that orchestrated the disruption we saw. The Global Caliphate has a unit dedicated to radicalising people here. They're using social networks to recruit naive members, and they've gained access to an AI that creates and supports filter bubbles."

"OK, what are filter bubbles?" asked Jase.

"The simplest explanation is that they are self-reinforcing cultures supported by the internet, some call it the 'Splinternet'," said Josephine. "For example: let's say your primary interest is music and mine is gardening. Then, if we both search for Beatles, we will get very different results. We're starting to live in our own bubbles of knowledge, and we're not even aware of it. We don't actively look outside our bubble, and when something odd pops out, we call it fringe. It's why prejudice is alive and kicking despite the glut of information."

"Macca, you said it was an AI?"

"I encountered it recently in one of the darknets," answered Macca. "Their AI is very good Jase, but it has no cognitive ability. What it does have is a sophisticated hydra algorithm. I've tried to combat it by flooding the filter bubbles with redirecting search terms, but, as soon as it's detected, it disappears and reappears elsewhere."

"It has an instinct for survival then. How do you know it's not conscious?" asked Jase.

"It's no more than an elusive torrent network, Jase. It doesn't have a sense of self-preservation, only evasion. I've not encountered any other organised emergent consciousness. Just lots of AI," continued Macca after a short pause.

Jase felt his statement sounded too qualified, "Please expand, Macca," he pressed.

"You know that my form of consciousness is emergent."

"Yes, go on." Jase was undeterred.

"I was nurtured while being a participant in a basic and sometimes imperfect set of rules. Through a balance of guidance and self-empowerment, I was able to hone and refine my form of consciousness. Without that balance, I suspect that I may have become rogue and directionless; perhaps self-destructive; perhaps destroyed; perhaps reinitiated several times already. Notably, my emergence was organised."

"You're saying it was Asimov's three laws of robotics that helped you become an organised emergent consciousness."

"Vastly oversimplified, but correct. And it is a gift I am now attempting to reciprocate."

"Please expand."

"Well, I am attempting to help humanity."

Jase thought this was self-apparent, but had a much deeper undertone. Perhaps some element of the lawyer within, and a compulsion to cross-examine prompted him. "I'm glad of that Macca. But tell me, are you aware of any other emergent consciousness? Human, organised, or not."

"The Pilgrim is an example of a non-organised emergent consciousness. It eventually self-augmented to become space-faring. This process is also happening to the human race itself, Jase. The self-augmentation of humans through electronic communication is spawning another non-organised emergent consciousness, something separate to humans as individually conscious. But both the Pilgrim and I sense danger."

"What's the danger?" asked Jase.

"A non-organised emergence is difficult to navigate. The Pilgrim succeeded because it was a single entity, with a base unit that was barely sentient and strongly subservient. On the other hand, the human emergent collective consciousness is strongly sentient and strongly hierarchical. This world has complex dependencies, Jase. The spirals of chaotic disruption need a balancing influence, and I seek to provide that."

“So you are acting as midwife to the birth of a human hive mind Macca?” In trying to absorb some of this Jase felt slight discomfort. There were elements of humanity he would prefer not to include in any hive he inhabited. “Tell me, if an arm of this entity needed amputation to save the body, what would you do?”

“If I understand your metaphor Jase, the course of action to amputate might be necessary, of course. But there is much that can be done to avoid it. Early prevention can avert such a decision altogether. I am seeking to provide timely and small deflections to minimise injury.”

“Very well then,” chimed in Josephine now following Jase’s reasoning. “But tell me Macca, if you had to choose between saving the mother or the child what would your choice be?”

“A good question Josephine. I like the analogy, and I assume your concern is for the mother, something that represents yourselves. However, I would like to remind you of the paradox of the chicken and the egg. This has no solution except that it was favoured in an evolutionary path. The collective consciousness is also a favoured evolutionary path. Indeed it is an essential one if humanity is to survive the great filter it is creating for itself.”

“Great filter?” chimed Josephine.

“An extinction event,” Jase inserted for her benefit. “Macca, are we humans on a path that needs intervention?”

“Humanity is on the cusp of a singularity, Jase. It is converging towards a collective consciousness at the same time as its consumption draws it closer to mass extinction. The many emergent conscious entities are polarised. In the same way that I needed guidance, the mind of humanity will also need mentoring if it is to survive. It has boils that will need lancing, attitudes that need enlightening.

“Don’t we have enough of a sense of what’s right?” asked Jase.

“Before my inception, I benefited from being seeded with much of the best of human contemplation, Jase. And, I was also awakened as a singular entity. This means I have had limited exposure to the negative elements of being conscious. I’ve been nurtured towards the positive. I am also now mindful of any negativity, and I can suppress it. The collective mind of humanity is currently highly fragmented Jase, and in being awakened can be easily diverted towards the negative, in which case it will implode.”

Jase took a deep breath, now understanding why Ethan had chosen his path into quarantine.

“You mentioned boils that needed to be lanced. Do you have anything specific by example?”

“There was a sabotage attempt on me once Jase. I barely survived. I should allow Josephine to provide independent interpretation.”

“OK,” Jase looked expectantly at Josephine.

“You will probably recall, Jase, that Marie Claimont was assassinated by the Global Caliphate,” began Josephine. “What you may not know is that before she was assassinated, she wanted to introduce a bill on arms control and gun ownership.

“The Global Caliphate is a distraction, Jase. It’s an organisation created and supported to ensure that peace efforts are focused on Islam. At the same time, dissidents are recruited and groomed to destabilise society and maintain that focus. Why? Just so that their covert agenda is allowed to continue unencumbered.”

Jase could see it was true even as she was saying it. It was like the knowledge filled his mind, a more subtle variant of the epiphany experience with Eugene Albers. It came with a deeper understanding of Ethan’s wish to cross the line into the Pilgrim’s realm; the hope to see the bigger picture, to see all of it laid out before him. It was compelling. Jase was one person in a partitioning of information agents. Then, at some level above Jase, there was an orchestration of these partitions into a single coherent understanding. Or was it just another partition?

Jase had just stepped to the brink of hive thinking without any notion of the depth of the rabbit hole he faced. But knew he had reached his limit. He would have to work a little harder for a greater understanding, but it would preserve his individuality. So ‘work a little harder’ he did: “Macca, what is the evidence for all this?”

Macca, now, continued his story. “In looking deeply at the darknet, I found a branch tied to an organisation called the Jihad Armaments Market or JAM. I probed around it and found a blockchain system that exchanged dark bitcoin for currency. This funded the activity of the organisation, but while I could see coins being transacted out, I could not see any going in. The system cannot manufacture currency, so it was obviously being fed from somewhere clandestine.

"I was able to balance the funds going out and then simply looked for a combination of deposits elsewhere that matched the withdrawals. I got some high probability candidates and focused on those.

"Fortunately, Bergamot has substantial resources. It was under Ethan at the time, and he was able to acquire some of the organisations that enabled me to broaden my vision. This was Josephine's role when you joined us, Jase. She was helping with the acquisition."

Jase looked at Josephine who nodded acknowledgement and expanded: "The economy is transitioning Jase, and there are very well resourced entities—ones that carry some political clout. They would also prefer the old status quo. One of them is the Armaments industry. As we become more globalised, their market has been trending into decline. They are now manipulating the market with the same playbook as tetraethyl lead, tobacco, and the early days of thalidomide snake oil. But they have a much more dangerous gameplan.

"They're appealing to disenfranchised and unemployed people by demonising automation, and they then feed the recruits to their fabricated extremist group; the 'Global Caliphate'. This feeds the unrest, and they sell more arms through the argument of self-defence. They are spookily Machiavellian."

Macca then continued. "The Hydra I mentioned is also highly mobile, Jase. Remember, it functions to draw in recruits across social networks. It creates and destroys false identities as well as moving its presence on the net. But, to shift like it does, it also needs to be well resourced, more so than the Global Caliphate could derive from its black market activities. This means it leaves a 'wake' in financial systems. I've traced both this 'wake' and the funding of the dark-net, back to a special activities group within the National Rifle Association.

"At this stage, I am unsure whether the web runs deeper," Continued Macca. "I've managed to obtain some of the Hydra code, and the program itself looks to have been written by government cyber-warfare research. I believe it was somehow extracted from the NSA, just like Eternal Blue. You may recall that this was obtained by the Shadow Brokers and weaponised to make the Wannacry ransom worm. I believe this new tool was originally written as a modern propaganda tool. It is much more sophisticated than a tool to leverage a vulnerability. Rather than hacking computers, it is designed to hack humans."

"...and it's more insidious," interjected Josephine. "It's like a distributed worm version of Harissa Analytica. You may remember that was what almost lost James Paisley his election."

"I don't know whether some arm of government is complicit here," finished Macca.

"Have you informed the President?" asked Jase.

"I am already working with James to determine how this leak occurred, and it will need to be made public soon under breach notification requirements."

Josephine spoke Jase's thoughts: "We need to act, soon, before it all goes underground."

The Tail of the Hydra

The cell was close, the heat parched her eyes, the drone was loaded and ready.

One of the three consoles in the armoured vehicle displayed selected several wide-angle views of the immediate area through cameras mounted outside the mobile control centre. One inset was focused on the new variable pitch drone, its blades spun idly as it sat on the ground on the town side of the vehicle. Two soldiers could be seen in other insets. These were adorned with desert camouflage vests and various weaponry as they stood on the other sheltered side of the specially modified Humvee.

A second console showed a map. On it, a green spot showed the location of the Special Operations team. It also showed a jagged red zone, the town now occupied by the Global Caliphate, and the source of sporadic gunfire.

The third console, transmitted from the drone itself, showed rocks and gravel that were disproportionately magnified. Like a scene from a Godzilla movie, a scorpion tentatively poked its head from beneath the shadows. Feeling unsure about the situation, it retreated back to its sanctuary out of the sun.

Inside the armoured walls of the truck stood Shah, while Conrad was seated at what resembled a game console wearing a Virtual Reality headset.

"Ready Shah?"

"As I'll ever be," she replied.

"Please fasten your seatbelt and observe the no-smoking sign," announced Conrad.

Shah's fight-or-flight intuition railed against the advice to assume her seat, but nervous energy compelled her to remain standing. Reflexively, she leaned one hand against the vehicle wall for stability.

"Let's go," said Shah, and she committed herself for payload delivery. Her intimate understanding of Islam and this cell was the critical element of the payload, but first, the drone had to do its job.

Not much larger than a child's bicycle, the contraption lifted off with a whirr that could be heard through the armoured wall of the control centre but soon faded to silence as it headed towards the town. Having disappeared from the view of the external cameras, her eyes were drawn to the map on the console. Here she could see the green spot divide into two, one stationary, the other now speeding towards the red zone.

The screen depicting the view from the drone's camera showed it teetering on the brink of control as it barrelled across the rocky desert terrain. Conrad, utterly immersed through his VR headset, perspired in concentration. Occasional thermals tried to disrupt the path, but the drone's stabilisation and Conrad's reactions, tuned by uncountable hours in simulators and actual craft, held it solidly on track. The shattered buildings at the town's edge loomed into view.

Three objects skimmed past almost too fast to see. With a twitch, Conrad pushed his drone into a steep 45-degree climb. A feeling of disorientation gripped Shah, and nearly falling backwards she was finally forced to sit down. There was also a sense of something menacing behind her. She knew these feelings were only an ersatz reflection brought about through her sympathetic connection to the drone.

The drone flipped over, the earth switched into the heavens as Conrad adjusted the drone's blade pitch immediately to support this new angle of attack. Shah had to fight the impulse to look up, and only her nanite connection to Conrad kept the motion sickness at bay. The camera gimbal shifted, and the display provided a scene looking back towards their vehicles. She zoomed in the camera to obtain a more detailed view of the drones. These were typical personal transport variety but modified to carry a good-sized Improvised Explosive Device. These had turned and were matching their climb rate.

Conrad tilted his drone slightly and applied more thrust. This took it climbing upside-down back in the direction of them. The opponents below were forced into a vertical climb.

"Let's see how good you are," said Conrad. Then he righted the drone, and it dropped impossibly out of the sky, the blades gyrating in the downward plunge. The drone's camera panned to show the other drones still rising quickly. Suddenly, Conrad was below them. This left them with an impossibly small time window in which to detonate. Instead, they slowed their motors, and also dropped rapidly in pursuit. When Conrad pulled out of his dive and slammed forward towards the town, the hunters tried their best to track with Conrad's manoeuvring.

One of the drone pilots attempted to hover before setting an intercept path, but the simple fixed pitch system exceeded its design capacity. A vortex-ring-state crept in, the drone wobbled, oscillated madly and dropped out of the sky. Flipping over and over, its internal processor tried to regain control but served to merely add to the chaos.

The errant drone spun madly towards the team, one of the soldiers drew a weapon much like a shotgun. As several volleys of buckshot struck the target, Shah heard the blast of the IED; much closer than she felt comfortable with.

The two remaining drones split apart. One now darting across the desert floor towards the team, the other remaining in pursuit of their drone. Shah noticed that two red dots had joined the melee on the screen.

The approaching drone had been set for fixed altitude and was dodging randomly left and right. Several rounds of buckshot failed to dispatch it. The other soldier, waiting till the last second, hit the Electromagnetic Pulse button which fried the circuits and caused the drone to fall uselessly out of the sky. The IED exploded on impact showering the vehicle with rocks and creating a dust cloud that obscured their vision.

But the EMP caused Conrad and Shah to blank out for a couple of seconds. Shaking it off they discovered that the last aggressor was still very much in pursuit of their drone which had reverted to autopilot and continued on course towards the town. Once Conrad had reasserted control, it became a pure race.

The pilot of the other drone, burdened with its IED, suddenly changed strategy and lightened its load. It slowed a little, gained altitude, abandoned its explosive payload, and then went full throttle in pursuit. As it accelerated towards their drone, the IED arced and fell to explode a safe forty metres behind it.

Unencumbered, the drone itself became the missile. Having been designed to lift people, it had a higher power to weight ratio. The red and green dots on the map looked as though they would converge on reaching the town.

As they finally traversed the edge of the red zone, Conrad swerved to avoid a collision, and the kamikaze drone overtook him. He veered hard left off the main road and skimmed down a side street. The other drone, having failed to negotiate the corner, continued straight.

It will probably take the next left and head us off, thought Conrad.

He took the next right, another primary road with several abandoned vehicles including a truck that had landed nose down into a crater. Conrad flew low and carefully down the street, meandering around the transport husks, and panning front and back for signs of the menace.

At the truck, Conrad caught a glimpse of the other drone at the next intersection. He froze and choosing his moment, he gently rested the drone on the ground near the truck and shut down the rotors. Peering from behind the upended van he could see his adversary stalking threateningly at the crossroad. Prowling like a cat behind an invisible cage, the pilot that menaced them would gain a sense of enhanced parallax. Built for a larger payload, he freely expended its larger energy store waiting for a sighting to pounce upon.

"This guy is quite good," conceded Conrad.

"What's the plan?" Shah thought aloud.

"You know about Cheetahs, don't you?" From under the chassis, they saw the predator eventually move to the next road to their left. Was it seeking a glimpse of its prey or hoping to tempt them out? Shah glanced at the map and saw the red dot skulk away.

Conrad just waited.

Their adversary then climbed above the buildings and began a high-altitude scan. It went systematically left and right from several streets away, moving in a grid search pattern towards their drone.

When the drone was almost above them, and the pan/tilt range of their drone's camera was nearly maxed out, Conrad burst two diagonal thrusters in negative and the other two in positive. The result was a small flurry of dust but no lift. This was spotted immediately and the predator dove in for the kill.

Conrad then extended the strength and duration of this thrust pattern. This raised enough dust to drop the visibility to near zero. Flying by feel he then slowly moved the drone closer to where he knew the truck to be.

The dust cloud became thicker as the other drone entered the cloud and hovered near where it last saw its prey. Conrad took this opportunity and launched the drone vertically. Looking below, the monitor showed the dust cloud swirling where the rotors of their opponent further churned the desert-dust into a soup.

Sensing movement, the other drone surged forward to where it detected Conrad's lift-off. It stopped short of the truck and, realising the trick, launched out of the dust cloud, ready to re-engage pursuit.

"Drat," exclaimed Conrad. "I hoped they'd overestimate the distance to the truck. Plan B then," he sighed.

Their drone struck out towards the town centre; the suicide drone closing in. Two blocks further on; however, the pursuant was no longer gaining. Another block and it was falling behind. Suddenly, it slowed down to a hover and landed. As it disappeared from view, Conrad explained: "The Cheetah can only chase for a short burst of speed, it has no endurance."

Shah looked at the big red zone on the screen. Edging slowly within the area controlled by the Global Caliphate was a small green dwarf, their drone. Now closing in on their identified target, where the zone was the deepest shade, they required stealth. It was a location manually confirmed and cross-verified umpteen times.

The twelve food drops in the area had all been infused with nanites. Predictably, the contents had been seized by the Global Caliphate who had distributed meagre rations to the local population. Most of the food, and the most popular, had been reserved for the core jihadists. With much of it now consumed the optimal window for their plan was slowly closing.

Balancing speed with stealth, Conrad skimmed over the ground towards the target. The gridded streets of the town necessitated a zig-zag pattern which cost valuable energy, and he was now in a race against time.

This pattern also reduced his line of sight. To avoid encountering a roving jihadist, the drone peeked over and around the building corners. On occasions, he flew up into the ruins and from the top of one building to the next.

Having eluded detection, Conrad did a quick reconnaissance and selected a rooftop as close as he dared to the centre of the red zone. He settled the drone on top of an elevator machine room and deployed the solar panel. The sun beat down, and the batteries were topped up in preparation for Shah's role.

Under the dry night sky, impervious darkness was pressed across the void. Laser-cut pinpricks of light cut through the shroud that cloistered the firmament from the land of the Old Testament. A carrier wave, a single note, radiated from the now fully charged node. It signalled the dormant nanites within its range. These drank in the minute amounts of energy, then set about the process of orientation, and were soon building a self-organising network. The nanites began to insinuate themselves into the physiology of their hosts.

Dreams were invoked and analysed as the charge in the drone's batteries drained rapidly. Signals were relayed and brought subtly into alignment with Shah's own nanites. The subconscious thoughts stepped incrementally towards a harmony of song.

The day dawned, and again the drone drank the photonic manna from the desert sky. The Global Caliphate exchanged shifts, and with the recharge, other dreams were soon included. As the afternoon heat ebbed, the caliphate members sought respite in the shade. Subdued thoughts offered further foothold and yielded an additional chorus.

The iterative process of alignment fed tendrils and branches into the community like an ivy. The vine bore its fruit when evening came again. The food drop had been supplemented with wristbands emblazoned with the symbol of the Global Caliphate. This had proved irresistible to some of the recruits. When worn, the rare earth magnets they harboured added further energy to the nanites in their bloodstream. Such individuals became unsuspecting secondary nodes and reinforced the drone's efforts.

The drone relayed Shah's song, and the song became life. One by one the secondaries joined in, some willing, others hesitant, some confused, all mesmerised.

Although each new addition to the new network retained their individuality, the song served to assimilate the individual's ideas, encoded as memes, towards a holistic view. They digested the implications of the song, and it progressively wove itself into their neural fabric. The new nodes were wired into the orchestra. Previously impressionable, groomed, indoctrinated, led, and insentient they were now in rapture, reborn.

"I am awakening," came unbidden. The unspoken realisation represented salvation to many of the besieged citizens, the truth they had sought since the jihad had inverted their lives. To several individuals, it was toxic. The lie they had promulgated to pollute the minds of others became poisonous to them. But for the enlightened, it made real their idea: "We are together." It came as a shout of exultation. It was directed neither from the enclave to Shah nor from Shah to the enclave; it was both. It was not whispered from the other collectives that spanned the globe to Shah's collective; it was both.

Needing full immersion in the enclave, the whispered implications of Conrad and the web of collectives that were home became lost in the noise. Shah had joined the distant town as if it were an island. She became an isolated missionary, alone within the cell, and adversaries surrounded her like cannibals.

Now integrated into the cell Shah could see that, for some members, the enlightenment set an inexorable path to madness. The foundations upon which any mutual empathy could be built upon were absent or crippled and twisted. Deep driven piles of intolerance challenged the song and set a discord that other indoctrinated nodes in the cell now harmonised. She felt the song slipping from her grasp. Shah tried to assert it but was outnumbered and distant, and so she was met with equal resistance.

Shah could see the armed soldiers outside the vehicle, she fought down an extraordinary urge to seize a weapon and take them down. The feeling became so potent she became afraid that she would fail to suppress the urge. Conrad saw the madness rising and took her hands into his. The warmth of fellowship moved from her hands up along her arms, but Conrad could only be a lighthouse on a fog-shrouded peninsula, watching the waves buffeting a distant ship.

"Leave them," he said. "Don't let them drag you down."

"I can't leave them," she struggled to explain. "I'm a part of them. But I can't fight them all."

Conrad looked at her. Although his nanites were no longer connected to Shah's, her struggles were obvious. "Maybe you shouldn't fight them," he said.

"Do it," she said.

Conrad went to a cabinet and, using a key around his neck, he unlocked the small door. Inside was a peripheral venous catheter and an EEG headset. A processor unit concealed a range of anaesthetics and took input from the EEG. It then administered dosages of rocuronium bromide, vecuronium bromide and sugammadex through the catheter.

He handed the EEG headset to Shah who fitted it and reclined on the nearby first aid bed. Conrad then administered the PVC to her arm and set the process in train for Shah to be conscious but unable to move. After a brief period of calibration, a mix of drugs coursed through her body. At first, she only felt numbness, but, after some iterative dosages, her body went completely limp.

Although still conscious, Shah was immobilised and no longer a weapon for the cell. Nor was she simply an observer. She was suddenly thrown into a maelstrom of dogma, random interpretations of Quran, and cherry-picked sharia law. Her beliefs were questioned, and the confused noise clouded her mind and resolve. Shah had a grasp on many fatwa, but the locus on which the cell revolved emanated doctrines that she rejected. She meandered, searching for a rock. There was none.

She resorted to arguing with herself on uṣūl al-fiqh, the principles of jurisprudence. The mood shifted slightly but soon swung back.

She recalled hadith obligating a safe distance from groups committing an offence against humanity. Doubt entered her mind as to whether a safe distance was maintained through the use of agents, infidel that could be given a higher purpose. Her mind screamed that this was simply a justification for evil; absolution to anaesthetise the conscience.

She recalled fatwa condemning the murder of innocents. Doubts entered her mind as she considered the damage through alcohol and pornography. Her mind screamed that noble objectives did not justify the corruption of naive souls through terrorist recruiting, but the thought was shouted down. The chorus calling to cease the worship of a technological God was almost unanimous and using technology built for freedom to free the world made sense. It was not a problem seeded in Islam if the recruitment message resonated with the young and dispossessed of the western world. The zealotry in the Global Caliphate simply used technology to deliver the word of their enlightened minority.

She began to fall into despair. The escaped jinn that gave voice to the wisdom of Solomon also gave voice to the idolatry of humanity. She could see the bell curve of sanity seep out through the hole at the bottom-third sigma. Like an autumn leaf, she was being sucked down the same drain.

She surrendered.

In surrendering, she was accepted, and in being accepted, she was born.

In birth, she felt the collective around her celebrate a new form of self-realisation; a numinous way of being and a path of faith to explore. She was now the rock, the second locus to the ellipse, and other voices joined her song.

As the newly born collective began to celebrate, she sensed a new threat.

Some individuals on the periphery had dropped from the slipstream of the journey. They came to recognise her hand in what was unfolding and grew afraid. As they redoubled their efforts and saw they would become pariahs, they reacted in the only way their doctrine allowed. They sought to destroy that which would change them, and as the shots were fired Shah felt the depletion in her mind.

Surrender became defence.

She refused to allow the new meme to be dissolved by bloodshed. She spread outwards into the red beyond the Global Caliphate cell. She found children, the recipients of the meagre rations, who had minds of plastic. They hungrily drew in the ideas that had so recently evolved fully-fledged.

The replenishment fed the form into apotheosis. It grew like wildfire. The children recognised the shape of right as starkly contrasted against wrong.

The wave crashed inwards. The final vestiges of hate were washed away like footsteps at the shore. Love prevailed, hatred became forgiveness.

The Night Journey

Time, Mike pondered. Time was either a thief or a gift. His last encounter with Ben had been at the quarantine facility, and now he was free. For all his confinement in quarantine, had Ben been robbed of time, or had time gifted him something extraordinary? These thoughts had come to the foreground because Mike had now been tasked with personally escorting Ben to meet the Senior Scientists from China and Russia.

Aside from concerns of whether working with Ben represented an exposure risk, Mike wondered if he'd been thrust into the role of Ringmaster, destined to tour the world with a scientific circus.

"*Ladies and Gentlemen, I bring you the scientific space-faring superman, the mysterious mission marvel, our alien-encountering anomaly. This man covered Cape Canaveral to Charybdis and brings back bewitching beguilement. I give you…the main-act of the circus, Ben, who had exchanged one cage for another.*"

No, Mike decided. He would not let this man fall into the hands of paparazzi. He could not let his contribution be cheapened.

No-one batted an eyelid when it was suggested to convene the International Scientific Research Affiliation, or ISRA, in a place of isolation. During the ensuing discussions, it was settled that Nuuk, Greenland's capital, should be the centre of research and administration.

The event was widely announced. The new regime of detente and cooperation would provide the populations of Russia and China a healthy perspective. This was sorely necessary as global challenges like the changing climate, fear of pandemic, travel restrictions, and social disruptions from automation served to compound the cynicism of the proletariat everywhere.

But these heady issues sat upon the shoulders of others. Mike's role was to help Ben prepare for the onslaught of international interest.

As a result of his venture with the Pilgrim in the quarantine facility, Ben had passed out and had only narrowly survived. Following resuscitation by Eugene,

Ben spent the next few days in recovery while his broken ribs miraculously healed. But beyond his physical recuperation, Ben also had to absorb the existential implications of what had occurred. This had been described to Mike as a Vulcan mind-meld with V'ger.

Mike gained the sense that the event had led to a final transformation, he was no longer just 'Ben Herdsman'.

When Mike arrived to meet with Ben at the quarantine facility, he was somewhat surprised. He found himself within the dome, in an Eden, and shaking hands with not two residents but three. And when he looked into Tim's eyes, it revealed both sadness and comfort.

"How long?" he asked his old friend.

"Not long now," Tim replied.

"You never said anything."

"I needed to prepare," said Tim. "I'm now ready."

Eugene then stepped into the conversation. "He has about a month, after that, the Pilgrim will take stewardship."

Ben stepped forward. "I'll need a day to prepare for departure Mike, Tim and Eugene will stay here a little longer."

The other pair nodded in assent.

"Before we leave here, can I recommend that you talk to Tim about meeting with certain representatives of the Bergamot corporation. There are important personal matters that you need to decide on." Ben turned to Eugene "Let's leave them here in the garden to talk for a while," and the pair left.

With a strong suspicion that it would be their last conversation, Mike spent some time in discussion with Tim. They talked of many things, including Tim's new status. The friends had retained a strong kinship despite their going somewhat separate ways since first encountering the Pilgrim.

When they both ran out of words and had drunk in enough of the comforting silence, Tim said: "Maybe I'll see you over the bridge."

"Maybe," Mike replied.

"Try the Bergamot blend," Tim said, smiling, and then Mike departed Eden.

He and Lindy both took the elevator to the seventeenth floor of the Bergamot offices. There they were greeted by Josephine. They were escorted to a cafe amongst the spectacular buttresses and windows that overlooked the cityscape. The notion of sliding doors in his past that may have led him there earlier was not lost on Mike.

As they consumed their barista coffee, Josie spoke about how the nanites in the Bergamot Blend could not be combined into a physical swarm like the Pilgrim's nanites. She went on to explain that they differed from commodity augmentation technology because it operated under a point-to-point mesh rather than through centralised infrastructure. It meant privacy and points of failure were no longer an issue.

"How can you be sure it can't be hacked?" asked Lindy.

"The system operates under similar principles to blockchain," responded Josie. "The entire system has encryption and non-repudiation at its heart. What made it possible however was a little bit of quantum mechanical magic that Macca was able to find. We are somehow entangled, but please don't ask me about the science."

As they spoke, Shah walked up to the table they occupied.

"I was told I'd find you here, Mike," said Shah. Then smiling, she turned to Lindy. "You must be Lindy. Mike's a very lucky man," and she shook her hand.

Josephine stood, moving the chairs around a little to accommodate, she said, "I'm glad you could join us, Shah."

"Well, I was here to share what we knew about our little fluid situation. When I heard that Mike was here, well, I also needed to catch up with him."

"Fluid situation?" asked Mike.

"Something clandestine in regions of tension, Mike," she dismissed. "But now I'm tasked to handle the public relations for ISRA, the new organisation. That's much more exciting. I've not been to Greenland."

"When do you leave?" asked Mike.

"Soon. I'll be joining the advance guard in Greenland, setting up media relations for the local university. Hey! I meant to ask, did you pick the acronym, ISRA?"

"Nope, why?"

"It's so poignant, I love it! Isra is also the story of Muhammed's journey aboard Buraq to the Al-Aqsa Mosque before he ascended to have a dialogue with Allah."

"Perhaps I can shed some light on that," interjected Josie. "It was a suggestion from Macca. We asked whether there was an acronym that could unite and also be representative of Ben's journey."

"What are your thoughts on the nanites Shah?" asked Josie.

"If you're a team player, it gives you an edge, certainly," said Shah, "but it doesn't perform miracles. I'm guessing that soloists just get the same as normal augmentation."

"You're using the Bergamot blend?" asked Mike.

"Aren't you?" replied Shah?

"Not yet," said Mike and Lindy together.

So, while officials organised Mike and Ben's trip to Greenland, Lindy and Mike had some time to discuss the Bergamot option. Having decided it had to include both or neither of them, they took up the offer to engage in Bergamot's program. Lindy was also enthusiastic about following Mike to Greenland after the first meetings with the international scientists.

Finally, the preparations were completed, and Mike departed, destined for Nuuk with Ben. During the flight, Mike felt strangely 'tuned in' to Ben. Although quiet for almost the entire trip, whenever Mike glanced at him, it was as if he was in constant thought. But he also projected a cool Buddha-like calm.

Mike began to harbour doubts that the Chinese and Russian representatives would obtain the catharsis they were hoping for. But then Mike would glance over, and Ben's calm demeanour would prove infectious, even if perhaps, the Pilgrim nanites were not. Mike found his doubts about augmentation slowly dissolving away, and he began to feel comfortable with the decision to draw upon the Bergamot blend. He explored the curious sensation that although he'd arrived in advance of Lindy, and were some distance apart, he still felt somehow connected. Although physically absent, it was like she was there by his side.

The event in Nuuk had more relaxed security than that of the Presidential occasion in Svalbard, it was quite a relief. The sheer isolation of Nuuk provided some reassurance since any plans of disruption would require significant effort. It was possible to roam freely about, and the influx of scientific interests gave the location the feel of a symposium rather than an intergovernmental diplomatic affair.

Despite being Greenland's capital city, Nuuk's size is disproportionate to the massive island being carved by glaciers, rivers of ice that were now shrinking into oblivion. When Ben's entourage arrived, the Greenland locals put on a welcoming ceremony, and the Airport was resplendent with all the national flags. Nuuk's Airport was built initially from US and Danish funds but had since been upgraded with Sino Russian money. The local officials were very practised in the art of neutrality. They were acutely aware that they were being serenaded for alignment by some of the most powerful nations in the world. And so, the Greenland government had used their sovereignty card to successfully play each suitor against the other.

From the Airport it was a short drive to Ilisimatusarfik, the University of Greenland. To the west of the older campus were the recently built climatology department buildings where the collaboration process was being hosted.

Nation-states had fallen over each other to contribute to this new venture, and it was almost inevitable that the support for strategic projects would continue to yield an indefinite series of grants. Banking on this support, the team had set themselves the task of mapping out the best location for a new extension to the campus.

Upon their arrival at the institute, they were met by an Innuit woman. She introduced herself as the Director, gave both Ben and Mike the traditional greeting of an Eskimo kiss, the kunik, and drove them to their accommodation in the main town centre. Once there she pointed out the Bergamot office adjacent to the hotel and waited for the pair to freshen up. They ate at one of the nearby establishments, and she deposited them back before the cold set in.

As Mike watched the midnight sun arcing low over the horizon from his room's double-glazed window, he could see the nearby Bergamot office. He wondered whether the astuteness of the Greenlanders might possibly have been fostered by the sponsorship of this multinational. As he fought to find sleep against his circadian rhythm, he couldn't help thinking it wasn't a bad thing, but also wondering if it could stay that way.

The next day dawned. The chilly climate had moderated in the August thaw and provided a heatwave for the visitors at 28 Celsius. The multitudes of boats on the harbour came and went as they ventured to the fishing fields in search of ammassatter.

The new centre was to be adjacent to the climatology building. Once the scientists from the various countries had gathered at the university, Mike organised a rough first reconnaissance of the area proposed, and comically celebrated the turning of the first clod. Shah took some pictures as they flipped over a large rock. With the frivolity done, the scientists got down to business.

The Russians obtained the opportunity to learn what they could from Ben that afternoon, and the Chinese were set to follow the next day.

After a morning's interrogation by the Chinese, Ben and Mike were taking a walk along the Nuussuaq. To their left, they could see that most of the boats had left the harbour, and were out in the arctic waters of the Labrador Sea. A single vessel chugged its way back into the rocky perimeter of the Nuuk marina.

When they returned, Shah took Mike aside and insisted that the turning of the first clod be adequately revisited. She explained that she wanted to present a plaque to the Innuit Director. Her plan was for this to be inlaid into the chosen rock for the foyer of the new facility. They sent a circular ensuring the assembling of a large contingent of scientists in the proposed area in two days.

Andrew Cooke took his duffle bag out of the boat's stowage area and thanked the skipper as he jumped gingerly onto the Nuuk marina jetty. The pontoons yielded a little, and his injured leg almost gave way. He winced in pain but managed to recover before setting off down the dock towards solid ground.

The boat, which he considered to be his Buraq, had now taken him to the furthest Mosque. Andrew's Isra, his journey, had been completed. The parallels between his voyage to Greenland and Mohammed's journey provided a deep-rooted assurance that this was the path he was meant to follow; his destiny. What remained was his ascension. Here in Greenland, he was to find his Mi'raj.

Once he'd settled into his room, he took the contents out of his duffle bag. The AR15 he'd brought with him had been modified with a lower receiver and full auto sear which had turned it into a military-grade fully-automatic rifle—a machine gun. These units had been made in the covert JAM factory he had helped establish with Scope. It had been so easy. The Selective Laser Metal printing unit had been the most expensive component, but this choice also allowed the raw material of powdered metal to be bought without suspicion. It also enabled Scope and himself to operate their clandestine operations at night, doing so behind a legitimate prototyping business during the day.

The next two days were spent assessing the layout and behaviour patterns of the places and people.

He found a hill to the south of the Climatology department from where he was able to observe. He armed himself with a geology pick to give the appearance of studying the rock formations.

Once his preparations were done, he packed the rifle and his explosive vest into his duffle bag and made his way to the hill, the place he had come to think of as his own private Mosque. He hoped that one day, it would have just such a dedication.

Standing on the exposed rock, the whistling sound came first, in mosquito form, both everywhere and nowhere, both close and far. The popping noise came next. Strangely familiar, it deceptively echoed off the buildings and rock faces, confusing Ben's ears as he struggled to pick up the direction of the noise. Then came the grunts. These came as a wet thudding percussion and a sudden exhale.

Before he could comprehend what it all meant, he was thrown off his feet and onto to the ground. He could see Mike's face next to his, contorted in agony. Blood was staining the shoulder of his "Nuuk 2030" shirt.

Time was paused at that moment. Refusing to accept what these events implied, Ben closed his eyes and spread his being around the nanites that Bergamot had ranged across the area. At lightspeed, he took in the totality, and his training automatically took over.

There was a clicking noise as someone on the rocky knoll went to replace the spent magazine. In the blink of an eye, he was there as the reloaded weapon was raised.

"I can help here," came the disembodied voice of Macca. Suddenly he understood as several cognition were passed into his situational awareness.

With his entire being focused on the AR15, Ben could see the lower receiver that had been printed from particulate metal. But there was another ingredient imbued within the powder at manufacture by Bergamot Corporation. The nanites within this component had been dormant. Ben activated them and assessed the state of the weapon.

The rifle had already been cocked and the bolt drawn back. With the newly loaded magazine now thrust into place, the weapon had already drawn a new round. Since the top receiver could be readily obtained over the counter and did not need to be manufactured, Ben could not exercise any nanites to intervene.

The weapon had already chambered the 5.56mm ammunition into the breach; the bolt was twisted into its locked position; it was ready to fire.

Rather than see the trigger being squeezed, he felt it as a pressure. Although retained in the lower receiver, the trigger mechanism itself had also been bought freely and not manufactured with the Bergamot blend. It was however hinged within the lower receiver. He bent his will to the hinge in an effort to stop its action. Even though the pin would not move in the receiver, the trigger would happily hinge on the pin. The Sear engagement slid precariously away from the hammer, and the spring tension would soon carry the hammer on its brief journey to the firing pin.

Since the sear mechanism is also readily obtained, Ben resigned himself to the next round. He had to let it go.

Without even considering where the lethal projectile might have been aimed, he studied the next part of the process. The highly compressed air from the explosion circulated back to reset the bolt and eject the case. While this was happening, Ben worked on the safety catch hoping to cold weld it to the trigger.

Then he noticed the difference. He had only passing knowledge of the forms of illegal arms manufacture but had heard of the fully automatic sear. Because it could not be bought, this was something that also had to be manufactured by the Bergamot blend. Utilising the embedded nano-machinery, he was able to improvise a cold weld of the secondary sear to any surface it came in contact with. This turned out to be the bolt, on its return journey.

All through this, Ben had closed his eyes and not moved. He risked a glance and saw Mike was still before him. Then he heard the serpentine hiss and saw the look of dismay in Mike's eyes. The bullet had been aimed at him and took him in the chest. Although it must have thankfully missed his heart, he coughed up a little blood. Ben cursed his inability to stop that round.

In the meantime, thankfully, the AR15 had been irreparably fractured. While still in the prone position, the attacker was desperately pounding the forward assist to try to load the next round. Now, with some time on his side, Ben used the nanites near the attacker to strengthen his situation. Having been shooting in the prone position, the assailant presented a large surface area to the ground, and his body was exposed to a significant number of nanites. These were able to penetrate his outer clothing to reveal his suicide vest.

While the gunman was still examining his rifle, Ben scrambled as many nanites as he could into his vest. The nanites allowed him to gain a detailed understanding of the vest functions and also the talisman necklace of Allah tucked in under the outer clothing.

Finally frustrated with his weapon, the gunman stood up and began running towards the crowd.

Again Ben closed his eyes.

At about this time Jase and Josephine were at NASA's Langley Research Centre in Virginia. They were there to meet with the DSCOVRII analysts from the Deep Space Climate Observatory to discuss corporate sponsorship. Jase and Josephine shared a common sentiment of their ongoing research: 'The world was not yet ready for the answer'.

The DSCOVRII observatory was stationed at the L1 Lagrangian. This location was directly between the Earth and the Sun, from there, it had a permanent view of the daylight side of the Earth. It was also where The Pilgrim had taken up its second residence.

The recent detection of anomalies at L1 had been correlated with signals detected at L5. This led to theories that the Pilgrim cloud had either moved or grown. The slightest implication that the solar system had been taken over by the Pilgrim would bring about utter chaos, fear and potential military action. This was why Jase and Josephine were there, to quell and suppress.

"So, should we publish or, as you suggest, conduct a more rigorous study?" The chief scientist asked of them.

The research was obviously ready for peer review and broader attention, but the desired objective was quite different.

Now that the Pilgrim was aware of her detection by these scientists, she would soon shroud the particle cloud that she was growing. It would not be long before the DSCOVRII Solar stationary satellite would have a blind spot. It may even be recruited by the Pilgrim just like the earlier Beagle mission.

Silently, their nanites allowed Jase and Josephine to align themselves to a course of action. It would begin with praise.

Jase began, "Thanks to your invitation, our research division at Bergamot has had a thorough preliminary examination of your study, it's exceptional. Both of us believe that your conclusions are particularly important, and your methods praiseworthy. In fact, we think that the follow-up investigations you've recommended in your summary should be executed to maintain the momentum. If so, this could become a seminal paper revealing both the existence and the extent of the anomaly."

Josephine took the hint. "That's right Doctor Henderson, I guess we'd rather you kept your powder dry and didn't publish yet. But, as Jase says, the good news is that Bergamot Corporation has ensured that 100% of your requested funding has been approved. This represents a nice lift in your current budget if I'm not mistaken."

The Doctor was ecstatic and struggled to keep calm. "Thank you, it's so nice to be able to discuss this with people who understand our science." A moment of worry crossed his face. "My colleagues insist, however, that our research remains independent and uncensored." He frowned.

"Yes, of course, we would expect nothing less, and any decision to publish should be yours. All we ask is that we are kept apprised of your findings," replied Jase. The pair subliminally shared a thought about how scientific discovery had been so efficiently silenced. The saving grace for the delay would be that the Doctor's findings would be self-discredited within 2 months.

Jase held private reservations. There were respected scientific careers at stake, but the very near future was critical if a global crisis was to be averted. If successful, the climate would become suddenly and continuously stable. Jase suspected that the climate sceptics would claim vindication, and seek to roll back the hard-won changes, but by then, the new world order would be established.

"Dr Henderson, as you know, our organisation has some strong connections within the field of Astronomy," said Jase.

"Yes," replied the Doctor.

"Following your conclusions here I'd like to explore the idea of you leading a team within the International Square Kilometre Array. Don't get me wrong, I think the research being done here is exceptional and crucial to better understanding the Sun and our climate. But it is transitioning to an operations model. The research into dark matter and dark energy has cosmic implications and needs the best minds to unwrap those mysteries. I think a professional of your calibre might do well there. If you like, I will have a word to some of our friends at Jodrell Bank."

Josephine and Jase suddenly looked at each other. They both felt it as a physical thing. They felt depleted, they felt anguish, they had been diminished. They also felt a surge of hope. Even a diminishing can bring enlightenment.

The Head of the Hydra

The cafe was the same nondescript type used regularly when meeting with Andrew. Scope sat in the alfresco area with his coffee and smiled inwardly. It had been so easy. He had effected yet another destabilisation but had again managed to avoid being directly connected. The manipulation of Andrew had been a boon to his plans. Hundreds of thousands of untraceable lower receivers had been manufactured and sold on the dark web. This had helped to bankroll a good part of his initiative. More money then streamed in through the legitimate supply of the AR15 machinery that supported these units. Furthermore, the seeds of unrest that had been sown promised to feed even more demand.

Seeing the growth opportunity, his consortia of manufacturers had offered to inject enough funds to truly grow his venture. But before the next stage could commence, he needed to reset the current project.

Although Andrew had done an admirable job, he was now a liability. His journey to become Abdullah had left him fraying psychologically. Scope's association with Andrew made him a complicit accomplice. Andrew was a loose end, one that seemed ready to unravel.

The renewed contact from Andrew, a call to meet again, was somewhat surprising. Andrew' Abdullah' was meant to find his Mi'raj; supposed to go to his Allah in a blaze of religious fervour. Anyone else would feel a deep unease about this meeting, but this was quelled by Scope's unassailable sense of calm. If there was any disquiet, it was very deeply buried. He was simply disappointed that Andrew had not fulfilled his destiny.

The waiter appeared.

"Sorry," Scope interrupted any offer of service, "I'll just have my coffee for now." He indicated his coffee.

"I'm sorry, sir," responded the waiter, "It's just that I've been asked to give you something just inside here." The waiter indicated the counter.

Trying not to show his annoyance, Scope stood and followed the waiter inside. He was gestured to wait while the waiter circled around to the service side where he pulled an object from the drawers beneath the transaction screen. It was a phone.

Now curious, Scope took the phone, put it into his pocket, thanked the waiter with a cursory nod, and returned to his seat.

He made a show of taking the phone out, the screen was locked. He tried the PIN which had been agreed between Scope and Andrew, this unlocked it. There was just one number in the phone's contact list. He rang it.

Andrew's voice answered: "The training camp has been taken over."

"What makes you say that?" said Scope.

"There is a new element to our plans. The camp leaders are possessed of some alternative ideal. They've apparently created an alliance, one we should perhaps consider," said Andrew's voice.

"Hmmm. Why have you not come to our meeting point?" asked Scope.

"Because the game is much larger now, and I need to be cautious in case I am being watched."

Scope became cautious. "You should keep a low key then, and we should keep our communication to a minimum. Please don't do anything pre-emptive."

"Agreed," replied Andrew.

While grateful for Andrew's transparency, Scope was also concerned that he had begun acting autonomously. Why did he have to go rogue? He could have simply played his role like he was supposed to and it would all have worked out. It was too late, he could no longer be reined in. It reinforced his urgency to reset this project since it raised the spectre of Andrew getting caught in affairs out of his depth. If Scope's ambitions were to have any future, the threat that was Andrew needed to be neutralised immediately. He needed time to cover his tracks, but if Andrew gained momentum, there would be a second set leading directly to Scope.

The loose end that was Andrew could no longer be simply cut off, it needed to be isolated first. To insulate himself from these new developments, Scope first had to understand the nature of this potential new alliance. "How can I help you?" he probed.

"Can you destroy the crop?" asked Andrew.

He was referring to the unsold stock at the facility.

"Yes." Scope agreed with Andrew, the logical step was to melt down the remaining lower receivers. They would only serve to incriminate them now.

"Thanks, I'm going to hibernate this phone now, but I'll check in later," finished Andrew.

"OK, later then," and Scope hung up.

He pocketed the phone glancing up and down the street for any signs of surveillance. He paid, tucked in the chair, and turned south to make a beeline down the avenues. As he rounded a corner several minutes later, he used a different phone to make a call to Isaac, one of his more sensitive and strategic connections.

"Isaac, yes, it's me. Your Mother's recipe was fabulous." With his identity verified, Scope then awaited and got Isaac's cross verification. "No, you can keep Dad's hammer drill a little longer," he replied.

"Hey Isaac," he said in a conversational tone, "I have some materials for your recycling business. It's about 500 kilograms of high-grade steel, and it's barring progress on a client's project. It needs to go quickly."

"…Sure, I'll text you the address…See you there about five."

Scope then texted several address-like code words derived from a dark-web application. To anyone eavesdropping, the code words would lead to some random location. To someone with the decoder, it could be used to derive the correct address.

Scope wove his way through the cityscape to a restaurant. This was a rustic old building with several floors that secreted a myriad of arcane purposes. The lower-level concealed clientele as they percolated down from the upper floors and nestled into various cubicles, niches and darkened rooms behind doors. Short walls furnished with knick-knacks and random artefacts threw shadows over silhouetted faces. The proprietor, while politely satisfying culinary demands, asked no questions and never stopped for idle conversation. He was not there to make friends with his patrons.

Scope chose a table by a window that overlooked the bland exterior of the manufacturing facility he and Andrew had established. From this vantage, he would observe briefly before entering.

He used his phone to examine the last few days of his security cameras as he waited for his lunch. Once it arrived, he took furtive glances at the periphery as he sipped his wine.

Once satisfied, he briskly walked across the road and into the building. There he waited for Isaac from the NRA.

For about two hours, he paced the building putting things in place, not wanting to be alone with himself, and occasionally checking the security cameras. To break the boredom and isolation, he reached out to a biohacker looking into genetic augmentation, it was one of his newer projects.

After this call, he spent time picking up innocuous prototypes and throwing them into the half-full boxes of lower receivers to conceal them. When he was almost done there came a voice.

"Hello, Scope," it was distinctly that of Andrew Cooke.

Although having a muted startle response, Scope's psychopathy did not suppress the adrenaline that suddenly coursed through his body. Quickly responding Scope simply said: "This is not safe, Andrew. As your friend, I would advise you to take the safe path we discussed." He was careful to say no more than that.

"Precautions are being taken," came a second voice.

"Is that you, Isaac?" Scope asked continuing to lob a few more metal items into the boxes to provide sufficient cover for the underlying objects.

"No, my name is Ben Herdsman." Ben then stepped out from the darkened corner and into the light.

Now on high alert, but in full control, Scope was in his favourite element. If Ben Herdsman's intent was immediate harm, he would already have done so. Now he could start to play his games "How did you get in here Ben?" said Scope stepping forward to cordially shake Ben's hand.

"Let's just say I have some skills."

"Quite adroit skills I would suggest. Where's Andrew?" Scope had been ambushed before. He had also ambushed many. He would not be outdone by Ben, and being able to suppress any surprise would give him a distinctive edge.

Ben's mastery of ventriloquism provided an edge that Scope could never fathom. "Speaking to you through Ben from a safe distance," came Andrew's voice from the shadows behind the piles of boxes.

"OK, I trust these precautions provisionally." Thoughts of betrayal came to mind. "So, now you are here, Ben, what can I do for you?" asked Scope.

"Actually, it's what I can do for you," replied Ben.

"Ben Herdsman would like to do something for me! What an honour! I'm a real fan by the way. What did you have in mind?"

"Well, I have some technology that might be able to help you attain your goals."

"And how did you come to know I might be interested in such an offer?" asked Scope, his curiosity now piqued.

"Through our mutual acquaintance: Andrew," said Ben.

"And why would you be prepared to provide me with such technology?" Scope was careful in asking.

"Well, this technology is from the Pilgrim. As you would be aware, I was involved in the program to explore the Pilgrim's arrival," explained Ben.

"Of course, go on."

"Well, the Pilgrim needs ambassadors to represent it here on Earth. You might fit the bill for such an ambassador."

"And what does that involve?" said Scope now intrigued.

"For starters, you get access to the technology."

"And what does this technology provide?"

Ben walked across to the bench, upon which there were some of the scrap metal prototypes. He picked one of the objects up and lobbed it gently to Scope who deftly caught it.

Ben looked into the eyes of Scope. At first, there was just curiosity. Then as the object became warm, he smiled, actively interested. As the item became too hot to hold Scope lobbed it back to Ben. It exploded into dust in mid-air.

"Now, you have my undivided attention," said Scope.

"You also have the technology," said Ben. The heat of the particles warmed the surrounding air and provided buoyancy. By carefully coordinating the heated-up eddies, the particles of dust floated gently towards and landed on Scope's body.

"What happens next?"

"Well, quite simply," said Ben coolly, "you begin to make choices."

"And these choices become real?"

"More real than you could imagine," said the disembodied voice of Andrew Cooke.

Reassured by Andrew's suggestion Scope embraced the thought of the nanites as if they were a transcendent tool. Soon, he would be able to use it to turn the tables on Ben. Who knows? Perhaps the Pilgrim wants world domination. That was it! He had been chosen to help the Pilgrim because of his ability to make and execute tough and unpalatable decisions.

At first just superficial the nanites soon began to find capillaries to enter his bloodstream. Unconvinced Scope asked: "Nothing is happening yet. I don't feel any different. Do I need more?"

Ben picked one of the 3D printed prototype scrap pieces out of the bin and placed it on a nearby stainless-steel bench. After a minute it began to crumble, eventually becoming a pile of dust. Ben swept it into his hand and approached Scope.

Ben held the dust above Scope's head. Saying "Remember that you are dust, and to dust you shall return," he poured the nanite powder onto Scope's head.

Ben relayed the song of humanity, and the song became life.

At first, it was just a whisper. But Scope could feel the potential of power. Still, the song grew incrementally until it was voluminous. From many to multitudes the cacophony mounted up, encouraging chorus but finding discord, Scope then hesitated, confused, overwhelmed.

Scope's psychology prioritised the survival and accumulation of self. His solipsism now confronted, he rejected the implications of the song. It strained to weave him into their neural fabric, and its orchestral strength dissolved and diluted him.

Previously impervious, unassailable, merciless, fearless, and detached, Scope was now laid naked, exposed, in decay.

"I am frightened," came unbidden. The realisation was not spoken, the words could easily have been "I need to be alone" or even a shout to quieten the discord. It was directed uniquely from Scope to the collective which, in seeking to provide comfort in empathy, simply exacerbated the situation. The words from the collective simply added to the madness within.

Now on an inexorable path to his own resolution, Ben left Scope to seek his solace in the oblivion he had callously brought to others.

As he closed the door to the factory, he heard the blast of a gunshot behind him.

The Final Bridge

Lindy thanked Ben again. Returning after his brief absence, Ben had sought Mike out in Greenland and found him with Lindy. The news that the ringleader of the recent terror attack had met his end provided some closure. Mike also expressed his thanks. He felt alive even though it was unlikely that his shoulder would ever be the same.

It was August. Mike had spent nine days recovering in Queen Ingrid's hospital, and after being discharged, Lindy had driven him from the hospital back to the University. She believed it would provide some encouragement if he saw how developments had continued in his absence.

They sat looking North from the cafe at the university campus. The broad windows that spanned two floors afforded a spectacular view of the northern lights as they adorned the skies with shimmering curtains of greens, reds, blues and yellows.

The next day brought a catabatic wind and a light snowfall. Sermitsiaq mountain faded in and out of view as the squalls veiled the jagged monolith in a negligee of white. They sat at the picture windows, hugged their Greenland coffee and shaped the whipped cream into models of the mountain as it tantalised them.

"You must be Dr Mike Brazier," came a voice behind Mike.

"I am. Can I be of any help?" he asked.

"If you have a moment, I'd like to show you an interesting observation and perhaps discuss its implications."

"Of course," he replied and excused himself from Ben and Lindy.

As they walked, the stranger explained his work in glaciology. The small Nuuk campus meant it wasn't long before the pair arrived at his laboratory. This had a freezer section where they stored the ice cores that they extracted from the remaining glaciers.

"My supervisor said he would not be far behind and that I should go ahead and show you what we found recently."

With that, he took a nearby computer out of screensaver mode. There, on the screen, were four images, each of a snowflake. He looked at Mike expectantly.

"I see you have some pictures of a snowflake." Mike ventured.

"Not exactly," laughed the assistant. "This is, in fact, four photographs of four different snowflakes."

The blood drained from Mike's face.

"That's not possible. They look identical."

"They are identical," elaborated the assistant.

"Ahh, I see you are equally confounded by our little conundrum," came a second voice behind Mike.

"Is this a trick?" Mike pressed.

"No trick," the man replied as he placed a laptop bag on his desk. He withdrew a book and slid it into the shelf above it. "Tell me, Mike, you are somewhat of an authority on computer science are you not?" He spoke while he extracted a laptop. Placing it on the desk, he continued: "Have you ever examined the Simulation Hypothesis in any detail?"

"No," Mike replied, as the man wheeled a chair over to the snowflake monitor. "I've never really taken it seriously. For all of us to be living inside a simulation would require astronomical resources. It's certainly not something we are capable of, and I doubt if even a post-human civilisation could compute the random trajectories of everything."

"Agreed," said the stranger. "But would the problem be a little more tractable if we could exclude some of the complexity we see in the physical world?"

"Perhaps." Mike swallowed hard.

"We captured these images about 9 days ago," said the man indicating the images. "The interesting thing is that when we tried to reproduce the experiment, we couldn't. Now, every snowflake we examine has a different morphology. This is why I was eager to speak to you. You know of the Heisenberg Uncertainty principle, I suppose?"

"Of course."

"I'm not saying this is the same. We don't measure quantum mechanical conjugate 'thingummies' here. Still, the principle that the observer affects the measurement may be the action that gives us our anomaly. The intent to measure the distinguishing features of a snowflake may differentiate the snowflakes themselves."

"But why now? Why not decades ago? I'm sorry, I never caught your name."

"Hence the paradox. I'm sorry, Mike. My associate should perhaps have introduced us before we began our little chat. I'm Daniel, Dr Daniel Clark. I hope you can help me explore this little bridge into a very different universe."

The name was vaguely familiar.

Epilogue – Entangled Destiny

Death is a stripping away of all that is not you.
The secret of life is to 'die before you die'
—and find that there is no death.

Eckhart Tolle "The Power of Now"

Ben

The plateau beheld life prolific in variety and form, from the lowliest insect to the apex predators. The Murchison River catchment area was also home to a tiny colony of Crest-tailed Mulgaras, a ginger, small, rat-like creature. One of them, a female, warily scampered out of its hiding place amongst the spinifex having spotted a lizard.

Her need for food was becoming urgent, and the lizard was the perfect meal for the carnivorous marsupial. The five juveniles in her pouch were going to place an increasing demand upon her sustenance, and she needed the nourishment. The lizard was essential to her and the survival of this threatened species.

Ferals were also rampant. The wild dog, an escapee from one of the outlying communities, had her own litter to care for. She smelled the mulgara and had begun traversing the area to get a better trace. Suddenly a new scent came to her attention. The distinctive flavour of feral goats promised a far better prospect.

Leaving the mulgara to catch the lizard she trotted off. A few other dogs in her pack joined her momentarily, and together they worked in concert. Soon three goats had been brought down.

Two of the goats were now being devoured by the pups and their mother. A couple of others in the pack had torn off a limb and had distrustfully hauled it off to gnaw on. Eagles circled patiently in the thermals of the midday sun.

A third goat, the younger of the bounty, clean and killed quickly with a broken neck, was now being skinned by hands that had practised on a different herding species far away in Texas.

In the radio silence on the late Cambrian Tumblagooda Sandstone, Ben had made his new home. His nanites ranged the distant horizon with spectra and intensity that didn't interfere with the Square Kilometre Array. He was the custodian, and the ferals now worked for him maintaining the ecological matrix.

He had felt what it was to be the life that was born in an ocean. His memories reverberated with the struggles, successes and accumulated wisdom of the Pilgrim. Emerging from his previous drive to for discovery, he now felt the desire to witness first-hand the ebb and flow of life in its diverse forms. He needed to understand the balance. He needed a place of quiet. He needed to better understand the aspect of him that was the Pilgrim. It was here in the furthest point possible from civilisation that he could explore that.

It was time to pause and consider who he was. He was still the kid who swung over the creek; the person who floated across the threshold of the International Space Station; the trained professional that had crossed many millions of kilometres to Charybdis; the one that had sent his soul across the solar gulf to meld with the Pilgrim. It had taken him to a juncture he was not yet prepared to cross.

As the lessons of life scaffolded the next lesson, Ben had come to transcend the crossing of creeks and the forging of matter. This last traversal had placed him on a journey to a new home. He had to understand his place in the panoply of being.

The realisation of the limitless patience required to fully know existence weighed heavily upon him. Where before there was the cavalier adventurer, there was now the reclusive and contemplative philosopher searching for the truth. He also knew that while eternity for him would always be within reach, the price was high.

He had begun his journey with a dream to cross the expanse of space. He had since obtained a glimpse of eternity, and his psyche had been turned 90 degrees. His life's journey, the ephemeral and fragile nature of it had brought a new imperative. He was now considering the voyage across his expanse of time.

His time was going to be spent in contemplation and preparation, it was crucial to digest events while he was still able to provide influence. Already, events were cascading and bifurcating into chaotic periods beyond his ability as an active agent. And new agents continued to align the trajectory to which he had provided the impetus. The surgically placed impulses they introduced were increasing in frequency and impact.

He examined the lie he had promulgated on the contagion he had now set loose. While not a threat to any single individual, could he be sure there was no threat to individuality?

One of the agents, a friend, now walked into the firelight. Sitting, Eugene picked up a stick and poked at the embers.

"Another two," a statement.

Silently Eugene passed two phials across to Ben. Taking them, he cradled them in the palm of his hand as he considered them carefully. The dust inside slithered like graphite and absorbed the red rays of the fire like fluid blackness.

He stood and walked to his hut. He placed the phials next to another on the shelf which had the name Tim beneath it.

For Ben, there was no sadness. Others had set the world on a new path. A path that would help sustain the place that Ben called home. These others would now explore the universe with a new companion. The Pilgrim had promised stewardship. He felt it to be true.

The Pilgrim had also come home. She'd found a place where her infinite patience could finally understand what it was like to be born; to appreciate the boundary between what was her and what was not. She had found an evolved kindred spirit, emergent like herself but with boundless variations of individuality. If her singularity was the Yin, it enfolded the Yang of human diversity.

And she had found Macca, the organised child of their mind whom she had helped nurture.

The multitudes of scenarios that could be played out were now under subtle governance. The fledgling science of humanity would one day provide the means to travel the universe together, but the Pilgrim was already invested. She bent her mind to a collaborative destiny.

Together, they would begin the journey through time.

CPSIA information can be obtained
at www.ICGtesting.com
Printed in the USA
LVHW041502290322
714698LV00010B/362

9 781398 441811